LOU EADE

The Found

The Molly Chapman Series

First published by Lou Eade Author 2024

Copyright © 2024 by Lou Eade

All rights reserved. No part of this publication may be reproduced, stored or transmitted in any form or by any means, electronic, mechanical, photocopying, recording, scanning, or otherwise without written permission from the publisher. It is illegal to copy this book, post it to a website, or distribute it by any other means without permission.

This novel is entirely a work of fiction. The names, characters and incidents portrayed in it are the work of the author's imagination. Any resemblance to actual persons, living or dead, events or localities is entirely coincidental.

Lou Eade asserts the moral right to be identified as the author of this work.

Lou Eade has no responsibility for the persistence or accuracy of URLs for external or third-party Internet Websites referred to in this publication and does not guarantee that any content on such Websites is, or will remain, accurate or appropriate.

Designations used by companies to distinguish their products are often claimed as trademarks. All brand names and product names used in this book and on its cover are trade names, service marks, trademarks and registered trademarks of their respective owners. The publishers and the book are not associated with any product or vendor mentioned in this book. None of the companies referenced within the book have endorsed the book.

First edition

ISBN (paperback): 978-1-0687887-0-3
ISBN (hardcover): 978-1-0687887-1-0

Editing by Andi Eade
Cover art by Ben White
Illustration by JH Illustration

This book was professionally typeset on Reedsy.
Find out more at reedsy.com

For My Husband and Children
Andi, Tianny, Kieran, Tom, Emi, Ben and Millie

"That's the thing about books. They let you travel without moving your feet."

— Jhumpa Lahiri

Contents

Preface	iii
Acknowledgments	v
Chapter 1	1
Chapter 2	11
Chapter 3	21
Chapter 4	31
Chapter 5	42
Chapter 6	53
Chapter 7	64
Chapter 8	75
Chapter 9	86
Chapter 10	96
Chapter 11	107
Chapter 12	117
Chapter 13	128
Chapter 14	139
Chapter 15	149
Chapter 16	159
Chapter 17	171
Chapter 18	182
Chapter 19	192
Chapter 20	203
Chapter 21	214
Chapter 22	225

Chapter 23	236
Chapter 24	247
Chapter 25	258
Chapter 26	269
Chapter 27	282
Chapter 28	293
Chapter 29	304
Chapter 30	315
Chapter 31	326
Chapter 32	333
Chapter 33	346
Chapter 34	357
Chapter 35	368
Chapter 36	379
Chapter 37	391
Chapter 38	402
Chapter 39	413
Chapter 40	423
About the Author	430
Also by Lou Eade	432

Preface

Welcome to the culmination of a journey that began with "The Fall" and continued with "The Forgotten." As you hold this book in your hands, you are about to immerse yourself in the final chapter of the Molly Chapman Series. "The Found."

It feels like just yesterday when the seeds of inspiration for this tale were planted in the fertile soil of my subconscious mind back in 2020. From the depths of recurring dreams emerged the enigmatic figure of Molly Chapman, her silhouette etched against the canvas of uncertainty.

"The Fall" introduced you to Molly and the mysterious circumstances surrounding her life, set against the backdrop of Blackpool's iconic promenade. In that gripping narrative, you witnessed the convergence of fate amidst the pulsating lights and bustling crowds as Molly's destiny teetered on the edge of oblivion.

Then, in "The Forgotten," the journey continues. As Molly grapples with amnesia, the forces of law and order race against time to uncover the truths buried within the shadows of Blackpool's streets. But as the mysteries deepen, so too do the bonds between dreams and reality blur, revealing profound insights into the nature of existence itself.

Within these pages, you will find the resolution to the questions that have lingered since the inception of Molly's story. Prepare to be captivated by the twists and turns of fate as the final revelations unfold, propelling you into the heart of a world where nothing is as it seems.

As we bid farewell to Molly Chapman and the world of "The Found," I extend my deepest gratitude to you, dear reader, for accompanying me on this unforgettable journey. May the echoes of Molly's tale resonate within you long after you turn the final page.

Welcome to the thrilling conclusion of the Molly Chapman Series.

Acknowledgments

To all my cherished readers,

I extend my deepest gratitude to each and every one of you who has embarked on the journey through three of my books.

Your unwavering support and enthusiasm for my work mean the world to me. It is your encouragement and feedback that fuel my passion for storytelling, and I am profoundly grateful for your continued presence on this literary adventure.

I also want to express heartfelt appreciation to my beloved husband and children. Your unwavering support and understanding throughout the process of writing these books have been my anchor and inspiration. Your patience, encouragement, and belief in me have sustained me through the challenges and triumphs of the creative process. I am endlessly grateful for your love and encouragement.

With deepest thanks and warmest regards,

Lou

Chapter 1

Wednesday Early Evening

The team disperses. Each member heads to their designated vehicle. Carter and Poker step forward, assuming control of Gerry and Rachel, respectively, leading them in opposite directions.

As they approach the cars, an unspoken tension hangs between them, visible in Gerry and Rachel's silent exchange of glances.

Their faces are a canvas of mixed emotions, fear, and apprehension etched into every line as Carter and Poker lead them towards the awaiting vehicles.

Despite the silent tension, their expressions convey volumes, revealing the weight of the moment.

Carter opens his car door, guiding Gerry inside with a gentle yet firm hand, while Poker does the same for Rachel on the opposite side of the driveway.

Their hands rest reassuringly on their heads, offering support amidst the turmoil as they lower them into the seats.

In this charged moment, anticipation thick, the gravity of

their situation casting a sombre shadow over the scene.

It's a pivotal moment for all involved, where the consequences of their actions loom large, setting the stage for what lies ahead.

* * *

The crackle of the radio disrupts the stillness in the room, and Dixie's heart quickens as he hears Carter's voice on the other end. Carter's tone carries an unmistakable excitement, signalling a breakthrough in the case.

With a sense of anticipation, Dixie listens intently as Carter relays the news of Gerry's arrest.

Dixie's pulse quickens further as he absorbs the significance of the moment.

Not only have they apprehended Gerry, but there's another development — Rachel has been arrested at the same location.

A surge of pride fills Dixie as he realises the extent of his team's accomplishment.

As he turns the radio off from Carter, Dixie's face breaks into a rare smile. The weight of the recent events settles upon him, and he leans back in his chair, crossing his legs at his ankles.

Weariness washes over him, a testament to the intensity of the investigation, but there's no time for rest.

Dixie knows he must see this through to the end.

Despite his fatigue, Dixie's mind races with anticipation.

The upcoming interrogations promise to be some of the most challenging he's encountered in his career as a Lead Detective Inspector. Yet, he is determined to navigate the

CHAPTER 1

complexities with skill, driven by a steadfast commitment to justice.

Dixie's phone abruptly interrupts the quiet of his office, the caller ID revealing an oversight that sinks his heart. He forgot to call his sister about his hospital appointment.

With a resigned sigh, he answers the call, bracing himself for the conversation he knows will follow.

"Hello," he greets, his voice carrying its usual matter-of-factness.

"Hey, did you forget to phone me?" The tremble in his sister's voice is noticeable through the phone line.

Lucy has been battling Parkinson's Disease for three long years, relying on Dixie for assistance with her daily routine as her condition worsens. Though he's reluctant to label himself as her caregiver, Dixie has taken on the role of aiding her through the challenges posed by her illness.

Their bond goes beyond mere familial ties.

In their youth, Dixie and Lucy made a pact to support each other should life deal them a cruel hand.

Tragically, their family has been besieged by terminal illnesses, leaving them no choice but to confront the harsh realities together.

In hushed conversations, Dixie and Lucy have grappled with the unthinkable: the prospect of his cancer worsening and the difficult decisions it would entail for Lucy's future.

Despite Dixie's heartache, Lucy has steadfastly resolved that, if necessary, she will journey to Switzerland to seek a humane end to her suffering.

"I did, and I am sorry that I forgot," Dixie admits, his tone carrying a hint of remorse.

"I have a lot on at work, and the meeting with the consultant seemed less important," he explains, feeling the need to defend himself.

"Oh, that's alright. I know that you have distractions there, which, Robert, is a good thing, I might add!" Lucy exclaims warmly, her voice echoing their mother's comforting presence.

Dixie's affection for his sister swells in his chest; she truly is the heart of their family.

"Well, what did they say?" Lucy asks, her breath deep down the phone betraying her concern.

"Are you alright, Lucy?" Dixie interjects, his worry evident.

"Yes, I've just folded the washing, so I'm a bit out of breath, but I am alright. You carry on," Lucy reassures him, her determination shining through.

"I did tell you to leave it until I got home," Dixie gently scolds.

"I know, but I was fed up and needed something to do," Lucy responds without hesitation.

"OK, well, they have given me less than a few months," Dixie reveals, his words hanging in the air.

Lucy gasps audibly, her shock discernible.

"What on earth? I didn't realise it was tha…" she begins, her voice trailing off.

"It's OK, Luce. I half expected it. I've been feeling shit lately, and seeing the consultant has made me realise why," Dixie interrupts, his attempt to reassure her halted by distance.

"It's so unfair, Robert. You are too young to be dying from this horrible disease," Lucy cries out in anguish, her words cutting through the space between them.

If Dixie were at home, the first thing he would do is wrap Lucy in a tight cuddle, letting her tears flow as he whispers

CHAPTER 1

words of comfort in her ear. But the demands of work keep him tethered, a physical distance that feels insurmountable in moments like these.

He can already imagine the weight of her sadness, the longing for his presence tangible through the phone line.

"That's all I can tell you at the moment Sis. I need to take it easy and face each day as it comes, Luce," he assures her, his voice filled with a mixture of resolve and vulnerability.

"And I know you'll do everything you can to make that as easy for me as possible."

Their words linger, heavy with unspoken emotion.

Despite the physical separation, their bond remains unbreakable, a source of solace in the face of life's cruel twists. As they navigate the uncertainty ahead, Dixie finds strength in the knowledge that Lucy will always be there, a steady presence in the storm.

Dixie's focus shifts abruptly back to the investigation, his mind already racing ahead to the tasks at hand.

Without warning, he brings their conversation to an end, cutting Lucy short of any further exchanges they might have had. It's a habit of his, always hanging up before the conversation has truly concluded.

His gaze drifts out the window, where he spots the convoy of police cars making their way back into the station's car park.

Among them, he anticipates the arrival of their nemesis, Gerry Penwald, and his accomplice, Rachel Houston. Dixie knows instinctively that this will mark the beginning of a very long evening.

As he watches the cars pull in, a sense of determination settles over him. Despite the fatigue that weighs heavily on his shoulders, Dixie is ready to face whatever challenges lie ahead.

With Gerry and Rachel in custody, the real work is only just beginning.

* * *

In the lounge, Elizabeth sits, cradling a steaming cup of coffee, her gaze fixed on Chase as he prepares his notepad to document her statement.

Their proximity is close, just a few feet apart, yet the distance between them feels insurmountable amidst the weight of the circumstances.

Chase is accompanied by PC Gilbert, a seasoned female officer with years of experience in handling serious crimes like sexual assault and murder.

The decision to have Gilbert present during Elizabeth's questioning is rooted in providing her with professional support from a female perspective.

Chase and Gilbert share a long history; they were once romantically involved but mutually agreed that their relationship worked better as a friendship.

Despite their past, they've maintained a close bond akin to that of brother and sister.

While admiring Gilbert's competence, Lambert harbours a hint of jealousy toward the stunning blonde officer with piercing blue eyes and long eyelashes.

Chase's expression softens as he looks at Elizabeth sympathetically, his voice gentle as he asks, "How are you feeling?"

"Not good, to be honest," Elizabeth responds, her voice strained with the weight of her emotions. The fear in her

CHAPTER 1

eyes is detectable, reflecting the immense impact the ordeal has had on her.

Anxiety courses through her veins, her heart pounding with palpitations, sweat beading on her brow, and her breaths coming in ragged gasps. The sensation of lightheadedness washes over her, making it difficult to focus on anything but the tightness in her chest, a precursor of impending doom.

"Just take some deep breaths, Elizabeth," Gilbert urges, her tone reassuring as she tries to calm Elizabeth's escalating panic.

"I... I... I am having trouble breathing," she stammers, her words punctuated by the strain of her laboured breaths.

"It's alright. It's a panic attack. I need you to put your head between your knees and take some deep breaths in through your nose, OK?" Gilbert offers her voice a beacon of stability amid Elizabeth's storm of anxiety.

The last thing Gilbert wants is to add to Elizabeth's burden by rushing her off to another hospital. She understands that what she needs most at this moment is reassurance and support, and she's determined to provide just that, offering a steady hand to navigate the storm of emotions that threatens to overwhelm her.

Elizabeth follows Gilbert's guidance, lowering her head to her knees and inhaling deeply as she counts along with her, the rhythm of her breaths gradually steadying.

With each exhalation, she releases some of the tension that has gripped her, feeling a sense of calm wash over her in its wake.

But as the tight knot of anxiety loosens, a flood of overwhelming emotions rushes in, and tears spill from her eyes, mingling with the turmoil within.

The shock of the arrests leaves Elizabeth reeling, her mind racing as she grapples for answers.

She only met Rachel an hour ago, and Gerry has always been by her side. The sudden intrusion of the police into their lives leaves her bewildered and frightened, and she struggles to comprehend what could have prompted such drastic action.

Into this fragile moment steps Lambert, clad in her white Tyvek suit, a forensics bag clutched tightly in her hand. She offers a brief apology as she interrupts Gilbert, Chase and Elizabeth, her focus singular as she addresses Elizabeth.

"Elizabeth, whose laptop is this, please?" Lambert's question is swift and direct, her urgency real as she seeks answers without intruding too deeply into their private moment.

"Erm, that's Gerry's laptop. I don't have any electronics," Elizabeth responds, her voice confused.

Chase and Lambert share a knowing glance, a silent acknowledgement passing between them.

It's no surprise that Elizabeth doesn't possess any electronics.

In the wake of recent events, it's becoming increasingly clear that there's more to this situation than meets the eye.

"Thank you," Lambert murmurs. Her attention shifts back to the task at hand as she turns away to resume her search for further evidence.

Elizabeth watches her for a moment, grateful for the investigator's diligence in uncovering the truth, but she is unaware of what.

As Lambert continues her meticulous sweep, Elizabeth's eyes wander to the pile of evidence scattered on the hallway floor. Among the array of items, her gaze locks onto

CHAPTER 1

something familiar — her diary.

A surge of unease grips her as she realises that her most personal thoughts and secrets are now laid bare, exposed to scrutiny in the unforgiving light of investigation.

"Do they need to take my belongings? I don't feel comfortable knowing that people are snooping through my thoughts," Elizabeth voices her concern to Chase, her tone full of apprehension.

He turns towards her, his expression sympathetic as he addresses her worries.

"I'm afraid we can take whatever we feel will help us with our investigation," Chase responds, his manner as understanding as possible given the circumstances.

Curiosity tugs at Elizabeth's thoughts, prompting her to enquire further.

"So, what is the investigation?" she asks, genuinely interested in understanding the situation.

"We are investigating the disappearance of a woman, Molly Chapman. Does the name ring any bells with you?" Gilbert probes gently, watching for any sign of recognition in Elizabeth's eyes.

"I recognise the name," Elizabeth admits, her eyes widening with a hint of fear at the mention of Molly Chapman's disappearance.

"Where do you think you recognise the name from?" Chase prompts, sensing her unease.

"I don't know, it's odd..." Elizabeth's voice trails off, uncertainty clouding her thoughts.

Chase places a reassuring hand on Elizabeth's arm, encouraging her to open up.

"What is odd, Elizabeth?" he presses gently.

"I know the name like I know who she is or that I should do," Elizabeth confesses, her voice confused.

Absentmindedly, Elizabeth wipes her nose on the sleeve of her top, then quickly wipes away the slimy trail with her other sleeve.

She sniffs, trying to compose herself in the flood of emotions.

"Can you please confirm your name and date of birth for me?" Chase interjects, changing the subject momentarily.

"I'm guessing you know what it is already," Elizabeth responds, attempting to stall the questioning.

"I do, but I need you to confirm them for me. Please," Chase insists gently, his eyes fixed on hers.

Meeting Chase's gaze, Elizabeth answers firmly, "My name is Elizabeth Mollyanne Penwald, and my date of birth is the 11th of April 1981."

"And who is your partner?" Chase enquires, searching Elizabeth's eyes for any sign of recognition.

"Gerry Penwald. My husband," Elizabeth replies without hesitation.

Chase continues his line of questioning, his concern growing as he delves deeper.

"And what is his date of birth?" he asks.

"I… erm… I don't know," Elizabeth admits, her memory failing her.

"You do not know when your husband's birthday is?" Gilbert asks, her concern transparent.

"No, I don't remember," Elizabeth replies, tears welling up in her eyes once again, a perceptible sense of distress riding heavy on her emotions.

Chapter 2

Wednesday Early Evening

As the cars glide into the station car park, they ease to a stop just outside the entrance to the Custody Suite, the engines purring softly as they settle.

Carter quickly emerges from his vehicle, his movements purposeful as he strides towards Gerry's side of the car.

With a swift motion, Carter opens the door, revealing Gerry seated inside, his hands bound in cuffs.

Gerry shifts, endeavouring to manoeuvre himself out of the seat, while Carter offers a steadying hand, assisting him to rise.

Once Gerry is upright, Carter gently eases the door shut before positioning himself beside Gerry, a supportive presence as they begin the short journey towards the station entrance.

Carter's firm grip on Gerry's arm serves as both guidance and reassurance, ensuring Gerry's steady progress.

Meanwhile, from the car behind them, Poker observes the scene with keen focus, his attention unwavering.

As Carter nods in his direction, a silent understanding

passes between them, a wordless affirmation of their shared purpose and determination. Poker returns the nod with equal conviction, his commitment to the mission clear in the resolute set of his jaw.

Poker glances in his rearview mirror, catching sight of Rachel's tear-stained face as she stares out of the window, her gaze searching for a glimpse of Gerry.

Poker senses her deflation, the weight of resignation settling upon her shoulders as she braces herself for whatever the next couple of hours may bring. The silent turmoil etched on her features speaks volumes, a poignant reflection of the uncertainty and apprehension that pervades the atmosphere within the car.

Poker watches as Carter takes Gerry through the large glass doors of the Custody Suite; he shuts them behind himself and walks out of view.

This evening, PC Dobinson is on the desk. She is a stocky, pretty woman with dark brown hair tied tightly in a bun at the nape of her neck.

"Evening Carter," she says in a jovial manner.

Her piercing blue eyes catch the light from the luminous lighting overhead.

"Evening Dobby, you alright?" Carter asks, smiling back at the attractive brunette.

"Yeah, thanks, all good. How are you?" she asks in return.

"All good, all good," Carter replies, looking at Gerry as they both make their way to the desk.

Still handcuffed, Gerry places both of his hands on the booking-in desk and leans against it, exhausted from his ordeal of being arrested.

Gerry is asked to write down his next of KIN and a person

CHAPTER 2

whom he would like to contact.

"I don't have anyone," says Gerry quietly.

"No one at all? that you can contact?" asks Dobby.

"No, my ex has been arrested, and my current partner, well, that's why I am here," he says, barely audible.

"Sorry, what was that?" Carter asked, almost sure he knew what Gerry had just said but needed to clarify the words.

"My wife, I don't want her bothered; she has enough to cope with."

"Oh, I see." says Dobby as she writes down 'Refused a phone call' on Gerry's booking-in papers.

Carter nods at Dobby as she continues to ask Gerry some formal questions whilst she registers him into custody.

Gerry complies and is quick to answer, simply so that he can be shown to his holding cell and not have to face anyone just yet.

"And do you know why you have been arrested, Mr Penwald?" asks Dobby.

His nerves are taut, stretched thin like a wire under tension.

Never before has he experienced the cold grip of fear that now coils around his heart.

'Arrested?'

The word echoes in his mind, alien and ominous. He had always considered himself an upstanding member of the community, a beacon of respectability untouched by the law.

The mere thought of speaking to a police officer sends a shiver down his spine. Until recently, such encounters were unimaginable, confined to the realm of distant possibilities.

But now, with the memory of those house-to-house calls still fresh in his mind, he can't shake the feeling of unease that gnaws at him.

He had never anticipated being caught up in the tangled web of suspicion and scrutiny.

To him, the police were a distant presence, like figures in a play unfolding on a stage. But now, they stand before him, their questions piercing through the facade of normalcy he had meticulously crafted.

In the blink of an eye, his world has been upended, his sense of security shattered.

The pillars of his identity crumble under the weight of uncertainty, leaving behind only the stark realisation that he is no longer immune to the long arm of the law.

"Yes, I believe so," he responds, feeling unnerved by the questions now.

Dobby regards him with a mix of empathy and understanding, her gaze softening as she recognises the vulnerability in his eyes.

Without hesitation, she extends a gesture of kindness, offering him respite in the form of a drink.

Gerry politely asks for some water.

"Sure thing," she replies warmly, her voice sincere.

"Water coming right up."

Dobby disappears behind the desk and into the room beyond. The sound of running water fills the air as she fills a plastic cup to the brim, ensuring it's refreshingly cold.

Gerry's gratitude is appreciable as he accepts the cup, the cool liquid a balm to his parched throat. Gerry is thirsty, and he drains the cup in a few swift swallows, the sensation of hydration a welcome relief.

Dobby's presence is a comforting reassurance as she offers him more. Gerry nods gratefully, relinquishing the empty cup into her waiting hand. Once again, she disappears into

CHAPTER 2

the back, emerging moments later with another cup filled to the brim.

"Alright, Mr Penwald, let's get back to the formalities," Dobby announces, her fingers dancing over the keys of her keyboard, the rhythmic clicking of her acrylic nails drawing Gerry's attention like a hypnotic melody.

Lost in his thoughts, he drifts away into a daydream, his mind wandering to Elizabeth and the uncertainty of her feelings towards him.

"So if you can sign there where I have put the cross," Dobby directs, her voice breaking through Gerry's reverie as she points to a designated spot at the bottom of the paperwork.

She draws another cross that she wants Gerry to sign next to.

Startled from his thoughts, Gerry fumbles for comprehension.

"Sorry, what am I signing again?" he asks, his embarrassment evident.

With a subtle click of her tongue, Dobby patiently explains with a hint of exasperation that he's signing for his personal belongings, which will be placed in a holding safe until his release.

Realising his lapse, Gerry offers a sheepish smile.

"Right, yes, sorry," he mumbles, hastily scrawling his signature at the bottom of the form.

"And one more signature here, please. This indicates your waiver of the right to a phone call," Dobby adds, gesturing to another section of the document.

Gerry complies, his hand moving almost mechanically as he signs the papers. Stepping back from the desk, he takes a moment to collect himself.

"Would you like a solicitor Mr Penwald?" asks Dobby seriously.

"Erm, Yes, I think I would, please."

"Ok, so if you can, just sign the last one here," she says as she points to the empty box at the top of the paperwork.

"That gives you the freedom to choose your solicitor, I have a few names here unless you have your own one?"

"I would like to use my family solicitor if that is at all possible, please." requests Gerry, waiting patiently for Dobby to write the details down on the form.

"Chatsworth & Brenner. Please." he asks.

Dobby looks at him and asks him to spell the solicitor's name so that she can get the right one. Gerry complies and signs the last piece of the paperwork.

Carter, ever the authoritative presence, gives Gerry a reassuring pat on the back before ushering him down the corridor toward the cells.

"You'll be placed in one of the cells until we need to question you. We can come and get you for questioning at any time. However, we need to go through your solicitor first, so unless they say we can interview you, we can't just come and haul you out for questioning. You are advised not to say anything until you have spoken to them." Carter pauses for breath.

"Is all of that clear?" he asks Gerry.

"Yes, crystal," Gerry answers, smiling at Carter.

Carter returns the smile.

"Until then, I suggest you get some rest, as it's likely to be a long evening," Carter advises his tone firm but not unkind.

Carter hands Gerry over to PC Dobinson, who proceeds down the corridor, footsteps echoing against the cold walls

CHAPTER 2

as they approach a cell tucked away in the corner.

Dobby produces the key to the cell, unlocking the door with a metallic click.

She motions for Gerry to extend his hands, indicating the removal of the cuffs.

Gerry complies, a sense of relief washing over him as the cold metal restraints are loosened.

He massages his wrists, grateful for the freedom of movement.

"Thanks, officer," Gerry acknowledges, offering a small smile.

Dobby returns the smile, her tone lightening the atmosphere.

"You're welcome. They're not exactly the most comfortable accessories, are they?" she remarks with a chuckle.

Gerry nods in agreement.

"Definitely not."

"Feel free to make yourself comfortable in here. The toilet is just on the side. Is there anything else you need? Perhaps something to eat?" Dobby's voice is calm but firm, her eyes reflecting a hint of sympathy for Gerry's predicament.

Gerry feels vulnerable as he contemplates the gravity of his situation.

"I suppose I'll be here for a while if you're offering me food," he replies uneasily.

Dobby nods, maintaining a delicate balance between seriousness and reassurance.

"At least 24 hours, minimum. After that, we'll decide whether to charge you or release you," she explains, hoping to allay Gerry's fears without downplaying the seriousness of the situation.

Admitting his queasiness, Gerry agrees.

"Alright, yes, please. I'll have something. It might settle my stomach," he admits, grateful for the offer.

"We have sandwiches available. Do cheese and ham sound alright to you?" Dobby offers her tone polite but with a hint of resignation.

As she extends this gesture of hospitality in the tense atmosphere of the cell, Dobby can't help but reflect on the irony of the situation.

In her years of service, Dobby has often found it strange how the pursuit of suspects can span weeks, months, or even years, only to culminate in their arrest and subsequent detention. Despite the severity of their alleged crimes, suspects are still entitled to basic rights and humane treatment, including meals and drinks prepared by the very officers tasked with bringing them to justice.

While Dobby fully understands and upholds the principles of human rights and the presumption of innocence until proven guilty, she can't shake the bitter irony of serving those who may have caused irreparable harm to others. The contradiction between providing care and catering to the needs of suspects, some of whom are accused of heinous crimes, and the emotional toll it takes on her conscience is not lost on her.

Nevertheless, Dobby remains committed to her duty of ensuring the welfare of all prisoners in her care.

Over the past year as a Custody Officer, she has diligently performed her role, navigating the delicate balance between empathy and duty, even when it leaves a bitter taste in her mouth.

Gerry walks over to the bed, his footsteps echoing softly

CHAPTER 2

in the dimly lit cell. With a heavy sigh, he reaches for the blue mattress resting against the wall and carefully unfolds it, letting it cascade onto the cold, unforgiving concrete base. This makeshift bed, little more than a thin layer of padding, will be his only refuge in the stark confines of the cell for the next twenty-four hours.

He sits down and brings his knees up and under his chin as he wraps his arms around his shins.

Dobby closes the door locks it behind herself, and makes her way to the small kitchen to prepare some food for Gerry.

Poker swings open the car door, gesturing for Rachel to exit. She shuffles across the seat, her movements slow and deliberate, before finally stepping out into the car park. He offers a steadying hand, guiding her gently as she rises to her feet and inhales the crisp December air with a deep breath.

A heavy sigh escapes her lips, laden with tension and uncertainty.

"I'm not involved in whatever this is," Rachel pleads, her voice desperate, as if seeking absolution from an unseen judgment. But Poker's response is firm and unwavering.

"Please save it for the interview," he interjects, his tone professional and clipped. But Rachel persists, her words tumbling out in a rush of emotion.

"I know how it looks," she insists, her voice trembling as she struggles to contain her emotions.

"But you have to believe me, I didn't know that Molly was there." She pauses, wiping away tears with the sleeve of her arm before continuing, her words a jumble of anguish and frustration.

"Jesus Christ, I don't even think that Molly knows she is there!"

"I said save it," Poker interrupts sharply, his patience wearing thin. He's not interested in entertaining Rachel's pleas or engaging in idle conversation. There are more pressing matters at hand, and he's determined to focus on the task without distraction.

Chapter 3

Wednesday Early Evening

In the dimly lit custody suite, Rachel leans heavily against the counter, her breath forming a warm mist on the glass partition separating her from the Duty Officer. The additional screens, hastily erected during the height of the COVID-19 pandemic, create an invisible barrier, further isolating Rachel as she grapples with the gravity of the situation unfolding before her.

Tremors course through her body, betraying the fear and vulnerability gnawing at her insides.

As the charges are read aloud, Rachel listens in silence, each word striking her like a blow.

"Conspiracy to abduction... Conspiracy to coercive behaviour... Perverting the course of justice..." The accusations cast a shadow over Rachel's already fragile state of mind. She knows she's innocent, but the weight of uncertainty threatens to suffocate her.

Faced with the daunting task of proving her innocence, Rachel struggles to comprehend the whirlwind of events that led her here.

'Was Molly with Gerry willingly, or was she a victim of coercion?'

The questions swirl in Rachel's mind, each one more confounding than the last.

At least by her being charged, she knows roughly what Gerry is being charged for.

With a resigned nod, Rachel answers PC Dobinson's enquiries and signs the paperwork, her hand trembling slightly as she does so.

"Would you like a drink, Miss Houston?" Dobby's voice cuts through the tense atmosphere, offering a momentary reprieve.

"No, thank you," Rachel replies tersely, her gaze fixed on the floor.

"I just need to sit down, if I may."

As Rachel sinks to the ground, her legs threatening to give way beneath her, Dobby's expression softens with concern.

With a gentle hand, Poker helps Rachel to her feet, guiding her towards a nearby cell where she can rest.

"Come on, Rachel," Poker says soothingly, adjusting his curt attitude toward her.

"I'll get you settled in. We'll take care of you."

After conducting a brief well-being check, Dobby leaves Rachel to her thoughts, promising to arrange for a solicitor and a phone call to her father.

Alone in her cell, Rachel grapples with the uncertainty of her fate, clinging to the hope that they will believe her.

* * *

Ray finishes overseeing the children's bedtime routines,

CHAPTER 3

ensuring teeth are brushed and showers taken care of. Looking forward to a bit of relaxation, he contemplates watching a movie, perhaps continuing with the 'Taken' series starring Liam Neeson.

Despite recent events involving Molly, he refuses to let her disappearance dampen his evening.

As he settles into the living room, Bonnie appears at the doorway, interrupting his thoughts.

"Do you need the toilet before I use the bathroom, Dad?" she asks politely.

"No, I'm good. Thanks, Bonnie. You go ahead," he smiles, appreciating his daughter's consideration.

Since Rachel departed from their lives, Ray has found himself bonding more with the children.

Bonnie sits on the sofa, and Ray braces himself, sensing that their conversation will delve deeper than their usual goodnight exchanges.

"Where do you think Mum might be?" Bonnie enquires, her concern obvious.

Ray takes a moment to consider his response, not wanting to appear indifferent.

Lately, he finds himself caring less, especially since learning of Molly's involvement with another man.

"I don't know, Bonnie. But the fact that she hasn't tried to contact any of us says something, doesn't it?" he muses.

Bonnie defends her mother, suggesting that Molly's absence might be due to memory loss rather than a deliberate choice.

Ray's voice turns bitter as he responds, "No, it means she's happy with this 'Gerry' bloke. That's what it means."

"Dad, do you honestly believe that?" Bonnie challenges,

her tone earnest.

"I don't know what to believe anymore," he admits, his frustration noticeable.

"The fact that she walked out and left us is one thing, but pretending to be missing, that's a whole different kettle of fish."

Bonnie looks puzzled.

"What do you mean, kettle of fish?"

"It's just an old saying. Don't worry about it now. You go have your shower so that I can then have mine. I want to settle down for the evening," Ray instructs.

"Alright. So long as you're OK, Dad. I do worry about you, you know," Bonnie expresses her concern.

Ray leans over and pats her knee reassuringly.

"I know you do, but I'm fine. Thank you."

Bonnie stands up, leaning in to give her dad a hug goodnight.

"I love you, Dad," she whispers.

"Ditto," he replies softly.

Ray has always struggled to express his emotions, especially love, towards his children. Molly used to criticise him for it, but he would attribute it to his upbringing, lacking the affection he now struggles to show. Despite Molly's arguments, Ray finds it difficult to break free from the emotional barriers he's built over the years.

Oliver stands at the doorway, his presence noted as Bonnie brushes past him, playfully poking him in the ribs.

"Ouch! That hurt!" Oliver exclaims, rubbing his side.

Ray, seated nearby, sighs and rolls his eyes upward.

"Will you two ever quit?" he yells in exasperation.

"Sheesh, Come on, Dad, we're just messing around," Oliver

CHAPTER 3

retorts, surprising both Ray and Bonnie.

Ray, taken aback by his son's cheek, responds, "Excuse me, young man?"

Bonnie lets out a quiet "Uh oh."

"We were just joking," Oliver defends himself.

Ray snorts disapprovingly, "Who do you think you're talking to like that?"

Bonnie quietly urges Oliver to apologise, but he ignores her.

"Forget it. I was just coming to say goodnight, but I won't bother now," Oliver says, turning on his heel and storming out of the living room, stomping up the stairs.

Ray rises from his seat and follows Oliver, determined to address the behaviour.

Reaching his room, Oliver slams the door shut behind him. Ray, unfazed by the show of temper, takes a deep breath, grasps the door handle, and forcefully swings it open.

"You need to come out here right now," Ray demands, pointing to the space before him.

Oliver throws himself onto his bed, burying his face in his pillows and beginning to cry.

Ray, showing no signs of remorse, continues to scold him.

Meanwhile, Lillie emerges from her room, a towel wrapped around her head and wearing a bathrobe, resembling 'Stay Puft' from the 'Ghostbusters' movie.

"What's happening?" Lillie asks concerned.

Bonnie trails behind her dad up the stairs, anxious about his reaction to Oliver's behaviour.

Recently, their father had been in relatively good spirits, but the children sensed he was putting on a facade, masking his worries about their mother.

"Dad's on the verge of losing it. Oli was really cheeky downstairs, it caught me off guard too, so I get why Dad's suddenly got up to tell him off," Bonnie explains.

"What did he say?" Lillie enquires.

"Let's just say he might as well have told Dad to take a 'chill pill'," Bonnie chuckles, unable to contain her laughter.

"Oh dear, he's in trouble then," Lillie remarks.

The two girls stand in the hallway, their ears tuned to the escalating commotion. Suddenly, a slap reverberates through the air, followed by more shouting and Oliver's tears.

"I hate you, I hate you! I wish I lived with Uncle Reggie; he's more of a Dad to me than you are. I'm glad Mum left you," Oliver's anguished voice echoes from his room.

Lillie and Bonnie exchange shocked glances, wincing at each other's distress as another slap is heard, followed by sobs.

Ray emerges onto the landing.

"Did you just hit Oliver?" Lillie demands, her tone fierce.

"Why, do you want one too, young lady?" Ray retorts, his voice dripping with anger.

"Lillie, please don't," Bonnie pleads, fearing further confrontation.

Frozen in disbelief at being threatened by her father, Lillie remains rooted to the spot as Ray storms past them and descends back into the living room.

The girls rush into Oliver's room to check on him. He's curled up in the fetal position on his bed, clutching his pillow tightly.

"I miss Mum. I miss her so much," Oliver cries.

Lillie leans over, enveloping Oliver in a comforting cuddle. "It's OK; we're here for you," she reassures him softly.

CHAPTER 3

* * *

I know I must have a conversation with Sharpie about my remaining time. The worry gnaws at me faster than the cancer is progressing. I need to figure out what to say and how to say it.

I've already recommended Sharpie for the promotion to Lead Detective Inspector of the Blackpool Police and even suggested that Carter become a Detective Inspector at the end of this case. But considering my declining health, it seems those promotions might need to happen sooner than I anticipated.

I'm not even sure if I'll be able to see this investigation through. I can feel the cancer coursing through my veins, slowly consuming what little life I'm holding onto.

For me, it's too late for treatment. I should have pursued it months ago, but I firmly believe that when it's your time, it's your time.

I spot Sharpie walking past my office window, so I beckon him over, and he smiles at me.

I have a deep admiration for him; we've been through so much together in all the years we've worked side by side without a single disagreement.

"You summoned me?" Sharpie chuckles as he pokes his head into my office.

I nod and offer a smile.

"Yes, I did. I need to speak with you before the team returns."

"Oh, alright. Nothing bad, I hope?" he asks.

"When is it ever good news when I call you in here, Sharpie?" I reply, and we share a laugh.

"True," he agrees.

I begin to explain about the consultant and the prognosis. I can see the devastation in his eyes.

"I just can't believe it," he murmurs, avoiding my gaze.

Maybe I should have waited to deliver the news later. But I've never been one to withhold important information for too long.

"I know. It's pretty awful. I'm worried about Lucy. Please promise me you'll keep an eye on her, Sharpie." I ask, knowing it's a significant request but we don't have anyone else to look out for her.

"Of course I will. I've always liked Lucy, you know that," Sharpie says with a twinkle in his eye.

"Yes, and I think she feels the same about you. Who knows, you might even find love at your ripe old age," I jest.

"True," he says

Sharpie's face flushes.

"You were supposed to say, 'It's not like that!'" I tease.

"So, what are we going to do about the investigation?" Sharpie's concern is evident.

"Well, I've made my recommendations. You'll take over from me when the time is right, probably in the next week or so…" I'm interrupted by Sharpie's sharp intake of breath.

"A week?" he says, shocked.

"Are you that ill?"

"Yes, I am. I shouldn't even be here right now, but you know me. I won't retire to my bed unless I've taken my last breath."

"Oh, don't say it like that."

"What? But it's true, and you know it. When have you ever known me to call in sick?"

CHAPTER 3

"True, of course. I know you too well. You'll still be here the day they carry you out in a box," Sharpie says, half smiling, half grimacing.

I appreciate this type of humour; it keeps my spirits up and adds a touch of levity to an otherwise grim situation.

"So, I've recommended Carter for promotion, but I think it'd be best to see him promoted sooner rather than later. He's cut out for it, and he's proven his worth beyond a doubt with this case," I explain.

"Yeah, I agree. He's practically been leading it himself," Sharpie adds.

"Right. So, you'll be the Lead DI for the force, and Carter will step into your role. That way, there won't be any gaps in the team," I clarify.

Sharpie looks visibly relieved that I've sorted it out.

"When will you be leaving work?" Sharpie hesitates, trying not to pry too much, but we're good friends, and honesty is crucial.

"Well, it's almost the weekend, so I probably won't be coming back to work from Monday. It's a race against time," I reply solemnly.

"Alright, that makes sense. But if you're not up for it, just let me know. I can always borrow a wheelchair from downstairs," Sharpie jokes.

"I'll tell the team over the next couple of days. I don't want them knowing any sooner; I need their full attention on the case and these interviews," I suggest.

"Speaking of which, I need to call Chase and see how he's getting on with Molly or Elizabeth, whichever one he's found," I chuckle.

Sharpie joins in the laughter and extends his hand for a

shake. I accept, and we stand there in silence for a moment, knowing that no words are necessary.

Chapter 4

Wednesday Late Evening

Lambert enters the room, clutching hold of a small bouquet she had picked up from the floor just outside the front door.

"Would you like me to put these into water for you?" she offers Elizabeth.

Elizabeth shakes her head.

"Oh, they weren't for me. They were what Rachel had brought for Gerry's Mum. She hadn't realized his Mum had passed away when she turned up to visit her."

Lambert nods, understandingly.

"Well, I've bagged up the cellophane as there were some prints on it. I don't want the flowers to go to waste. Do you have a vase?"

"Just inside the kitchen cupboard under the sink," Elizabeth responds, mentally noting the location.

Lambert retrieves the vase and carefully untangles the flowers. She fills the vase with water, stopping just shy of the brim, and expertly arranges them into a beautiful display. Carrying the vase into the lounge, she places the flowers on the coffee table before returning to the hallway to continue dusting the door frames for prints and signs of blood splatter.

"They look stunning," Gilbert remarks.

Elizabeth nods in agreement.

"Yes, they do," she says.

The fragrance of the lilies fills the room, adding a touch of freshness to the atmosphere.

Gilbert offers Elizabeth a drink, but she declines. Feeling overwhelmed by the ordeal, all she wants is to be left alone.

Chase coughs and excuses himself, asking Elizabeth for directions to the bathroom.

"Yes, of course. It's just off the hallway to the right," she responds.

"Thank you. I won't be long," Chase replies as he heads toward the bathroom, side-stepping Lambert, who is on her hands and knees dusting the skirting board in the hallway.

"You missed a bit," Chase jokes as he passes her.

Lambert playfully slaps his legs as he walks past, and they both share a laugh.

Gilbert reaches into her bag, pulling out a notepad which she carefully places on her lap. Before leaning back, she rummages for a pen, retrieving the lid with her teeth before starting to write on it.

"I'm going to start by asking you some questions. Some might be difficult, and others might seem strange, but please don't hesitate to ask if you're unsure, alright?" Gilbert's tone is gentle, trying to ease Elizabeth's nerves about the impending interrogation.

"OK," Elizabeth replies, her voice filled with apprehension at what kind of questions she might face.

"Am I a suspect?" Elizabeth queries, her anxiety evident in

CHAPTER 4

her voice.

"No, dear god, you're most certainly not a suspect, but, we do need to determine if you're a victim of a serious crime," Gilbert reassures her, hoping to alleviate some of Elizabeth's shock at the gravity of the situation.

Elizabeth's expression reflects her surprise at Gilbert's words, but she remains composed and patiently awaits the onset of questioning.

"Can you tell me how you know Gerry Penwald?" Gilbert asks, diving straight into the interrogation.

Elizabeth takes a moment to collect her thoughts, surprised by the simplicity of the question. She had anticipated trickier enquiries designed to trip her up.

"He's my husband. We got married in August of this year," Elizabeth replies, her voice steady despite the underlying tension.

"And before then? When and how did you meet?" Gilbert notices Elizabeth's struggle and decides to wait until Chase returns to the room. She doesn't want to overwhelm her and risk missing out on vital information for the investigation.

"It's OK, Elizabeth, take your time," Gilbert reassures her, offering a moment of respite before delving deeper.

"I, uh, I have amnesia, total memory loss of anything before the accident that I had. I don't remember most things. I'm sorry," Elizabeth confesses, her voice tinged with worry, her face a canvas of concern.

"It's OK; I know it's difficult," Gilbert responds her tone gentle and understanding.

"I know that it all happened very fast. We met, dated, and then got married quickly," Elizabeth continues, her uncertainty observable.

"And do you remember that, or is that what Gerry has told you?" Gilbert probes, her pen poised over the paper, ready to jot down Elizabeth's response.

"It's what Gerry told me at the hospital. The staff adored him; he looked after me the whole time I was in there," Elizabeth recalls, relying on Gerry's account of their whirlwind romance.

"What happened the night you had your accident? Do you remember any of that evening?" Gilbert delves deeper, seeking clarity amidst the haze of Elizabeth's memory loss.

"I don't remember a thing, but I was told that I was knocked off the sea wall by our dog, Duke. It was an accident in which he drowned," Elizabeth reveals, a shadow of sadness crossing her features.

Chase re-enters the room and settles beside Elizabeth, his presence offering a sense of comfort.

"You both alright in here?" he enquires, casting a concerned glance between Elizabeth and Gilbert.

"Yes, we're good. I was asking Elizabeth about the night of the accident," Gilbert explains, her gaze shifting between Chase and Elizabeth.

"I wish I could remember something, but the first thing I have any recollection of is waking up from my coma. Gerry was standing there. He seemed familiar to me, but I would never have guessed he was my husband," Elizabeth recounts, her voice full of confusion and frustration.

Gilbert scratches her head, silently seeking Chase's approval to broach a delicate subject.

With his nod of affirmation, she proceeds cautiously.

"Elizabeth, would you be shocked to find out that Gerry isn't, in fact, your husband?" Gilbert poses the question

CHAPTER 4

gently, bracing for Elizabeth's reaction.

"Oh, don't be so ridiculous. Of course, he is. We live together, eat together, sleep together. Of course, he is my husband," Elizabeth responds, her laughter ringing hollow and full of uncertainty.

Chase and Gilbert exchange a silent glance, allowing Elizabeth a moment to process the implications of their revelation. As the pressure of the situation sinks in, Elizabeth's complexion pales, her conduct shifting to one of quiet contemplation.

"I would know, wouldn't I?" Elizabeth's voice wavers, her gaze shifting between Gilbert and Chase, seeking validation.

"Think back to the time you woke up. You were in a state of shock, unable to comprehend what was going on around you. You were in the hospital, wired up to machines that were keeping you alive. When did you first learn that Gerry was your husband?" Gilbert prompts, her tone gentle yet probing.

"When the nurse said to me, 'your husband is here to see you,'" Elizabeth recalls, her voice trailing off as she delves into the memories of that fateful evening when she regained consciousness.

As the recollection floods her mind, Elizabeth's senses reel, the events of that night seeming like a blur, a distant memory shrouded in fog. She feels a bead of sweat forming on her brow, the weight of uncertainty pressing down on her.

Elizabeth blurts out.

"He stood there in an open-collar shirt, radiating a certain charm and handsomeness that was hard to ignore."

She pauses before continuing.

"There was an aura about him, one that exudes kindness,

care, and concern. As I regained consciousness, I felt an inexplicable familiarity with him. He's one of the first people to speak to me, and his relief at my awakening was real."

Elizabeth wipes a tear from her eye.

"His hurt and disappointment when I failed to recognize him felt genuine, raw, unscripted. You can't fake those emotions, and you can't rehearse them; they're authentic and genuine. Unless he's a Hollywood-level actor, I refuse to believe he's putting on an act."

"Elizabeth. Is there anything else you can tell me about that moment?" Chase's voice interrupts her, pulling her back to the present moment.

"I needed a wee. I initially thought he was a doctor, so I asked him to take me to the toilet, but he said he would get a nurse."

She pauses again.

"He was so kind to me, so understanding of me being anxious."

Wiping her eyes, Elizabeth asks, "Can I see my husband? I want to see him now. He's the only part of reality I understand. Please, can you take me to see him?"

The tears now fall down her cheeks.

"This is ludicrous. I don't know what you want from me, but I'm not playing along with your silly games," Elizabeth retorts, frustrated and upset.

Lambert enters the room, drawn by Elizabeth's raised voice.

"Everything alright in here?" she enquires.

"No, I'm being told that my husband isn't actually my husband, and what else? That I'm not Elizabeth Penwald? Is that what's coming next?" Elizabeth stands up, her hands

CHAPTER 4

trembling with emotion, and excuses herself to use the bathroom.

She leaves the room, leaving Chase and Gilbert to grapple with the weight of her obvious disdain.

"This is going to take some convincing," Chase remarks to Gilbert, concern in his voice.

"At the end of the day, the poor woman has been through weeks of an ordeal. She's just about got her life on the straight and narrow, and then we come barging in, arresting her supposed husband, and then start firing questions at her about who she is, like she's a suspect or the one who's done wrong," Gilbert muses, echoing the unease.

"She is going to have to answer the questions, though. She may not be a suspect, but she is a victim in all this," says Chase.

Gilbert pauses, considering Chase's suggestion for a moment.

"Let's approach this from a different angle," Chase proposes.

Intrigued, Gilbert asks, "OK, and what approach would that be?"

* * *

Elizabeth stands before the bathroom mirror, her eyes still glistening with tears. She reaches for the plush towel hanging on the rail, gently dabbing at her cheeks.

Peering into her reflection, she brushes her fringe away from her face, attempting to compose herself with a determined smile.

"I can do this," she whispers to herself, her voice barely

audible in the quiet room.

"You've held it together this long; just a little while longer. You knew this day was going to come eventually"

A soft tap on the door interrupts her thoughts, and Lambert's voice penetrates the silence.

"Are you OK in there, sweetie?"

Elizabeth clears her throat before responding, "Um, yes. I'm fine, thank you. Just... having a moment."

"Is there anything you need?" Lambert's concern is obvious in her gentle tone.

"No, I'm OK, thank you. I'll be out soon," Elizabeth assures her.

As she hears the latch slide across and the door creak open slightly, Lambert catches sight of Elizabeth standing in the narrow gap, her eyes red-rimmed from crying.

"I know it's overwhelming, but you're handling it so well," Lambert offers, her words filled with understanding and support.

"Thank you. I just... I'm still trying to process everything," Elizabeth admits, her voice aches with uncertainty.

"Just take each question as it comes and answer as honestly as you can. It'll all work out in the end," Lambert reassures her.

Elizabeth's eyes fill with tears once more as she wipes away a stray tear falling down her cheek.

"But will it? Will it really?" she says aloud.

Lambert's heart aches for Elizabeth.

One moment, she was living her ordinary life with her husband, and the next, the police burst in, turning her world upside down with uncertainties and unbelievable tales. Elizabeth is lost in a sea of confusion, unsure of what to

CHAPTER 4

believe.

Silently, Elizabeth follows Lambert back to the living room where Chase and Gilbert await on the sofa.

"Are you OK, Elizabeth?" Gilbert enquires, concern etched in her expression.

Elizabeth meets her gaze briefly, managing a fleeting smile.

"Yes, I think so," she replies softly.

Chase interjects, breaking the tension.

"Are you ready for me to continue with my questions?" he asks.

"Yes," Elizabeth nods.

"Tell me about your husband and how he's been since you woke from your coma," Chase prompts.

"He's been my rock, my support. Gerry's been there for me through everything since I regained consciousness. I woke up in that hospital not even recognizing my name, and he's stood by me ever since," Elizabeth explains gratefully.

"Has anything occurred that's made you question your life with him?" Chase probes gently.

"Absolutely not!" Elizabeth's response is immediate and firm. But then, she begins to recount her flashbacks.

"They feel so real, yet disjointed. And the name Molly... In my memories, I hear the name Molly mentioned. I've always believed, and still do, that because it's my middle name, it was used as a nickname in those fragmented recollections," she reveals.

"Someone called out Molly in your dreams?" Gilbert clarifies.

"Not in my dreams, but in my flashbacks," Elizabeth corrects.

"So, if I understand correctly, you're experiencing flashbacks where someone is calling out the name Molly?" Gilbert seeks confirmation.

"Yes, that's correct. I initially thought it was because my middle name is Mollyanne," Elizabeth explains, her expression thoughtful.

Chase appears puzzled.

"Who informed you that your name is Elizabeth Mollyanne?" he enquires.

"Gerry and the hospital staff did. It was on my records," Elizabeth responds, her confusion visible as she tries to piece together where this conversation is leading.

"Doesn't it strike you as odd that we're searching for a missing person named Molly, and yet in your flashbacks, that's the very name you're being called?" Chase probes delicately, trying to unravel the mystery.

"Yes, it does seem strange, but considering that is my name," Elizabeth responds, her tone somewhat uncertain.

"You mean your middle name?" Gilbert seeks clarification.

"Huh?" she replies.

"You said, considering that is your name," Chase interjects.

"I'm getting confused here. Are you trying to tell me that my name isn't even Elizabeth Mollyanne? I don't know where you've got that information from?" Elizabeth's voice rises slightly, frustration creeping into her tone.

Sensing Elizabeth's growing distress, Chase shifts gears, opting for a different line of questioning.

"Do you have any children, Elizabeth?" he asks gently.

"No?" Elizabeth's confusion deepens.

"Are you sure?" Chase persists, observing Elizabeth's reactions closely.

"I'm sure," Elizabeth replies firmly.

CHAPTER 4

"How can you be so sure, you have severe memory loss?" Chase continues cautiously, monitoring Elizabeth's conduct. Seeing her relatively calm, he decides to press on with the line of enquiry.

"Because we can't have children. Gerry is unable to have them, he disclosed that information to me just recently when I questioned him about it" Elizabeth explains.

Chase consults his notes, pointing to some writing for Gilbert to read, then gestures to Gilbert; signalling for her to ask Elizabeth the next question that he had written in his notes.

Meeting Elizabeth's gaze directly, Gilbert asks, "Elizabeth, how would you explain the Cesarean scar across your tummy if you haven't had any children?"

Elizabeth's eyes widen in shock as she slowly lifts her top to her belly button, pulling down her trousers slightly to reveal a neat white scar stretching across her abdomen.

Chapter 5

Wednesday Late Evening

Confinement to these four walls, it's like a descent into madness.
    Within this space, all my demons converge, and there's a dark interplay between conscience and immorality. Here, you grapple with the realisation that only one version of yourself will emerge through that door, but the question is, which one?

I find myself pondering if I've done wrong. Who holds the authority to judge the morality of my actions?

Society labels me an abductor, a person who forcefully takes others against their will. Yet, Elizabeth willingly came home with me. She chose to be by my side, to be my wife, to let me care for her.

The weight of the accusation hangs heavy on me—am I truly a bad person?

The lines between right and wrong blur within these walls, leaving me questioning the morality of my choices and the person I've become.

Do I craft a story to align with the accusations, or do I dive

CHAPTER 5

in with the unfiltered truth? It's a dilemma gnawing at my conscience.

The longing to see Elizabeth consumes me. It's maddening not knowing her whereabouts. They've likely whisked her away to the hospital for examination. The thought crosses my mind—have I inadvertently caused her harm? Perhaps they're scrutinizing her wrists for any sign of restraint, any hint of coercion on my part.

But deep down, I know the truth.

There's no malice in my heart, no coercion in my actions. Elizabeth is with me out of her own free will, out of love. Surely they'll see that, won't they? She chose to be by my side, to share her life with me.

The love between us is pure, untainted by force or manipulation.

I lay my head back on the mattress and pull the itchy woollen blanket over my head to block out the luminous lighting above.

I close my eyes and replay the past few weeks over in my mind. The hospital, the house, making love. I think for a moment about losing my Mum.

"Shit!" I exclaim

"My Mum!" I say aloud in a panic.

I have her funeral to plan for next Friday.

The door unlocks and I sit up letting the blanket drop to the floor, I bend down to pick it up and fold it onto my lap. I don't stand up, my legs feel like jelly and I naturally feel sick.

A petite-framed woman with glasses enters my cell.

"Mr Penwald?" she asks me.

"Yes?" I reply shakily.

"I am your solicitor," she holds out a delicate hand for me

to shake.

"Miss Brenner. You can call me Emily."

I take her hand in mine and gently squeeze it.

"Nice to meet you, Emily," I say as a smile creeps nervously across my face.

"Please call me Gerry," I ask.

"OK. Gerry, it is," she says.

Emily is an attractive woman with beautiful long red hair, she has cute freckles covering her nose and cheeks and has expertly applied her makeup accentuating her beauty.

I have used Chatsworth and Brenner before, they are the solicitors who are dealing with Mum's estate.

I have not met Emily before. I assume she is the daughter or the wife of the partner.

"May I take a seat here?" she asks, pointing towards the end of my makeshift bed.

"Of course, I'm sorry, I should have offered." I hold my hand out to the space next to me.

As I shift further down the bed, I can't help but wonder if Emily's distance is a sign of mistrust towards me. If she doesn't feel comfortable sitting next to me, this whole situation is bound to go downhill.

"How are you doing, Gerry?" Emily's voice breaks through my thoughts, it is filled with genuine concern.

"Yeah, as good as can be expected given the circumstances," I reply, trying to sound as composed as possible.

"Can I get you anything? And have you had your phone call yet?" she continues, her kindness notable.

"No, I've refused my phone call. There's no one to call. They won't let me speak to Elizabeth, so there's no one else I can contact," I explain, frustration in my voice.

CHAPTER 5

"I'm sorry about your Mum. How are you holding up?" Emily's words bring back the weight of recent events.

"It's very raw still," I reply quietly, my sorrow lingering.

"Is there anything you need, Gerry?" Emily's eyes hold a sincerity that touches me.

"I'm alright, thank you," I assure her, trying to maintain composure.

"They're bringing me something to eat soon," I add, hoping to shift the focus away from my emotions.

"That's good to hear. Eating something might help clear your mind," Emily offers, her tone comforting.

"So, would you like to tell me in your own words what has brought you here today?" Emily's question prompts a moment of hesitation.

I resist the urge to make a sarcastic remark about the police bringing me here and instead opt for a more serious tone. Emily seems professional and now isn't the time for jokes.

"I've been accused of abducting a woman called Molly Chapman," I confess.

"Did you abduct her?" Emily's direct question catches me off guard.

"No, of course not! I would never take someone by force or snatch them from their home," I reply vehemently, surprised by her straightforwardness.

"That's kidnapping, Gerry," Emily reminds me gently, a small smile playing on her lips.

"Well, what's the difference?" I ask, genuinely curious.

"I had to look into that myself. I have some information for you to study, so you can understand the difference between the crimes," Emily says, handing me a printout of research material.

```
Kidnapping and abduction are often used
interchangeably in casual conversation, but there
are legal and conceptual differences between the
two:
1. **Kidnapping**: Kidnapping involves the unlawful
taking and carrying away of a person by force,
fraud, or deception, with the intent to hold the
person against their will. It typically involves
the use of force or threat of force to physically
remove a person from one place to another without
their consent. Kidnapping is a serious criminal
offence in most jurisdictions and is often
associated with ransom demands or other illicit
motives.

2. **Abduction**: Abduction, on the other hand, is
a broader term that encompasses a wider range of
actions. It generally refers to the act of taking
someone away without their consent or the legal
authority to do so. Abduction can involve various
circumstances, such as taking a child from a
custodial parent without permission, transporting
someone across borders unlawfully, or even removing
someone from a location under false pretences.
Abduction doesn't always involve force or coercion;
it can also occur through fraud or deception.

In summary, while both kidnapping and abduction
involve the unlawful removal of a person,
kidnapping specifically entails the use of force or
threat of force, whereas abduction can involve a
broader range of actions and circumstances.
```

"OK, so I didn't kidnap anyone, but it looks like I may have committed abduction," I mutter aloud, instantly regretting

CHAPTER 5

the admission.

A wave of sickness washes over me as I realize the severity of my actions. I hadn't even grasped the gravity of what I was doing when I decided to keep Elizabeth with me.

I had been driven by fear, fearing she might be found with me and wrongly accused of kidnapping, but I hadn't truly comprehended that I was committing a crime myself.

For a few moments, I'm lost in worry, fully absorbing the weight of the situation. I know deep down that the only way forward is to come clean, but the thought sends my head spinning.

The possibility of facing prison time looms ominously before me.

"What sentence could be passed for a crime like this?" I ask Emily, my voice trembling with anxiety.

"Honestly, anything from a custodial twelve months to life imprisonment," she responds matter-of-factly.

"There are a lot of contributing factors, like previous convictions, remorse, etc."

"I've never even spoken to a police officer before now, let alone been in trouble with one," I protest weakly, grasping at the hope that my lack of prior encounters with the police might somehow mitigate the severity of my situation.

"That will stand in good stead for you; it will make the judge look at you more favourably," says Emily, her tone carrying a hint of reassurance.

She seems to be trying to convey her approval that I have maintained a clean record with the police until now.

"I also think that if you go for a guilty plea, it will keep the prosecution from having a trial. You really don't want a trial, do you? It would mean that you plead guilty though," Emily pauses for a moment, her words heavy with implication.

"Are you happy with that?" she asks, momentarily distracted as she rubs her eye and fusses with an imaginary stray eyelash.

I can't help but notice the small quirks of her behaviour, like the way women often open their mouths when they're adjusting their eyelashes or applying mascara. I push aside the distracting thought and focus on Emily's question.

"I'm not happy with any of it. I don't feel like I've committed a crime, to be honest. Elizabeth came home with me voluntarily. She didn't have to get in the taxi with me," I explain, frustration in my tone.

"But did she believe that you were her husband?" Emily gazes at me, waiting for my response.

"OK, so I might have led her to believe that I was her husband. The hospital staff did it before I did; I just carried it on. I didn't want to cause her any anxiety or fear. I wanted her to have someone whom she could trust whilst waiting for her to wake up!" I exclaim, defending my actions.

"The hospital staff?" quizzed Emily.

"Yes, they had already made the assumption. In actual fact, the first people to assume that I was Elizabeth's husband were the ambulance crew and the police officer on the night of her accident," I continue, recalling the events with a hint of annoyance.

Gerry's mind drifts back to the chaotic evening on the beach. He remembers them referencing Elizabeth, who at the time was still called Molly, and how they referred to her as his wife.

'Your wife is alive' and 'Your wife will be taken to Preston Hospital via Air Ambulance.'

CHAPTER 5

Not once had I told them that she was my wife.

"I only lied the minute we got to the hospital. I had to fill in some forms. I was in total shock. I had just watched my dog push the woman whom I cared a lot about into the sea. My dog drowned for fuck's sake," I vent, unable to contain my frustration.

"I'm sorry, I didn't mean to swear," I quickly apologise, feeling a pang of guilt.

"It's OK, Gerry. I think under the circumstances, you are allowed to be a little bit vocal about what you went through that evening," says Emily, her voice understanding and sympathetic.

"Tell me what happened next," Emily asks gently, her voice prompting me to recount the events.

"I was by her bedside day and night while she was in her coma," I begin, pausing to collect my thoughts.

"Elizabeth was watched constantly in the intensive care unit. The staff got used to me being there; I would never want to leave. Sometimes they had to force me to go home. I was scared she would die through the night or while I was away from her side."

I pause again, wiping my eyes. I feel embarrassed getting emotional in front of Emily, but I need her to understand that I'm not a bad person.

"Go on," she encourages me gently.

"My Mum took ill while I was at the hospital with Elizabeth. I received a call from Mum's neighbour to say that Mum had collapsed outside next to the pond. I thought I had lost her, to be honest," I continue, shifting on the bed to find a more comfortable position.

"She had a stroke and ended up in a hospice. I knew then

that my Mum would never return home," I explain, feeling the weight of sadness settling over me.

Emily shifts on the mattress too. The blue cushioned surface is bare, and it gets uncomfortably warm. I offer Emily my blanket to sit on, but she declines. It's probably for the best, as it's a woollen mix that can be quite itchy.

I imagine Emily squirming with discomfort and feeling a flicker of amusement.

"Did you ever confide in your Mum about Elizabeth?" Emily asks, bringing me back to the conversation.

"Yes, I told my Mum everything. She knew I had fallen in love with Elizabeth and that I wanted to take care of her. Elizabeth was living in an abusive marriage, both physically and mentally. She had become a shell of the woman I had first bumped into while I walked my dog, Duke" I explain, feeling sadness and longing.

Emily smiles at me, a reassuring gesture that I desperately need as I recount my story. "Did you ever converse with Elizabeth before the accident?" she continues.

"There was an occasion where we sat down together and started to talk, but her daughter showed up and told Elizabeth she needed to get back home," I recall, taking a deep breath.

"Other than that, we didn't speak to each other."

"Can you explain to me what started this fascination with Elizabeth?" Emily asks, her tone soft but probing.

"Long story short, my ex-fiancé was having an affair with Elizabeth's husband Ray. I ended our relationship and vowed to ruin the life of the man, who had taken my life away from me," I admit bitterly.

"I see," says Emily, her expression sympathetic.

CHAPTER 5

"You wanted revenge but ended up falling for his wife."

"Yes, that's pretty much it in a nutshell. I didn't really want to hurt anyone, but I kind of followed her and overheard the arguments when I walked past their home," I confess, feeling a pang of guilt.

"You stalked her?" Emily points out.

"Yes, I guess I did. But it was never malicious or weird or anything like that. I was genuinely concerned and worried about Elizabeth, and then I fell in love with her," I explain, feeling a mix of shame and vulnerability.

Emily interrupts me.

"How do you feel about her now?" she asks, her gaze steady but questioning.

"I miss her, and I love her more than life itself. I just want to be back with her, taking care of her. I promised her that," I reply, my voice breaking with emotion.

"Gerry, you do realize that after today, Elizabeth is going to know that she is, in fact, Molly Chapman and that she has a husband and three children waiting at home for her," Emily reminds me gently.

"Yes, I know, I know. I just wish I was the one who could tell her everything. I would be able to explain myself at the same time. With the police being the ones to tell her, it is going to blow her mind and probably set her right back in her recovery," I confess, tears welling up in my eyes once more.

"They are using the top psychologically trained officer to deal with it. But it will be a huge shock to her," Emily admits, her voice filled with empathy.

"I am just so sorry for everything that I have done. I only wanted to love her," I say, my voice barely above a whisper, overwhelmed with guilt and regret.

Chapter 6

Wednesday Late Evening

Chase and Gilbert position themselves relatively close to Elizabeth, their proximity serving both to reassure her and to ensure her comfort as they prepare to disclose the impending revelation.

Their demeanour is gentle yet attentive.

"Elizabeth, we really must talk to you about all of this now," says Chase solemnly.

"OK?" Elizabeth replies, her voice laced with shyness and curiosity.

"Firstly, let me introduce myself formally to you. My name is PC Jason Chase, and I am a Forensic Psychologist," he explains.

"What does that mean exactly?" asks Elizabeth, seeking clarification.

"It means that first and foremost, I am a police officer, but I am also a police psychologist. So, I have a PhD in Psychology and a Master of Science in Forensic Behavioral Science," Chase elaborates.

"And what does that mean to me exactly? With respect, of

course, officer" Elizabeth asks politely.

"It means that you are in the best hands possible at this moment in time. My colleague here, PC Alice Gilbert, is a specialist in therapy and operational support of serious crime," Chase reassures her.

"Why do I need officers with such experience in dealing with major crime? I am not a victim of, nor have I committed a serious crime," Elizabeth tries to rationalise the situation.

"That is just it, Elizabeth. You are a victim," Chase interjects firmly.

"Of what?" she laughs, her voice slightly raised, betraying her growing unease.

Lambert approaches the room.

With her evidence bags safely stowed away in the van ready for dispatch back to the lab at the station she hovers in the doorway, receiving a nod from Chase, indicating that she can stay for the remainder of the interview with Elizabeth.

"Elizabeth, can I get you anything to drink?" Gilbert offers, trying to ease the tension.

"No, thank you. I just want to know what is going on, and want to see my husband" Elizabeth replies, her tone reflecting her growing apprehension.

Chase continues, his expression grave.

"We have reason to believe that you are not Mrs Elizabeth Penwald."

Elizabeth looks at Chase vacantly, her mind struggling to process the information.

"I don't understand what you are talking about," she replies, shaking her head in confusion.

"We have reason to believe that you are the missing young woman whom we have been looking for, Mrs Molly

CHAPTER 6

Chapman,"

Chase drops the bombshell.

The weight of his words becomes an obvious burden on Elizabeth.

The room goes deadly silent except for the sharp inhale of breath from Elizabeth's mouth.

"Don't be so bloody ridiculous," Elizabeth gasps, her voice trembling with shock, her mouth still agape as she continues to speak.

"You have the wrong person. It is a coincidence that I have the same name as a middle name, but that is the only thing in common that we share."

"Elizabeth, Molly, I will need you to give me a sample so that we can compare it against the DNA that we have for the missing young woman." Lambert interrupts from the doorway.

"Take what you want, you won't find a match," Elizabeth retorts defiantly, her disbelief distinct in her voice.

"I'm afraid that is exactly what we are going to need to do, to confirm your identity, as you have a severe case of Amnesia. It is the only way we can confirm who you are other than having you identified by your family," Chase explains, his expression serious.

"My family?" Elizabeth's eyes widen with surprise and confusion.

"Yes, Elizabeth, your family," Chase confirms, offering her a reassuring smile.

"Gerry is my family. I don't have any other living relatives. I only have Gerry," Elizabeth repeats, her voice trembling with emotion as if trying to convince herself of the truth.

"No, Elizabeth, you have a husband and three children,"

Chase reveals gently.

The words hit Elizabeth like a bolt of lightning. The colour drains from her face, replaced by a look of real shock and horror. She had not expected Chase to come out with that.

She sits for a moment, speechless, grappling with the sudden and overwhelming revelation.

"I am sorry, I refuse to believe what you are saying," Elizabeth replies with disbelief and defiance.

Lambert makes her way toward Elizabeth, a Buccal Cell DNA kit in hand, ready to take a sample. She methodically puts on a pair of gloves in preparation, ensuring the utmost care in handling the procedure.

"I need your permission to take the swabs from you, please, Elizabeth," Lambert requests politely, opening up the kit under the watchful gaze of Chase and Gilbert.

Elizabeth stares at the kit in Lambert's hands, shaking her head in disbelief.

"I give you permission, but you are wasting your time," she asserts defiantly.

"With respect, Elizabeth, how do you explain the scar on your tummy?" Lambert enquires gently, as she holds the swab in front of Elizabeth's mouth.

"Open wide, please. I will just swab inside your cheeks. That will collect your sample, which we can then process and match up on our database."

"I believe it happened during the accident. I was wedged between two rocks and was winched up out of the water; it probably happened then," Elizabeth surmises, her voice full of resignation.

Lambert expertly swabs the inside of Elizabeth's mouth, noticing the dryness, and offers her a drink of water once

CHAPTER 6

she has collected a sufficient amount of DNA on the swab.

Elizabeth refuses again.

Lambert carefully places the swab into the test tube and tightens the lid. She meticulously writes on the sticker affixed to the side of the tube and inserts it into the forensics bag, diligently noting Elizabeth's details on the front.

"That is it, that is all that I need," Lambert announces, gathering the waste and making her way into the kitchen to dispose of her gloves and packaging, leaving Elizabeth to contemplate the implications of the DNA sample.

"How will you know if you have a match or not?" Elizabeth asks, her mind racing to anticipate the sequence of events before they unfold.

"We already have the DNA for Molly Chapman on our database," Lambert explains as she walks back into the room, her tone calm but resolute.

Elizabeth looks visibly confused.

"But how?" she presses for clarification.

Lambert and Gilbert exchange a glance, silently urging Chase to fill in the blanks. They don't want to be the ones responsible for revealing the grim truth to Elizabeth.

Taking the cue, Chase steps forward.

"We are investigating the disappearance of 'Molly,'" he begins cautiously.

"Yes, I know that, but how will you know if my results match hers?" Elizabeth interrupts, her voice impatient.

Chase clears his throat before responding.

"Because we already have Molly's DNA on our database. We suspect foul play took place at her home the night she disappeared."

Elizabeth's confusion deepens.

"Foul play?" she repeats, her brows knit together.

"What does that mean exactly?" she presses for further clarification.

"There was an altercation between Molly and her husband. Moments later, Molly left their home and never returned," Chase explains, carefully choosing his words.

"That doesn't explain the DNA," Elizabeth persists, her frustration mounting as she seeks straight answers.

"We found blood-stained clothing at the house," Chase admits, his voice grave.

Fear grips Elizabeth's features, evident in the pallor that washes over her face. She visibly pales, her lips turning a shade of pale grey as the severity of the situation sinks in.

* * *

Everything goes dark in front of me, except for the little specks of glitter floating gently in front of my eyes, each time I blink.

I sense that I'm somewhere familiar, a feeling of being at home. I open my eyes, it doesn't look how I remember it.

Where is Gerry?

His absence leaves a void in my thoughts. I hear a voice, a chill running down my spine as it penetrates through me.

I recognise the voice, but I push it out of my mind.

A stinging sensation spreads across my face, followed by a sharp pain in my back as I lose my footing and fall backwards, hitting the door.

The pain intensifies, sending waves of discomfort through my body.

I open my eyes, and I am still standing here, in the kitchen, facing the black glossy kitchen worktop.

CHAPTER 6

I see the familiar kettle, the lid appears to be broken off, and a cup sits under the water spout. There is a bottle of milk on the side.

Shouting fills the air, but I can't see anyone in front of me. Where am I? I've been here before, but I have no idea where 'here' is. It's not home, but it feels like it should be.

The sound of a young girl calling "Mum" echoes in the distance.

And then again, his voice; deep and degrading, cuts through the air, filled with accusations and scorn.

I am not lazy. I am not attention-seeking. I am not... I am not... The words linger in my mind, unfinished, as I struggle to make sense of my surroundings.

* * *

"Elizabeth, are you alright?" Chase's voice breaks through the haze, his arm resting gently on her shoulder.

"Huh?" She responds, startled, and then instinctively wipes her forehead with the back of her hand. Sweat gathered just above her brows, evidence of the turmoil within her.

"We lost you for a moment there. Is everything alright?" Chase's concern is palpable as he gazes at Elizabeth intently.

"Oh, I'm sorry. It happens sometimes," She replies, attempting to brush off the disorientation.

Chase's expression remains concerned. "What happens? Blackouts?" he asks gently, probing for more information.

"They are sort of flashbacks. They never make much sense, and to be honest, if I don't write them down, I forget them. But you have my diary now, so I can't write it down," She explains, feeling a sense of vulnerability in revealing this aspect of herself.

"Would you like to talk to us about it?" Chase offers, his tone gentle yet insistent, clearly worried by what she must have just experienced.

"No, it's OK. I would rather not go over it," Elizabeth declines, feeling the weight of the memories pressing down on her.

Lambert interjects, breaking the tension with her practicality.

"I'm going to head back to the station and get these samples fast-tracked," she announces with a smile directed at the trio, offering a sense of reassurance amidst the uncertainty.

"OK, Lambert, I will stay here as I have a lot more questions and things to discuss with Elizabeth. Will you call me the minute you get the results, please?" Chase requests, his tone earnest.

"Yes, of course," Lambert replies promptly, her expression professional yet sympathetic.

Gilbert stands up and turns to face Elizabeth.

"I will go back with Lambert if you will be OK here with Chase unless you would like me to stay?" she offers, with concern in her eyes.

"No, I will be OK. But please, can you find out when I can see Gerry?" Elizabeth's voice trembles with worry.

"We have never been apart from each other, and I am worried about him."

Gilbert understands the predicament but knows the protocol won't allow them to be together.

"I will see what I can do," she promises, offering a glimmer of hope.

"Thank you," Elizabeth murmurs gratefully.

"Can I ask you something else before you both go?"

CHAPTER 6

Elizabeth continues as Lambert steps back into the living room.

"Yes, of course," Lambert responds, her demeanour gentle yet firm.

"What will happen if the samples do match up? What will happen to me?" Elizabeth's voice wavers with uncertainty.

"Let's worry about that if or when it happens. Until then, please continue to answer all the questions that PC Chase asks you," Lambert advises, her words offering a sense of reassurance amidst the uncertainty.

"OK, I will do my best," Elizabeth replies, though her confidence seems to falter, doubts cloud her mind.

Lambert and Gilbert bid their farewells to Chase, and Lambert rounds up the rest of her forensics team. They clear the house and make their way back to their cars, parked strategically on the driveway, leaving Elizabeth and Chase to confront the looming uncertainties together.

Chase and Elizabeth find themselves alone in the living room, the air thick with tension and unanswered questions.

"Am I alright to make us a coffee?" Elizabeth breaks the silence, her voice carrying a hint of uncertainty.

Chase nods in agreement, grateful for the prospect of a brief respite.

"I think that is a great idea," he says, his tone warm and encouraging.

"You're welcome to come out with me," Elizabeth offers a small attempt to bridge the gap between them.

Chase follows Elizabeth out into the kitchen, the atmosphere shifting slightly as they leave the confines of the living room.

The kittens emerge from their hiding spot under the table,

their curiosity piqued by the newfound activity.

Era, the more vocal of the three, meows loudly, demanding attention from Elizabeth. She responds with a gentle smile, reaching for the food to satisfy the hungry feline.

Elizabeth sources the food and distributes it into two large bowls, placing them on the floor.

The kittens waste no time in lapping it up eagerly, their tails twitching in contentment. Era, however, takes her time, savouring each bite with deliberate care.

"Cute kitties," Chase remarks, his voice soft as he bends down to stroke Era. She responds with a graceful arch of her back, enjoying the attention as Chase's hand moves gently along her spine.

"Officer, can I ask you something please?" Elizabeth's voice carries a weight of sadness, her eyes reflecting the turmoil within.

"Of course," he responds, his tone gentle yet firm, ready to offer whatever information he can.

"What exactly has Gerry supposed to have done?" she questions.

"Well, it's a tough one," he begins, scratching an imaginary itch on his head before continuing.

"Your supposed husband has been arrested for abducting you. He has coercively manipulated you into thinking that you are his wife and that you have a home together. When you lost your memory, you had no recollection of your previous life. All you knew was what you were told at the hospital and the nurses and doctors who were looking after you were none the wiser either. It sounds to me like the whole thing has got out of hand."

He pauses, allowing Elizabeth a moment to absorb the

CHAPTER 6

gravity of his words.

"Abduction. How can a husband abduct his wife?" she asks.

"Elizabeth you are not his wife. Gerry Penwald is not a married man."

The kitchen falls silent.

Chapter 7

Wednesday Late Evening

Lambert and Gilbert stride into the station, their expressions serious as they spot Carter and Poker enjoying a coffee at the front of the desks.

"Where is Dixie?" Lambert enquires, her voice cutting through the quiet hum of the station.

"In with Sharpie. They've been in there for a couple of hours now," Carter replies, his tone reflecting the situation.

"What's the update?" Lambert presses, eager for any information.

"The update is that Gerry is with his solicitor. Rachel is on her own in her cell. She's declined a solicitor, claiming she's done nothing wrong—just in the wrong place at the wrong time," Carter explains, his words punctuated by a sip of his coffee.

"What do you make of it all so far, Carter?" Lambert asks.

"To be quite honest, it's a mess. Gerry is undoubtedly guilty of the crime of coercive behaviour and abduction," Carter admits, his expression sombre.

"But he's in no way your typical predator."

CHAPTER 7

"It doesn't sound like he's done anything to harm Molly or Elizabeth. Can we agree on what we're going to call her? It's confusing the hell out of me," Lambert suggests, frustrated.

"OK, from now on, we refer to her as Molly, as that is who she is," Carter decides firmly.

"I agree," Dixie affirms as he enters the main office, Sharpie trailing behind him.

"Me too," Sharpie adds, nodding in agreement.

"OK," Lambert acquiesces, accepting the decision.

"So, Molly is in denial of what Gerry has done to her. She's still claiming she's his wife and that we're all making this story up for the fun of it," Poker remarks, his tone tinged with disbelief.

"I don't think it's quite like that. The poor woman is in shock at the moment. She doesn't know what to believe," Gilbert interjects, her voice filled with sympathy as she joins them, clutching a cup of coffee.

"I think we can all agree that Gerry is not your typical abductor. But he is an abductor, nonetheless," Carter concludes, his tone grave.

"True," Dixie acknowledges, his expression thoughtful.

"So where do we go from here?" Sharpie prompts.

"I believe the immediate priority while waiting for the DNA results is to bring Molly in. Along with that, we should also reach out to her brother, Reggie, and request that he come in to formally identify her, as he is her next of KIN."

Gilbert interrupts, "But what about Ray? He's her actual husband. Shouldn't we be involving him in this process?"

Carter sighs, "We can't bring Ray in just yet—he's still under investigation because of the blood-stained clothing we found. Damn, this situation is turning into a real mess."

Sharpie interjects, "Well, regardless of our next steps, we need to inform the families that we've located Molly. But we can't do that until Reggie has been notified."

"I'll go," Carter volunteers. "I've formed a personal connection with him, and I want to be the one to break the news."

"Alright, lad, you go," Sharpie agrees. "But be sensitive about it. Remember, this could all just be a coincidence, and his sister might still be out there, missing."

"Do you want me to call Chase and have him bring Molly in?" Lambert asks.

"No, I'll handle that," Dixie responds.

"You focus on getting that sample to the lab and make sure they mark it as urgent. We need those results as soon as possible."

"Got it, boss. I'm on it," Lambert replies, heading off to the lab with Gilbert.

Carter grabs his coat and phone, the weight of the task ahead pressing on him as he leaves the office. His heart pounds full of nerves and anticipation as he heads toward the car park. Knowing how delicate the situation is, he decides to call Reggie first, hoping to avoid alarming him and Yvonne by showing up unannounced at their home again.

As Carter drives along the quiet streets, the usual hustle and bustle of the day has faded, leaving an eerie calm. The dark sea merges with the night sky, creating a seamless expanse of black beyond the promenade. He notices a lone cherry picker up ahead, its basket holding a stocky man who is diligently changing the bulbs on one of the illuminated displays, adding a faint glow to the otherwise dim surroundings.

He selects Reggies number on the hands-free.

It starts ringing.

CHAPTER 7

* * *

Yvonne closes the blinds in the living room, shutting out the darkening evening. The room is spotless, a reflection of the hours she spent tidying every corner, dusting her collection of expensive ornaments, and ensuring the furniture gleamed. Earlier, she had even baked a coffee and walnut cake, the sweet aroma still lingering in the air.

A bottle of Rosé sits on the table, beads of condensation forming on its surface from being taken out of the fridge and left in the warm room. Reggie relaxed on the couch, pats the space beside him and smiles as Yvonne approaches. She gracefully tucks one leg behind her and sits on her foot, a habit Reggie has always found curious.

"How is that even comfortable, love?" he asks, just as he does every time.

Yvonne chuckles, giving him the same answer she always gives.

"I don't know, I just do it by habit," she replies, smiling back at him, her eyes twinkling with warmth.

Reggie gazes at Yvonne, his heart swelling with affection as he takes in her beautiful, though ageing, face.

Her hair is neatly tied back into a bun, with delicate ringlets cascading down the sides, framing her features in a way that makes her look timeless.

Unable to resist, he reaches out and gently strokes her cheek

"I do love you, Vonnie," he says softly, his voice filled with sincerity.

"You know that, don't you?" There's a tender anticipation in his eyes as he waits for her response.

Yvonne smiles warmly, her eyes sparkling.

"Of course, I know you love me, and I love you very much too. Or should I say… ditto?" she teases, a playful giggle escaping her lips as the iconic scene from the movie; Ghost, flashes in her mind.

With a contented sigh, she places her hand over his, their fingers intertwining for a moment. Then, they both turn back to the television, settling in to watch The Lost Boys—a movie they've seen countless times, yet it never seems to lose its charm.

Reggie's phone rings, and he quickly grabs it when he sees PC Carter's name on the caller display.

"Hello? PC Carter… Is everythi—?" Reggie's voice trails off as worry creeps in.

"It's nothing to worry about," Carter interjects, trying to ease the tension.

"Oh, well, how can I help you?" Reggie asks, still sounding concerned.

"I'm on my way to see you," Carter explains. "I didn't want to spook you by showing up unannounced."

Yvonne, overhearing the conversation, interjects, "Reggie, is everything alright? Is it Molly?"

"I don't know yet, love. Give me a minute, please," Reggie replies gently as he stands and walks toward the window, seeking a bit of privacy. He curls his toes into the plush carpet beneath him, trying to ground himself as he processes the unexpected call.

"OK, we're both here. Come on round," Reggie says, his tone softening, relieved to hear from Carter.

Carter, driving along Red Bank Road into Bispham, reassures him, "I'm just two minutes away, Reggie. I won't be

CHAPTER 7

long."

"Alright, great. I'll get a cup of tea ready for you," Reggie offers, trying to maintain a sense of normality.

"That would be lovely, thank you," Carter responds.

"See you shortly."

With that, he ends the call, focusing back on the road.

Yvonne, watching Reggie's face closely, asks, "I hope everything is alright?"

"Me too," Reggie replies, his expression clouded with worry. He tries to stay calm, but the uncertainty gnaws at him.

"Let me put something decent on if Carter's coming around. I'm sure he doesn't want to see my milk bottle legs in this nightie," Yvonne adds with a playful smirk.

"Von, your legs are gorgeous," Reggie chuckles, "but you might give him a heart attack if he sees you in that silky number with your boobs hanging out."

Yvonne grins mischievously and grabs her breasts, squeezing them together to create a tantalizing cleavage.

"Behave yourself, woman," Reggie laughs, his face flushing crimson.

"You've got two minutes before he gets here, off you go."

"Two minutes for what?" she teases, giggling.

"Go!" Reggie insists, laughing out loud as he watches her.

Yvonne gives her bum a cheeky wiggle as she leaves the room, making Reggie shake his head with a grin. As she disappears through the living room door, Reggie heads into the kitchen, preparing the cups and setting up for their drinks, still smiling at his wife's playful antics.

* * *

The doorbell rings, and Reggie, already prepared, opens the door almost instantly.

"PC Carter, good to see you, my friend. What brings you out here this evening?" Reggie asks politely, a warm smile on his face.

"Hello, Reggie, good to see you too," Carter replies offering to shake Reggies hand.

"Is that tea ready yet? I'm parched."

Reggie takes Carter's hand into his and shakes it gently.

"Yes, yes, come in and sit down. We were just watching a film. Are you alright?" Reggie asks, leading Carter into the cosy living room.

"I'm good, thank you. And how about you two? Keeping well, I hope?" Carter inquires, his tone light but with a hint of concern as he glances around the room, taking in the familiar surroundings.

"We're both good, thank you," Reggie replies, settling back into the conversation.

"And the children? How are they doing after going back with their father?" Carter asks.

"Yes, as far as I know, everything is alright— all quiet on the western front, as they say."

"Good, I'm glad to hear it," Carter responds, relieved.

Reggie gestures toward an armchair, where a cup of tea is already waiting. Carter takes the seat just as Yvonne enters the room, now fully dressed.

Carter stands again, greeting Yvonne with a polite nod before she sits down beside Reggie, her expression curious and a little anxious.

"We have a development," Carter begins, his tone serious.

"OK," Reggie says, leaning forward slightly. "Go on."

CHAPTER 7

Carter takes a breath.

"We've located a woman who we believe to be Molly." He pauses, choosing his words carefully. "She's with our police psychologist as we speak."

Yvonne gasps, her hands flying to her mouth.

"You've found her! Oh my god, is she alright?" she exclaims, eyes wide with shock.

"Yes, Yvonne. We think it is her and she is fit and well, it seems," Carter confirms, nodding reassuringly.

"This is the reason I am visiting you, I need to ask you to do something for us."

"Bloody hell," Reggie mutters, stunned by the unexpected news.

"Anything, we will do anything to help you and the investigation," Yvonne says urgently.

"Yes, of course, anything," Reggie reiterates, his tone resolute.

Carter nods.

"As you are Molly's next of KIN, we need you to formally identify her for us. She's currently denying her identity. We've taken samples for DNA analysis, but that will take some time, as you can imagine."

Reggie and Yvonne both nod in understanding.

"I must warn you," Carter continues, "she has complete memory loss and is unlikely to recognise either of you. We'll start with a remote identification to accommodate this."

"Do we need to come into the station?" Reggie asks.

"Yes, if that's alright with both of you," Carter replies.

"Does Ray know yet? Or the children?" Reggie enquires, searching Carter's face for answers.

"You are the first to know," Carter responds.

THE FOUND

"Please, just give us a moment to sort ourselves out, and we'll be ready to come along with you," Yvonne requests.

"Great, that gives me just enough time to drink my tea," Carter replies, picking up his cup and taking a satisfying mouthful of the warm drink.

As Carter savors the tea, Reggie and Yvonne move quickly around the room, Reggie grabs his jacket and keys from a nearby table, while Yvonne checks her phone and slips into her coat.

Carter lets out a contented sigh, watching them with a mixture of sympathy and anticipation, knowing the importance of the task ahead.

* * *

Chase's phone rings, displaying Dixie's name. He answers promptly.

"Chase, can you talk?" Dixie asks.

"Yes, boss. I'm just having a coffee with Elizabeth," Chase replies.

"Good. In your opinion, is she calm enough and fit enough to be brought into the station? We're bringing Reggie in for obvious reasons," Dixie says cautiously, ensuring his words are discreet in case he is overheard.

"Yes, she's actually doing really well," Chase confirms.

"That's good to hear. Can you bring her in, then, as a matter of urgency?"

"I will. Give me twenty minutes, and we'll be there," Chase assures him.

"Thanks, Chase."

"No problem," Chase replies before ending the call.

CHAPTER 7

Chase hangs up.

"I need to take you in and get you checked over by our doctor before we ask you any more questions," Chase tells Elizabeth gently.

"I want to make sure you're fit enough to handle any sensitive topics that might come up."

Chase pauses for a moment, considering his words carefully.

"I can't promise that you'll be able to see Gerry right away, as this is a serious situation," he says, his tone sympathetic.

"But I promise I'll ask on your behalf."

"OK," she responds, her voice tinged with resignation.

"If I have to, I guess I don't have a choice, do I? But thank you. I hope I can get to see my husband. I will do anything I can to clear his name"

Chase helps Elizabeth gather her belongings, his actions gentle and reassuring. As they prepare to head to the station, Molly's mind is a whirlwind of anxiety.

She is consumed with fears about what lies ahead. The uncertainty of why the police doctor needs to examine her unsettles her further, and she can't help but worry whether the authorities suspect Gerry might have harmed her in some way. The thought weighs heavily on her, adding to her confusion and apprehension about the entire situation.

Chase escorts Molly to the car, his presence steady and quiet.

As they drive, Molly gazes out of the window, her thoughts racing.

The streets pass by in a blur, but her focus remains on the vast blackness of the sea. The dark, seemingly endless expanse makes her reflect on her survival, the enormity of her ordeal sinking in. She finds herself marvelling at how she managed to endure the fall, her mind struggling to reconcile the traumatic event with her present reality.

Chapter 8

Wednesday Late Evening

The girls buzz with excitement as they prepare for a sleepover with Oliver.
    Their father, finally calmed down after a tense moment, gives them the green light to spend the evening and night downstairs. The girls are thrilled, eagerly gathering their favourite snacks to create the perfect cosy setup.

Meanwhile, their father, relieved to have some peace, retreats to the kitchen to grab snacks before spending the evening in the other room. He's content to let the kids enjoy their night while he catches up on social media and reviews some prospective clients. The familiar soft glow of the screen provides a comforting background as he settles into his evening, happy to give the kids their space.

The house buzzes with laughter and playful chatter as the children busily haul their bedding down the stairs, blankets and pillows trailing behind them. Amid the chaos, stuffed animals tumble down the steps, only to be scooped up again with giggles.

Oliver, always eager for a bit of adventure, suddenly has

an idea.

He grabs his well-worn, slightly lumpy pillow and positions it at the top of the stairs, envisioning a thrilling slide down to the bottom. With a determined look, he sits on the pillow, ready for the ride of his life. But instead of the swift descent he imagines, the pillow stubbornly stays in place, clinging to the step beneath it. Oliver wiggles and squirms, trying in vain to scoot himself downward, but the pillow remains unmoved, much to his disappointment.

Bonnie, noticing his predicament, flashes a mischievous grin.

"Hey, if you sit on the end of the duvet, I'll pull you down the stairs on it. Try it—it'll be fun!" she suggests, her eyes sparkling with the promise of a new adventure.

Oliver hesitates for a moment but, with a huge smile, shifts from his uncooperative pillow to the edge of the duvet, positioning himself just as Bonnie suggests.

Bonnie grabs the other end of the duvet, bracing herself for the pull. With a quick tug, she begins to drag Oliver down the stairs. The duvet slides smoothly over the steps, carrying him along with it. He lets out a joyful whoop as he bumps and bounces gently down, the ride far more thrilling than he anticipates. Bonnie laughs along with him, her plan a success.

The two of them end up in a heap of blankets and giggles at the bottom of the stairs, their sleepover off to a fun and adventurous start.

Lillie joins them in the hallway, her face concerned. She quickly bends down to help gather the scattered bedding, expertly scooping up pillows and blankets. Together, they carry the load into the living room, where they plan to set

CHAPTER 8

up their cosy camp for the night.

The air fills with the excitement of the sleepover, their laughter echoing softly through the house.

Just as they begin to spread out the blankets, a sharp voice cuts through the hallway like a knife.

"What's all this noise?" their father's stern voice booms from the kitchen. Ray has been particularly short-tempered with the children lately, with little patience for any disturbance.

The sleepover was only agreed upon after a tense negotiation between Ray and Lillie. The deal is clear: any noise or mischief, and there will be serious consequences, starting with Lillie being grounded.

Lillie reluctantly accepts the responsibility of keeping an eye on Bonnie and Oliver for the evening. She knows all too well how much noise the two of them can make when having fun together. As she watches them giggling and playing, a bitter thought crosses her mind: *'A laugh. If only Dad knew the meaning of it.'*

Trying to keep things under control, Lillie puts a finger to her lips, signalling her brother and sister to be quiet. But they're too wrapped up in their fun to notice her silent plea.

The tension in the air thickens as Ray's heavy footsteps echo closer, and before Lillie can do anything, he appears in the doorway.

His face twists with anger, eyes narrowed as he takes in the scene.

"I don't understand how you kids can make so much fucking noise while making a bed!" he snaps, his voice rising with barely contained fury.

His temper, always quick to ignite, is beginning to boil

over, and Lillie feels the heat of it directed straight at her.

She braces herself, knowing what's coming, but before she can utter a word, Ray's gaze locks onto her.

"And you, young lady, you're supposed to keep them under control! I can't ask you to do one fucking thing without there being drama about it, can I?" He wipes the spit from his lips, his anger making him tremble.

Desperation wells up in Lillie as she tries to find the right words to defend herself. "But Dad!" she exclaims, her voice trembling with the weight of the situation.

"I don't want any excuses, Lillie. I warned you…" he seethes.

For what feels like an eternity, the silence in the room is thick with tension, pressing down on them like a heavy weight.

Bonnie and Oliver, sensing the shift in the atmosphere, instinctively lower their voices to barely a whisper. The carefree laughter that filled the house just moments before evaporates, replaced by anxious, darting glances between their sister and father.

Ray stands there, his face a mask of barely contained fury. His mouth opens, ready to unleash a torrent of anger, but he suddenly pauses. Something in Lillie's eyes—a silent plea for mercy—gives him pause. The intensity of her gaze cuts through his rage, forcing him to wrestle with the storm of emotions raging inside him. He inhales deeply, the air seeming to shudder as it fills his lungs. The effort to control his temper is visible in every taut muscle of his body. His jaw is clenched so tightly it seems as though it might crack, and his fists, curled up tight at his sides, open and close in a futile attempt to release the tension coiled within him.

CHAPTER 8

For a few agonizing moments, Ray stands there, teetering on the brink of an outburst, his mind a battlefield between fury and restraint. The children stand frozen, their wide eyes fixed on their father, bracing themselves for the explosion they know is just one breath away.

But then, with a frustrated exhale, Ray spins on his heel. The motion is sharp and abrupt. He turns his back on his children, retreating into the kitchen, his footsteps heavy and deliberate. The echo of his departure lingers in the hallway, mingling with the children's held breaths, as they wait in tense anticipation for the outburst that, miraculously, doesn't come.

Relief washes over Lillie, though it's tinged with the bitter awareness that this reprieve could be fleeting. She catches Bonnie and Oliver's eyes and offers them a small, reassuring wink, trying to restore a sense of normalcy. With a quiet understanding, they set to work, pulling the cushions off the sofa and arranging them into makeshift beds on the floor in front of the TV.

The sleepover resumes, but the shadow of Ray's temper lingers ominously, a constant reminder that they must tread carefully for the rest of the night.

As the three of them settle in, the fragile peace is broken by a soft, hesitant whisper from Oliver.

"I need a wee."

Bonnie's head snaps around, her heart sinking as she looks at her brother. She hopes she misheard, but the urgency in his eyes tells her otherwise.

"I really need to go, Bon," he insists, his voice trembling slightly as he meets her gaze.

Bonnie glances nervously toward the hallway, her mind

racing.

"Be quick then," she whispers urgently. "And sneak up those stairs—if Dad catches us out of this room again, we're dead meat!"

Her words hang in the air like a dire warning, breaking the uneasy silence. But Oliver remains rooted to the spot, his face pale with dread. Before he can muster the courage to move, a warm, damp sensation spreads between his legs, soaking through his pyjama bottoms. The realization hits him like a wave of shame, leaving him frozen in place, tears welling up in his eyes as he stares at Bonnie, utterly helpless.

* * *

Chase parks the car in his usual spot, right next to Carter's vehicle. The tyres crunch over the gravel, the sound echoing softly in the stillness of the evening. As the wheels slow to a stop, they brush against the white line that neatly marks out his designated parking space. Chase stops the engine, and the quiet hum of the car fades, leaving an almost eerie silence in its wake.

Elizabeth sits quietly in the passenger seat, her gaze drifting out the window. The surroundings are unfamiliar, and she takes in the scene with a growing sense of unease.

The police station is just ahead, its exterior cold and imposing, while the starkness of the almost empty car park only adds to her turmoil.

She can feel her heart beginning to pound in her chest, each beat echoing louder in her ears. Her breath quickens, deepening with every inhale as a wave of anxiety washes over her, tightening her grip on the edge of her seat. She

CHAPTER 8

glances over at Chase, who meets her gaze with a warm and reassuring smile. Though his expression is full of comfort and support, it does little to soothe the growing unease gnawing at her insides. Her fingers, resting tensely beneath her, begin to tremble subtly as the anxiety creeps up on her. Chase, noticing the subtle quiver in her hands, gently reaches over and places his warm hand over hers, trying to steady her.

"It will be OK," Chase murmurs, his voice etched with sympathy and a quiet determination to ease her worries.

Elizabeth doesn't respond.

Instead, she turns her face away from him, the tension still tight in her chest, and directs her gaze out the car window. Her eyes fixate on a single droplet of water that slowly forms on the glass, the condensation gathering and sliding down in a delicate path. She follows its journey intently, her mind distant and detached from the moment, lost in the simplicity of the droplet's descent.

Elizabeth instinctively closes her eyes, retreating into the depths of her mind.

> *'I've been here before', she thinks, a sinking sense of déjà vu washing over her. The warmth of the car seeps into her skin, grounding her in the present, yet the eerie familiarity of this moment pulls her away. It isn't quiet anymore; the sound of screeching tyres pierces the silence, sharp and jarring. She's felt this before, like a recurring nightmare that she can't escape.*
>
> *Her body reacts on its own, curling up tightly as if bracing for an inevitable impact. The image*

81

flashes before her: the lights of a passing motorcycle cutting through the darkness. She tries to focus, to see the number plate, but it's impossible. The darkness swallows everything, and the blinding glare of headlights from passing cars only adds to her disorientation.

Then, she hears a voice—a soft, angelic voice, familiar yet distant.

"Mum."

The word echoes in her mind, pulling at something deep within her, but she can't place it. She knows the voice, but the memory slips through her fingers like sand.

Desperately, she tries to picture the face that belongs to it. A girl with long blonde hair and a heart-shaped face comes to mind, but the features are blurred as if seen through rippling water.

"Mum, are you OK?" the girl asks, her tone full of concern.

'But I don't have children...' Elizabeth's thoughts spiral into confusion. The situation feels too surreal, too disjointed from reality. Her shoulder begins to shrug involuntarily as if fighting against the haze that engulfs her.

"Elizabeth," a male voice breaks through the fog, calling her name.

"Elizabeth?" the voice repeats, more insistent this time but she doesn't recognize him.

'Who are you?' she wants to ask, but the words won't form.

CHAPTER 8

> *Then, there's a pause—a hesitation—and the voice tries again, "Molly?"*

At the sound of the name, Elizabeth's eyes snap open, startled and wide. Her pupils are dilated, the confusion and fear still gripping her tightly as she tries to make sense of the world around her.

Elizabeth buries her face in her hands, her sobs erupting uncontrollably, her body shaking with the force of her desperation. Tears stream through her fingers, and her chest heaves with each ragged breath.

Chase, wanting to comfort her, reaches out gently, placing a hand on her shoulder with a soft, reassuring touch.

"It will all be alright," he whispers, his voice tender and calming.

"I think you were having another flashback." His words trail off as he watches her, seeing the turmoil in her eyes, the way her mind is spinning, lost in a chaotic whirlwind of emotions and memories.

"I just want it all to stop," she cries, the words spilling out in a sob.

Chase begins to rub her shoulder, trying to soothe her further, but Elizabeth recoils, shrugging off his touch as if it burns. She turns to him, her face flushed with emotion, her eyes bloodshot, and her cheeks streaked with tears. Her nose is running, leaving a trail of snot on her top lip, which she absently sniffs back before wiping her nose on her sleeve. Without a second thought, she glances down at the damp cuff and wipes it on her jeans, indifferent to whether Chase sees her or not.

"I want to see my husband," she demands, her voice trembling.

Her face is now blotchy, her tear-streaked cheeks flushed with anger and desperation.

Chase hesitates for a moment, understanding the depth of her need.

"Let me see what I can do," he says softly, his tone steady as he tries to bring her back from the edge, hoping to calm the storm of emotions raging within her.

"Why wouldn't I be able to see him, Chase?" Elizabeth asks, her voice full of genuine curiosity and a hint of frustration.

Chase hesitates for a moment, searching for the right words.

"Your husband," he begins, clearing his throat as if trying to prepare her for what he has to say, "Gerry... Gerry is facing some pretty serious charges. The decision to keep you apart is to protect you."

Elizabeth stares at him in disbelief.

"That man couldn't hurt a fly, Chase. He's never touched a hair on my head," she insists, her voice rising with indignation.

"This is just so ridiculous, and the sooner you all realise you have this all wrong, the better." She snorts as she crosses her arms defiantly.

Her eyes flash with a fierce determination, unwilling to accept the narrative being laid out before her.

"Come on," Chase says gently, nodding toward the building ahead.

"We should get ourselves in there. We have a full team of experts anticipating your arrival."

He tries to keep his tone light and encouraging, but there's

CHAPTER 8

a seriousness in his eyes that Elizabeth can't ignore. The weight of the situation presses down on her as she realises the gravity of what lies ahead.

She takes a deep breath, trying to steady herself, but her mind is still spinning with unanswered questions and doubts.

Reluctantly, Elizabeth gets out of the car and starts walking toward the entrance with Chase, knowing that whatever awaits her inside could change her life as she understands it.

Chapter 9

Wednesday Late Evening

Rachel idly flips through the pages of a women's magazine she wouldn't normally give a second glance. Her eyes catch on a particularly bold headline:

'Husband Cheats with My Best Friend's Sister.'

She clicks her tongue in mild disapproval, yet something about the scandalous title piques her curiosity. She folds the magazine at the centrefold and rests it on her knees, leaning in closer to read.

I'm no different she muses silently, a wry smile tugging at the corners of her mouth. As she licks her thumb, preparing to turn the page, her eyes scan the salacious details of yet another tabloid story—a tale of betrayal that someone, somewhere, has been paid handsomely to publish.

But her mind drifts to her situation.

'What would the headlines say if this all goes tits up?' she wonders. A bitter laugh escapes her as the thought solidifies in her mind.

'Mistress's Ex, Cheats with Current Lovers Wife'—'Now that

CHAPTER 9

would be fitting.' She imagines the words in bold print, splashed across the cover of a magazine just like this one. The irony isn't lost on her, and for a moment, the weight of her choices settles heavily on her shoulders.

The door clinks as a set of keys are inserted into the lock, the sound echoing in the small room. With a creak, the door swings open, revealing the imposing figure of the Duty Officer.

"Rachel, your solicitor has arrived. Will you follow me, please?" His voice is firm, leaving no room for hesitation.

The officer, fittingly named Biff, bears an uncanny resemblance to Biff Tannen from the 'Back to the Future' movies—broad-shouldered, towering over six feet, and built like a bulldozer he casts a long shadow over Rachel's petite frame.

Rachel glances up at him, feeling small by his presence, before obediently setting the magazine back on her bed. The blanket at the foot is crumpled, evidence of the restless hours she'd spent there.

With a quiet sigh, she stands and follows Biff out of the room, the cool, sterile corridor stretching out before them. Her footsteps are silent on the lino floor as they walk, the weight of what lies ahead pressing down on her with every step.

They reach the interview room, and as the door opens, Rachel's eyes fall on the man waiting inside—her solicitor.

"Miss Houston, please take a seat," he says, his voice strong and commanding, yet with a warmth that immediately draws her in.

If a voice could have a look, Rachel would have described it as 'handsome.' She squints slightly, trying to place where she's seen him before, but the memory eludes her.

"My name is Benjamin—Benjamin Swift," he introduces himself, pausing to let her absorb the name. His presence is confident, and the way he carries himself suggests he's used to taking charge.

"I'm from Swift and Pope, the solicitors down on Central Drive. You may have heard of us. We specialize in high-profile cases—mostly human trafficking and kidnapping."

Rachel nods slowly, her mind racing as she tries to keep up with what he's saying. Benjamin pauses again, giving her a moment to process.

"Your case is unique and appeals to us. I think we can help you, but you've got to be straight with me—about everything," he says, his tone turning serious as he leans slightly closer, the intensity of his gaze making it clear that he means business.

Before Rachel can respond, Benjamin reaches out, his large, warm hand enveloping hers in a firm shake. The contact jolts her memory.

"College," she blurts out, her voice brightening with the sudden realisation.

Benjamin raises an eyebrow, puzzled.

"I beg your pardon?" he asks, his professional demeanour faltering for a moment.

"College," she repeats, a small smile tugging at her lips. "That's where I know you from. We took Public Service together."

A flicker of recognition crosses Benjamin's face, and then he smiles—a brilliant, white, perfectly straight smile that sends a flutter through Rachel's stomach.

"Oh, right. Well, yes, I suppose we did," he replies, a touch of amusement in his voice as he vaguely remembers.

Rachel feels a warmth spread through her that has nothing

CHAPTER 9

to do with nerves. She realises with a start that she's still holding onto his hand, the moment lingering longer than it should. Benjamin gently releases her hand and gestures toward the chair.

"Please, take a seat," he offers again, his smile never wavering.

She sits down, her mind racing not just from the gravity of the situation, but from the unexpected attraction she feels toward the man who's supposed to be her advocate. Concentrating on the case ahead suddenly seems a daunting task with someone like Benjamin Swift sitting less than two feet away.

* * *

The Duty and Custody Officers, Biff and Dobby, are in the thick of a hectic night, the station buzzing with activity. It's rare for them to be this busy, but tonight it seems like the whole town is converging on their doorstep.

"So let me get this straight," Dobby begins, trying to wrap her head around the situation.

"We've found the missing woman, and she's coming through the doors as we speak. We also have her supposed husband in custody for abducting her, and he's in with his solicitor, Miss Brenner."

She pauses to catch her breath before continuing, "And his ex-fiancée is in room six with her solicitor, Mr Swift."

"That's right," Biff confirms, his expression serious.

"And we're bringing in the brother of the missing woman to hopefully give us a formal identification."

"Bloody hell," Dobby mutters, shaking her head in disbelief.

"It's all happening on Bonny Street tonight."

"I know," Biff agrees, rubbing the back of his neck.

"We go weeks with nothing but minor crimes, and then bang, we're landed with a high-profile case like this."

Dobby nods, the weight of the night settling on her shoulders.

"Best make sure we keep the paperwork in top-tip condition tonight, Biff."

Biff lets out a deep, hearty laugh, the sound echoing through the corridor.

"You mean tip-top, Dobby."

Dobby squints at Biff, confused for a moment.

"I could have sworn it was top-tip. You best check that while I check the next one in."

Shaking his head in amusement, Biff watches as Dobby heads off to handle the next arrival. Despite the chaotic night ahead, he can't help but smile at his colleague's quirks.

It's going to be a long night, but at least there's a bit of humour to keep them going.

Elizabeth walks beside Chase as he gently pushes against the Custody Suite door, which swings open with ease. Standing in the doorway, Chase holds it open, allowing Elizabeth to step inside first.

The moment she enters, she feels the weight of several pairs of eyes on her, their gazes following her as she makes her way toward the check-in desk. The air in the foyer is thick with a mix of curiosity and tension, and she can't help but feel exposed to the scrutiny of the officers and staff around her.

Chase gives a quick nod to the officers, acknowledging them as they return to their routine, dealing with cases far

CHAPTER 9

less complex than that of Elizabeth Penwald.

Elizabeth clears her throat, trying to loosen the phlegm that has gathered at the back. As they approach the desk, Dobby catches sight of Chase and offers him a warm smile.

"Evening, Chase. Another late one for you, I see," she says, her tone light and friendly.

"Dobby, good to see you're still holding down the fort," Chase replies, returning her smile with one of his own.

Dobby's gaze shifts to Elizabeth, her curiosity piqued.

"Who do we have here with you tonight?" she asks, knowing all too well who the woman standing before her would be, her eyes flicking between the two of them.

Chase glances at Elizabeth, a subtle, reassuring glint in his eye as if to say, *'Trust me.'* Elizabeth's mind races, wondering what name he'll use to check her in, the tension in her chest tightening.

"Mrs Elizabeth Mollyanne Penwald," Chase says, his voice steady as he smiles at Dobby.

"She's here to see Doctor Granger," he adds, his tone casual but purposeful.

Dobby's eyebrows lift in recognition.

"Ah, right, she's expecting you. I'll take you straight to her." With that, she lifts the makeshift counter that separates the officers from the public, motioning for them to follow.

"Follow me," Dobby instructs, leading the way.

Elizabeth's stomach churns as she trails behind Chase and the officer, her nerves tightening with each step. They pass through a set of double doors at the end of the foyer, the atmosphere shifting to something more clinical.

Dobby turns left, stopping in front of a small room marked with a plaque reading 'Medical Room.'

Dobby knocks on the door, and after a moment, it swings open to reveal a strict-looking woman with a no-nonsense demeanour. Elizabeth immediately guesses that this must be Doctor Granger. The doctor's eyes briefly scan Elizabeth, taking her in with a discerning gaze, before she steps aside to allow them entry.

* * *

Gerry and Emily follow Biff down the corridor toward an interview room, his broad frame leading the way.

"The Sergeant will be down to see you both in a moment or two. Please bear with us—we're extremely busy tonight," Biff says, his voice as jovial as ever.

Despite his stocky build, Biff is known as a fair and professional officer, always on the ball. Many people say that he and Carter could be brothers, given how similarly they approach their work. But unlike Carter and most of the staff who move through different roles in policing, Biff has always remained a fixture in the Custody Suite. It's where he's found his niche, handling the constant flow of people with a blend of authority and approachability that puts even the most anxious at ease.

"Who have we got tonight, Biff?" Emily asks with a mischievous grin, her eyes sparkling with curiosity.

"You've got the arresting officer, Carter," Biff replies, his smile just as charming as hers.

Biff has always had a soft spot for female solicitors. He admires their strong will and resilience, qualities that stand out in the often tough environment of the Custody Suite. Unlike the police officers he works with daily, these women

CHAPTER 9

are on the side of the 'Innocent until proven guilty' clientele, and Biff respects the tenacity they bring to their work. His tone softens slightly whenever he interacts with them, a subtle nod to the respect he holds for their role in the justice system.

Gerry watches the playful banter between the two professionals, feeling almost invisible in their world. To them, it's just another day—same shit, different day—but for him, this is completely alien.

The sterile environment, the formalities, and the tension all make him feel out of sorts like he's out of his depth in a place he doesn't belong.

As his breath deepens, anxiety tightens his chest, he has to stop just short of the door that Biff has left open for them. The empty, stagnant room waits its air heavy with a sense of foreboding. Gerry hesitates, feeling like he's about to step into a space where everything will change, where nothing will feel normal again.

Emily gestures for Gerry to take a seat, and he gratefully accepts, slumping down onto the hard plastic chair. The legs scrape loudly against the floor as he awkwardly shuffles himself under the desk. With a heavy sigh, he puts his head in his hands, the weight of the situation gnawing away at him.

Emily and Biff exchange a knowing glance, both too familiar with the sight of someone crumbling under the strain of an unfamiliar and stressful situation.

"Can I get either of you a drink?" Biff asks politely, his voice gentle but breaking the silence.

"Two strong coffees would be lovely, please," Emily replies, her tone calm and supportive.

"I won't be long," Biff says, giving a reassuring nod before stepping out of the room. He heads back to the desk, slipping behind the counter and into the small kitchen to prepare the drinks, leaving the door ajar as the smell of coffee begins to fill the air.

"I don't know if I'm strong enough to do this, Emily," Gerry's voice barely rises above a whisper, the words creeping into the quiet room.

"Yes, you can," Emily responds firmly, her voice steady and reassuring.

"You just need to tell them what you've told me. Let them be the judge of what, if any, crimes have been committed."

Gerry shakes his head, the fear and doubt gnawing at him.

"They're going to find something to pin against me. Even if Elizabeth willingly came home with me, I coerced her, didn't I? And I never told her the truth about who she is. She's going to despise me. Hell, I wouldn't be surprised if she's in the other room right now, helping them build a case against me."

Emily leans in slightly, her voice dropping to a conspiratorial whisper.

"Look, I shouldn't be telling you this, but for all you know, she could be on your side."

Gerry's brow furrows in confusion.

"What do you mean?"

"She may be more sympathetic toward your situation than you think," Emily explains, choosing her words carefully.

"She might see things from a different perspective, might understand that there's more to this than meets the eye. And she might not want to press charges against you."

Gerry stares at her, the tension in his chest easing just a

little as he considers the possibility that Elizabeth might not see him as the villain he's made himself out to be.

"OK, but if the police still want to press charges, they'll do so," Gerry says, his voice trembling.

"And then it'll go to court, and a jury will see me for the monster that I am."

He exhales deeply, his breath catching as he struggles to hold back tears.

"Gerry, you are not a monster," Emily reassures him, her voice steady and kind. She places a comforting hand on his arm and gives it a gentle squeeze.

Just then, Biff reenters the room, carrying two steaming cups of coffee. He catches sight of Emily's hand resting on Gerry's arm and raises an eyebrow in silent acknowledgement. Emily quickly withdraws her hand, offering a small, apologetic smile to Biff before he sets the coffee cups down on the desk.

"There you go," Biff says, his tone neutral but attentive.

"Two strong coffees, just as requested."

Emily nods gratefully, her gaze shifting back to Gerry.

"Let's focus on the present, Gerry. Take it one step at a time."

There is a knock at the door, and Sharpie enters the room.

"We won't be too long, I am just waiting for my colleague PC Carter to return then we can get started," says Sharpie.

"Oh great, they've pulled out the big guns," Emily mutters under her breath, her frustration noticeable as she watches the senior officer enter.

Chapter 10

Thursday Early Hours

Yvonne and Reggie, both steady and composed, exit the car in unison.
Reggie gently closes the door behind them and circles around the back of the vehicle, ready to join Carter.

The night air is cool, and the gravel crunches under Yvonne's feet as they walk toward the entrance of the large building, their purpose clear but unspoken.

Carter, already at the door, turns to check in on them.

"Are you guys feeling alright? Still happy to go through with this?"

Yvonne's voice is light, and speaking for the two of them, she responds, "We're as ready as ever."

The trio moves forward, each step echoing softly in the quiet night.

The moon, half-hidden by clouds, casts a faint, eerie glow over the scene, giving the car park an otherworldly feel. As they reach the building, Carter leans against the door, holding it open for Yvonne and Reggie to enter. The shadow of the moon stretches out behind them, adding to the sombre

CHAPTER 10

atmosphere.

Inside, the sound of the gravel is replaced by the soft hum of a computer.

Dobby is busy typing away but looks up as they approach. She greets them with a warm smile, which Carter returns as he steps closer to the desk.

Reggie, feeling the weight of the moment, takes Yvonne's hand in his. His thumb circles gently in her palm—a gesture they've shared countless times, a silent expression of their love and support. Yvonne smiles softly and mirrors the gesture, a silent agreement that they are in this together.

"I have Mr Reggie Draycott and Mrs Yvonne Draycott here to formally identify Mrs Molly Chapman," Carter states with a professional tone, his words clear and concise.

Dobby, her fingers still on the keyboard, looks up and nods.

"Mrs Penwald—Chapman—is currently with the police doctor," she informs them, opening a new tab on her screen to pull up Molly's details.

"Penwald?" Reggie echoes in surprise, the name unfamiliar to him.

Carter turns to Reggie, his expression calm.

"It's the name she believes she goes by at the moment," he explains.

"Oh, right. Yes, that makes sense," Reggie says, though there's a hint of unease in his voice. The situation is becoming more complex than he anticipated.

"Are we putting everyone in the visitors' lounge?" Dobby asks, her tone practical as she begins to make the necessary arrangements.

"Yes, I think that would be the most comfortable place," Carter agrees.

"Is Chase still with Molly?" he enquires, his concern for the logistics showing.

Yvonne, who had been trying to keep up with the conversation, felt a wave of nervousness wash over her. The different names, the formalities, and the pressure of the situation are beginning to overwhelm her. She starts to feel out of place, like a fish out of water, as if she's struggling to keep her footing in a situation that's spiralling out of her control.

Sensing her discomfort, Reggie tightens his grip on her hand, his thumb continuing its gentle, reassuring circles in her palm. The familiar gesture anchors her, reminding her that she's not alone in this. Yvonne takes a deep breath, trying to focus on Reggie's touch and the love it conveys, rather than the swirling thoughts in her mind.

"OK, you are all checked in. Can I get any of you a drink?" Dobby asks with a warm smile, her tone light as she takes pride in her role as a hostess.

Reggie glances at Yvonne for confirmation before replying, "We would love a coffee, if you don't mind, please."

Yvonne nods in agreement, her voice soft but appreciative.

"Yes, a coffee would be most welcome."

"Sugar? Milk?" Dobby asks.

"Just milk for both of us please," replies Yvonne.

"Great! I'll take you to the lounge first so you can get yourselves comfortable, and then I'll bring your drinks to you," Dobby says, her enthusiasm evident as she steps out from behind the desk.

"I'll wait here as I need to pop in to see Sharpie, who's expecting me," Carter says, his tone businesslike as he leans over Dobby's desk to sign the open book. The pen glides smoothly over the paper, the quiet scratch of his signature

CHAPTER 10

filling the brief silence.

Dobby nods, acknowledging his comment with a smile.

"Of course, Carter. I'll make sure Reggie and Yvonne are comfortable in the lounge until you're ready."

Carter straightens up, giving Reggie and Yvonne a reassuring glance.

"I won't be long. Just a quick check-in with DC Sharpie, and then I'll be back."

Reggie nods in understanding, still holding Yvonne's hand.

"Take your time, Carter. We'll be fine."

With that, Carter heads down the corridor, leaving Reggie and Yvonne in Dobby's capable hands as they prepare themselves for the emotional encounter ahead.

Dobby leads them down a short hallway, the soft hum of the building's ventilation the only sound accompanying their footsteps.

As they enter the visitors' lounge, the room is quiet and warmly lit, offering a small measure of comfort amidst the tension.

Unbeknownst to Reggie and Yvonne, just across the hallway in the opposite room, Molly is undergoing her medical examination.

The room is sterile and clinical, a stark contrast to the cosy visitors' lounge. The police doctor methodically checks Molly's vitals, her voice calm and professional as she asks Molly routine questions.

Molly, or Mrs Penwald as she currently believes herself to be, sits on the edge of the examination table, her expression distant. The soft buzz of the fluorescent lights hums overhead, filling the silence between the doctor's enquiries. She answers in short, polite responses, her thoughts seemingly elsewhere, perhaps lost in the confusion of the different names and faces she's been presented with.

The hallway that separates Molly from Reggie and Yvonne is quiet, a thin barrier of walls and doors hiding the proximity of their reunion.

In the Visitors' Lounge, Yvonne and Reggie remain unaware that the person they've come to identify is so close, yet so far in the sense of identity and memory. The weight of the situation hangs in the air, oblivious to the fragile state of the woman just a few steps away.

"Please, make yourselves at home," Dobby says, gesturing to the plush chairs arranged around a low table that is scattered with magazines.

"I'll be back with your coffees in just a moment."

Reggie and Yvonne settle into the chairs, the tension in their shoulders easing slightly as they take in the room's calming ambience. Yvonne leans into Reggie, grateful for his steady presence, as they wait for the next step in this difficult process.

Reggie gently wraps an arm around Yvonne's shoulders, pulling her close. She nuzzles into the warmth of his embrace, drawing comfort from his presence and the familiar scent that soothes her during this unsettling time.

"Are you alright, Vonnie?" Reggie asks softly, his voice filled with concern.

"I will be," Yvonne replies, her voice muffled against his shoulder.

"I just don't like these places. I'm right out of my comfort zone being here."

Reggie nods, understanding her unease.

"I know, love. It won't be long before we can find out if it

CHAPTER 10

really is Molly. But where we go from there, I don't know."

"I hope we can take her home with us," Yvonne says, her voice tinged with hope and anxiety.

"I'm sure she'll be able to come home with us," Reggie reassures her.

"They won't be keeping her here for questioning much longer. They just need to go through the formalities."

"Time will tell, love," Yvonne murmurs.

She clings to his words, hoping for a resolution that will bring them closer to bringing Molly home while navigating the uncertainty of the situation with him by her side.

* * *

I knock on the door of the interview room and wait for the all-clear from Sharpie. Once I hear his voice, I push the door open and step inside. The room is brightly lit, and the sudden contrast makes my eyes squint for a moment as I adjust to the light.

Across the table sits Gerry, looking tense, with his solicitor, Miss Brenner, by his side. She's engrossed in some paperwork, her eyes sharp as she guides Gerry through the documents, which he signs without hesitation.

Sharpie turns to me as I enter, his face breaking into a wide grin.

"Carter, young man! Welcome back," he says, his voice cheerful and warm, a stark contrast to the tension in the room.

"Hey," I respond, keeping my tone measured. I don't want to come across as too casual, given the weight of the situation bearing down on Gerry. There's a lot at stake here, and I need to stay focused.

I acknowledge everyone else in the room with a polite nod and a friendly smile.

"Mr Penwald, Miss Brenner."

Gerry looks up briefly, his eyes tired, but he acknowledges my presence with a slight nod. Miss Brenner glances up from her paperwork, offering a professional, curt smile before returning to her task.

I take a seat, ready to assist with whatever needs to be done, fully aware that the atmosphere in the room is thick with unspoken tension. It's clear that Gerry's situation is serious.

I decide to start the recorder, the familiar click and whir of the machine filling the room as it begins to capture every word. I look at Gerry, maintaining a neutral but approachable expression.

"Alright, Mr Penwald, I just need to get the customary information before we begin. Can you please state your full name, date of birth, and address for the record?"

Gerry obliges, his voice steady but with a hint of apprehension as he provides the details. As he speaks, I make a mental note of his demeanour, looking for any signs of stress or nervousness.

"I won't keep you long," I continue after he finishes, leaning forward slightly to convey a sense of understanding.

"I just want to keep you up to date with where we are at with regards to your case, Mr Penwald."

"Please, call me Gerry," he responds, his tone a bit more relaxed, almost as if he's trying to bridge the gap between us.

"Thank you, Gerry," I say, nodding appreciatively.

I always prefer when suspects allow us to use their first names—it creates a more informal atmosphere, which can be

CHAPTER 10

crucial in these situations. When the boundaries are slightly more relaxed, people tend to let their guard down. They're more likely to be open and honest, which is exactly what I need to make progress in the case.

As the interview starts, I focus on maintaining that balance—professional yet approachable, firm yet fair. It's a delicate dance, but one that often leads to the truth.

"To make you aware, we've brought in two of Mrs Chapman's family members to formally identify her while we await the results from the sample we took earlier," I say, keeping my tone neutral as I observe Gerry's reaction closely.

His eyes flicker between Sharpie and me, searching our faces as if trying to gauge how much we know or what we're thinking. There's a hint of desperation in his gaze, as though he's grasping for something to hold onto amid all this uncertainty.

He looks utterly lost, the weight of the situation seemingly pressing down on him from all sides.

"She is Molly Chapman," he blurts out, his voice strained but clear.

The confession hits like a bolt of lightning, sudden and unexpected. For a moment, the room seems to freeze, the air thick with the impact of his words. I hadn't anticipated such an early admission, and the significance of it struck me instantly.

This was gold dust—something every investigator hopes for but rarely gets so quickly.

Sharpie and I exchange a brief glance, both of us registering the gravity of what Gerry has just admitted.

I keep my composure, not wanting to betray the surprise or the importance of his confession too openly.

"Thank you for your honesty, Gerry," I say calmly, leaning forward slightly.

"This is an important step in understanding everything that's happened."

Inside, my mind is racing, already piecing together how this changes the landscape of the case. But outwardly, I maintain the same steady, composed demeanour, knowing that Gerry's sudden confession could open the door to more crucial information if handled correctly.

"I didn't abduct her though," Gerry says, his voice trembling slightly as he looks at his solicitor, Miss Brenner, searching her face for reassurance. Her expression remains composed, but she gives him a slight nod, encouraging him to continue.

I lean in, my tone careful but probing.

"But did she go with you knowingly, Gerry?" I ask, watching his reaction closely. The room feels charged with tension, every word carrying weight.

Gerry hesitates, his eyes flickering with uncertainty.

"She... she came with me willingly," he repeats, but there's a hesitation in his voice now, as if he's questioning his own words.

I keep my gaze steady, allowing the question to hang in the air. It's a pivotal moment, and I need to see if Gerry will clarify or if his conscience will push him to reveal more. The subtle difference between willingness and informed consent could be critical here, and I want to give him the space to grapple with that realisation.

"What do you mean by 'knowingly,' Carter?" Miss Brenner interjects, her voice calm yet pointed, seeking to protect her client but also aware of the delicate line we're walking.

"Knowingly, as in fully aware of who you were and what

CHAPTER 10

the situation was," I clarify, keeping my tone neutral.

"Did she understand who she was, where she was going, who you were, and why she was with you?"

Gerry's face tightens as the implications of the question sink in.

His silence speaks volumes, and the room seems to close in around us as we wait for his response.

"No, she was not in the know about any of that information," Gerry admits, his voice barely above a whisper as he hangs his head low.

And there it is—the full confession we needed. The force of his words settles over the room like a heavy blanket, and I feel the weight of the moment. This admission is the final piece that confirms everything we suspected, solidifying the case against him.

I exchange a quick glance with Sharpie, who gives a subtle nod, both of us acknowledging the significance of what Gerry has just confessed.

This is the point where the investigation pivots from gathering information to moving forward with formal charges.

"Thank you, Gerry," I say, keeping my tone steady, though inside I'm already shifting gears.

"We appreciate your honesty. We'll need to go over this in more detail, but you should know this is enough for us to proceed with charges."

Gerry doesn't respond, his head still bowed, the weight of his confession pressing down on him. Miss Brenner places a hand on his arm, a small gesture of support, but it's clear that he understands the seriousness of what he's just admitted.

I stop the recorder and the silence that follows thick and heavy with the finality of the situation. This is the moment where the case transitions from suspicion to certainty, and it's now a matter of ensuring that justice is served.

Chapter 11

Thursday Early Hours

The camera flashes, each click capturing still images of the scars that cover my arms. The lens zooms in, documenting every detail of the scars, which snake from my shoulders down to my wrists. They resemble a chaotic map, an array of marks that suggest more than just random injury. The scarring is old and uneven, some more pronounced where I might have needed stitches.

I hadn't given these scars much thought until now, but deep down, I know they didn't come from the fall. They tell a different story—one of pain and self-inflicted harm.

The doctor's voice cuts through my reverie.

"Self-injury," she says, her tone clinical yet gentle.

"Huh?" I look up, startled. Her eyes meet mine with an intensity that feels almost penetrating. I'm suddenly aware that she might see into the darkest corners of my mind. Her gaze is unwavering, and I find myself unable to look away.

She has beautiful brown eyes with flecks of green around the pupils, framed by short lashes coated in a thin layer of mascara. A few strands of hair have fallen loose from her gently tied back bun, brushing against her face. I notice the faint freckles peeking through her foundation, adding a touch of natural charm.

"Self-injury," she repeats.

"Do you remember how you got these scars?"

I snap back to the present moment, her question grounding me in reality. The tears that had started forming in my eyes now threaten to spill over, and I blink them away, struggling to maintain composure.

Her words are a harsh reminder of my past actions, and the reality of facing them in this clinical setting feels overwhelming. I know I need to answer, to confront the truth, but it's a difficult task, dredging up memories that I've tried to keep buried.

She looks me up and down, her gaze clinical but not unkind.

"Please go behind the curtain and remove your clothes down to your underwear," she instructs.

I nod, feeling a flush of embarrassment rise to my cheeks.

The curtain rustles as I step behind it, the small space providing a scant barrier between my vulnerability and the outside world. As I strip down, I can hear Chase making his excuses, his footsteps fading away from the room. His departure adds to the sense of isolation I'm feeling.

When I emerge, she begins her meticulous examination. With each mark, blemish, and bruise she documents, I feel more exposed, both physically and emotionally. Her pen moves steadily, capturing every detail.

The doctor's gaze remains focused on me, and I can't shake the feeling that she's probing deeper, searching for something beyond the surface—a truth that she hopes I'll

CHAPTER 11

reveal willingly. The pressure to open up is evident, but the idea of sharing my inner struggles with a stranger is daunting.

I feel the weight of her unspoken expectation, and a part of me wants to comply, to release the burden that's been weighing me down. Yet, the fact that she is a stranger, someone I don't know or trust, makes it nearly impossible to open up.

But then I think of Gerry. He was a stranger too. Has he confessed his truth, however reluctant he might be? If he does face the truth in front of someone he doesn't know, why does it feel so much harder for me?

The internal conflict churns within me as I stand there, exposed and vulnerable. I want to be honest, but the fear of judgment and the discomfort of being so raw and uncovered in front of a stranger keeps me from speaking.

I place my hand gently on my tummy, cradling it as if nurturing an unborn child. "Apparently I have children," I say, my voice trembling slightly as I struggle to reconcile this new piece of my identity.

"Apparently you do, Elizabeth. Three of them, in fact," the doctor confirms, her tone calm and reassuring.

I glance down at the scar on my abdomen. "They say that I had a C-section, that this scar is from giving birth to them," I continue, searching her eyes for any hint of the truth beyond her professional demeanour.

"Yes, that is correct," she responds, her eyes meeting mine with a steady gaze. "You were led to believe that the scar on your tummy was from a fall—that you were trapped between some rocks and injured yourself. Is that right?"

I swallow hard, grappling with the disconnect between

what I'm being told and what I remember.

"Yes that's right, I believe" I reply, my voice barely above a whisper, seeking confirmation that what she's saying aligns with my fragmented recollections.

The room feels heavier as I wait for her response, the weight of my uncertainty and the pressure of facing the truth creating a suffocating atmosphere. The doctor's calm, authoritative presence is a stark contrast to the turmoil inside me, and I'm left to navigate the chasm between what I thought I knew and the reality being presented to me.

"As far as I'm aware, all of the scars on my body are from the fall," I say, frustration creeping into my voice.

"It was a life and death accident, apparently." It feels like my words are falling on deaf ears. The doctor is focused on her own observations, not on what I'm trying to convey. But then again, she is the expert.

"Elizabeth," she begins, her tone gentle yet firm, "These scars are not from your accident. They are too neat and methodical. And you have hesitation scarring on your thighs."

"Hesitation scarring?" I ask, my voice betraying my nervousness. I know what she means, but I'm stalling, hoping to buy some time before she explains further.

"Yes," she replies, her eyes meeting mine with a blend of compassion and clinical detachment. "Hesitation scarring is characteristic of self-injury. It occurs when someone has started to harm themselves but has stopped before the act was completed. The scars are often more jagged and uneven, showing hesitation and the internal conflict of wanting to hurt oneself but ultimately not following through."

I feel a lump forming in my throat. Her words hit close

CHAPTER 11

to home, making the reality of my situation even more noticeable. The scars she's describing—those jagged, uneven marks—are indeed present on my body. They represent moments of struggle and fear, a reflection of internal battles that I've tried to keep hidden.

The doctor's assessment, though clinical, strikes a chord deep within me. I can no longer deny the truth she's laying out. The scars are not just remnants of a fall; they are markers of a painful journey with self-harm.

A journey that only Molly Chapman could know exists.

* * *

Oliver moves quietly over Lillie, carefully tucking the corner of the duvet into the cushion of the sofa laid out on the floor. He makes sure everything is snug and secure, creating a cosy space. The chairs around them are bare, their flame-resistant tags still visible, while the floor is strewn with bedding, creating a makeshift bed large enough for all three children and their dog, Daisy.

Daisy, content and oblivious to the commotion, happily munches on cereal crumbs and bits of biscuits scattered across the floor. Her presence adds a comforting, homey touch to the scene. Despite shedding her fur, Daisy is a cherished companion on the bed with the children. The warmth she provides, along with her comforting presence, makes her a part of their cosy arrangement.

Bonnie sits cross-legged on the floor, a few feet away from the makeshift bed. In front of her, three bowls are laid out, filled with bags of crisps and bits of broken-up chocolate. She carefully portions out the treats, sharing them between herself and the children. Careful not to touch a bite until it has all been shared out.

"I saw that!" Oliver squeaks, his voice full of accusation and surprise.

"Saw what?" Bonnie responds, turning to face Oliver with a look of faux innocence.

"You ate a bit of chocolate!" Oliver insists, his eyes narrowing in determination.

"I swear I didn't! I just licked my fingers; they were salty from the crisps," Bonnie defends herself, her voice rising slightly in protest.

"You did, I saw you put it in your mouth," Oliver retorts, sticking to his claim.

Bonnie, feeling unjustly accused, screws up her face in defiance. She opens her mouth wide, sticking out her tongue as far as she can to prove her point that nothing had entered her mouth.

"Urgh, that's gross," Oliver whines, turning away in disgust.

"Will you two pack it up?" Lillie chimes in, clearly frustrated.

"You're going to get us all in trouble with Dad if you keep arguing."

"Dad won't hear us; he's watching a movie in the other room," Oliver argues, trying to deflect.

"Maybe, but you know what will happen," Lillie counters.

"You'll start arguing louder, it'll turn into a fight, and then it'll end in tears, which Dad will definitely hear."

Both Oliver and Bonnie exchange a knowing glance. Lillie's logic is hard to dispute, and they reluctantly acknowledge the truth in her words. They decide to call a truce, settling down under the duvet with their bowls of treats.

CHAPTER 11

Daisy, sensing the calm after the storm, sniffs around Lillie's bowl with eager anticipation.

"No, you can't have any of this," Lillie says firmly, gently shooing Daisy away.

"It's not good for you."

Daisy whines softly but backs away, her tail wagging hopefully.

With the argument truced and everyone settled under the duvet, the cosy nest of bedding becomes a haven of peace once more.

* * *

I swear, if I hear those kids making another peep, I'm going to storm in there and rip apart their little camp, and send them all to bed with a good smacking. Why do they have to be so damn noisy and bicker constantly? One minute they're the best of friends, laughing and playing, and the next, they're tearing each other's hair out. It's infuriating.

It's the whining that really gets under my skin.

Lately, it seems like Oliver has turned into a whining, snivelling brat ever since he got back from Reggie and Yvonne's house. It's as if being there transformed him into a completely different child. I can't stand it.

I'm the first to admit that I have a short temper, but right now, I'm having to put on this facade of being the doting, carefree dad.

It's all bullshit!

The truth is far from that. I love my kids, of course I do, but at this moment, I'm absolutely fed up with them. They're constantly under my feet, mouthing off, refusing to eat the meals I've cooked for them, and leaving the house in a state of utter chaos. It's like they don't have a clue about the effort it takes to keep things running smoothly.

I'm starting to realise just how much Molly did around the house. I used to think she spent her days lounging around, doing her coursework whenever she felt like it, but now, as a single parent, I'm seeing firsthand how the mess doesn't clean itself up and how lazy the kids can be. They're downright slobs, and it's driving me to the brink.

I hear the living room door creak open for what feels like the hundredth time tonight. I'm tense, ready to snap, but luckily for them, it's just Lillie. If it had been one of the other two, they would've gotten a hiding, no question about it. It's nearly midnight, and I have to drag myself out of bed early tomorrow to price up another job. I know I shouldn't be sitting here watching this damn film—especially one I've seen a dozen times—but I need something to take my mind off Molly.

Will they ever find her?

That question haunts me.

Is she happy in this new life, wherever she is, without me and the kids?

If I were in her shoes, I probably wouldn't want to come back to this mess either. But everything Molly did, she did for us. For me and the kids.

And what did I do?

I betrayed her.

My thoughts drift back to that parents' evening.

How callous could I have been, dragging Molly along and sitting her right across from the woman I was screwing behind her back?

CHAPTER 11

I was a real bastard to her. And then there was that argument. If we hadn't fought, maybe things wouldn't have fallen apart so completely.

But that's just me lying to myself, isn't it?

Because even if we hadn't fought, I was still cheating on her, still unhappy with what I had, always chasing after something more.

I didn't just have a one-time fling; I was carrying on a long-term affair with our daughter's teacher. And now, I doubt I'll ever hear from Rachel again. Maybe I rushed everything, pushed too hard, and it all blew up in my face. God, what a stupid, stupid mess I've made of everything.

The guilt weighs on me like a ton of bricks, and no amount of late-night movies or distractions can make it go away. I caused this. I did this. And now, I'm left with nothing but regrets and a house full of reminders of the life I shattered.

"Ahem." Lillie's soft voice breaks through the silence.

"Dad? Are you alright? You've watched this film loads of times before."

"No shit, Sherlock, as you kids would say…" I grunt, the irritation slipping out before I can rein it in. I know I'm being sharp, but I'm not in the mood for chit-chat, especially not with my teenage daughter at this ridiculous hour.

"OK, I'm sorry I even bothered to check on you," she mutters, her voice small, like a puppy that's just been scolded.

I immediately regret it.

"No, I'm sorry, that was uncalled for," I say, trying to soften the blow, to pull her back from the edge I just pushed her toward.

"You want me to leave you alone?" she asks, hesitating, clearly not sure whether to stay or go.

"No, it's OK," I offer, feeling the guilt gnaw at me.

"You know you can talk to me about Mum, right?" Lillie's voice is steady, but the weight of her words hits me hard. Suddenly, I feel like the child in this conversation, like she's the one holding the reins.

"Yeah, I know. I just… erm… find it difficult, that's all, Lills." The words come out haltingly as if admitting this weakness will crack something inside me wide open. But I can see she's seeking that vulnerability, wanting to shoulder some of the burden I've been carrying alone. It feels like I'm surrendering a bit of control, letting my guard down in front of her.

"They will find her. If she wants to be found, she will be." Lillie's words are calm and mature—more grown-up than anything I've ever heard her say. There's a quiet wisdom in her tone that both reassures and unnerves me.

"Anyway, I'm going to get some sleep now," she says, turning to head back into the living room.

"Night, Lills," I call after her, my voice barely more than a whisper.

I turn my face into the pillow, feeling the tears well up, and I finally let them fall. The sobs come quietly at first, then wrack my body as I bury myself in the pillow, allowing the grief and regret to wash over me. There, in the silence of the night, I cry myself to sleep, hoping the tears will bring some small measure of relief, though deep down, I know they won't.

Chapter 12

Thursday Early Hours

I feel their eyes on me, heavy with judgment as if they're peeling back the layers of my soul, searching for the monster they believe me to be. I can sense what they're thinking, that I've committed some heinous crime, something unforgivable. And maybe they're right. Maybe I am that monster they see, but all I've done is speak the truth.

Carter just laid it out for me, blunt and final—my confession is enough. Enough to charge me, enough to seal my fate. He says they've pretty much got me, that there's no way out now. I can see it in his eyes, the certainty, the satisfaction of a job nearly done. But despite it all, I don't feel like I've committed any crime, not really. Not in the way they think.

Yet, deep down, I know I have. I know there's something wrong with what I've done, even if it doesn't feel that way. It's a strange, hollow realisation as if the reality of my actions is something distant, something I can't fully grasp.

I've said too much and confessed to more than I should have, but it's all out there now. And still, I can't shake this feeling—that I'm somehow both guilty and not guilty at the same time.

The door creaks open, and a dishevelled-looking man steps into the room. He scans the room with sharp, tired eyes before introducing himself.

"DCI Dixie," he says, his voice low and gravelly.

Without wasting a moment, he beckons to Carter, a subtle nod of his head indicating the need for a private conversation. Carter, who has been sitting across from me, scrapes his chair back across the floor, the sound grating against the tension in the room. He stands up, gives me one last look, and then follows Dixie out into the corridor.

* * *

Carter barely has time to register the abruptness of DCI Dixie before the man dives into the heart of the matter.

"Carter, we need to move this forward," Dixie begins, his voice laced with irritation. "We've got Molly in with the Doc right now, and her brother and sister-in-law are sitting in the visitors' lounge, waiting to give a formal identification. Lambert's upstairs with Poker, chasing up the lab reports on her sample to confirm if the DNA matches Molly's."

Dixie takes a deep breath, his frustration barely contained as he continues, "So, where are you at?" There's a sense of urgency in the air, a pressure that Carter can feel bearing down on him, knowing that every second counts.

"This is all on you lad, you know you can bring it to the table."

"Yeah, I know, but before you make a judgement, we have had a result."

"Go on," says Dixie

CHAPTER 12

"Gerry Penwald has only gone and admitted that the woman is in fact, Molly Chapman."

"Get the hell out of here?!"

"Seriously boss, he fessed up," Carter tells him.

They both know that they need to wait for Lambert's results and the identification from Reggie and Yvonne before they can take the case to the next level.

The door to the corridor swings open, and a young man steps out, his demeanour calm but his eyes alert. Dixie and Carter, both standing a few feet away, exchange nods of acknowledgement as the man approaches. Benjamin Swift, a solicitor known for his recent high-profile case.

"Hi, I'm Miss Houston's solicitor," he says, extending his hand in a polite, yet firm manner. Dixie reaches out first to shake it, followed by Carter, who grips it briefly before releasing it.

"I don't want to be a nuisance," Benjamin continues, his voice carrying a note of concern, "but is anyone coming to interview Rachel tonight? It's extremely late, and the poor woman has been waiting for hours."

Carter's expression tightens as he responds, "I'm really sorry about the delay. We've had a significant breakthrough in the case, and all our officers are tied up with various urgent tasks related to it."

Benjamin scratches his head, a gesture that reveals his growing confusion and frustration.

"Then why call her in for an interview if there's no one available to speak with her? It's not fair to keep her waiting; we could have gone back to her cell."

Dixie steps in, his tone a mix of apology and explanation. "We understand your frustration. Unfortunately, the nature of our work in a busy custody suite means that sometimes things don't go as smoothly as planned, especially with a major case on our hands."

Benjamin, clearly agitated, adds, "Please don't think I'm being patronizing. It's just that I wouldn't expect such treatment for a young woman under caution. She hasn't even had her phone call yet."

Dixie takes a deep breath and offers a compromise.

"Look, here's what we can do. I'll take Rachel down to make her phone call now. You're welcome to come with us if you'd like. By the way, what's your name again?"

"Swift. Benjamin Swift from Swift and Pope down on Central Drive," he replies, his voice steady despite his irritation.

"Oh, right, I know the company," Carter says, his tone warming slightly.

"You recently handled the Janie Jackson case, the missing teenager?"

"Yes, that's the one," Benjamin replies, a note of pride in his voice as he nods.

The three men fall into a brief, contemplative silence, each processing the situation from their perspective. Dixie, sensing the need to move things along, gestures towards the corridor.

"Alright then, follow me. I'll take you to the reception area where Rachel is waiting."

Dixie turns to Carter.

"I'll catch up with you later lad, carry on as you were," he says.

With that, Dixie turns and begins walking back down the corridor, his pace deliberate. Benjamin follows, the

CHAPTER 12

atmosphere charged with urgency and the quiet hope that the situation can be resolved swiftly.

Benjamin pokes his head back through the door to Rachel's waiting area, his expression concerned and frustrated.

The door swings open, and Rachel's eyes meet his immediately, her face a mask of anxious anticipation.

"Any luck?" she asks, her voice full of hope.

Benjamin shakes his head, his face falling slightly.

"Not yet for the interview, but you can make your phone call now."

Rachel glances at him with confusion.

"What time is it?" she asks.

Benjamin glances at his watch, his eyes widening as he realises the hour.

"Bloody hell," he mutters, adjusting his sleeve to cover his wrist.

"It's just gone two in the morning."

Rachel's eyes widen in alarm. "I can't call my dad at this hour!"

"Why not?" Benjamin asks, puzzled. "Will he not hear his phone?"

"Ringing him at this awful hour will give him a heart attack," Rachel protests, her voice rising with frustration.

Benjamin tries to remain calm and authoritative.

"Rachel, you have to call him now. They're waiting for you down at the reception."

Rachel's frustration peaks.

"Oh, for God's sake, my dad will go spare if I wake him up now!" she huffs.

With a loud scrape of chair legs against the floor, Rachel pushes her chair back and stands up, her movements sharp and defiant. Benjamin observes her, struggling to maintain his professionalism. He can't help but think, somewhat uncharitably, that she's acting like a spoilt child.

"Rachel, please," Benjamin says, trying to keep his voice steady and reassuring.

"It's important you make this call now. It's part of your rights."

Rachel takes a deep breath, visibly upset but aware of the necessity.

She follows Benjamin out of the room as they head towards the reception area, Rachel's frustration is unmistakable in each step. Benjamin follows her, his irritation simmering beneath the surface, but his focus remains on ensuring that Rachel gets her phone call and the process continues as smoothly as possible.

* * *

Margaret and Philip Houston are nestled together in bed. The soft glow of the bedside lamp casts a gentle light over Margaret's side, illuminating the quiet room with a comforting, golden hue.

Her book 'The Van', which Margaret had been engrossed in earlier, now lies discarded on the floor, its pages slightly splayed open as if frozen in time. Her glasses, still perched on the bridge of her nose, are askew, one lens catching the faint light and casting a small, distorted reflection.

At the foot of the bed, their cat is curled up in a cosy ball of fur, its body contorted into an oddly adorable shape, resembling a fluff ball that has been zapped by a static charge. The cat's rhythmic breathing creates a soft, comforting purr

CHAPTER 12

that mingles with the steady rise and fall of Margaret and Philip's breaths, adding to the peaceful ambience of the room.

The night is still and quiet, the world outside oblivious to the small, tranquil scene unfolding within the Houston's bedroom.

The silence of the night is abruptly pierced by the sudden illumination of Philip's mobile phone, which buzzes insistently on the bedside cabinet. The caller display clearly shows 'unknown' in bold letters. The phone's traditional ringing melody begins softly, its faint chimes gradually growing louder with each ring.

The initial quiet beeps are almost inaudible, but they steadily crescendo, becoming increasingly urgent and penetrating. The rhythmic ringing fills the space, jolting Philip and Margaret from their peaceful sleep.

Margaret stirs first, her eyelids fluttering open as she reaches out helplessly to silence the intrusive sound, while Philip, still half-asleep, fumbles groggily for the phone.

"What in the hell," Philip mutters as he reaches for his phone, Margaret trying to lean over him to grab it first.

"Who on earth is calling at this hour?" Margaret asks groggily, rubbing the sleep from her eyes.

"It's OK, love. I've got it," Philip says, his voice thick with sleep.

"I don't know, Who on earth would call this time of night?"

"Rachel?!" Margaret exclaims, fully awake now.

Philip quickly answers the call, bringing the phone to his ear.

"Rachel?" he asks, his voice filled with concern.

"Hi, Dad, it's only me. Don't panic, I'm alright," Rachel says quickly, her voice steady but trying to reassure him.

She holds the phone close to her mouth, while the Custody Officer beside her holds another phone close to her ear, listening in.

Philip frowns, glancing at the clock on the bedside cabinet.

"Where on earth are you? Have you seen the time?" he demands, his worry palpable in his tone.

"Yes, Dad, I know it's late. I'm sorry, but I'm at the police station," Rachel replies, the reality of her situation hitting her with each word.

"There's been a massive mix-up, and I've been arrested in connection to a missing person."

For the first time, Rachel feels the weight of her words and the seriousness of her predicament. Her voice wavers slightly as she processes the gravity of her situation.

"At the police station?" Philip exclaims, his voice rising with shock and disbelief.

He pushes himself upright in bed, throwing the duvet aside as he swings his legs over the edge. He stands up, moving around to Margaret's side of the bed, and flicks on the main light, flooding the room with brightness. Margaret shields her eyes with her hand, squinting against the sudden glare.

"Yes, Dad," Rachel continues, her voice apologetic.

"I'm so sorry to call you at this hour, but this was the first chance I've had to reach you."

Philip's mind races as he tries to comprehend what he's hearing.

"How long have you been there, love?" he asks, his voice softening with concern.

"All evening," she admits, the exhaustion clear in her voice.

Margaret sits up fully now, her face pale with worry.

"What happened, Rachel?" probes Philip.

CHAPTER 12

"I don't know," Rachel replies, starting to feel overwhelmed.

"It's all a big misunderstanding, but they think I'm involved in this missing person case. I didn't do anything, I swear."

Philip exchanges a worried glance with Margaret, his mind already racing with what they need to do next.

"OK, Rachel, stay calm," he says, trying to sound reassuring despite the anxiety tightening in his chest.

"We're coming to the station right now."

"Thank you, Dad," Rachel says, her voice barely a whisper. "I'm so sorry."

"Don't worry about that now, we'll sort this out," Philip replies firmly, already grabbing a pair of trousers from the chair beside the bed.

"Just hang tight. We're on our way."

Rachel clutches the phone tightly, pressing it closer to her mouth, her voice trembling as she speaks to her father. Tears well up in her eyes, threatening to spill over.

"Dad," she pleads softly, her voice barely holding steady.

"Can you please hurry up? I need to see someone who knows me. It's horrible down here. They put me in a cell and…"

Before she can continue, Dobby, who is standing nearby, shakes her head subtly, reminding Rachel to keep to the formalities of the call. Rachel wipes her tears and takes a deep breath.

"I'm allowed a visitor to bring me some belongings," she continues, trying to keep her voice even.

"Can you ask Mum to bring my washbag that's on the sink in my ensuite? It has all my toiletries in it. Please, Dad," she begs, her desperation evident.

Philip's voice is steady but strained as he responds, "Yes, erm, of course. I'll sort that for you now."

There's a pause as Philip tries to piece together what he's hearing.

"When you say missing person, do you mean the woman they came to the college about the other day? When they took you in for questioning?" he asks, a hint of urgency creeping into his voice.

"Yes, Dad, it's about the same woman. I'll explain everything later. I have to go now. My time is up," Rachel says hurriedly, handing the phone back to Dobby with a reluctant sigh.

Dobby takes the phone and addresses Philip.

"Mr Houston, your daughter is under caution, so she can't reveal too much, but you are welcome to come in and see her with her belongings."

Philip's anxiety sharpens.

"Has she been charged with anything?"

"I can't provide any more details over the phone," Dobby replies calmly, "but you can speak to her solicitor when you arrive."

"Who is her solicitor?" Philip presses.

"I'm sorry, Mr Houston," Dobby says, maintaining a professional tone, "I can't give out that information over the phone."

Philip exhales heavily.

"OK, OK. I'll come down and see her shortly."

"Thank you, Mr Houston. Goodbye." Dobby says before hanging up the call. She places the receiver back into its cradle and then does the same with her phone.

Philip sits there for a moment, stunned, trying to absorb

CHAPTER 12

the news.

"I don't believe what I've just been told, Mags," he mutters, turning to Margaret.

Margaret, already sitting up and alert, her worry etched deeply into her face, asks, "What on earth is going on, love?"

"It's Rachel," Philip replies, his voice tight with anxiety. "She's been arrested in connection with the disappearance of a woman."

"What the hell?!" Margaret exclaims, her voice shocked. She leans back against the headboard of the bed, pulling her knees up to her chest in a protective gesture. She pushes her glasses back up her nose, trying to focus on the situation unfolding.

Philip starts pacing the room, his mind racing with thoughts and fears.

"I need to get dressed and head down there now. She sounded so scared, Mags. I've never heard her like that before."

Margaret nods, swallowing hard to keep her composure. "I'll get her washbag and anything else she might need."

Philip moves quickly, pulling on a pair of trousers and grabbing a shirt from the wardrobe. Margaret gets up, her movements are frantic yet purposeful, gathering Rachel's belongings as her mind races with worry and confusion.

The quiet, sleepy peace of their bedroom has been shattered, replaced by a sense of urgency and dread.

Chapter 13

Thursday Early Hours

The doctor finishes taking the photos and, with Elizabeth's permission, proceeds with a forensic physical examination. The room is quiet except for the faint sound of gloves snapping and the soft rustle of paperwork. Elizabeth remains calm, answering more intimate questions with a steady voice. The doctor's demeanour is professional yet gentle, ensuring Elizabeth feels as comfortable as possible throughout the process. After what feels like an eternity, the examination concludes.

"You're all set," the doctor says softly. Elizabeth nods, grateful for the end of this ordeal. The doctor steps out of the room, leaving Elizabeth to gather herself.

The doctor heads down the hallway and spots Chase at the check-in desk, sipping a cup of tea, his posture relaxed but his eyes alert.

"She's good to go," the doctor informs him.

Chase looks up, his brow furrowed with concern.

"And what do you make of it all?" he asks, leaning in slightly.

CHAPTER 13

"She's not showing any signs of physical abuse," the doctor replies thoughtfully.

"Honestly, I don't think she's even suffered emotional abuse. She's clear and concise with her answers and seems to understand everything perfectly. She's even acknowledging the fact that she possibly has children."

"Wow, you've gotten a lot out of her," Chase remarks, clearly impressed and grateful for the insight.

The doctor smiles softly, a hint of pride in her eyes.

"I've been doing this a long time. You learn to ask the right questions," she replies. Her smile is warm but knowing, a subtle acknowledgement of the complexities she navigates in her line of work.

"So what happens now, Doctor?" Chase asks, his concern for Elizabeth's well-being obvious in his tone.

"Now, I write up my report," the doctor replies, her face reflecting empathy and professionalism.

"I can have it back to you within the hour. DCI Dixie has asked me to fast-track it so they can determine what charges, if any, they can present to the suspect." She glances at Chase, sensing his unease about Elizabeth's situation.

"OK, that's great. But is she fit enough to meet with some family members? Or will that cause her too much trauma?" Chase asks, his voice filled with a genuine worry for Elizabeth's state of mind.

The doctor considers his question carefully before responding.

"In my professional opinion, I'd recommend keeping her at a distance for now. Meeting family members face-to-face could potentially be overwhelming or traumatic for her, given her current condition. Maybe use the video link instead? I can set it up in my room if you like."

"That would be really helpful," Chase agrees, nodding.

"I can wheel the video link screen into the Visitor's Lounge since that's where her brother and sister-in-law are waiting. I'll go in and speak with them shortly. But first, I want to go and check on Elizabeth, see how she's doing."

"Of course," the doctor says, understanding the weight of the situation.

"I'll get everything set up for the video link. Let me know if you need anything else."

"I think she might be the missing girl you're looking for," the doctor continues, her voice serious and thoughtful.

"It can't all be coincidences. The scarring suggests a life full of emotional ups and downs, but without a deeper dive into her psyche, we won't truly understand what's been happening in her marriage with her *'real'* husband."

"Thank you, Doctor. That's really useful to know," Chase says, appreciating her insights.

She gives a brief nod.

"I'll let you get on with it. My door is still open, and Elizabeth is expecting you."

With that, the doctor turns on her heels and walks back down the corridor toward another part of the building. Chase watches her go for a moment, gathering his thoughts before making his way back to the medical room. His thoughts focused on how best to support her through what is clearly a delicate and emotional situation.

He stops outside the door and gently knocks.

"Hello?..." Elizabeth's voice comes softly from inside.

"It's only me, Elizabeth. Can I come back in?" Chase asks, trying to keep his tone calm and reassuring.

CHAPTER 13

"Yes, of course," she answers, her voice sounding a bit steadier than before.

Chase slowly opens the door and steps inside, closing it quietly behind him. He sees Elizabeth sitting there, her posture showing exhaustion and wariness, but also a glimmer of hope. Chase gives her a small smile as he approaches.

"I wanted to check in with you," he says gently, taking a seat across from her.

"How are you feeling?"

"Yes, I'm feeling OK, thank you," she says, a small smile creeping onto her face, her eyes brightening ever so slightly.

"That's good to hear," Chase responds warmly, nodding his head.

Elizabeth's expression shifts to one of hopeful anticipation.

"Am I done here now? Can I see Gerry, please?" she pleads, her voice carrying showing longing and anxiety.

Chase's face softens with understanding, but he shakes his head gently.

"I'm sorry, but Gerry is currently being questioned. However, I do have some good news for you," he says, pausing to gauge her reaction.

"Some of your family members are here to see you."

Elizabeth's eyes widen with surprise and uncertainty, her hands gripping the edge of her seat.

Chase continues, "Rather than meeting with them face-to-face right now, we'd like to set up a video link first. It'll be a bit less overwhelming and give you some space. But, of course, I need your permission to do that. Do you give me your consent?"

Elizabeth hesitates for a moment, her gaze dropping to her hands as she processes this new information. After a few seconds, she looks back up at Chase, having curiosity and apprehension in her eyes.

"Yes, I give you my consent," she finally says, her voice steady.

"I want to see them… even if it's just through a screen."

"That is great," Chase exclaims, visibly relieved by Elizabeth's agreement. He shifts from his position, turning towards the door with a renewed sense of purpose.

"I'll get that sorted for you now. Would you like a drink while you wait?" he asks her, his tone gentle.

"Water would be lovely," she replies softly, then adds, "And Chase, thank you… for everything."

Chase gives her a reassuring smile.

"You don't need to thank me for anything. I'm just here to help. I'll get the video link set up and bring it through to you here, where you're comfortable."

With that, Chase steps out of the room, closing the door quietly behind him, allowing Elizabeth a moment of solitude before facing the next challenge. She lets out a long breath, her mind racing with thoughts of who might be on the other side of the screen, and what seeing them might bring. As the room falls silent, she finds herself grappling with jumble of hope and anxiety, her heart pounding in her chest.

She takes a deep breath, trying to steady herself for whatever comes next.

* * *

Chase knocks on the door to the visitors' lounge and steps inside. Reggie and Yvonne are sitting close to each other on the plush chairs, sipping their coffees. As he enters, they

CHAPTER 13

both look up, curiosity evident on their faces.

"Hello, my name is PC Jason Chase, or Chase for short," he introduces himself, giving them a warm, professional smile.

Reggie and Yvonne nod in unison, Reggie setting his cup down on the small table in front of him.

"Hi, I'm Reggie, and this is my wife, Yvonne," he adds.

"I'm pleased to meet you both," Chase replies, extending his hand. They each shake it politely, the tension in the room noticeable.

"So, I believe you are Elizabeth's brother?" Chase asks, then quickly corrects himself, "Excuse me, I mean Molly's brother."

Reggie nods.

"Yes, that's correct. We're here to identify her."

"God, Reggie, that sounds awful saying it like that," Yvonne says softly, placing a hand on her forehead in disbelief.

Reggie looks at her, slightly exasperated.

"You know what I mean. What else am I supposed to say?" he asks, his voice filled with genuine confusion and frustration.

"I'm sorry, I know," Yvonne mutters, shrinking back into her seat, her expression one of worry.

Chase senses the tension and steps in to ease the moment.

"We're going to set up a video link," he explains calmly.

"I'll bring the monitor in here, and you'll be able to see each other on the screen. I'll turn it on for you first, so you can identify Molly. Once we have the OK, I'll turn the screen on, on her side so she can see you both. Does that make sense?"

Reggie and Yvonne exchange a quick glance before Reggie nods.

"Yes, that makes sense," he replies, his voice steadier now.

Yvonne takes a deep breath.

"Thank you for setting this up. We just want to see her, to know she's alright."

Chase nods empathetically.

"I understand. I'll go get everything ready now. It won't be long."

He gives them a reassuring smile before stepping out of the room to make the arrangements. Reggie and Yvonne sit back, their fingers intertwined, preparing themselves for the emotional moment ahead.

* * *

Lambert is in the forensics lab, focusing intently on the samples she had taken from Molly earlier.

The various machines and computers around her hum with activity, processing data, and conducting analyses.

She taps her fingers nervously on the counter, her eyes flicking between the digital clock on the wall and the whirring machine in front of her. The tests are nearly complete, and anticipation bubbles within her. The stakes are high, and she knows the significance of what she's about to uncover.

Finally, the machine grinds to a halt with a soft beep. Lambert exhales slowly, her breath fogging the glass in front of her. She carefully removes the slide from the slot and places it under the microscope. Adjusting the focus, she zooms in on the sample, her trained eyes scrutinizing every detail. Her heart beats faster as she moves the slide, comparing it to the control samples of blood taken from Molly's family. The digital screen beside her displays the

CHAPTER 13

magnified images, and she overlays them, aligning markers and sequences.

Then, the result pops up on her laptop screen in bold, unmistakable text:

MATCH FOUND

A surge of adrenaline rushes through her. The DNA matches that of Molly Chapman. Lambert can hardly contain her excitement.

"We've got her!" she shouts, her voice echoing off the sterile walls of the lab.

She quickly hits enter on her laptop, sending the confirmation data to the printer. The machine immediately whirs into action, spitting out several sheets of paper filled with the DNA analysis results. Lambert rushes over, grabbing the freshly printed pages, her fingers trembling with exhilaration. She shuffles them into order, barely glancing at the text she already knows by heart.

Bursting out of the lab, she makes her way down the corridor, the papers clutched tightly in her hand. As she rounds a corner, she spots Chase coming up the stairs, heading towards the office where the rest of the team is gathered.

"You are looking very pleased with yourself," Chase remarks, raising an eyebrow as he sees the gleam in her eyes.

"You would not believe how happy I am right now," Lambert replies, a wide grin spreading across her face. Her voice is practically vibrating with excitement.

"I bloody love science!" she whoops, throwing her head back and laughing with relief and joy. The realization that they've found Molly at last hits her fully, and she can't help but feel a sense of triumph.

Chase chuckles at her enthusiasm, a grin breaking across his own face as the force of her words sinks in.

"Great work, Lambert. Let's get this to Dixie and the rest of the team. They'll want to know immediately."

Lambert nods, still beaming as she follows Chase towards the office, the precious papers in hand, carrying with them the truth they've all been desperately seeking.

* * *

Dixie sits in his office, staring at the screen as the interview between Gerry and Carter plays out. His eyes narrow, analyzing every word and movement, searching for any crack in Gerry's demeanour. He rewinds the recording, focusing on a specific moment where Gerry's voice falters, a subtle shift that seems to suggest he's hiding something. But before he can replay it again, a burst of noise erupts from the office outside his door.

He quickly gets to his feet, moving towards the sound. As he reaches the doorway, Lambert appears, her face flushed with excitement and her eyes practically glowing. She's holding a stack of papers, and the triumphant look on her face says it all.

"We've got her, Boss," she exclaims, her voice bubbling over with excitement.

Dixie feels a rush of relief and adrenaline.

"Bloody well done, Lambert," he says, patting her firmly on the shoulder.

"I know," Lambert says, her words tumbling out quickly.

"I sort of knew it already, but it's the confirmation we've been waiting for. Her DNA matches with her family, and

CHAPTER 13

it matches with the blood we found on her nightie and her diary." She waves the papers in her hand as if the physical evidence itself were proof enough.

"That is terrific news," Dixie says, his voice filled with emotion. The weight of the investigation, all the long hours and the uncertainty, suddenly feels lighter. His knees feel weak under the sudden release of tension, and he stumbles slightly, catching himself on the door frame.

Lambert notices immediately, concern flashing in her eyes.

"Shall I get you a chair, Boss?" she asks, stepping forward as if ready to catch him.

"No, no," Dixie waves her off, trying to stand tall.

"I'll be alright, thank you." He rejects the offer with a hint of pride, unwilling to show weakness in front of his team, especially not in a moment like this.

"Alright, Boss, but you need to take care of yourself too," Lambert insists gently, but she respects his decision and steps back.

Dixie nods, taking a deep breath to steady himself.

"Right," he says, trying to refocus.

"Let's get this over to Chase and the others. This changes everything. We need to prepare for the next steps—there's a lot to do."

Lambert nods eagerly.

"On it, Boss. I've just seen Chase, but I will go and let the others know." She turns quickly, heading back down the corridor, already thinking of what needs to happen next. Dixie watches her go for a moment, then squares his shoulders and heads back into his office, feeling the weight of responsibility but also a renewed sense of purpose. They're finally getting somewhere, and for the first time in a long while, he feels a spark of hope.

Dixie pauses at his office door and glances back over his shoulder, watching Lambert as she makes her way back into the office. Her confidence is undeniable, almost contagious, as she strides past Poker and Gilbert, who are both buried in piles of paperwork, their desks cluttered with files and documents.

Poker glances up, noticing Lambert's upbeat demeanour.

"What's got you all fired up?" he calls out, raising an eyebrow.

Lambert flashes a grin, waving the stack of papers triumphantly.

Gilbert, half-hidden behind a tower of files, looks up with a hint of curiosity.

Lambert nods, still moving briskly past them.

"DNA match confirmed. It's Molly," she replies, and her words hang in the air like a spark ready to ignite.

Poker and Gilbert exchange glances, their expressions shifting from weary concentration to a shared look of hope. The atmosphere in the office seems to lift, the gravity of the situation feeling just a bit lighter with the news.

Dixie, still watching from the doorway, allows himself a small smile. Lambert's enthusiasm is exactly what the team needs right now. He turns back into his office, the sounds of renewed chatter and movement behind him a comforting reminder that, for once, things are going their way.

Chapter 14

Thursday Early Hours

Chase knocks on the door to the interview room where Carter and Sharpie are finishing up their questioning of Gerry. Carter is needed to sit in with Reggie and Yvonne while they identify Molly. Although they already have the evidence needed to formally identify her, they believe it's best to conduct the formal identification to observe Molly's reaction in a controlled environment. This way, they can offer immediate support if any trauma surfaces when she is reunited with her brother and sister-in-law.

Carter makes his excuses to Gerry, preparing to leave the room.

"I won't be too long." he says, standing up.

"OK," Gerry replies, watching as Carter exits, leaving him in Sharpie's hands.

Outside the room, Chase is waiting, barely able to contain his excitement.

"The results? They're in?" Carter asks, eyes wide with anticipation.

"They sure are pal," Chase confirms, a grin spreading across his face.

"I'm guessing by the look on your face that we do have the right person?" Carter asks, trying to temper his excitement.

"Yes, she *is* Molly. It looks like the amnesia isn't as bad as we first thought," Chase explains.

"In what way?" Carter asks, intrigued.

"In the sense that she's already beginning to accept that she has children," Chase replies.

"Oh wow, really? Did that come out during the doctor's assessment, or when you were with her earlier this evening?" Carter enquires, leaning in closer.

"Not with me. She was flat-out denying that she had children when I spoke with her, but the doctor managed to get her to open up more," Chase says, clearly relieved.

"That's brilliant that the doc managed to do that. She really is great at her job, isn't she?" Carter says, clearly impressed.

"Yes, she is," Chase agrees.

"Anyway, the reason I came to get you is that I need you to sit with Reggie and Yvonne. I'm setting up a video link from the medical room where Molly is to the visitors' lounge. The doc thinks it'll be better for Molly's mental health if we do it remotely at first."

"Aha, that makes sense," Carter nods, understanding the caution.

"Just give me a minute," he adds, before popping his head back through the door of the interview room.

He catches Sharpie's eye and gives him a quick nod, motioning for him to come over. Sharpie approaches, and Carter quietly informs him, "I'll be about half an hour. Let Gerry go back to his cell and get some sleep."

Sharpie nods in understanding and moves to escort Gerry

CHAPTER 14

out of the room.

Carter turns back to Chase, ready to follow him to the visitors' lounge for the video link session.

* * *

Whilst Molly is in the toilet Chase and Carter adjust the video links' monitor height, ensuring the camera is positioned at Molly's eye level. They want the identification process to go smoothly, without any issues. For now, the two men decide to hold off on announcing the results of the DNA test. They are more interested in observing the natural interaction between Molly, Reggie, and Yvonne.

"If you could text me when they've identified Molly, then I can turn this monitor on. Is that alright?" Chase whispers, looking to Carter for confirmation.

"Yeah, that makes sense. I'm sure it will all run smoothly," Carter replies, nodding in agreement.

Despite his calm demeanour, Chase's stomach churns with nerves and a hint of anxiety. He worries about how Molly will react to the reunion and what emotions might surface.

Molly re-enters the room.

Carter turns to her and asks gently, "Are you alright, Molly?"

"Yes, thank you. I think I am," she replies, her voice steady. "I'm actually quite looking forward to meeting my relatives."

Carter finds her response a bit strange. He expected her to be more overwhelmed by the situation, given the circumstances. It's almost as if she is anticipating recognizing them immediately, without any hesitation.

"So, the relatives are your brother, Reggie, and your sister-in-law, Yvonne. Do either of those names mean anything to you?" Chase asks gently.

Molly shakes her head.

"No, they don't. I'm sorry," she replies, her voice soft and apologetic.

"That's alright," Chase reassures her.

"They might come back to you when you see them."

"I hope so," Molly murmurs, her eyes closing slightly to shield them from the harsh light of the monitor as Carter switches it on. The screen fills with a bright, white light, and Molly stares into it, almost as if she's in a trance.

Her mind begins to drift back to the day she woke up in the hospital. She remembers the unfamiliar faces surrounding her, everyone smiling and clapping, though none of them seemed recognizable. She recalls needing the bathroom and asking Gerry for help, mistaking him for a doctor. She remembers his look—his smile tinged with something else, something like fear. She hadn't seen him before that night, at least not that she could remember.

"I just want to see my husband," she says aloud, her voice filled with confusion and longing.

"We know you do, but I've explained the circumstances around why you can't see him right now. That's not to say that tomorrow you won't be able to see him for a short while. We're working on getting you the necessary permission from higher up," Chase explains patiently.

"Thank you, Chase," Molly replies, her voice blend of resignation and hope.

"Right, well, if the machine is all set up here, I'm going to head back next door and set up the other monitor," Carter

CHAPTER 14

says, preparing to leave.

"OK, Carter. Thank you for your help," Chase responds.

With a nod, Carter turns to head back down the hallway, leaving Chase and Molly to prepare for the video link with her family.

As Carter crosses the corridor, Emily, Gerry's solicitor, calls out to him.

"PC Carter," she shouts.

Carter stops dead in his tracks.

"Yes?" he replies, turning around to face her.

"Off the record," she pauses, taking a deep breath, "where does he stand?"

"Miss Brenner, you know I'm not privy to that kind of information just yet," he says cautiously.

"I just need to know," she persists, her voice carrying a note of desperation.

"This poor man is due to bury his Mum in a few days. Is he likely to get bail?"

Carter sighs. "I think he might be able to get bail. It's his first offence, and the woman he's accused of abducting is not on the same page as us. She's still insisting he's her husband."

"Damn, that's some memory loss she's got there. Is that normal for this kind of accident?" Emily probes, pushing for more information.

"I don't know," Carter admits, shaking his head slightly.

"I'm waiting for the medical report. But professionally speaking, anything is possible. We never fully understand the human body, let alone the brain."

Emily hesitates, then asks, "Is there a chance she could be faking it, PC Carter?" Her words feel sharp, like a needle pricking at an uncomfortable truth.

"Faking it?" Carter repeats, surprised by her suggestion.

"No, I can't see her faking it at all. But then again, I'm not the expert—Chase is."

"Just food for thought," Emily says, turning away. She walks down the corridor, her heels clicking against the floor.

Carter watches her go, unable to help himself as he murmurs under his breath, "Nice arse."

* * *

Back in this bloody place, with just the four walls and a small window with bars on it. I wonder if this is what prison is like, or if the rooms are smaller. I know they have bunk beds and a sink and toilet all in the same room—or is that just in the movies, where they give you grey, itchy blankets and a plastic bowl so you can wash yourself?

I feel tired.

I know I'm going down for this, so I take in and accept my surroundings.

Damn, I would have no visitors. I have no more living relatives; I only have Elizabeth. Rachel isn't going to want to see me again after being arrested too. I bet my name is shit in her interview. The good thing is, she doesn't know too much anyway—she'd only been around twenty or thirty minutes before the police turned up.

Elizabeth is not going to visit me when she realizes what's going on. She's going to hate me, more than she's hated anything in her life. I love that woman so much; everything I have done is because I love her.

Fuck it.

If I go down, I go down. I am not going to sit here dwelling

CHAPTER 14

on something I have absolutely no control over.

I wipe my hands over my face and feel the urge to pee. I walk into the tiny room with the toilet. I look over my shoulder and up to the camera, wondering if they actually watch us taking a piss. I imagine them back at the desk, laughing at my pearly white ass on the camera in front of them.

My mind races—the kittens, what are we going to do about Era and her babies? They're going to need feeding, and there is no one that I can call on.

What am I going to do about my poor Mum?

The thought of her lying in that cold, sterile morgue alone, without me there to hold her hand one last time, breaks my heart. Will I even get the chance to say my final goodbyes, or are they going to take that right away from me too?

She deserves better than this—she deserves a proper farewell, not to be left unkempt and forgotten in some drawer. The guilt gnaws at me, knowing I might not be there for her when she needs me the most, even in death.

And what about Elizabeth?

By admitting that I know she's actually Molly, I'm basically signing my own confession. The moment those words left my mouth, I was as good as guilty in their eyes. They don't need to dig any deeper or piece together the evidence—I've handed them everything they need on a silver platter. They could skip the whole investigation, even bypass a trial, because I'm not denying any of it.

I've already sealed my fate, and now all that's left is to face the consequences.

* * *

THE FOUND

The monitor flickers on, casting a pale glow across the room as a ghostly image of Molly appears on the screen. I adjust the button on the back of the monitor, and the picture sharpens, bringing Molly into clearer view. Her face fills the screen, and for a moment, time seems to stand still.

Yvonne gasps, her hands flying up to cover her mouth, her eyes wide with disbelief.

"Oh my God, it's her, it's Molly," she cries, tears streaming down her face.

I turn to Reggie, who is frozen, staring at the screen as if he's seen a ghost. His hand reaches out instinctively, fingertips almost brushing the glass as if he could reach through and touch her.

"Reggie?" I ask gently, bringing him back to the moment.

"Is she really here, in another room?" he asks, his voice trembling with hope and fear.

"Yes," I reply softly, nodding to reassure him.

"She's alive and well."

On the screen, Molly shifts in her seat, straightening her top, her eyes focused on the camera. She tries to muster a smile, but it's clear she's struggling to understand what's happening. Her confusion and vulnerability are evident.

I quickly pull out my phone and send Chase a text to confirm that Molly has been identified and that he can connect his screen so Molly can see Reggie and Yvonne.

A few moments later, we see Molly's calm and collected demeanour crumble. Her face falls, and she covers her eyes with her hands, her shoulders shaking as she begins to sob uncontrollably.

"What does that mean?" Reggie asks, panic rising in his voice as he steps closer to the monitor, his hands hovering

CHAPTER 14

just above the screen as if he could comfort her from afar.

"They can hear you," I warn him softly, not wanting him to say something he might regret later, now that he knows the microphone works both ways.

"Molly, Molly, it's me, Reggie," he says, his voice thick with emotion.

"Please, tell me you remember us," he pleads, desperation seeping into every word.

Molly lifts her gaze to the camera, her face fuse of confusion and pain. She wipes her eyes with her sleeve, taking a deep, shaky breath.

"H-h-hello," she stammers, barely managing a single word.

Reggie's face crumples as he leans closer to the screen, his eyes glistening with unshed tears.

"Sweetheart, tell me you remember who I am. Please," he begs, his voice breaking, his eyes locked on the image of his sister. His hands rest on the table in front of him, knuckles white from clenching them so tightly, hoping against hope for a sign of recognition in her eyes.

* * *

The camera faces me, and I feel numb inside. I look at the screen and see the two people sitting on a sofa. They look kind and are smiling, but I can see the pain breaking through the façade they're putting on. I hear them saying, "Molly, Molly," but even though I've been told that's likely my name, it doesn't feel right.

It doesn't resonate with me very well.

I just want to go home, to my bungalow, with the kittens and the beautiful garden and the fish in the pond. I don't want to be sitting here on display like this.

What on earth has happened tonight?

I feel like I've been ripped out of my own existence. I'm already trying to find my way in life, and this—this has completely shattered the reality I know.

I don't recognise the man, nor do I recognise the woman but they are still familiar.

To me now, they are strangers.

I stare hard at the screen, hoping for some flicker of memory or recognition, but nothing comes.

Tears well up in my eyes, and I begin to cry, bringing my hands to my face to hide my embarrassment and frustration.

I watch the man as he pleads, "Sweetheart, tell me you remember who I am. Please." His voice is thick with emotion, and I can see the desperation in his eyes.

"I'm sorry," I say softly, the words barely escaping my lips. It's the most I can manage.

I feel Chase close by, watching me, trying to figure me out, but he won't find the real me. How could he? Even I don't know who the real me is anymore.

Chase clears his throat and starts to speak.

"Elizabeth... ahem, Molly," he says carefully, his tone gentle but probing.

"Do you know these people who are claiming to be your relatives?"

I shake my head slowly, feeling overwhelmed and lost.

"No... I don't recognise them," I reply, my voice trembling with uncertainty.

I glance at the screen again, searching their faces for a sign of recognition, but in my world, they remain strangers.

Chapter 15

Thursday Early Hours

I turn away from the monitor and look at Chase, who is sitting right next to me. I can see the concern in his eyes, and before I even say a word, he senses how overwhelmed I am. He stands up quietly and switches off the video link, understanding that I've reached my limit.

"Are you alright, Elizabeth?" he asks gently, his voice filled with concern.

"No, I don't think I am," I reply, my voice shaky and uncertain. My emotions feel like a tangled mess, threatening to unravel at any moment.

Chase places a reassuring hand on my arm. It's a small gesture, but I don't pull away. Instead, I put my hand over his, seeking some kind of comfort in the contact.

"I didn't recognise them, not in the slightest," I say, my voice barely above a whisper.

"It can be a daunting experience," Chase says softly, trying to comfort me.

"Especially when it's the first time you're seeing a family member after some time."

But his words don't soothe the turmoil inside me.

"I really just want to see my husband now," I confess, my voice breaking.

Chase sighs, a look of sympathy crossing his face.

"I'm sorry, but I don't think you'll be able to see him tonight," he explains gently.

A wave of panic washes over me.

"How can I go back home without him?" I cry, my voice filled with desperation.

"He's all I know right now."

Chase squeezes my arm a little tighter, trying to provide some comfort.

"It's OK," he says softly.

"We can have someone take you back home and stay with you for a while, at least until you feel comfortable being alone. Is there anyone else we can call for you?"

I can feel the weight of his question, sensing that he's probing to see what I might remember. I shake my head, tears streaming down my face.

"There is no one, Chase," I sob.

"I don't know what else to say to make you all believe me." Chase looks at me, his face full of empathy.

"I believe you, Elizabeth," he says quietly.

"We'll figure this out together, OK?"

But I can't shake the feeling of being lost, alone in a sea of faces I don't recognise, memories I can't recall, and a life that feels like it's slipping further away with every passing second.

I can see him thinking hard, his brow furrowed as if he's trying to decide whether or not to say something. His hesitation makes me uneasy. Is he waiting for Carter to come

CHAPTER 15

back in? Is there some big reveal they're holding back, some secret they've been hiding from me? Maybe the DNA results are in. Well, at least when they see those, they'll know I'm not this 'Molly Chapman' woman they keep talking about.

Chase takes a deep breath, breaking the silence.

"It's not that we don't believe you, Elizabeth," he starts, but then hesitates again, choosing his words carefully.

"But there is something I need to tell you."

I look at him, feeling a knot tighten in my stomach. He knows something I don't, something important.

Are they planning to charge Gerry?

Will they keep him here, locked away from me? The thought makes my heart race, and I hate the feeling of being kept in the dark, of everyone tiptoeing around me like I'm some fragile thing.

"We've had the test results back from the samples you provided us," Chase says finally.

"OK," I reply, my voice wavering. I hold my breath, anxiety coursing through my veins, making me feel light-headed.

"And what do they tell you? That you've all been wasting your time and now I can go home with Gerry?" I try to keep my voice steady, but there's a tremor in it.

Chase looks at me with a consort of sympathy and something else—something heavier.

"It's quite a bit more complicated than that," he says, his tone serious.

I brace myself, almost instinctively knowing what he's about to say, but refusing to let my mind fully grasp it. I don't want to hear the words. I want to close my ears, shut out everything around me, and pretend none of this is happening.

"There's no easy way to say this," Chase continues, his voice soft but direct, leaving no room for misunderstanding. He doesn't sugarcoat it, doesn't try to soften the blow.

"You are Molly Chapman."

The words hit me like a sledgehammer. They echo in my mind, loud and jarring, like a blaring alarm that won't stop. My ears are ringing, and I feel as if the ground has just been ripped out from under me. Everything around me goes silent, except for those four words that keep repeating in my head, over and over again.

You are Molly Chapman.

I feel my world spinning, my identity slipping away from me like water through my fingers. How can this be?

How can he say that? I look at Chase, searching his eyes for some sign that this is a mistake, a cruel joke, anything but the truth. But all I see is his sincere gaze, filled with empathy and an unspoken apology.

The room starts to blur, and I realise I'm shaking, my breath coming in short, shallow gasps. The name, that name I hardly recognize, feels like a shackle being clamped around my ankle, anchoring me to a reality I don't understand. I am not Molly Chapman. I won't be.

But the certainty in Chase's voice, the finality of his words, makes it clear that everything I thought I knew is about to change forever.

This shouldn't be true. It just can't. Why is Chase saying this? My mind races, trying to reject the words he just spoke. I bury my face in my hands, my shoulders shaking uncontrollably as I sob, overwhelmed by the weight of it all.

Chase stands up and wraps his arms around me, pulling me into a tight embrace. For a moment, I let myself sink into his comforting hold. I can smell his aftershave on his shirt, a

CHAPTER 15

mingle of citrus and woodsy notes that should be calming, but it just makes everything feel more surreal.

As he pulls away to give me some space, I catch a glimpse of a trail of snot stretching between his shirt and my face. Embarrassment washes over me. I quickly wipe it away and mumble an apology for getting so close, for breaking down.

He gives me a small, understanding smile, a look that's gentle and forgiving. He knows this is an awkward, raw moment for me. I wipe my nose again, trying to pull myself together, but I feel like I'm falling apart.

"I know this has come as a massive shock to you," Chase says softly, his voice steady and measured, "but you need to understand that you are the missing person we've been searching for. We've had task forces out day and night looking for you, and your family... they've been out of their minds with worry. They've been forced to stay home, waiting for any news about your disappearance."

His words start to sink in, and I feel a weight pressing down on my chest, making it hard to breathe. My brother and sister-in-law—the people I saw on the screen—are my family. The reality of the situation is like a heavy anchor, pulling me deeper into confusion and fear.

I try to stand up, to get a grip on myself, but my legs feel like they're made of jelly. They buckle under the weight of this new truth, and I slump back into the chair. I don't know who I am anymore.

Everything I knew about myself is crumbling around me, and I'm left clutching at straws, trying to hold on to some semblance of reality.

"It's OK, Molly," Chase says softly, but the name feels wrong—almost alien. It doesn't resonate with me at all like it's meant for someone else entirely.

"Please don't call me that, Chase. It doesn't feel right," I plead, my voice shaky and desperate.

He hesitates for a moment before replying, "But that is your name. Your DNA proves it, and Reggie and Yvonne have confirmed in the other room that it's you."

His words wash over me without meaning, like background noise in a dream. It feels like some kind of elaborate conspiracy like they've found a convenient person to fill the role of this missing woman just to tick some boxes and close a case. But why would those people—the ones I don't remember—say I'm their sister? The weight of this situation is crushing me, pressing down until I can't breathe.

I turn away from Chase, unable to face him and lean my head against the cold, sterile examination bed. My sobs shake my entire body as I cry hard, feeling the isolation and confusion swallow me whole.

"Would you like me to give you a moment?" Chase asks gently, his voice steady and calm amidst my storm.

I nod, my face buried in the crinkling paper sheet of the bed, and manage to whisper through my tears, "Yes, yes please."

"I'll be just across the corridor," he says, his tone reassuring.

"I'll be in with your brother and sister-in-law. And I'll have someone wait outside the room, so you're not completely alone."

"Thank you, Chase. Thank you," I manage to say, my voice barely audible over my sobs.

As Chase quietly leaves the room, I feel a hint of gratitude and despair. I'm thankful for the space he's giving me, but the enormity of what he's said and what I'm feeling is overwhelming. I need time, space, and something—

CHAPTER 15

anything—that makes sense in this upside-down world I've found myself in.

Chase leaves the room, and the door closes softly behind him, leaving me in an unsettling silence. I wipe my eyes on the crinkled paper sheet of the examination bed, but it's already soaked through with my tears. My nose is running again, so I manage to stand and head to the small sink in the corner, tearing off a strip of rough paper towel to wipe it.

My mind is spinning, frantically trying to piece together everything that's happened tonight. What are the police officers thinking?

Do they believe I'm some missing woman just because the DNA says so?

What if they're wrong, what if I am wrong, so very very wrong?

And then there's Gerry—what's happening to him?

My heart aches with the thought of him locked away somewhere, alone, maybe scared, maybe confused like I am. But if I am who they say I am, then Gerry... it means he has been lying to me the whole time, but then I know that deep down, don't I, or do I, Oh I just don't know anymore?

The thought sends a fresh wave of pain through me, and I start to cry harder, my sobs echoing off the sterile walls. I refuse to believe this. I won't be Molly. I know who I am. I know my life, my memories, my love for Gerry. I won't let them take that away from me.

Anger bubbles up inside me, fierce and hot. I kick the floor with my toe, the small act of defiance doing nothing to soothe the turmoil within me. My hands curl into tight fists at my sides. The urge to lash out, to hit something, anything—even myself—builds. I want to feel something other than this

155

overwhelming confusion and betrayal.

I raise my fist, but a flicker of hesitation stops me. Instead, I press my fingernails into the palms of my hands, pushing harder and harder until I feel a sharp sting. I welcome the pain as it pierces through the numbness, grounding me in the moment.

My nails dig deeper into my skin until I feel the warmth of blood pooling in my palms.

I stare down at the small crescent-shaped cuts, the physical pain offering a brief distraction from the chaos in my mind. But the relief is fleeting, and the questions come flooding back.

Who am I?

Who is Gerry?

And what is the truth?

* * *

I catch a glimpse of Biff down the corridor, so I give him a shout.

"Hey, Biff! Can you come over here for a second?" I call out.

He turns around, a grin already forming on his face as he walks back towards me. "What's up, mate?" he asks.

"I need you to stand outside Molly's door for a bit, please. Just keep an eye on things while I check in with Carter and her relatives,"

"Sure thing," he replies without hesitation, leaning against the wall next to the door. I'm grateful for his willingness to help, knowing he'll keep things steady while I step away.

I head across the corridor and gently knock on the door

CHAPTER 15

to the room where Carter, Reggie, and Yvonne are waiting. Carter opens it and greets me with a friendly, "Hey, pal," stepping aside to let me enter.

"Hello again, everyone," I say as I step inside, nodding at Reggie and Yvonne, who look up with a mix of hope and anxiety etched across their faces.

Reggie is the first to speak.

"How is she, officer?" he asks, his voice tinged with worry.

I take a deep breath before responding.

"She's not in a good way. I informed her that the DNA test results have confirmed she's Molly and that you both have identified her as your sister," I explain carefully, watching their reactions.

Carter, who's been listening intently, leans forward, concern on his face.

"How did she take the news?" he asks softly.

I shake my head slowly.

"She didn't take it very well at all. She's overwhelmed and struggling to process everything," I reply.

"I've given her some space to have a moment of reflection, to try and come to terms with everything that's happening."

Yvonne looks distraught, her hands clasped tightly in her lap.

"I just want her to remember us," she whispers, her voice barely audible.

Carter clears his throat, trying to bring the focus back to the practicalities.

"So, what's the plan now?" he asks.

I take another deep breath, considering my words carefully.

"Well, Molly is going to need some time to calm down and begin to accept that she is who we've told her she is. The realisation that the suspect, the man she believes to be her husband, has been lying to her all this time—it's going to be the biggest shock for her," I say, feeling the weight of the situation pressing down on all of us.

Reggie nods, though he looks pained.

"We just want to help her through this, however we can," he says earnestly.

"I understand," I respond.

"Right now, it's a matter of giving her some space and time. Once she's had a moment to breathe, we can gently start to guide her back to who she really is. It's going to be a process, and we'll all need to be patient and supportive."

Yvonne nods, tears welling up in her eyes.

"We'll do whatever it takes," she says firmly, her voice quivering with emotion.

Carter places a comforting hand on her shoulder.

"We're here to help, all of us," he reassures her.

"We'll take it step by step."

I nod in agreement, feeling the room's collective determination to bring Molly back to herself.

"That's the best we can do for now," I say softly.

"Take it step by step and give her the time she needs."

Chapter 16

Thursday Early Hours

The moon hangs low in the sky above the police station, casting an eerie silver glow across the relatively empty car park.

Down the side of the building, two officers are busy with jet washes, cleaning their police car. The powerful streams of water spray against the vehicle, the officers' laughter and banter echoing in the still night air, a stark contrast to the otherwise quiet surroundings.

Inside the station, Margaret and Philip step through the main entrance into the reception area. A young woman sits behind the desk, her eyes briefly meeting theirs as they approach.

"We're here to see Rachel Houston," Philip says, his voice calm but strained with concern.

"She's our daughter. We have the belongings she requested."

The woman, whose name tag reads PC Brighton, nods and begins typing swiftly on her keyboard. She glances at the screen in front of her and looks back up at them with a reassuring smile.

"Right, I see here that you've been given the all-clear by DCI Dixie to spend a moment with your daughter," she confirms, continuing to type for a few moments longer. Then, she picks up a phone and makes a quick call.

"Biff, could you come to the front desk, please? I have Miss Houston's parents here to see her"

"Please, just take a seat over there," Brighton says, pointing to a small seating area by the entrance.

Philip and Margaret nod and move to the table and chairs indicated. They sit down. Margaret clutches Rachel's wash bag in her lap, her fingers gripping it tightly as if it were a lifeline.

As they wait, Philip's eyes wander around the room, noticing the tiredness etched on other visitors' faces and the quiet hum of activity within the station.

Benjamin Swift, Rachel's solicitor, had left the building not long before, promising to return sharply in the morning. He had lodged a formal complaint at the front desk about the handling of Rachel's case, emphasising her vulnerability as a young woman who had been brought in for questioning twice now without any charges.

His frustration was noted, and he made sure his concerns were recorded before departing for the night.

In the meantime, DCI Dixie had reviewed the complaint and decided to allow Rachel's parents a brief visit to bring her some much-needed toiletries. He knew this wasn't standard procedure, especially given the ongoing investigation, but with the delay in officers being available to question her, he felt it was only fair to show a bit more leniency in this instance.

CHAPTER 16

Margaret and Philip exchange worried glances. The ticking clock in the reception area seems loud, each second stretching into eternity as they wait for Biff to escort them to the Custody Suite.

A few more moments pass, and a stocky man enters the reception area from the corridor, his eyes scanning the room.

His gaze settles on Philip and Margaret, who are sitting by the entrance door, their faces lined with worry.

The man strides over to them with a purposeful gait, his broad shoulders pinned back, exuding a sense of authority.

"Mr and Mrs Houston?" he asks, his voice calm but firm.

"Yes, that's us," Philip replies, rising to his feet, with Margaret following suit.

The man extends a hand.

"Biff," he introduces himself, offering a firm handshake to each of them in turn. Philip and Margaret introduce themselves as they shake his hand.

"Please, follow me," Biff says, gesturing down the corridor. "It's just a short walk to the custody suite."

Philip and Margaret exchange a quick, apprehensive glance before nodding and following Biff down the narrow, dimly lit corridor. Their footsteps echo on the hard floor, amplifying the tension in the air. The walls are lined with notice boards filled with police bulletins and missing persons posters, adding to the unsettling atmosphere.

After a brief walk, they arrive at the Custody Suite.

Dobby is already there, waiting behind her desk. She looks up from her paperwork and gives them a polite nod.

"Good evening," she says, her tone professional but not unkind.

"I'll need to check you both in."

Dobby hands them each a visitor's badge, which they clip to their clothing.

"And if you could just let me take a quick look inside your handbag, Mrs Houston," she adds, gesturing to Margaret's bag.

Margaret hesitates for a moment, clutching her bag a little tighter, but then she nods and hands it over.

"It's just a formality, Mrs Houston," Dobby assures her, speaking softly as she opens the bag and quickly scans the contents. Her hands move efficiently, but with a certain delicacy, showing she respects the personal nature of what she's doing.

After checking the handbag, Dobby takes the toiletry bag Margaret fetched for Rachel and does the same. She unzips it and peers inside, carefully inspecting the contents. Finding nothing of concern, she zips it back up and hands both bags back to Margaret. "Thank you," she says with a small smile.

"You're all set."

Margaret gives a tight-lipped smile in return, clearly anxious but grateful for the smooth process.

Philip nods his thanks, and Biff gestures for them to continue.

"Alright, you're clear to see your daughter now. Let's head to the visiting area."

They follow Biff further into the open room eager yet apprehensive about seeing Rachel again and learning more about the troubling situation she's caught up in.

"Just wait in here while I go and collect Miss Houston for you," instructs Biff.

A few more minutes pass and then the door to the visiting area swings open, and Rachel rushes in, her face lighting up

CHAPTER 16

when she spots her parents.

Philip and Margaret rise quickly from their seats, their arms outstretched to welcome their daughter.

"I can't tell you how grateful I am to see you both," she says, her voice breaking as tears well up in her eyes.

"I am so sorry for this mess."

"Don't cry, love," Margaret says softly, wrapping her arms tightly around Rachel. She hands her daughter the wash bag full of toiletries.

"We're here now. Everything will be OK."

"Please, take a seat," instructs Biff, who stands watchfully at the end of the table, his expression sympathetic but professional.

"Can we go somewhere more private?" Philip asks, glancing around the open visiting area, which is far from ideal for a sensitive conversation.

"I'm sorry, but this is the only space we have available for an authorised visit right now," Biff responds apologetically, his tone conveying his understanding of their need for privacy.

Philip sighs and nods, reluctantly taking a seat.

"So, what's happening?" he asks, looking directly at Rachel.

Rachel sits down, across from them. She takes a deep breath, speaking quickly, almost in a rush to get everything out.

"So, I turned up at Gerry's Mum's bungalow to take her some flowers. And when I knocked on the door, this woman answered. I've seen her before—she's the Mum of one of the girls I teach at school."

Philip and Margaret listen intently, their faces etched with concern.

"Go on," Philip urges gently.

163

"Well, it turns out this woman has been missing," Rachel continues, her words tumbling out in a hurry.

"But somehow, she's... she's hooked up with Gerry!"

"Hooked up?" Margaret asks, confused.

"Together, Mum," Rachel clarifies impatiently, "in a relationship."

Margaret's confusion deepens.

"But I thought you and Gerry..."

Rachel interrupts her, not wanting to get sidetracked.

"It's not like that, Mum. I went there just to drop off some flowers. But half an hour later, the police show up—loads of them. They just burst into the bungalow, start searching all the rooms, and then they arrest Gerry and me for kidnapping this woman!"

Margaret and Philip exchange a shocked glance. Philip leans forward, his voice low and serious.

"You mean to say they think you and Gerry are involved in her disappearance?"

Rachel nods, her eyes wide with fear.

"Yes! I'm caught up in this whole ugly mess, and I don't even know what's going on." She lies, hoping her parents won't see through her words, trying to protect herself and them from the full truth of what she knows.

Philip looks at her with a combination of disbelief and concern.

"Rachel, are you sure there's nothing more to this? Are you telling us everything?"

Rachel nods emphatically, trying to maintain her composure.

"I swear, Dad, I don't know anything about what's happening. I'm just... I'm scared. I don't understand why this is

CHAPTER 16

happening to me."

Margaret reaches across the table, taking Rachel's hand in hers.

"We'll figure this out, sweetheart. Whatever it is, we'll get to the bottom of it. You're not alone in this."

Biff watches from his position at the end of the table, ready to intervene if necessary but giving them this moment together. The tension in the waiting area is strong, with fear, confusion, and the desperate need for answers.

* * *

Chase decides to head back to the medical room to be with Molly.

He glances over at Reggie and Yvonne, who are still visibly shaken but seem to be in good hands with Carter.

Chase notices a change by the medical room door. Instead of Biff standing guard as before, PC Gilbert is there now. She stands with her arms crossed, alert and attentive, her gaze scanning the corridor. It appears that Biff has been called away on another task, and Gilbert, who was looking for Chase earlier, has stepped in to take his place.

Gilbert catches sight of Chase approaching and offers a slight nod.

"Chase," she says in a calm, steady voice, "I was looking for you earlier, but it seems you were with the Draycotts. Biff got called away, so I thought I'd keep an eye on things here. Molly Chapman is still inside, having some time to herself. I knew you wouldn't be too long, so I figured I'd wait here until you came back."

Chase nods, appreciating her initiative.

"Thanks, Gilbert. I just want to make sure Molly's alright. It's been a rough night for everyone, but she's taken it particularly hard."

"Of course," Gilbert replies, stepping aside to let Chase pass.

"Take your time. I'll be right here if you need anything."

With a quick, grateful smile, Chase gently opens the door to the medical room and slips inside.

It is quiet inside.

Molly sits on a chair in the corner, her posture tense and her eyes distant, lost in her thoughts.

"Molly?" Chase begins softly, trying to gauge her state of mind.

"Yes?" she replies, her voice full of exhaustion.

"Are you alright? Can I get you anything?" he asks, his tone gentle and concerned.

"No, thank you. I'm alright," she says, though her tone suggests otherwise.

"I just want to go home."

Chase nods, understanding her desire to escape the environment of the police station and return to somewhere familiar and safe.

"Would you like to meet with your brother and sister-in-law?" he suggests, trying to offer a semblance of normalcy.

"NO!" Molly exclaims, her voice sharp and immediate, filled with a mixture of frustration and fear.

Chase is taken aback by the intensity of her response.

"And can I ask why not?" he enquires, keeping his tone as neutral as possible.

Molly's eyes flare with a sudden anger.

"How about because I don't know them?" she snaps.

CHAPTER 16

"They are strangers to me, Chase. I have never seen them before in my life."

Chase senses Molly's agitation rising and quickly decides to ease off.

"That's OK," he says soothingly.

"I'm not going to force anything on you tonight. You've been through enough for one day."

Molly's expression softens slightly, and she asks again, her voice small and almost childlike, "Does that mean I can go home?"

Chase hesitates, then nods.

"Well, yes. I can't see any reason why you shouldn't be able to go home," he reassures her.

He moves a bit closer to her, noticing the way she looks up at him, her eyes searching his for answers he wishes he could provide.

Tonight's events have thrown him completely.

He had been so certain that seeing her brother would trigger some recognition in Molly, some emotional response. But there had been nothing—just blankness, a void where memories should have been.

"Molly," he says softly, "I know this is all confusing, and I'm sorry for everything you're going through. But we're going to figure this out, OK? One step at a time."

Molly nods, though she looks far from convinced.

Chase notices a subtle shift in Molly's demeanour. She's no longer asking him to stop calling her by that name—Molly. It's a small change, but he takes it as a step forward, a sign that perhaps she's beginning to accept some part of what he's been telling her.

"Can I ask you a question before I arrange for you to go

home?" Chase asks carefully, knowing full well that they might not get another chance to question her unless she's formally brought in tomorrow.

"Yes, of course," Molly replies, her voice calm but guarded.

"I'm just going to bring in my colleague, PC Gilbert. You met her earlier at your home. She's just outside the door. I won't be a moment," Chase explains.

He steps out into the corridor and quietly pulls Gilbert aside.

"I need you to back me up on this. We need to get some clarity on her connection to Rachel and this whole situation," he murmurs.

Gilbert nods, understanding.

Together, they re-enter the room.

"Hi, Molly," Gilbert says with a reassuring smile.

"Hi," Molly replies, her eyes flickering between Gilbert and Chase.

Chase decides to get straight to the point.

"Molly, the woman we arrested at your house tonight—"

Molly cuts him off, her expression sharpening.

"Rachel?"

"Yes, Rachel," Chase confirms, pulling out his notebook and pen from his back pocket.

"What about her?" Molly asks, her tone neutral but curious.

Chase leans forward slightly, focusing on her.

"What exactly was she doing at your home this evening?"

Molly looks thoughtful for a moment before answering.

"Oh, she was hoping to see Gerry's Mum. She didn't know that his Mum had passed away recently. She had brought some flowers for her. She's Gerry's ex-girlfriend, did you know that?" Molly's voice is calm.

CHAPTER 16

Chase and Gilbert exchange a quick glance.

"Have you met Rachel before tonight?" Chase asks, maintaining eye contact with Molly, watching her closely for any signs of recognition or deception.

"No, definitely not," Molly responds, her voice steady but with a slight edge, as if bracing herself for what might come next.

"At least, not that I remember if that is where you are going with this questioning?"

She shifts her gaze to Gilbert, searching for some hint of what's really going on, but Gilbert's face remains impassive, giving nothing away.

Chase takes a deep breath.

"Molly, we just want to understand what happened tonight and how everyone involved is connected. If there's anything else you can remember, anything at all about Rachel it could help us a lot."

Molly hesitates, her eyes narrowing slightly as she thinks.

"I've told you everything I know. I don't remember meeting Rachel before, and I don't know why she was there tonight beyond what I've said. I'm as confused as you are, Chase."

Chase nods, feeling the tension in the room tightens again. He knows pushing her too hard could backfire, but he also knows they need more answers.

"Alright, Molly. Thank you for being honest. We're just trying to piece everything together, and your cooperation is really important."

Molly gives a slight nod, still looking wary. Chase senses that's as much as they're going to get for now. He steps back, signalling to Gilbert that they should wrap things up for the moment.

"We'll arrange for you to go home now," Chase says gently. Molly just nods again, her expression closed off.
Chase knows this is far from over.

Chapter 17

Thursday Early Hours

Dixie and Sharpie are sitting in Dixie's jam-packed office, the dim overhead light creating shadows on the desk. Dixie rubs his tired eyes and leans back in his chair, which creaks under his weight.

"You really should get yourself home to bed, Dixie," says Sharpie examining his boss's face.

"You look whacked out."

Dixie gives a tired smile, waving off Sharpie's suggestion with a dismissive hand.

"I'll be alright. You know me—I work on overdrive," he replies, trying to sound more energetic than he feels.

Sharpie, not quite convinced, gives him a sceptical look but moves on.

"So, where are we at now?" he asks, shifting in his chair to get more comfortable.

"It looks like Gerry Penwald is settled down for the night. Rachel Houston is in with her parents at the moment, but she'll be taken back to her cell soon. We'll start the interviews with them first thing in the morning," Sharpie reports, leaning forward slightly as he speaks.

He takes a deep breath, collecting his thoughts before continuing.

"Chase and Gilbert are with Molly Chapman right now. She'll be going home shortly, and Gilbert will stay with her overnight until we can bring her back in for questioning tomorrow," he adds, watching Dixie's reaction closely.

Dixie nods, his mind working through the logistics.

"And where do we stand with Molly and her memory? How did the identification go?"

Sharpie pinches the bridge of his nose, a sign of his weariness setting in. He sighs heavily before responding, "She didn't recognize the brother, but both he and the sister-in-law gave an identification that she's Molly Chapman."

Dixie's shoulders relax a fraction, and he nods again.

"Good, good. That's something solid, at least."

There's a brief pause as Dixie's gaze drifts to his desk, scattered with paperwork and case files. Then he looks up with a frown.

"Where's Poker? I haven't seen him all evening."

Sharpie shifts in his seat, adjusting his posture.

"I sent him home. I want some fresh eyes in with Gerry tomorrow. Instead of having Carter and myself handle it, I thought it'd be better to have Carter and Poker run the interview. If that's alright with you, boss?" he asks politely, carefully watching Dixie's reaction.

Dixie considers this for a moment, tapping his fingers on the desk.

"Yeah, that makes sense. Poker's sharp when he's had some rest. We'll need that if we're going to make any headway tomorrow."

CHAPTER 17

Sharpie nods in agreement, relieved that Dixie is on board with his plan. The two men sit in silence for a moment, the weight of the day pressing down on them.

"You sure you're OK, Dixie?" Sharpie asks again, softer this time.

Dixie offers a tired smile.

"I'll be fine. Just another long night at the office, right?"

Sharpie doesn't argue, but his expression says he's not fully convinced.

"Alright then. I'll check in with you in the morning."

Dixie nods, watching as Sharpie stands up and heads for the door. He leans back in his chair again, staring up at the ceiling for a moment before letting out a deep sigh.

It's going to be another long night.

* * *

Doctor Granger sits at a cluttered desk in the forensic lab, typing away on her laptop with a focused expression. Across from her, Lambert is organising files and preparing her report. The room is dimly lit, with the only sounds being the soft hum of the overhead fluorescent lights and the tapping of keys.

"She's a tough cookie," Lambert remarks, glancing up from her work.

"That she is," Doctor Granger replies, not taking her eyes off the screen.

With a few final keystrokes, she finishes her report.

"Well, that's my clinical report all written up for Chase and the team," she says, leaning back in her chair and stretching her arms.

Lambert nods.

"With your report and my forensics report, we can give Chase the all-clear for her to go home now."

Doctor Granger frowns slightly, her brows knitting together in concern.

"Is she not going to go home with the Draycotts?"

Lambert shakes her head.

"Nope. She's denied knowing them and refuses to meet with them. We can't force her to go with them if she's not comfortable."

Doctor Granger sighs, her expression softening with empathy.

"Based on her mental health, we shouldn't be asking her to do very much at all. She's too fragile to be interviewed, that's for sure."

Lambert nods in agreement.

"All she wants is to see Gerry, her 'supposed husband.'"

Doctor Granger shakes her head slowly.

"Well, that's a real difficult one. She's been made aware that she's not Elizabeth Penwald, that she has another husband and children, but she's not pursuing those avenues."

"It's a tough situation," Lambert agrees, rubbing the back of her neck thoughtfully. "What's your clinical diagnosis?"

Doctor Granger pauses for a moment, choosing her words carefully.

"She's suffering from severe anxiety. I'd suggest she also has depression, and she's showing signs of PTSD. Her mental health is in a poor state, so her well-being is our utmost concern. She shouldn't be left alone tonight."

Lambert nods, understanding the gravity of her assessment.

CHAPTER 17

"That's why Gilbert is going home with her tonight?"

"Yes, that is good" Doctor Granger confirms.

"I suggested that. She's too delicate to be on her own right now. She needs someone there to support her, at least until we can get a clearer picture of her mental state and what she needs moving forward."

Lambert sighs, closing the folder she is working on.

"It's such a complex case. Hopefully, with some time and support, she can start to piece things together."

Doctor Granger nods, a look of concern still etched on her face.

"I hope so. But it's going to be a long road for her. We need to handle this with care."

The two fall into a contemplative silence, both reflecting on the challenging situation Molly Chapman finds herself in.

"Right, well, I'm going to get this report in to Dixie, and then I'm calling it a night. It's been a long few days," Doctor Granger says, her voice weary as she starts packing her laptop and papers into her bag.

Lambert nods, feeling the fatigue as well.

"I think I'm done too. I'll walk with you if that's alright," she replies, gathering her things and zipping up her bag.

The two women step out of the forensic lab and into the dimly lit corridor, their footsteps echoing off the walls as they head toward Dixie's office. The station is quiet at this late hour, with most of the staff having already clocked out or moved to other duties.

As they turn a corner, they see Sharpie just leaving Dixie's office.

He looks up, surprised to see them still around.

"Ladies," he greets them with a tired smile.

"Burning the midnight oil?"

"Just wrapping things up," Doctor Granger replies with a nod.

"We've got our reports ready for Dixie," Lambert adds.

Sharpie steps aside, holding the door open for them.

"He's in there. Go on in."

Doctor Granger and Lambert enter the office, where Dixie is sitting behind his desk, looking over some paperwork. He glances up as they come in, his eyes tired but alert.

"Evening, Dixie," Doctor Granger begins.

"We wanted to give you our updates on Molly Chapman."

Dixie sets his papers aside and leans back in his chair, giving them his full attention. "Alright, let's hear it."

Doctor Granger goes over her clinical findings while Lambert provides a summary of the forensic report. Dixie listens intently, nodding occasionally, his expression growing more serious as he takes in the details.

When they finish, they both hand over their written reports.

"Thanks for getting these done," Dixie says, accepting the documents.

"I'll go through them tonight and see where we stand."

"We're only a phone call away if you need anything else," Lambert says.

"Appreciate it," Dixie replies.

With that, Doctor Granger and Lambert turn to leave. They exit the office, bidding goodnight to Sharpie, and make their way down the corridor, ready to finally head home and get some much-needed rest.

Dixie, meanwhile, remains in his office, already absorbed

CHAPTER 17

in their reports, knowing that the next day would bring another wave of challenges and decisions.

* * *

"Alright, guys, I'm sorry, but your time is up," Biff says as kindly as he can, though his tone is firm.

Philip frowns and checks his watch.

"But officer, we've only been here fifteen minutes," he protests, a hint of frustration in his voice.

Rachel looks devastated, clinging to her mother like a small child in desperate need of comfort. Tears stream down her cheeks, as she holds her mother tightly, her knuckles turning white from the intensity of her grip.

"Please, can we just have a few more minutes?" Rachel asks softly, her voice trembling.

"I'm really sorry," Biff replies, feeling a pang of guilt as he looks at Rachel's tear-streaked face, "but you've already had longer than the five minutes you were supposed to have." His words are gentle but unwavering.

"Five minutes? That's not long enough for a visit," Margaret exclaims, surprising even herself with the assertiveness in her voice. She gently strokes Rachel's hair, trying to soothe her daughter's anxiety.

Biff sighs and explains, "Again, I'm sorry, but you were only allowed to hand over Rachel's belongings. You're fortunate they let her out to see you both at all. Normally, we'd just take the items from you at the desk." He looks around, trying to soften the blow of his words with his expression.

Rachel looks up at him with pleading eyes.

"Just five more minutes, please, officer," she begs.

Biff shakes his head, this time looking less than pleased. "It's more than my job is worth. I'm sorry."

Philip looks at his distraught daughter and sighs.

"Alright, let's do what the officer asks. We don't want to cause any trouble that might make things worse for you, love," he says softly. He reaches out, putting his arm around Rachel, pulling her close to him as she cries into her father's chest.

He leans down and whispers into her hair, "It'll all be alright. Just tell the truth, and you'll be out of here in no time."

Rachel shakes her head, her voice muffled by her father's embrace.

"I don't know how Dad. I don't know how I can prove I have nothing to do with it. I was there, after all." Her words are heavy with worry and fear, her mind racing through the possibilities, trying to figure out how she ended up in this mess and how she might ever get out of it.

Rachel looks at her parents, her eyes wide with a fusion of fear and frustration.

"When can we visit again?" asks Margaret.

"I am sorry but there will be no more visits now," he answers.

"No more visits?" Rachel whispers, her voice trembling. The thought of being cut off from her family is almost too much to bear.

Margaret steps forward, her face lined with worry.

"Please, there must be something we can do," she pleads with Biff.

"We're her parents. She needs us right now."

Biff sighs, looking genuinely sympathetic.

CHAPTER 17

"I'm sorry, Mrs Houston, but it's out of my hands. This is standard procedure until the investigation moves forward. You can call the Custody Suite for updates, but that's all I can offer at the moment."

Philip puts a comforting arm around Margaret's shoulders, gently pulling her back. "Let's not make things harder for Rachel," he says quietly.

"We'll call, and we'll stay on top of things, alright?"

Rachel gives a weak nod, trying to muster a brave smile.

"It's OK, Mum, Dad. I'll be alright. I just need to sort this out. Hopefully, it won't be too long."

Margaret's eyes well up with tears again, but she forces a smile, trying to be strong for her daughter.

"We love you, Rachel. We're here for you, no matter what."

"I love you too," Rachel responds, her voice thick with emotion. She turns to follow Biff down the corridor, casting one last glance over her shoulder at her parents.

She musters up a handheart for them which they reciprocate lovingly.

The heavy metal door closes behind her with a loud click, leaving Philip and Margaret standing in the empty visitor's area.

Philip takes a deep breath, trying to keep his emotions in check.

"Come on, Mags," he says softly.

"Let's go home and get some rest. We'll figure out our next steps in the morning."

Margaret nods, wiping her tears away with the back of her hand. Together, they make their way back toward the reception area.

Philip puts his arm around Margaret's shoulder and pulls

her in close to him, his warmth comforting her as they walk out of the Custody Suite towards the main reception of the building.

They pass by PC Brighton who is still on the desk.

"Oh excuse me," she shouts over to them just as they approach the exit.

"Huh?" Philip says as he looks back over his shoulder.

"Your visitor badges please, we take them back at the end of each visit," she asks politely.

"Oh right," he says as he unclips the badge from his shirt and hands it to the officer.

"Thank you," she responds as she takes the badges from Philip and pops them back into her drawer.

"Have a good morning," Brighton says.

They both nod at her.

Philip and Margaret step out into the cool, damp morning air. The chill hits them, and Margaret instinctively pulls her coat tighter around herself, trying to ward off the early morning cold and the anxiety that lingers in her chest.

Philip keeps his arm around her, holding her close as they walk slowly toward their car.

The car park is mostly empty, the streetlights casting long shadows across the wet pavement. For a moment, they stand beside the car, neither of them saying a word, both lost in their own thoughts.

"I can't believe this is happening," Margaret finally whispers, her voice barely audible over the faint hum of traffic in the distance.

"Our Rachel… in a cell."

Philip squeezes her shoulder gently, trying to offer some comfort.

CHAPTER 17

"I know, love. It's a nightmare, but we have to stay strong—for her and ourselves. We'll get through this. We have to believe that."

Margaret nods, but her face is still etched with worry.

"Do you think she'll be OK? I mean, in there… alone?"

Philip hesitates before answering, choosing his words carefully.

"Rachel's strong, Mags. Stronger than we sometimes give her credit for. She'll get through this. And we'll make sure she knows we're here for her, no matter what."

Margaret looks up at him, her eyes filled with uncertainty. "What if they don't let her out? What if she's stuck in there for days, weeks?"

Philip opens the car door for Margaret, guiding her into the passenger seat. He takes a deep breath, trying to steady his nerves.

"We'll do everything we can to help her, alright? We'll make calls, we'll keep pushing until she's home with us. But for now, we need to stay strong and keep it together."

As Philip gets into the driver's seat and starts the car, they both glance back at the police station, a heavy silence hanging between them.

The building looms in the rearview mirror, a stark reminder of the uncertainty that lies ahead.

"Let's go home," Philip says softly, his voice steady but tinged with determination. "We need to rest and be ready for whatever comes next."

Margaret nods, her eyes still on the station as Philip pulls out of the car park.

The drive home is quiet, each lost in their thoughts, both holding onto the hope that this nightmare will soon be over.

Chapter 18

Thursday Early Hours

Carter walks over to the video monitor, his movements deliberate and careful. He bends down to unplug the device from the wall socket, the plug coming out with a soft click. He begins to coil the long cord around his hand, taking his time as if the methodical action might somehow ease the tension in the room. Pushing the monitor on its wheeled stand toward the door, he glances back at Reggie and Yvonne, trying to gauge their reactions.

"So, that's that, then, is it?" Reggie asks. His eyes are fixed on the floor, unable to bear the weight of the situation any longer.

Carter pauses, looking at Reggie with genuine sympathy.

"That was tough, Reggie. I can only sympathise with you," he says softly, finishing with the cord and resting it next to the monitor on the stand. He knows there's little he can say to ease the pain that's written all over Reggie's face.

Yvonne's eyes are red and puffy from crying, she wipes away a stray tear with the back of her hand takes a shaky breath and rises from her chair, her body tense and restless.

CHAPTER 18

She starts pacing the back of the room, her feet making soft, muted sounds against the cold lino floor. Her thumb circles the palm of her opposite hand repeatedly for comfort.

"Vonnie, please, sit down. You're making me nervous," Reggie says, his voice wavering slightly. He looks at her with concern and exhaustion, his patience stretched thin by the night's emotional strain.

He rolls up his sleeves, exposing his forearms to the cool air of the room. Crossing his arms tightly across his chest, he feels the fine hairs on his skin stand on end—a visceral reaction to the anxiety that's building inside him. He tries to steady his breathing, focusing on the slow rise and fall of his chest, but his worry for Molly, and for Yvonne, makes it hard to stay calm.

Reggie sighs heavily.

"So what now… if she doesn't recognise us, how can she come home with us?"

Carter leans against the wall, folding his arms, his expression sympathetic but firm. "I'm sorry, but she won't be able to go home with you. She can't be expected to go with people she feels are complete strangers to her."

Reggie shakes his head in disbelief, a bitter laugh escaping his lips.

"That's the ironic thing, isn't it? She *did* go home with a stranger. She went home with Gerry!" His voice rises in frustration.

Yvonne's composure finally breaks, and she begins to sob, her shoulders shaking as she tries to hold back the tears.

"Oh, this is all such a damned mess, Reggie," she cries, her voice cracking with despair.

Reggie gets up from his seat, walking over to Yvonne with

a weary expression. He wraps his arms around her, pulling her into a tight embrace. He strokes her back gently, trying to provide some comfort even though he feels just as lost as she does. He looks over Yvonne's shoulder at Carter, his eyes filled with frustration and helplessness, silently pleading for any solution.

"So, what do we do?" Reggie asks.

"Just go back home and what… wait for her to get her memory back?" He glances between Carter and Yvonne, searching for any sign of hope in this bleak situation. His mind is racing, struggling to grasp the reality that his own sister doesn't recognise him, that she might never remember who she is.

"I think home is your best bet for now. I can run you back if you like?" Carter offers gently, his voice filled with empathy.

"That would be good, please, Carter," Reggie responds with a tired nod.

"We appreciate everything you have tried to do."

Carter gives a quick nod of understanding.

"I'll just run this monitor back to the office, and then I'll come and get you to take you back home."

Reggie glances down at his watch, his eyebrows meet in the middle as he realises how late—or rather, early—it is.

"No wonder we're both so tired and emotional. It's nearly four o'clock, Vonnie," he mutters.

Yvonne wipes her eyes with the back of her hand, blinking away the last of her tears. "Christ, have we been here that long already?" she sniffs, looking equally shocked by the time.

Carter, now holding the video monitor securely, turns and backs out of the room, his footsteps echoing down the

CHAPTER 18

hallway as he disappears from view.

Reggie stands up and stretches, feeling the fatigue in his bones.

"I'm going to find a toilet, I'm busting," he says, giving Yvonne a weary smile.

"OK, love, don't get lost," Yvonne replies, attempting a small smile despite her exhaustion.

"I'll try not to," Reggie answers, chuckling softly as he heads towards the door.

Reggie opens the door and steps out into the dimly lit corridor, pulling the door shut behind him with a soft click. Just as he starts down the hallway, he hears the door to the medical room open nearby. He pauses mid-stride, something tugging at the edge of his awareness, and turns around.

He stops dead in his tracks.

There, standing just a few feet away with her back to him, is Molly. Her hair is slightly dishevelled, and she appears tense as if caught in a moment of indecision.

"Molly! Molly!" Reggie shouts, his voice full of hope and urgency, the sound echoing through the quiet corridor.

Startled, Molly swings around to face him. Her eyes widen as she recognizes his voice, but she remains frozen in place, a look of confusion and hesitation clouding her features. For a long moment, neither of them moves, the space between them charged with a blend of disbelief, hope, and the unspoken weight of the past.

* * *

I stand here, staring at him. My mind races. I gaze at him, and it feels like time stands still. My breath comes in shallow gasps, barely noticeable.

He's smiling at me, taking slow steps in my direction.

Instinctively, I back away, inching closer to Chase and Gilbert, needing the comfort of their presence. I grab hold of Chase's arm, gripping it tightly as I step slightly behind him, using him as a shield against the confusion and fear welling up inside me.

"Molly, it's me, Reggie," the man says, his voice gentle but filled with urgency.

Before I can react, the door on the right swings open, and a striking woman with long blonde hair, hastily tied up, appears in the doorway, obviously hearing the commotion.

"Molly?" she asks softly, her eyes searching mine.

"It's me, Yvonne."

Yvonne and Reggie exchange glances, their expressions that of hope and desperation. I feel trapped, unsure of what to do or how to respond.

"Sorry, Reggie, if you can excuse us for a moment, please," Chase interjects, stepping forward to intervene.

"But, Molly?!" Reggie pleads, his voice rising in desperation.

The fear in my stomach mounts, twisting into a nauseating knot. I watch as the man—my brother—walks toward me, extending his hand, an invitation to trust, to remember. But I can't. My body tenses, and I shy away, pressing myself closer to Chase, clinging to the only sense of stability I have in this moment of chaos.

My mouth goes dry, and beads of sweat form on my forehead as he calls my name again.

"Molly…" His voice is like a spark igniting a fire of panic within me. Every nerve in my body feels electrified, and my

CHAPTER 18

skin prickles with a cold sweat.

I instinctively hide my face behind Chase, seeking the sanctuary of his presence. He immediately senses my fear and steps forward, positioning himself as a shield between me and the approaching man.

"Reggie, this is not the way. Please, just keep walking," Chase says firmly, his voice steady and authoritative.

Reggie's face is a mixture of anguish and determination as he responds, "I am not walking away from my sister. She needs to see me, she needs to know it's me."

His cry of desperation echoes, a stark contrast to the tense silence that follows.

Gilbert, seeing the escalating situation, approaches Reggie with a soothing gesture. "Come on, Reggie, I'll walk with you," she offers, extending her arm toward him in a gesture of calm.

Reggie's frustration mounts and he yells, "I don't want to go anywhere. I want to see my sister." His voice is filled with a helpless urgency that reverberates through the corridor, amplifying the tension.

Yvonne, observing the unfolding scene, interjects with a pleading tone, "Reggie, please, you're scaring her."

My breath quickens, and I cling tighter to Chase, my eyes wide with fear and confusion.

"Chase, please," I beg, my voice trembling as I look up at him, desperately hoping for some resolution to this painful encounter.

Chase quickly guides us away from the chaotic scene, turning us towards the doors of the Custody Suite. My heart is pounding, and my breathing is shallow. I press on the doors, and they swing open effortlessly, though I keep my gaze fixed forward, unwilling to look back. The echoes of the man's voice calling my name—"Molly"—pierce through the growing haze of panic in my mind.

I don't want to be Molly; I want to be Elizabeth.

As we step into the Custody Suite, Chase asks gently, "Are you OK?" His concern is evident, and his voice is steady, offering a small measure of reassurance.

"I'm sorry," he continues, "I wouldn't have brought you this way had we known Reggie would be out there. ."

Dobby, who is tidying up her workstation, glances over and asks, "Everything alright, Chase?"

"No, not really," Chase replies, his frustration boiling over.

"Can you please go check on Gilbert? I left her with a relative who's causing a bit of a scene in the corridor."

"Sure," Dobby responds.

"Just keep an eye on things here for me please." She heads off, disappearing through the door.

I listen intently for any more sounds of shouting but hear only the subdued hum of the Custody Suite. It seems like Reggie has quieted down, at least for now. My thoughts race as I try to process what just happened.

Was that really my brother?

My sense of reality feels uncertain; I'm trying to piece together fragments of my identity and the surrounding chaos. My reflection in the plastic screen of the Custody Suite seems like a stranger as if everything familiar has been stripped away, leaving me disoriented and questioning everything.

I turn to Chase, my voice trembling with fear and frustration.

"Chase, what am I going to do?"

Chase meets my eyes with a steady gaze, his expression

CHAPTER 18

one of determined reassurance.

"We're going to get you better, that's what."

"But if that was my brother and sister-in-law," I continue, my voice cracking, "and I didn't even recognize them, how can I start to get better?"

Chase's eyebrow raises.

"Did you not recognise them at all? Not even a tiny bit?"

I shake my head slowly, the weight of the situation sinking in.

"No, Chase, I didn't."

Chase takes a deep breath, trying to offer me the most comfort he can.

"Alright, just take a seat over there," he gestures to a nearby chair, "until Gilbert is ready to take you home. Give yourself a moment to calm down."

I walk over to the row of seats and settle into one of the cold blue plastic chairs. The chill from the seat seeps through my clothing, and I try to focus on the view outside.

The moon has vanished, and the clouds are illuminated by a piercing shaft of light, casting intricate patterns across the sky. I watch as the shapes in the clouds shift and drift, my thoughts becoming as fluid and disconnected as the drifting formations.

My mind starts to wander, the exhaustion and anxiety weighing heavily on me. As I stare at the clouds, a sense of drowsiness overtakes me.

My vision begins to blur, and a deep cold envelopes me, making everything in front of me become a foggy haze.

I close my eyes, hoping to escape the frigid sensation, but instead, I am plunged into a different kind of cold.

> *I'm submerged in something icy and liquid, my chest heaving as I struggle to breathe. Panic grips me as I gulp desperately for air, the sensation of suffocation overwhelming.*
> *"Molly... Molly..." A familiar voice pierces through the chaos. It's Reggie's voice, filled with urgency and warmth. I can almost feel his presence reaching out to me, his voice a lifeline in the icy abyss. He's here to save me, to pull me from the cold water.*

"Molly?"

I snap my eyes open, startled by the sound. Gilbert is crouched down in front of me, her face a comforting presence against the backdrop of the dimly lit room. She has one hand gently resting on mine, her smile warm and reassuring.

"Are you OK?" Gilbert's voice is soothing, grounding me back to the present. I take a deep breath, the cold retreating as I focus on her calming presence. The panic from my vision slowly fades, replaced by the gentle reality of her concern.

"Are you ready to go home now?" Gilbert asks softly.

I nod, trying to shake off the lingering disorientation.

"Eh, yes, please."

I rise unsteadily to my feet, gripping the back of the chair for support. My legs feel heavy, but I manage to steady myself.

"Are you sure you're alright to go home?" Gilbert's concern is comforting.

"I can call the doctor back in to give you a quick check if

CHAPTER 18

you're not feeling up to it."

"No, I'll be fine," I say, trying to reassure both Gilbert and myself.

"As soon as I see my cat Era and the kittens, I'll feel a lot better."

Gilbert nods, understanding. We head towards the door together, and Chase meets us there.

"You may need to come back in for questioning," he says as he gives us a warm, supportive smile, "but for now, just rest up, OK?"

"Thank you, Chase. I will," I reply, grateful for his kindness.

Gilbert holds the door open for me, and I step out into the early morning chill. The breeze cuts through the air, making me shiver slightly.

The trees in the distance sway ominously in the wind, their silhouettes dark against the faint glow of the dawning sky. Leaves scattered across the car park, remnants of a windy night.

We make our way to Gilbert's car. I stand by the passenger side, feeling a deep sense of loneliness settle over me. I let out a long sigh, trying to expel some of the weight from my chest.

"This is all so very lonely, Gilbert," I admit, my voice sad.

"I know, love," Gilbert responds gently, her voice filled with empathy.

"It must be incredibly hard for you right now. I truly sympathise with what you're going through."

Her words offer a small comfort as we prepare to leave.

The drive home feels like it will be long and quiet, but for now, I focus on the small solace of returning to my familiar, if somewhat uncertain, world.

Chapter 19

Thursday Early Hours

Carter steps into the visitors' lounge and immediately senses the tension in the room. Reggie is hunched over, his face buried in his hands, while Yvonne gently rubs his back, her own eyes glistening with tears.

"It is her, Carter," Reggie says, his voice thick with emotion. "How can she not remember me? How can she not know her own brother?" His words are a mix of anguish and disbelief as if he's pleading for an explanation that will make all of this make sense.

"I don't know, Reggie," Carter replies gently, taking a seat across from them.

"It's one of the more severe cases of amnesia I've seen. It's not just her memory that's affected—her whole sense of self seems to have been altered." He pauses, searching for words that might offer some comfort but finds none.

Reggie takes a shaky breath, frustration bubbling up inside him. He wipes his eyes roughly with the back of his hand, trying to regain some composure.

"This whole bloody thing is a living nightmare," he mutters,

CHAPTER 19

his voice breaking.

"So, where has she gone now? What's happening to her?"

Carter hesitates for a moment before answering.

"She's gone home, back to the house she shares with the man she believes to be her husband. That's her reality now, Reggie. It's what she knows, what she believes to be her life."

"But it's not her life," Reggie snaps, his frustration spilling over.

"She has a real husband—albeit a tosser," he adds with a small, bitter laugh, "but he's still her husband. And her children… Lillie, Bonnie, Oliver… they all have a mother who's out there, and she doesn't even know them. She doesn't know any of us."

He pauses.

Yvonne squeezes Reggie's shoulder gently, trying to offer some comfort.

"We'll get through this," she says softly, though her own voice trembles.

"We have to believe that she'll come back to us. Somehow, she'll remember."

Carter nods, though he knows how difficult the road ahead will be for all of them.

"It's going to take time, Reggie. We have to be patient. Right now, she's safe, and she's being looked after. That's what matters."

Reggie shakes his head, the tears welling up again.

"It's just so hard to see her like this. So lost. So… different."

"I know," Carter replies quietly.

"But we're going to do everything we can to help her find her way back. You have to hold onto that hope."

Reggie nods, but the look in his eyes shows just how much

he's struggling to do exactly that.

"Maybe we should let her meet her children?" Reggie suggests.

Carter shakes his head firmly.

"No, that really isn't a good idea at this moment in time. It could be too much for her, especially when she doesn't remember who she is or who they are. It might cause more harm than good right now."

Reggie sighs heavily, his shoulders slumping.

"Yeah, I guess you're right. I just… I just want to do something, anything, to bring her back."

Yvonne, who has been quietly rifling through her bag to make sure she has all her essentials—her mobile, house keys, and purse—looks up.

"Even I can see that it wouldn't be a good idea just now, love. We need to take this one step at a time. She's fragile, and we can't push her too hard."

Reggie nods, albeit reluctantly.

"Yeah, OK. I'm just… It's hard to sit back and wait."

Yvonne gives him a small, understanding smile.

"I know. But we have to trust the process."

"Well, I'm ready to go if you are, Carter," Yvonne says, standing up and slipping her bag over her shoulder.

Carter stands as well, stretching a bit after sitting for so long.

"Yep, I'm ready. Are you, Reggie?"

Reggie takes a deep breath, trying to steady himself.

"Yeah, I'm ready. Thank you for everything, Carter. Really."

Carter gives a nod of acknowledgement.

"It's the least I can do."

The three of them head out of the police station, stepping

CHAPTER 19

into the cool early morning air.

The sky is beginning to lighten ever so slightly, hinting at the coming dawn. The streets are quiet, a stark contrast to the earlier flurry of activity.

Inside the station, Dobby sits at her desk, enjoying the rare moment of peace. With most of the night's work behind her, she waits for any new suspects that might be brought in. The station feels almost serene in its stillness, a sharp departure from the chaos that unfolded earlier.

Meanwhile, Biff moves between the cells, responding to the occasional request for a drink or a blanket. He maintains a quiet efficiency, his footsteps barely making a sound on the lino as he checks in on each of the detainees.

In their cells, Gerry and Rachel sleep soundly, oblivious to the night's events. The low hum of the station is a distant echo to them as they rest, unaware of the turmoil outside their dreams. They have a few more precious hours of sleep before the morning brings new questions, new interrogations, and perhaps, new revelations.

As the station settles into a quieter rhythm, the officers prepare themselves for another day—a new chapter in the unfolding mystery that surrounds Molly, and all those entangled in her life.

Y Y Y

Thursday Morning

Daisy barks loudly, her sharp, insistent yaps echoing through the quiet house as another bang comes from the front door. The sound jolts Ray awake from his makeshift bed—a setup of two dining room chairs pushed together, covered with a duvet and a flattened pillow. He blinks groggily, rubbing the sleep from his eyes, and quickly pulls on a pair of worn jeans, not bothering with shoes or a shirt. His bare feet slap against the cold floor as he makes his way to the front door, Daisy trotting closely behind him, still barking in alarm.

As he reaches the door, he opens it to find the familiar face of their regular postman. The postman, looking a bit tired but cheerful as always, hands Ray a small package. "Morning," he says with a nod.

"Got something for Molly today."

Ray accepts the package, the cardboard cool against his hands. He glances down at the label, noticing the neat handwriting and the return address in the top corner. The sender is a company named 'Lushes and Lashes,' which doesn't ring a bell. Curious, he gives the box a little shake, hearing a faint rattle from within. He frowns, wondering what Molly could have ordered from a place with such a peculiar name, but he doesn't dwell on it long.

"Thanks," he mutters to the postman, who nods and heads back down the path. Ray shuts the door with a short slam, the noise making Daisy jump slightly before she settles back down with the children in the living room.

Ray walks over to the kitchen and sets the package on the counter, deciding it can wait for later. He's too tired to think much about it now. He turns away, heading back towards his makeshift bed in the dining room. As he passes through the hallway, he glances back at the package one last time, then shrugs. There are more pressing things on his mind, and the mystery of 'Lushes and Lashes' can wait.

A few hours later, the sun is peeking through the curtains, casting soft morning light across the living room.

Oliver is already wide awake, engrossed in his Xbox game. He had brought it down from his bedroom last night, determined to spend the morning building his virtual world in Minecraft.

With the help of his sisters, he managed to set up the console in the living room. Now, he's fully immersed, sitting cross-legged on the floor, his fingers flying over the keyboard. Unlike most players who use a controller, Oliver prefers the precision and speed of a keyboard and mouse, a skill his sisters can't quite match.

Oliver loves the creative freedom Minecraft offers him. He spends hours mining for ores, crafting tools, and designing elaborate treehouses high in the digital canopy. His latest project is a sprawling farmyard, complete with stables and pens for the virtual animals he's collected. The screen is filled with vibrant pixelated blocks, and Oliver's eyes are fixed on every movement, every block he places, fully absorbed in his own world.

Lillie sits on the couch nearby, her feet tucked underneath her as she watches her brother play. She has no idea how to navigate the game herself, the controls and endless crafting recipes completely baffling to her. But she enjoys watching Oliver work, admiring his creativity and the way his mind seems to buzz with endless possibilities.

Bonnie, on the other hand, is the complete opposite of

Lillie. She's perched on the edge of the couch, leaning forward eagerly. She's not playing, but she's fully engaged, cheering Oliver on and offering enthusiastic encouragement every time he accomplishes something.

"Nice one, Oliver!" she exclaims as he successfully fends off a group of virtual monsters.

"You're getting really good at this!"

Ray, sitting in his usual chair with a cup of coffee in hand, watches the kids with a slight frown. He's never understood the appeal of video games or computers. In fact, he despises anything electrical. He always claims that if the internet were to go down or technology were to fail, he'd be one of the few who could thrive without it, living off the land and relying on his own two hands.

"All this tech nonsense," he mutters under his breath, though his words are drowned out by Bonnie's cheering and Oliver's clicking keyboard.

Ray takes a sip of his coffee, shaking his head slightly as he looks out the window, preferring the simplicity of the world outside to the digital landscapes that captivate his children.

Despite his aversion to technology, Ray can't resist the pull of his mobile phone, which sits enticingly on the side table. With a sigh, he picks it up and starts scrolling through his messages.

He has a familiar urge building up inside him—'an itch that he needs to scratch', as he likes to call it.

He quickly types out a message to Rachel, someone he hasn't talked to in a while.

» **09:48 am** *Hey Rachel, long time no speak. What have you been up to lately?*

He presses send and stares at the screen, waiting for the

CHAPTER 19

telltale ping of a reply. Minutes tick by, but his phone remains silent. Frustrated, he decides to scroll through his contacts, hoping to find someone else who might be up for a chat or more. As he swipes through the list, his finger hovers over a familiar name: *Tracy*.

"Tracy," he murmurs to himself, smirking at the memory.

He met Tracy a while back, during a printing job he was doing for his boss's sister's best friend.

She was hard to forget—a blonde-haired, busty woman who loved to have a good time. Their last encounter was particularly memorable. Tracy was bold, confident, and unapologetically forward. When they were together, she practically devoured him, leaving no room for Ray to be anything other than a willing participant. She was experienced, knowing exactly what she wanted, and took control in a way that left Ray breathless.

But there was something about Tracy that always felt too easy, too predictable. She was all about the physical—pure, unadulterated sex with no emotional attachment. And while Ray certainly appreciated the occasional no-strings-attached fling, he preferred a bit of a challenge.

He liked it when a woman desired him, and craved him, both physically and emotionally. It wasn't just about the act itself for Ray; it was about the game, the dance of seduction and mutual attraction.

With Tracy, it felt more like a transaction, a simple exchange of pleasure without any of the intrigue or build-up he craved.

Still, the itch was there, persistent and nagging. As he continued to scroll through his contacts, his mind wandered back to Tracy.

"If you've got an itch and it needs scratching, Tracy is a good call," he mutters quietly to himself, weighing his options.

He glances back at his phone, considering whether to send her a message. He knows exactly what to expect if he does, but maybe that's what he needs right now—a sure thing to take the edge off, even if it lacks the thrill he usually seeks.

He sighs, his finger hovering over her name, wondering if he'll give in to the temptation or keep searching for something more.

* * *

I lie awake in this empty bed, a bed that feels far too big without Gerry beside me.

I feel alone, adrift in a world that no longer makes sense. My mind is a whirlpool of confusion and regret, pulling me under with thoughts of everything that has gone wrong.

Gerry, the love of my life—or so I've been told—is locked up in a cell right now because of me.

Because I had that stupid accident on the sea wall.

Because I fell.

The memory haunts me.

I can still feel the cold, salty spray of the ocean against my face, the wind howling in my ears. I remember slipping, my feet losing their grip, and then the terror as I tumbled towards the churning water below. Duke, Gerry's beloved dog, had been there. I remember reaching out in panic, feeling Duke's fur beneath my fingers as he tried to save me, his weight dragging me down as he struggled to keep me afloat. I had to let go—I had to let him slip from my hands. His weight was

CHAPTER 19

pulling me under, and I knew if I didn't release him, we'd both drown.

So, I let go. I can still feel the moment his fur slipped through my fingers. The guilt is suffocating. Duke drowned because of me, and I can't shake the feeling that it's all my fault.

But what's worse than the guilt is the confusion. How can I not remember what has been happening to me?

There are flashes—certain events, certain things that come back to me in bits and pieces.

I remember waking up in the hospital and seeing Gerry there. But he was a stranger to me. My memory was vague. And yet, he's filled in the gaps for me, told me we are married, that we've shared a life together.

Restless, I throw back the covers and get out of bed. I need proof, something tangible to show everyone. I start looking for wedding photos—surely there must be more than the one I've seen. That single picture in a frame, the one I carefully wrapped up because I didn't want it to get damaged. It can't be the only one, he must have more printed out.

I check all the drawers in the bedroom, rummaging through clothes and papers, but there's nothing. I get down on my knees and peer under the bed, but still, I find nothing. Frustration builds inside me as I move to the wardrobe, pulling out boxes and going through every inch of space. I tear through the spare room next, opening every drawer and cupboard, and rifling through boxes. But again, I come up empty.

They keep telling me he's not my husband.

How did he just happen to be at the hospital when I woke up?

THE FOUND

He must have known me at the time; he would have been a part of my life to be there.

Everything feels surreal, like a dream I can't wake up from.

I keep searching, moving from room to room, my desperation growing with each empty drawer and every blank space where more pictures should be. But I find nothing. My heart sinks with every moment that passes, and I can't shake the feeling that something is terribly wrong. Why doesn't he have proof if he is to continue this lie?

Chapter 20

Thursday Morning

"I think we can grant Gerry bail, but the question is where," Dixie says, leaning back in his chair and rubbing his temples in frustration.

"He doesn't have any relatives he can go to, and we definitely can't let him go back to the bungalow where Molly is staying. Legally, I'm not sure what our options are."

He glances around the room, searching for any ideas from his colleagues. The room is silent for a moment.

"We can't just release him with nowhere to go," Dixie continues.

"We have to find a solution that ensures everyone's safety and complies with the law. But our hands are tied if he doesn't have a place to stay that's away from Molly."

A heavy sigh escapes his lips as he leans forward, his hands clasped tightly together on the desk. "Does anyone have any suggestions? We need to figure this out before we move forward."

Sharpie interjects, "Unless we don't grant him bail." He pauses, scanning the room to see if anyone agrees with him.

The silence is thick, stretching longer than he expected. He raises an eyebrow, waiting for someone to speak up.

"Anyone?" he asks, a bit louder this time, trying to stir a response.

"Poker, Chase, Lambert? Gilbert, Carter? Are any of you awake this morning?" His voice carries a hint of frustration, echoing slightly in the quiet room.

Poker leans back in his chair, arms crossed, looking thoughtful but saying nothing. Chase is staring at the table, lost in his own thoughts, while Lambert fidgets with a pen, avoiding eye contact. Gilbert looks up briefly but remains silent, her expression unreadable.

Carter sighs, rubbing his chin, clearly deep in contemplation.

Finally, Carter breaks the silence.

"It's not that we're not awake, Sharpie. It's just… complicated. Denying bail means keeping him here longer, but releasing him could cause more issues. We're in a tough spot."

"Exactly," Chase adds, finally looking up.

"If we deny him bail without a strong enough reason, it might come back to bite us on the ass. But if we let him go and something happens, we're liable."

Sharpie sighs, his patience thinning.

"I get that it's complicated, but we need to make a decision. We can't just sit here all day weighing the pros and cons. We have to act."

Dixie interrupts, "Carter, you make the call."

Carter looks up, his eyes widening in surprise.

"What? Why me?" he asks, clearly taken aback. He glances around the room, searching for a hint of why he was chosen

CHAPTER 20

out of everyone to decide whether Gerry should be granted bail or not.

"Because you're the one who's been closest to this case," Dixie replies firmly.

"You've seen the evidence, you've spoken to the witnesses, and you know Molly's situation better than anyone here. You're the most informed. It makes sense for you to decide."

Carter lets out a deep sigh, feeling the weight of responsibility settle on his shoulders. He rubs the back of his neck, thinking hard.

"Alright, but this is a big decision. We need to consider all the risks and implications. If Gerry's let out on bail, we have to make sure there's no chance he'll interfere with Molly or try to influence the case."

The room falls silent again as everyone waits for Carter to process his thoughts. He looks over at Poker, who nods slightly in encouragement, and then at Sharpie, whose expression remains stern but expectant.

Carter takes a deep breath.

"OK. Here's what I'm thinking…"

"We need to speak to Rachel first and eliminate her from suspicion," Carter begins, his voice steady and thoughtful.

"Once we've done that, our next step is to speak to Molly, to find out what she knows and fill in any gaps in our understanding of the situation. Only then can we make an informed decision about what we're actually going to charge Gerry with?"

Dixie nods, following Carter's train of thought.

"And once we have that, we send everything over to the CPS," he adds.

"They can make the final call on the charges and decide

the best course of action."

"Exactly," Carter agrees.

"If we decide to grant him bail, then we'll have to ensure that he stays somewhere away from Molly—like a hotel or something similar. There's no way we can risk him going back to the bungalow, especially with her state of mind and the confusion over who he really is to her," says Carter.

Sharpie leans back in his chair, nodding slowly.

"It's a solid plan. We just have to make sure that if he gets bail, it comes with strict conditions. He needs to be monitored closely to ensure he doesn't try to contact Molly or disrupt the investigation."

"Agreed," Carter says.

"Let's get moving on this. We've got a lot of work to do, and we need to act quickly if we want to keep things under control. I'll start by arranging the interviews with Rachel and Molly. The sooner we get their statements, the sooner we can put this all together." says Sharpie.

The team nods in unison, understanding the urgency of the situation.

The room buzzes with a renewed sense of purpose as everyone prepares to carry out the next steps in the investigation.

**

Carter and Poker have been tasked with interviewing Rachel, and with her solicitor arriving early as planned, they can get started right away.

Knowing that time was of the essence, Carter picked up the phone and dialled the extension for the Custody Suite, hoping to expedite the process.

CHAPTER 20

The phone rings twice before a voice on the other end answers, "Custody Suite, PC Wallace speaking. How can I assist you?"

Carter leans back in his chair, a hint of familiarity in his tone.

"Wallace, it's Carter from upstairs. How's it going? Long time, no chat."

"Hey, Carter! I'm doing well, thanks. It's been a while. What's up?" Wallace responds, his voice brightening at the sound of a friendly colleague. They exchange a few pleasantries, catching up briefly on the morning's events, before Carter shifts the conversation to the matter at hand.

"Listen, Wallace," Carter says, his tone becoming more serious, "we need to speak with Miss Rachel Houston this morning. Is her solicitor on-site yet?"

"Yes, her solicitor's been here for about an hour already," Wallace replies, a slight hint of eagerness in his voice.

He is a young officer, just four years into his service, and always eager to prove himself. This week he is covering the Custody Suite due to a staffing shortage, which is an opportunity he hopes to make the most of.

"Great, that's good news," Carter acknowledges.

"Could you arrange for Rachel to be brought into the interview room? We'd like to get started as soon as possible."

"Of course, Carter," Wallace assures him.

"I'll take care of it right away."

"Thanks, Wallace. You're doing a great job. Appreciate the help," Carter adds warmly before hanging up the phone. He turns to Poker, who has been listening to the conversation.

"Wallace is on it. Rachel will be in there shortly. Let's get ourselves ready."

Poker nods, already mentally preparing for the interview ahead.

"Perfect. Let's see if we can get some answers out of her today."

The two officers gather their files and make their way to the interview room, knowing that this could be a pivotal moment in their investigation. As they walk through the corridors, Carter can't help but think about the complexities of the case and the importance of what they are about to uncover.

* * *

Rachel sits in the chair opposite the two empty seats, feeling a tight knot in her stomach. The room is cold, but beads of sweat form on her forehead, trickling down slowly. She dabs them away with the back of her hand, trying to steady her breathing.

Benjamin, her solicitor, leans in closer, his voice calm but firm.

"Are you going to be OK, Rachel?" he asks, his eyes scanning her face for any sign of doubt.

She swallows hard, straightening her posture as if trying to convince herself as much as him.

"Yes, I'll be alright," she replies, her voice steady but with an edge of tension.

"I have nothing to hide."

Just as she finishes speaking, the door creaks open. Two men enter the room, their expressions serious, their presence commanding.

Rachel immediately recognises Poker, and a wave of

CHAPTER 20

heat rushes to her face. She feels the blood pumping harder, flushing her cheeks crimson. Memories of their last encounter flood her mind, creating discomfort and anxiety. She glances away quickly, trying to mask her reaction, but the sudden tension doesn't go unnoticed.

Benjamin, seated beside her, observes the awkward exchange between Rachel and Poker. His practised eyes catch the subtle shift in her demeanour, the way her eyes dart nervously. He makes a mental note but decides not to draw attention to it. The last thing he wants is to make Rachel feel cornered or agitated, especially before the interview has even begun. Instead, he maintains his calm composure, ready to guide her through whatever comes next.

Carter, steps forward, his expression professional yet approachable. He introduces himself to Rachel with a polite nod, reminding her of their earlier brief encounter.

"Miss Houston, I'm PC Carter, we've met before," he says formally, though his tone is not unkind.

He moves to the centre of the room and presses a button on the recording machine placed on the desk between them. The machine whirs to life, the small red light blinking steadily, indicating that the interview is officially starting.

"This interview is now being recorded," Carter announces, his voice clear and authoritative. "Present are PC Carter, PC Poker, Rachel Houston, and her solicitor, Mr. Benjamin Swift.

He continues to repeat the date and time after glancing at his watch.

Rachel shifts slightly in her seat, feeling the gravity of the moment settle over her, ready to face whatever questions come her way, knowing that this interview could change everything.

Rachel clears her throat and provides her personal details to the officers, her voice steady despite the churning in her stomach. She tries to project calm, but she can't ignore the sweat on her palms or the tightness in her chest.

"Thank you for that," Carter says, his tone polite but clipped, signalling a swift transition to the main subject.

He sits back slightly, giving Poker the cue to take the lead.

Poker leans forward, his eyes narrowing as he fixes Rachel with an intense gaze. The tension between them is deep, a silent standoff that seems to thicken the air in the small room. Rachel shifts uncomfortably under his scrutiny, her hands twisting in her lap.

"Rachel," Carter starts, breaking the silence and cutting straight to the chase, "what were you doing at the home of—let's say at the time—Elizabeth and Gerry?" The question is sharp, almost like a punch to the gut, and Rachel feels it land hard. She wasn't expecting them to dive in so directly, to skip over any easy questions.

She takes a moment to gather her thoughts, but the delay only makes her feel more exposed.

"I was taking Mrs Penwald some flowers," Rachel begins, trying to keep her voice even.

"I hadn't seen her for some time and wanted to visit her." Her explanation is quick, almost too quick, and she knows it. Her cheeks betray her, flushing a deep red that only seems to confirm her discomfort.

Poker doesn't let up.

"What made you want to go and see her?" he presses, his voice low and probing.

Rachel hesitates, her mind racing. She feels cornered like

CHAPTER 20

she's being forced to reveal something she isn't ready to share.

"I had been to see my ex-boyfriend," she admits, carefully choosing her words.

"I called at his house. His neighbour, Mrs Easton, told me that Gerry had moved out with his wife." She stops, swallowing hard as the memory surges up, raw and painful.

"I was angry," she continues, her voice a bit shakier now.

"I wanted to know what was going on. I couldn't believe he had gotten married, and I knew nothing about it. So, I decided to go to his Mum's home and ask her outright." Rachel takes a deep breath, trying to steady herself.

"Mrs Penwald and I were quite close at one time. I thought she would be OK talking to me."

Carter nods, his face giving away nothing as he takes in her words.

"And when you got to her house, what happened next?" he asks, his voice calm but insistent, pushing her to keep going.

Rachel's eyes flicker as she tries to recall the details, the memory of that day still fresh in her mind. She knows this is the moment where she needs to be careful, to choose her words wisely. She looks down for a moment, as if searching for the right answer in her lap, then looks up to meet Carter's steady gaze.

Rachel's voice trembles slightly as she recounts the memory.

"Molly opened the door," she says, her tone of voice lingering with disbelief. Even now, she seems shocked by the encounter, as if reliving the moment.

Carter leans in slightly, his eyebrows meeting with confusion.

"And who is Molly?" he asks, pressing for clarity.

Rachel takes a breath, steeling herself.

"Molly is the wife of the man I was having an affair with," she replies bluntly.

The room falls into silence.

Carter and Poker exchange a quick, glance, neither of them having expected her to admit this so openly. Benjamin, on the other hand, sits back with a slight smile of satisfaction on his face, as if he's been waiting for this moment to unfold.

Poker breaks the silence, his voice steady but his eyes intense.

"Are you saying that Molly Chapman is the wife of your lover?" he asks, needing to confirm for the recording what he just heard.

Rachel nods her face tight with frustration.

"Well, I *was* having an affair with him," she admits, a hint of anger creeping into her voice.

"I'm not anymore—not after he lost his shit with me one evening in front of the kids. *He's* the one you need to have in here, not me, not Gerry." She stresses each word, her agitation clear.

Carter senses the tension building and quickly steps in, trying to keep the interview on track.

"Let's stick to the formalities," he says calmly, although there's an edge to his tone, revealing his own unease with how the conversation is unfolding.

He takes a moment, then asks, "What happened when Molly answered the door?"

Rachel sighs as if the memory itself is exhausting.

"I didn't get to say much because Gerry appeared at the door," she explains, "and kind of pushed Molly out of the way so he could speak to me." Her eyes narrow slightly as

CHAPTER 20

she recalls the encounter, the tension between the three of them still fresh in her mind.

"He asked me to keep quiet," Rachel continues, "to not say that I know Molly—who was calling herself Elizabeth." She shakes her head, her frustration is evident.

"It's all too bloody confusing. I don't understand it myself. She was telling me how she'd been in an accident, how she's married to Gerry, and Gerry then told me that his mother was dead." Rachel's voice breaks slightly on the last word, and she takes a deep, shuddering breath, trying to steady herself.

"It's all so overwhelming," she admits, her composure finally slipping. Her hands tremble as she grips the edge of the table, her knuckles white.

"Can I stop, please?" she pleads, looking between Carter and Poker with desperation and exhaustion. Her eyes are wide, and for a moment, she looks vulnerable, the tough exterior she's maintained starting to crack under the weight of everything she's just revealed.

Chapter 21

Thursday Morning

Molly collapses onto the lounge floor, her body trembling with the weight of her emotions. Gilbert rushes in, her face full of concern. Without hesitation, she drops down beside Molly, wrapping her arms around her tightly, and pulling her close.

"Hey, hey, it's alright," Gilbert whispers soothingly, her voice gentle. She rocks Molly back and forth, holding her in a protective embrace. Molly feels small and fragile, like a child seeking comfort in the arms of a parent. Her body shakes as the sobs tear through her, her tears flowing freely down her cheeks, pooling onto Gilbert's shoulder.

"It's just too much," Molly cries, her voice barely audible. "I can't—it's all too much."

Gilbert pulls her in closer, resting her chin on Molly's head.

"I know, love. I know it's been a lot, but you're not alone. I'm right here with you," she murmurs, stroking Molly's hair softly.

Gilbert holds her, not letting go, knowing that sometimes words aren't enough—sometimes, it's the presence and the

CHAPTER 21

simple act of being there that makes all the difference.

* * *

Reggie rises with the early morning light filtering through the curtains and casting a gentle glow in the room.

The weight of the recent events on his mind stopped him from being able to get any rest.

He mentally prepares himself for the task ahead. He knows that his next steps are crucial, and he's resolved to face them head-on.

He takes a moment to scribble a brief note to Yvonne, letting her know that he has gone out and explained his plans. He places the note where she'll be sure to see it when she wakes.

With his plan set, Reggie grabs his car keys from the hook by the door, slipping them into his pocket.

Quietly, he exits the house, careful not to wake Yvonne. He opens the car door with a soft creak, slides into the driver's seat, and starts the engine.

The car hums gently, its engine a comforting purr as he drives through the quiet streets, making his way to Ray's house.

The early-morning traffic is light, and he reaches his destination in about twenty minutes.

Reggie parks the car in front of Ray and Molly's house, his eyes briefly surveying the familiar neighbourhood.

He steps out and approaches the front door, his footsteps muted on the pavement. He glances at the ring doorbell, a small frown creasing his brow as he presses it.

The door swings open almost immediately, and Ray appears, now dressed casually. His face brightens with a genuine smile as he sees Reggie.

He steps aside, gesturing for Reggie to enter.

"Come to see the kids?" Ray asks, his voice friendly as he ushers Reggie into the house.

"No actually, I have come to see you," says Reggie very matter of fact.

"Me?" laughs Ray.

"To what do I owe the pleasure?"

Reggie steps forward, his expression serious.

"Look, Ray, I'm not going to beat around the bush. I'm here to give it to you straight." His voice is steady, but there's an edge to it, a frustration bubbling beneath the surface.

Ray raises an eyebrow and takes a step back, his face blended with confusion and suspicion. "What's going on?" he asks, clearly bewildered by Reggie's sudden intensity.

"It's about Molly," Reggie says, his tone grave.

"She's been found. She's alive and well."

Ray's eyes widen in shock.

"What?!" he blurts out, his confusion deepening.

"I thought… I thought she was found already? What do you mean she's been found?"

Reggie sighs heavily, clearly irritated.

"She went from being one of 'The Forgotten' to 'The Found,'" he explains.

"It's a long story, and honestly, it's all very complicated."

Ray leans back against the wall, crossing his arms over his chest.

"I'm listening," Ray says, his tone neutral, almost detached.

Reggie can't help but feel a flicker of anger at Ray's lack of enthusiasm or relief. Any decent person would be overjoyed

CHAPTER 21

to hear Molly is alive, but Ray's indifferent response just solidifies Reggie's belief that he's an asshole.

"Last night, I did an identification," Reggie continues, a hint of irritation creeping into his voice.

"I saw her on a video link."

Ray frowns, confused.

"Don't you usually do that kind of thing for dead people?" he asks bluntly.

Reggie's face tightens, clearly unimpressed with Ray's tactlessness.

"Real nice, Ray," he mutters.

Ray shrugs, unapologetic.

"I'm just saying, that's how I thought it worked."

Reggie shakes his head, his frustration growing.

"Well, she's very much alive, but she's not the same. She has severe memory loss. Didn't even recognise me or Yvonne. She doesn't believe she's married, and worst of all, she doesn't believe she has children." Reggie's voice is strained, his anger at Ray's indifference mixing with his worry for Molly. He rubs his temples, trying to keep his composure as he continues.

"I thought you'd care more about this, but you're just proving me right."

Ray's expression remains stoic, and Reggie's frustration only grows. It's clear to him that Ray isn't going to give him the reaction he hoped for, and that realisation stings more than he cares to admit.

"I don't know how I'm supposed to act. First, I have you telling me the news and not the police..." Ray says, his voice dripping with scepticism.

Reggie interrupts him.

"Because I'm her next of KIN, and you know that."

"Fair enough," Ray scoffs, "but why haven't they come to see me yet?"

"Well, probably because I was only dropped off at nearly half past four this morning. They haven't gotten around to checking in with other relatives who need informing," Reggie answers, trying to keep his frustration in check.

"So why are you telling me?" Ray scoffs again, his tone more mocking than questioning.

"Because I want you to do something, Ray. Tell the police you want the children to see their mother. It might jog her memory or… or do something," Reggie pleads, feeling lost for words. He hates that he's asking for help from the one person he despises.

"I don't think we should push her," Ray replies calmly. "Let her memory come back on its own."

"Oh, that would suit you just fine, wouldn't it?" Reggie snaps, his voice rising.

"You'd love for her not to remember that last night she spent with you, wouldn't you?"

Ray smirks slightly, clearly enjoying the fact that he's getting under Reggie's skin. "We've all moved on, Reggie. We learned to live without Molly the day we found out she was with another man and didn't want anything more to do with us," Ray shouts back, spit flying from his mouth.

"She had an accident, you selfish bastard!" Reggie shouts, his voice raw with anger. "She lost her memory and ended up going home with someone completely different from her family. She's been coerced, abducted, or whatever the hell you want to call it."

"So she says!" Ray retorts, not backing down.

CHAPTER 21

Suddenly, a small voice cuts through their argument.

"They've found Mum?"

Both men turn to see Lillie standing in the doorway, holding three empty cups stained with congealed hot chocolate from the previous night's sleepover. Her eyes are wide, full of hope and with confusion etched across her face.

"Oh, Lillie, love, come here," Reggie says softly, holding out his arms.

Tears stream down Lillie's face as the reality of the news sinks in. She moves toward Reggie, walking straight past her father without a second glance, and collapses into her uncle's open arms. He holds her tightly, gently rubbing her back, waiting for the sobbing to subside.

Ray watches, bewildered by his daughter's actions.

"This is a joke, right?" he mutters, stunned that Lillie would so blatantly ignore him.

"It's how you treat them, Ray," Reggie replies sharply, not looking up from comforting Lillie.

"You have no respect for your own children. It's no wonder they don't come to you for comfort."

Lillie lifts her head, looking up at her uncle with tear-filled eyes.

"I can't believe they've actually found her. Where is she, Uncle Reggie?"

"She's at her new home," he says carefully, trying to gauge her reaction.

"New home? Her home is here," Lillie insists, confused.

Reggie takes a deep breath.

"Because she lost her memory, she's staying with a man who she believes to be her husband. He's been looking after her since the accident."

Lillie's eyes widen with shock.

"And you saw her?" she asks, her voice trembling.

"Yes, we did. But she didn't recognise us because of her amnesia," Reggie explains gently.

"She would recognise us," Lillie says firmly, her voice filled with hope and determination.

"That is what I am hoping for." Reggie conveys.

"I want to see her, Uncle Reggie."

Ray interrupts, his voice edged with frustration.

"Erm, I think you'll find that's up to me, not your uncle."

Reggie straightens up, his tone turning cold.

"Well, I think you'll find that since I'm listed as Molly's next of KIN, I have the authority regarding the children. You're not named anywhere in the legal documents, Ray."

Oliver and Bonnie stand quietly behind the door, having overheard the conversation about their Mum. They can hear Lillie's sobbing and feel a mix of emotions—fear, confusion, and longing—but neither is brave enough to enter the room and face everyone.

Oliver, still in his pyjamas, looks at Bonnie and tries to push her toward the door.

"You go in, Bonnie," he whispers.

"They're not going to tell you off for interrupting an adult conversation."

Bonnie shakes her head firmly.

"No way. You go. Besides, you're the boy—they'll probably be easier on you."

"I'm not going," Oliver whines, his voice low and shaky.

"You know how much Dad doesn't like me. He's always shouting at me. If I go in there now, he's going to shout at me like, well, bad."

CHAPTER 21

Bonnie glances at the door and then back at Oliver, sharing his hesitation. She knows he's right about their dad.

"Yeah, well... I don't want to get yelled at either," she mumbles, crossing her arms and leaning back against the wall.

Bonnie looks at Oliver, feeling a pang of sympathy for her little brother.

Lately, it seems like he's been taking the brunt of their father's frustration. Ray's temper has been so short, and his patience so thin, that all the children have become too scared to speak up or even be themselves around the house.

The carefree days of laughter and playing have vanished, replaced by a constant tension that hangs in the air.

They can't just be children anymore—not with their dad turning into a bully who seems to find fault with everything they do.

Bonnie reaches out and squeezes Oliver's shoulder gently, offering him a small, reassuring smile.

"We'll figure this out," she whispers.

"We just have to stick together, OK?"

Ray strides through the hallway and spots Oliver and Bonnie hiding behind the door.

A scowl darkens his face.

"Oh, great," he mutters, his voice dripping with irritation.

"Now I've fucking got all three of you involved in something you didn't need to know about yet."

The children flinch at his harsh tone, but Ray doesn't seem to notice—or care.

"Don't start getting any ideas about seeing your mother and thinking everything's going to magically turn into some happy little family reunion. Life doesn't work that way." His words are sharp, carrying a bitterness that makes the air feel heavier.

Just then, the doorbell chimes its familiar tune, cutting through the tense silence in the house.

Daisy starts to bark.

Ray, feeling the sudden urge to use the bathroom and desperate for an escape from the situation, makes a quick detour towards the front door before anyone else can answer it.

He swings the door open, and there, standing on the doorstep, is Tracy. She's dressed provocatively in a low-cut top that shows off her cleavage and a short denim skirt that barely covers her thighs. If she were to bend over, Ray thinks, there would be no hiding what's underneath.

"Hi," she starts, a hopeful smile on her lips.

"I'm sorry, but I rushed over like you asked me to—"

Ray cuts her off, putting his foot in the doorway to block her from coming inside.

"Now really isn't a good time," he says, glancing over his shoulder to make sure the kids aren't watching.

Tracy's smile fades, disappointment settling in her eyes.

"Oh, right," she says, clearly hurt by his abruptness.

Ray sighs, growing more impatient.

"Yeah, but I've got family that just showed up, and now the kids are here. So, it's really not a good time," he repeats, his tone firm, leaving no room for negotiation.

Tracy's shoulders slump slightly, and she gives a small nod, realising she's not getting any further with him today.

Ray waits for her to leave, his mind already back on the mess unfolding inside the house.

He heads past the children and makes his way to the

CHAPTER 21

bathroom.

Oliver's eyes light up with a sudden realisation: this is the perfect moment to go into Uncle Reggie.

With a burst of excitement, he and Lillie swiftly dart out from their hiding spot behind the door. They make a beeline towards Uncle Reggie, who stands with his arms wide open, a welcoming smile on his face. As they reach him, they are enveloped in his comforting embrace.

With emotions running high, they cry out in unison, "Uncle Reggie!" Their voices tremble as they struggle to keep their tears at bay, weighed down by the heavy news they've just received.

Reggie turns to Bonnie with a questioning look.

"So, who was at the door?"

Bonnie shrugs slightly, her expression a blend of curiosity and concern.

"Some woman, all dressed up. She was there to see Dad. I think he was expecting her."

Just then, Ray reappears at the doorway, his face a mask of cold determination.

"Who I see and who comes to this house is no one's fucking business but my own. She's a client, if you must know."

Reggie raises an eyebrow, his tone laced with sarcasm.

"Oh, yes, Ray. We're all too familiar with the kind of clients you entertain, aren't we?"

Ray's face flushes with anger as he clenches his jaw.

"You know what, Reggie? I think you've overstayed your fucking welcome. Kids, go to your rooms. NOW!"

Reggie's eyes narrow, but his voice remains steady.

"It's alright, Ray. Just continue showing your true colours." Reggie snipes.

Ray's temper snaps.

"This is my house, Reggie! MY HOUSE!" He points toward the door, his voice rising.

"So get the hell out!"

Reggie takes a deep breath, his face softening as he leans down to kiss the children gently on their heads. As he turns to leave, he whispers to Lillie, "If you want to come over to ours after school, just send me a text, OK?"

"OK, we will want to come over to yours later. We'll pack up some things and give you a call when we are ready," Lillie replies quietly.

"Come on, we'd better go to our rooms," Lillie says, her voice steady but strained as she talks to her sister and brother.

The three children make their way along the hallway, disappearing upstairs and into their rooms and leaving Ray alone, simmering with frustration.

As Ray listens to the distant sound of the children moving about in their bedrooms, the rhythmic thump of their activity grows louder. He can hear them kicking around, gathering their things and preparing for school. Each sound heightens his sense of impatience. He eagerly anticipates the moment when they will finally leave the house, longing for a brief respite from the chaos and noise, craving a moment of solitude to gather his thoughts and regain his composure.

Chapter 22

Thursday Morning

In the dim confines of his cell, Gerry stirs awake as the first rays of light filter through the narrow window, casting a harsh glare directly onto his face. He grimaces and instinctively turns away from the intrusive brightness, burying his head under the thin, scratchy blanket. With a low groan, he slowly starts to rouse himself, his movements sluggish as he begins to face the reality of another day within the cold, unyielding walls of his cell.

The small window set into the door of Gerry's cell slides open, and a cheerful female voice filters through.

"Good morning, Gerry."

Gerry blinks awake, squinting against the brightness. He responds sheepishly, "Good morning."

The voice brightens further.

"Would you like some breakfast?"

Gerry stretches and shifts on the thin mattress, his bare feet meeting the cold, unforgiving floor. He lifts them instinctively, as if the chill were scalding, then gingerly sets them back down.

"Yes, please," he replies, his stomach rumbling in agreement.

The voice continues, "Any preferences? We have a variety of options."

Grateful for any nourishment, Gerry thinks for a moment. "Just some toast would be lovely, with butter, please."

"Toast it is," the voice responds warmly before the window closes, leaving Gerry to wait in the quiet anticipation of his simple breakfast.

Gerry waits patiently, using the time to get up and freshen himself as best as he can.

He shuffles over to the small, grimy mirror attached to the wall of his cell. As he gazes at his reflection, he sees the stark difference from the man he was just a few days ago. His eyes appear hollow and exhausted, and his face is unkempt, marked by the strain of recent events.

The basic toiletries he requested—just a flannel, a bar of soap, and a toothbrush with toothpaste—seem inadequate. The sink, devoid of a plug, offers little solace for his attempts at washing.

The harsh reality of his situation begins to sink in. The stark, unyielding conditions serve as a brutal reminder of what awaits him if he ends up in prison. The isolation, the lack of privacy, and the meagre supplies all point to a future devoid of comfort or dignity.

Gerry's resolve wavers under the weight of it all, but he fights to maintain control. He takes a deep breath through his mouth, then exhales slowly through pursed lips, trying to steady himself and push back the overwhelming sense of despair.

CHAPTER 22

* * *

"So are we all ready and in the know of what we are all doing this morning, yes?" questions Sharpie.

The team all agree in unison.

Lambert and Chase head to the lab with Dr Granger's report in hand, determined to piece together the evidence they have gathered. Their investigation has so far yielded little incriminating evidence against Gerry, but the report sheds light on a crucial aspect: the diary entries from Molly suggest a troubling situation. The entries reveal a pattern of flashbacks, with Molly struggling to differentiate between her past life and her current reality. This disorientation suggests that she is indeed grappling with memory loss, as she claimed.

As they sift through the evidence, it becomes apparent that Molly's diary does not contain any references that would indicate Gerry is involved in her abduction or imprisonment. Instead, it paints a picture of confusion and a disjointed sense of reality.

The forensic analysis of the bungalow reveals three distinct sets of fingerprints: Gerry's, Molly's, and an unidentified third set. The unknown prints are presumed to belong to Mrs Penwald, adding a new layer to the investigation but not directly implicating Gerry.

They notice the house had been scrupulously cleaned but they also know that Gerry and Molly have only just recently moved into the bungalow.

As Lambert and Chase delve deeper into the evidence, they discover a critical piece of information: the fingerprints found on the front door of the bungalow match those of

Rachel. These same prints are also found on the flowers she had previously brought for Mrs Penwald. This discovery adds a new dimension to their investigation, linking Rachel directly to the scene but also corroborating her story.

The correlation between Rachel's fingerprints on both the door and the flowers suggests her presence at the bungalow around the time of the incident only. Ruling her out as being a suspect of abduction.

With Molly's testimony and Gerry's partial statement now in hand, Lambert and Chase reassess their position. Molly's account, supported by her diary entries, and Gerry's clear statement suggests a lack of evidence linking Rachel to any wrongdoing. The information indicates that while Rachel's fingerprints were found on the bungalow door and the flowers, there is no substantial evidence connecting her to any criminal activities.

Given the current evidence and testimonies, the investigative team concludes that they no longer have sufficient grounds to hold Rachel which leads them to the decision that Rachel should be released.

"Who wants to be the one to tell her she can go?" Sharpie asks, glancing around at the team.

No one steps forward.

"Alright, Poker, you're up. Make sure you fill out the discharge papers completely—don't leave out any crucial details like where she'll be staying," Sharpie adds with a pointed look.

Poker's stomach churns. The last person he wants to be released back into the wild is Miss Houston—the very woman who had seduced him only recently.

CHAPTER 22

* * *

The heavy cell door creaks loudly as it swings open, and the Custody Officer on duty, PC Brown, steps into Rachel's small, dimly lit cell.

"You're up, Miss Houston. Please follow me," she says curtly, her voice devoid of warmth or emotion.

PC Brown's expression is stern, her lips pressed tightly together as if forcing herself to remain professional. Her demeanour suggests she's already had a rough start to her day, her eyes narrowed with irritation and a frown etched deeply into her face. Rachel glances up at the officer, noticing the unmistakable look of frustration clouding her features. She can't help but wonder who or what had managed to sour the officer's mood so early in the morning, making her appear as if someone had ruined her day before it had even begun.

"Where are we going?" Rachel asks, her voice full of apprehension.

"To the interview room," PC Brown replies curtly.

"Your solicitor is already there, waiting for you."

The rest of the walk is marked by an uncomfortable silence, neither woman willing to break it or engage in small talk. The echo of their footsteps in the narrow hallway is the only sound, reflecting the tension in the air.

When they reach the interview room, PC Brown knocks loudly on the door, a sharp rap that echoes down the corridor. A moment later, the door opens, revealing Benjamin Swift. His face brightens with a welcoming smile, a stark contrast to the officer's stern demeanour.

"I'll leave you with Mr Swift," PC Brown says, her tone still formal and distant.

"I'll be waiting just outside the door."

"Thank you," Rachel replies as she steps into the room, grateful for a familiar face.

"Rachel, please, take a seat," Benjamin offers, gesturing to a chair across from him.

Rachel sits down, leaning in slightly as she whispers,

"Am I glad to see you. She's one sour-faced cow, isn't she?"

Benjamin chuckles softly and responds, "I didn't pay much attention, to be honest."

"How have you been?" Benjamin asks her.

"Alright, I saw my Mum and Dad last night after you had left, they brought me my personal belongings." she sighs.

"Why the long face?" Benjamin asks, noticing the tension in Rachel's expression.

"Because we were only allowed twenty minutes if that," she replies with a sigh.

"To be fair, you were lucky to get even that much time," Benjamin says.

"You probably only got it because I filed a complaint before I left."

"Oh, right. Thank you," Rachel responds, her tone softening a bit with gratitude.

Benjamin leans forward, his voice dropping slightly as he prepares to deliver some news.

"OK, I have some important news to tell you." He takes a quick breath before continuing, "In a nutshell, they're going to be releasing you. Today." A smile spreads across his face.

Rachel's eyes widen in disbelief.

"Oh my god, are you serious?"

She leans back in her chair, trying to control the surge of

CHAPTER 22

excitement rushing through her.

"I just got a call from upstairs, the investigating team. I spoke with PC Lockman—Poker, I think his name is," Benjamin says, glancing down at the hastily scribbled note he took during the call.

"Yes, that's his name," Rachel confirms, though her excitement quickly shifts to unease. Her stomach flips, not from excitement, but from a wave of nerves and apprehension.

There's a knock on the door, and Poker steps in, holding a stack of paperwork. He sits down across from Rachel and Benjamin, giving them both a brief nod of acknowledgement.

"So, my client just needs to fill in this paperwork, and then she can go?" Benjamin asks as Poker hands him the documents.

"Yep, that's it in a nutshell," Poker replies.

Rachel stays silent, peering over Benjamin's shoulder at the thick pile of papers. He lays them out on the desk and retrieves a pen from the breast pocket of his blazer. He hands the pen to Rachel, who starts to read through the documents.

After carefully taking in each page, she fills in the required details on the forms. Once finished, she passes the completed paperwork back to Benjamin, who reviews them before handing them back to Poker.

"That's it then, Miss Houston. You are free to leave," Poker says, rising from his chair. "But please be aware that we may need to call you back if we think you can provide further assistance with our investigation."

Rachel nods, a jumble of relief and excitement washing over her as she contemplates what might come next.

Benjamin stands up and extends his hand to Poker, who takes it firmly and shakes it. The handshake is brief but cordial, a gesture of professional courtesy between them. Rachel, however, keeps her hands at her sides, avoiding any interaction with Poker as she walks past him and steps out into the corridor.

Once outside the room, she speaks quietly with Benjamin for a moment. They exchange a few words before heading down the hallway together, making their way back to the custody desk to retrieve her belongings—the few valuables that had been taken from her when she was arrested.

As they approach the desk, Rachel's eyes widen with surprise.

Standing there, waiting for her, is her father.

Sharpie had taken it upon himself to call him and inform him of Rachel's release. He thought it was the least he could do after she had been held in custody for so long. Seeing her father brings a rush of emotions, a mix of relief and gratitude, and she quickens her pace to meet him.

"Oh, Dad, thank God you're here!" Rachel exclaims, rushing forward and throwing herself into his arms. She clings to him tightly, feeling a wave of relief wash over her.

Her father hugs her back firmly, his voice soothing as he says, "Come on, love, let's get you out of here."

Rachel turns to the custody officer and collects her belongings—her watch, phone, and a few personal items that had been taken from her.

After making sure she has everything, she glances at Benjamin, offering him a grateful smile.

"Thank you for everything," she says sincerely.

"Take care, Rachel," Benjamin replies with a nod.

With one last look around the gloomy building, Rachel turns and heads for the exit, her steps quick and eager.

CHAPTER 22

She can't wait to leave the sombre atmosphere behind and breathe freely outside again.

* * *

Poker makes his way down the corridor and through the Custody Suite toward the cells. As he walks, he spots PC Brown making her rounds, collecting breakfast trays from the detainees.

"PC Brown," Poker calls out, catching up with her.

"I need Gerry Penwald in an interview room as soon as possible. I've already called his solicitor, and she's on her way. She might come down here to find him first, so if she does, please send her up to the interview room."

"Alright, will do. Any particular room you want?" PC Brown asks as she balances a stack of trays.

"No, any one will do. They're all empty," Poker replies, glancing down the row of doors.

"OK, Poker, will do," Brown answers with a nod.

With a brief nod of thanks, Poker turns and makes his way back along the corridor. He heads up to the offices to grab his paperwork, mentally running through what he needs for the interview. Once there, he spots Carter in a side room, busy in conversation with Dixie.

"Carter," Poker calls out, stepping into the room.

"I need you to come with me when you are free, please. We've got an interview with Gerry Penwald lined up."

Carter looks up, nods in acknowledgement, and quickly wraps up his discussion with Dixie, ready to join Poker for the next phase of their investigation.

THE FOUND

* * *

Carter and Poker sit side by side, trying to appear calm and collected as they prepare for what could be the most significant interview of their careers. The room is filled with a quiet tension, each of them aware of the stakes.

Carter feels the pressure weighing heavily on him; he knows there's no room for mistakes today. A successful interview could be his ticket to a long-awaited promotion, but any slip-up could cost him everything.

Across the table, Emily sits next to her client, Gerry, exuding quiet confidence. Her posture is upright, and her expression is composed and professional. She's prepared for any line of questioning that might come their way and is ready to defend Gerry with everything she has.

Gerry, on the other hand, is a bundle of nerves. His hands are trembling slightly, and his eyes dart around the room, unable to focus. He's exhausted, having barely slept the night before, and his stomach churns from his recent breakfast. The weight of the situation bears down on him heavily, and it's clear he feels like the world is closing in on him. He knows this interview could determine his future, and the anxiety is almost unbearable.

Emily sits calmly beside Gerry, her demeanour steady and unreadable. What no one else in the room knows, not even Gerry, is that she has a trump card up her sleeve that she's been keeping close to her chest, waiting for the perfect moment to unleash it. She is fully aware that she can soften the consequences for Gerry by presenting his actions through the lens of diminished responsibility. By arguing that Gerry's mental state was impaired at the time

CHAPTER 22

of his behaviour, she can portray him as less culpable for his actions. This approach would serve as a way to explain or justify his behaviour, potentially leading the police team to be more understanding or lenient, and reducing the severity of any punishment or criticism he might face.

She plans to hold off until the very last minute, using it as her ace in the case to turn the tide in Gerry's favour. The secret weighs heavily on her mind, but her expression remains composed and confident. She knows that revealing this information too soon could undermine its impact, so she waits, biding her time, ready to strike when the moment is right.

Chapter 23

Thursday Morning

The recorder beeps to life, signalling the start of the interview, and all eyes turn to Carter. He sits up straighter, feeling the weight of the moment settle on his shoulders. In the corner of the interview room, a red light on the video camera blinks to life, indicating that the live stream has begun. The feed is broadcast directly to Dixie's computer, which sits prominently in the middle of the bustling office. A small crowd of colleagues has gathered around, eager to watch the interview unfold in real-time.

Dixie leans back in his chair, quietly confident but showing signs of exhaustion from yet another sleepless night. Dark circles are visible under his eyes, and his posture is slumped as if the weight of his fatigue is too much to bear. He shifts sideways across the desk, trying to find a comfortable position while keeping his focus on the screen. Despite his tiredness, his eyes remained sharp, watching every movement and listening intently to every word, knowing how critical this interview could be for the case.

"Mr Penwald, Gerry," Carter begins, his tone measured

CHAPTER 23

and steady.

Gerry shifts in his seat, sitting up a bit straighter as he stretches his back, trying to shake off the nerves that are making his muscles tense. His hands rest uneasily in his lap, fingers fidgeting slightly.

"Yes," Gerry replies, his voice just above a whisper.

The recorder captures every sound, whirring softly as it documents the formalities at the start of the interview. Carter methodically goes through the necessary questions, and Gerry confirms his identity and personal details, his answers clipped and tense. The routine questions are meant to put him at ease, but they only heighten his awareness of the seriousness of the situation. Each word he speaks feels heavy, and he knows that everything he says is being scrutinised, not just in this room, but back in the office where his fate is being closely watched.

"On the night of October 26th, can you tell us where you were and what you were doing?" Carter asks, leaning forward slightly to emphasise the question.

Gerry glances at his solicitor, Emily, seeking reassurance. She nods at him encouragingly, signalling for him to continue. But Gerry hesitates, nerves tightening his throat. Emily offers a reassuring smile, and after a moment, Gerry takes a deep breath and begins to speak.

"I was out walking my dog, Duke, along the promenade," he says, his voice wavering slightly.

"It was something I did a couple of times a day."

Carter nods, jotting down notes.

"Did anything significant happen that evening? Again, in your own words, please," he prompts gently.

Poker leans back in his chair, his eyes fixed intently on

Gerry, watching for any sign of hesitation or deception.

"I was walking along the promenade when I saw a woman on the sea wall," Gerry continues, his gaze distant as he recalls the memory.

"She was standing on the edge."

"Did you know the woman?" Carter probes, his tone remaining calm but firm.

"Not at first," Gerry replies, shaking his head slightly.

"I couldn't see who it was, but as I got closer, I realised it was Molly Chapman."

Carter scribbles something down, his face unreadable.

"And what did you do?"

"I called out to her," Gerry says, his voice growing softer.

"She turned around, and our eyes met… I started to make my way toward her, but my dog, Duke, he—he started bounding toward her. The next thing I knew, she was gone… and so was my dog."

A heavy silence fills the room, each word lingering in the air. Poker's gaze sharpens, searching Gerry's face for any trace of a lie, while Carter sits quietly, waiting for Gerry to continue. The tension in the room is heightened, and everyone is aware that this moment could change everything.

"Go on," Carter prompts, his voice steady.

Gerry takes a deep breath, struggling to keep his emotions in check.

"I ran to the edge of the wall, but I couldn't see either of them," he continues, his voice cracking slightly.

"I was so scared. There was a fishing boat nearby, and they let off a flare. In a panic, I called the emergency services." He blinks rapidly to clear the tears that are threatening to spill.

Poker's eyes remain focused on Gerry, studying his reac-

CHAPTER 23

tion.

"Did you know Molly Chapman, Gerry?" he asks, trying to keep his tone neutral.

"Not really," Gerry replies, shaking his head.

"I'd seen her on my walks. She had the same breed of dog as me. It's not a popular breed, so it stands out when you see one like your own."

Carter leans forward slightly, his pen poised over his notebook.

"A Dogue de Bordeaux. Is that correct?"

"Yes," Gerry confirms, nodding.

The room falls into a tense silence as the weight of Gerry's words settles in. The details of his account are carefully noted by Carter and Poker, each piece of information scrutinised for its relevance and accuracy.

"Did you push her, Gerry?" Carter asks, his tone taking on a more intense edge.

"Were you arguing, and she slipped? Is that what really happened?"

The question hangs in the air, sharp and accusatory.

Gerry's face pales, and he looks visibly shaken by the directness of Carter's enquiry. He struggles to find his voice, his earlier composure giving way to an alloy of confusion and distress.

"No, absolutely not," Gerry says, his voice trembling.

"I didn't push her. We weren't arguing. I just—I just saw her standing there, and when I tried to approach, everything happened so fast. My dog started running towards her, and then… then she was gone. I didn't do anything to her."

His eyes well up with tears again, but he blinks them away, trying to maintain his dignity in the face of the accusation.

His hands grip the edge of the chair tightly, knuckles white with the strain.

Poker notices and so does Emily.

"So, let's rewind to before October 26th," Carter says, pausing for effect. His gaze is steady, making sure Gerry is fully attentive.

"Tell us how and when you met Molly before the night in question."

Gerry gulps nervously, his throat dry. He knows this is the moment he must come clean about everything if he wants his later account to be taken seriously.

He takes a deep breath and begins to speak, his voice low and hesitant.

"My fiancée was having an affair," he starts, the words spilling out in a rush.

"With a married man. I vowed to track him down and make his life a living nightmare for messing up my perfect little life."

Carter's eyes narrow slightly.

"Ah, I see. So, you thought you'd get *revenge* on him?"

"Kind of," Gerry replies, nodding, his voice barely above a whisper.

He continues, his words tumbling out as he recounts his actions.

"While I was keeping tabs on my ex, I started noticing that his wife walked her dog along the same paths that I walked mine. At first, I thought it was just a coincidence, but I felt for her. I knew she was being cheated on by my fiancée. I felt responsible in some way."

Carter and Poker exchange glances, processing the revelation. Poker leans in slightly, his voice firm as he asks, "And who was your fiancée?"

Gerry's shoulders sag, and he looks down at his clasped hands.

"Rachel. Rachel Houston," he admits, the name hanging heavily in the room.

The atmosphere in the interview room shifts as the confession settles, each participant absorbing the weight of Gerry's words. The connection between the people involved becomes clear, adding an interesting layer to the case.

"Did you ever talk to Molly?" Carter asks, his tone is methodical as he seeks to understand the dynamics between everyone involved.

Gerry nods, his expression thoughtful.

"Yes, briefly. One day, we had a short conversation, but it was interrupted by her daughter, Lillie, I think. She had to leave because her husband was causing a scene. Molly looked so sad."

Carter nods, taking in the information.

"And how did you feel towards Molly?" he prompts, trying to delve deeper into Gerry's emotions.

Poker shifts slightly, his gaze fixed on Gerry, eager to understand the full picture.

"I started falling for her," Gerry admits, his voice tinged with a a mingling of regret and vulnerability.

"I would walk past her house in the evenings and hear the arguments coming from inside. Her husband was a bully, a complete asshole towards her."

Gerry's gaze drifts as he continues, his voice growing softer.

"I'd see her sitting on the rocks, looking out to sea. She always seemed so sad. Sometimes, I would hear her crying through the open window as I walked past with Duke. She was clearly in a very unhappy marriage."

The room is silent for a moment, Gerry's words settling over everyone present. The details paint a vivid picture of Molly's distress and Gerry's growing concern, adding depth to the investigation as they piece together the complexities of the relationships involved.

"Take us back to the night of the accident," Carter presses, his voice steady but insistent.

"What do you think Molly was doing up there on the rocks that night?"

Gerry closes his eyes momentarily, trying to collect his thoughts.

"I truly believe she was going to commit suicide," he says, his voice trembling.

"She was without Daisy, her dog. I had never seen her out and about without Daisy. And I could see she had been crying, too."

As he speaks, Gerry's emotions overwhelm him. He buries his face in his hands and begins to sob quietly, his shoulders shaking with the effort to control his tears.

"I just wanted to save her, to bring her back down, but she fell... Duke jumped up at her, and she fell."

Emily, sitting beside him, places a reassuring hand on Gerry's shoulder. Her touch seems to help him regain some composure.

He takes a few deep breaths, trying to steady himself before continuing.

Carter watches him closely, waiting for him to gather his thoughts.

"Tell me what happened next, Gerry," he prompts, his tone

CHAPTER 23

encouraging but firm.

"It all happened so fast," Gerry begins, his voice cracking as he recounts the events. "There were ambulances, police cars, an air ambulance. They found my Duke. He had drowned. I believe he tried to save Molly; he was loyal till the end." His voice trails off, the weight of the memory almost too much to bear.

Carter nods, acknowledging the weight of Gerry's words but urging him to continue. "Then what happened?" he asks, prompting Gerry to move forward in his narrative.

"I sat on the beach with Duke in my lap," Gerry says, his voice trembling.

"There was a really nice officer who said he would stay with Duke while I was getting checked out by the ambulance crew. I was in total shock."

Carter takes a deep breath, leaning forward slightly.

"Would it surprise you to know that I was the officer who sat with your dog that evening?" he drops the bombshell, his tone steady and deliberate.

Gerry leans back in his chair, squinting at Carter, trying to process the information. "I'm sorry," he says, his voice confused, "I don't recognise you from that night, so yes, it would surprise me."

Carter nods thoughtfully.

"I sat with your dog until the vets arrived to take him away," he confirms, his voice softening.

"I remember it was a very difficult night for everyone involved."

The revelation adds another layer to the interview, and Gerry's gaze lingers on Carter, grappling with the unexpected connection between them. The room is charged with brew of emotions as Carter's admission sinks in, and the atmosphere becomes even more charged with the weight of the night's events.

"Bloody hell," Gerry murmurs under his breath, the realisation hitting him hard.

"So it was you who started all this, then?" Gerry asks, his voice frustrated

Carter looks genuinely puzzled.

"I beg your pardon? Started all what?" he responds, clearly not understanding Gerry's implication.

"All of this nightmare," Gerry says, his frustration mounting. He glances at Emily, who shakes her head subtly, signalling him to hold back. Despite her warning, Gerry continues.

"You were the one, that evening, who referred to Molly as my wife," Gerry accuses. "You thought we were a couple and had just had an argument. After speaking to the drunk witnesses, you knew that I didn't push her," he pauses, his voice quivering with emotion.

"But you kept referring to her as my wife."

Poker turns to Carter, who is now sitting there, stunned and unable to recall the specific details of that night. The realisation that he may have contributed to the confusion adds a new layer of tension to the room.

Carter shifts uncomfortably, feeling the weight of the team's collective gaze from the office upstairs, where the live feed captures every moment.

"It was an assumption," he admits, his voice heavy with regret.

"One that, given the circumstances, I shouldn't have made. But it is in no way, by far, my fault, Gerry."

CHAPTER 23

The room remains charged with tension as Carter's admission hangs in the room. Gerry's frustration and the impact of the mistaken identity continue to resonate, complicating the already intricate web of the investigation.

"It was then, in the ambulance and later at the hospital," Gerry continues, his voice strained and emotional.

"They all called her my wife. They were asking me for all of her details. I was in a state of shock, in a panic. I didn't know what to say or do. I needed her to be seen and checked, so I gave them the details. I wasn't thinking straight; it was a matter of life and death. I had to register her at the reception in the ICU ward. She was rushed in and operated on."

Gerry takes a shaky breath, his eyes welling up with tears.

"I said I was her next of KIN. I knew her husband wouldn't be there for her—he wouldn't care. She was probably up on that wall because of another argument. I was just doing what anyone would have done in those circumstances."

His words are filled with compoud of desperation and justification. The gravity of the situation and the mistaken identity have weighed heavily on him, and he tries to explain his actions, hoping that the truth of his intentions will be understood.

"She was in a coma, and I visited her every day," Gerry continues, his voice cracking with emotion.

"I fell more and more in love with her. I wasn't even thinking about her family, especially when I saw her husband still carrying on with my fiancée. Molly was a missing woman, and her husband was happily having an affair instead of being out searching for her. It was as if Molly Chapman had been erased from the world, and there, lying in that hospital bed was a new woman—Mrs Elizabeth Penwald."

Gerry's eyes glisten with tears as he speaks, the weight of his feelings and the complexities of the situation evident in his voice. He looks up at Carter and Poker, hoping they understand the depth of his emotions and the unintended consequences of his actions.

"I think we will leave it there for a short while Gerry, let's all get a coffee and stretch our legs," says Carter.

"Interview terminated at 10.38 am. We will reconviene at 11am."

Chapter 24

Thursday Morning

Carter and Poker stand by the coffee machine, the hum of the appliance above their conversation about the unfolding interview.

"So, we've still got some points that we need to ask him about," Carter begins, stirring his coffee absentmindedly.

"But he doesn't come across as someone who would intentionally hurt Molly."

Poker nods thoughtfully.

"I don't think this is a malicious case. It seems more like someone trying to get back at another person, and in the process, he's fallen for the woman. It's a complex situation."

Carter agrees but adds a note of concern.

"But it's still coercion. He's made her believe she's someone she isn't. That's a serious issue."

Poker frowns, his frustration noticed.

"Yes, that may be the case, but we're all guilty to some extent—me, the ambulance crew, the hospital staff. We all contributed to the idea that Molly was his wife. He was just living up to the expectations set by everyone around him."

Carter sighs, running a hand through his hair.

"Jeez, Poker, he's still abducted her and took her to his home. He's continued to lie to her. She has children, for God's sake."

Carter stops and scratches his head, trying to piece together the tangled threads of the case.

"Yes, I know. I'm still trying to get my head around it. But what can we actually charge him with? Molly will have to be brought in as a witness against him, and I can see that turning into a complicated situation."

Poker shakes his head.

"I can see that one going tits up," he says with a resigned tone. The reality of the case, with its mix of emotional entanglements and legal complexities, hangs heavy between them as they try to navigate the best course of action.

Everyone files back into the interview room, visibly refreshed from the brief break. The mood is tense as Carter resumes his seat, pressing the record button to continue the interrogation.

Carter's voice cuts through the room with a professional tone.

"Who else knew that you were visiting Molly?" he asks, his gaze steady on Gerry.

Gerry shifts uncomfortably in his seat, his expression sombre.

"No one. My Mum had a stroke while I was at the hospital with Molly. So, I was juggling visits between Molly and my Mum at the same time. My Mum didn't know anything about it at the time," he emphasises, his voice strained.

"At the time?" Poker interjects, raising an eyebrow.

Gerry looks down, fidgeting with his hands.

CHAPTER 24

"I told her eventually," he admits, his voice cracking.

"The stress of it all became too much to bear. I couldn't keep it to myself any longer, so I blurted it all out to my Mum one day." His desperation is evident as he recounts the moment.

Carter notices Gerry's eyes welling up with tears, his composure visibly shaken. Deciding to avoid further distress, Carter shifts the line of questioning.

"Have you and Rachel had any further contact since you separated? We're trying to build a complete picture and understand what she was doing at your house when we arrested both of you."

Gerry wipes at his eyes, trying to regain his composure.

"No, we hadn't had any contact," he replies, his voice subdued.

"I hadn't seen or spoken to her at this time since we broke up."

The room falls silent as Carter and Poker exchange glances, weighing Gerry's responses. The complexity of the relationships and emotions involved makes the investigation all the more challenging.

Gerry's expression becomes contemplative as he continues.

"We met up once, at the college. Rachel had arranged for us to meet. She wanted to tell me she was having a hard time with her new boyfriend and that his wife had gone missing. She said she knew the missing woman." Gerry pauses, struggling to piece together the details.

"She was picked up by the police for questioning, and I was there when they arrived."

Poker's eyes widen in surprise.

"You were the man Rachel was with at the college?"

"Yes, that's right. Why?" Gerry responds confused.

"No particular reason," Poker replies, masking his surprise. The realisation that their main suspect was so close to being identified at that meeting is unsettling. Carter shoots Poker a cautionary look, signalling him to redirect the questioning.

Carter takes over, his tone shifting to a more pressing note.

"So, what made you move house? There's only been one confirmed sighting of you and Molly, and that was at the hotel where you did a photography shoot for a wedding. Were you trying to conceal Molly from the outside world? Is that why you left the house you rented next door to Mrs Easton? Was your lie spiralling out of control to the point where you had to hide Molly away?"

Gerry shifts uncomfortably in his chair, clearly troubled by the line of questioning.

"It wasn't like that," he starts, trying to maintain his composure.

"The move was necessary for other reasons. We wanted a fresh start, and the new place was more suitable for me and Molly—Elizabeth. I didn't want to hide her away; I just wanted to keep her safe and start over."

Carter and Poker exchange looks, noting the tension in Gerry's voice and the contradictions in his story. The investigation is clearly more tangled than they anticipated, and the implications of Gerry's actions are becoming increasingly complex.

Carter leans in slightly, his gaze fixed on Gerry.

"But why the rush? Why the sudden decision to pack up everything and move?"

Gerry's face tightens as he struggles to find the right words.

CHAPTER 24

"My Mum passed away," he explains, his voice tinged with sadness.

"She left us the house in her will."

Carter raises an eyebrow.

"Left us? Who is '*us*'?"

Gerry looks pained, searching for the right way to explain.

"Me and Elizabeth—Molly. Oh, what do I even call her now?" he falters, clearly distressed.

Carter offers a reassuring nod.

"Her name is Molly. Why would your Mum leave the house to you and Molly?"

Gerry swallows hard, trying to steady his emotions.

"When I confided in my Mum about everything, she knew how much I loved Molly. She understood how much I wanted to look after her. It was a shock to me, just as much as it is to you. It was a very generous gesture, but it came from a place of love, not from any other reason."

Carter and Poker exchange glances, noting the emotional weight behind Gerry's words, questions still loom about Gerry's motivations and the truth behind his actions.

Poker leans forward, his eyes narrowing.

"So explain what Rachel was doing at your home?"

Gerry's face grows more strained as he tries to recall the details.

"Rachel had brought some flowers over for my Mum, not knowing she had passed away. Molly answered the door, and when I heard who was at the door, I panicked. I intervened and got to Rachel before she could say anything to Molly."

He pauses, collecting his thoughts.

"Rachel is an innocent party in all of this. She didn't know anything about the situation with Molly. She was shocked to see me with her, and honestly, I don't think she would be able to fully comprehend what's been going on."

Poker nods, making notes as he processes Gerry's explanation. Carter, however, remains sceptical and continues to probe.

"Rachel's visit was just a coincidence then?" Carter asks, his tone still probing.

"Yes, it was purely coincidental," Gerry confirms, his voice earnest.

"Rachel had no idea what was really happening. I tried to shield her from the situation as best as I could. She was only there to see my Mother, and she ended up stumbling into a much more complicated scenario than she could have imagined."

The room falls into a contemplative silence as Carter and Poker weigh Gerry's answers. The interview's complexity deepens with each new revelation.

Carter narrows his eyes, clearly intent on digging deeper.

"So Gerry, can you enlighten us on how you managed to maintain this fabrication? Surely Molly has asked questions about her family, friends, children, and so on."

Gerry looks down, his shoulders slumping as he wrestles with his guilt.

"Don't misunderstand me," he begins, his voice trembling.

"I've felt an immense amount of guilt since bringing her home from the hospital. But Molly is such a sweet, fragile person. She had lost her memory and had no one else to trust in the world but me. It was, dare I say it, surprisingly easy to 'deceive' her."

He twiddles his thumbs anxiously, his head hanging low as he speaks.

CHAPTER 24

"Molly trusted me implicitly. I told her what I thought she needed to hear to feel safe and secure. She was disoriented and vulnerable, and it was like she was searching for something familiar and comforting. I just… I just went along with it, even though I knew it was wrong. Every day I was confronted with the weight of my actions, but I convinced myself that I was helping her, that I was protecting her from a harsh reality she wasn't ready to face."

Gerry's voice cracks as he continues, "It was a terrible mistake, and I realise now how deeply I've wronged her and her family. I'm sick with guilt over what I've done. It's one thing to deceive someone, but to do it to someone so vulnerable—it's unbearable."

"OK, Gerry," Carter says, his tone softer now.

"I think we can leave it there for today. You've been extremely forthright, and we appreciate your cooperation. As you can imagine, this is a complex case, and I'll need to discuss it with my superior."

He turns to the recording device.

"Interview suspended at 12:15 p.m."

Gerry lets out a long sigh, the weight of the conversation visibly lifting from his shoulders. He spreads his arms across the table and rests his head down, the exhaustion and guilt etched into his posture.

Emily, sitting beside him, gently pats him on the back, offering a reassuring gesture. Her touch is meant to comfort him, acknowledging the emotional toll of the interview while remaining silent. Gerry appreciates the small gesture of support, feeling a flicker of solace amidst the turmoil.

"Can I go outside for some fresh air now, please?" Gerry asks Emily, his voice strained.

"Yes, of course," she responds warmly.

"I'll take you out if you like."

"Please, that would be nice. Thank you," Gerry replies, a hint of relief in his voice.

The two of them stand, and Poker and Carter head out of the interview room first, arms loaded with folders and files.

Outside the room, the four of them part ways: Carter and Poker head back to the office to debrief with the rest of the team, while Gerry and Emily walk toward the small, enclosed yard.

Stepping outside, Gerry feels the warmth of the sun on his face. He tilts his head back, closing his eyes for a moment as he breathes in the fresh air, watching the clouds slowly drifting across the sky.

Emily breaks the silence.

"You did so well in there, Gerry."

"Thanks," Gerry mutters.

"It didn't feel like it. I felt like a complete dick for what I've been doing to Molly." His voice trembles with guilt and remorse.

Emily places a comforting hand on his shoulder.

"It will all be over soon enough. I just need to make sure you end up on that side of the wall and not this side," she says, nodding toward the high brick wall surrounding the yard.

Gerry glances at the wall, understanding her meaning.

"Yeah," he sighs.

"I hope so."

Emily gives him a reassuring smile, though her eyes remain cautious.

"One step at a time, Gerry. We'll get through this."

CHAPTER 24

* * *

Thursday Afternoon

A woman appears at the reception desk of the police station. She is tall, with long, flowing blonde hair and stunning blue eyes that seem to catch the light. As she approaches, PC Johnson, the officer on duty, looks up from his desk and offers a polite smile.

"Hello, I would like to see PC Carter, please," the woman says, her voice steady but urgent.

"What is the nature of your visit?" PC Johnson asks, noticing the intensity in her gaze.

"I would like to make a confession," she replies, brushing her hair out of her eyes, and revealing a face marked by both beauty and a hint of distress.

"A confession?" PC Johnson repeats, surprised.

"We don't advise making a confession without your solicitor present. It's for your own protection."

The woman nods, her expression resolute.

"I understand. But I need to speak with PC Carter."

PC Johnson picks up his phone, preparing to call Carter, but first, he asks, "May I have your name, please?"

She hesitates for a moment, then says softly, "My name is Molly Chapman."

PC Johnson's eyes widen in recognition.

"Alright, Miss Chapman. Please have a seat, and I'll get hold of PC Carter for you right away." He quickly dials Carter's extension, knowing that this is about to take a significant turn.

Gilbert walks in behind Molly, her footsteps echoing slightly in the quiet reception area after she parks the car. She stands close behind her, her presence steady and reassuring.

"Have they phoned through to him yet?" Gilbert asks.

PC Johnson, still on the phone, glances up at her and nods.

"They're doing it now," Molly says.

Gilbert watches Molly carefully as she shifts her weight from one foot to the other.

Molly takes a deep breath, her fingers fidgeting slightly at her sides.

"Good," she murmurs, more to herself than anyone else.

Gilbert places a gentle hand on her shoulder, offering silent support.

They both know that the next few moments could change everything.

***

Lambert returns from the evidence room, carrying Molly's diary. She places it on the desk and begins to flip through the pages marked with brightly coloured Post-it notes. Each note marks a painful entry where Molly documented her experiences as a victim of emotional abuse. Her handwriting reveals a story of enduring manipulation and torment.

Lambert stops on a particular page, the corner creased and the ink slightly smudged from where her tears might have once fallen. She clears her throat, the room growing quiet as everyone waits to hear the words that Molly wrote in her darkest moments.

"She writes about his anger," Lambert begins, her voice steady but sombre.

CHAPTER 24

"How he would twist her words until she doubted herself. 'He says I'm too sensitive,'" she reads, "'that I'm imagining things. But I know what I heard. I know what he did. He tells me I'm losing my mind, but I'm not. I see him for what he is—a master at turning the truth into lies.'"

Lambert pauses, letting the gravity of the words sink in.

"She goes on to describe how he would gaslight her," she continues, "making her question her own reality, her own sanity. 'Every day feels like a battle for my own mind,' she wrote. 'He acts like he's the victim, but it's me who is being slowly erased.'"

The room is silent, filled with the weight of Molly's suffering. Lambert carefully closes the diary, her expression serious.

"These diaries paint a very clear picture of what she was going through," she says softly, "and they show just how calculated her husband's abuse was. We need to keep this in mind as we move forward with her statement."

Chapter 25

Thursday Afternoon

"Look, here is another entry." Lambert holds the book open for the rest of the team to read the diary entrance.

23rd of October
Dear Diary,
When life seemed overwhelmingly miserable and desperate, I stormed out of the house this afternoon. Ray's early return from work, demanding the loo, clashed with Oliver's bath time, leading to a demeaning exchange.
I couldn't bear another argument in front of the children, so immaturely, I left.
Perched on the sea wall, lost in my own world, anticipating the usual breathtaking sunset, a beautiful dog—reminiscent of my Daisy—approached and showered me with affection.
Surprisingly, it belonged to the man I often saw

CHAPTER 25

> *during our walks. Though our conversation was brief, I felt an odd sense of familiarity. Perhaps it was from our walks, but there's something about him. I can't put my finger on it, but his presence exudes calmness, and I sense understanding.*
>
> *It's not about contemplating an affair; I would end my marriage first. Yet, I couldn't deny a connection.*
>
> *Well, that's enough for tonight.*
>
> *TTFN,*
>
> *Molls xx*

The team sits in stunned silence. Lambert closes the diary slowly, the soft thud echoing in the otherwise quiet room.

"This diary entry alone paints a vivid picture of the cruel life she was enduring with Ray," Lambert says, her voice filled with a unity of sympathy and frustration.

"It's clear she was trapped in a cycle of emotional abuse. But there's more. She writes about her growing feelings for someone else, someone she found herself drawn to amidst all the chaos."

"The evidence is all here," she says.

"Molly was not just a victim; she was also desperately searching for an escape, for a sense of peace and affection that she wasn't getting at home. It's clear she was emotionally torn, caught between her fear of Ray and her feelings for someone else."

Carter leans back in his chair, processing the information.

"So, she was already looking for a way out," he muses.

"That explains a lot. The whole situation with Gerry… maybe she saw him as her way to escape from Ray."

Poker nods, deep in thought.

"It makes sense," he agrees.

"She wasn't in her right mind, not fully. She was looking for something, anything, that would make her feel less trapped."

The team exchanges glances, each of them contemplating the implications of Molly's diary. They know they have a complicated road ahead, one that will require careful handling of Molly's fragile state and a deeper investigation into Ray's behaviour.

"We need to dig deeper," Carter finally says.

"Into Ray, into their marriage, and into what happened between Molly and Gerry. This case isn't as clear-cut as it seemed."

Lambert nods.

"Agreed. Let's make sure we get it right—for Molly's sake."

* * *

Carter immediately snaps his attention to Gilbert, the urgency in her voice cutting through the thick atmosphere in the room. He straightens up, pushing the diary to the side.

"Molly Chapman is here? Right now?" he asks, his surprise evident

Gilbert nods quickly.

"Yes, she's downstairs in the reception area. She asked for you specifically. Said she wants to make a confession."

The room goes silent, everyone exchanging glances filled with confusion and curiosity. "A confession?" Carter repeats, trying to make sense of it.

"What could she possibly want to confess?"

Gilbert shakes her head, her excitement barely contained.

CHAPTER 25

"I'm not saying a word, but she is determined. This will be a game-changer, Carter. We need to go now."

Without wasting another second, Carter grabs his notepad and pen, shoving them into his pocket. He looks over at Poker.

"Stay here and keep going through the evidence. We need to know everything about her mindset, especially if she's about to drop some kind of bombshell on us."

Poker nods, eyes still on the diary, as Carter and Gilbert make a swift exit from the room. They move quickly down the corridor, Carter's mind racing with possibilities.

Why would Molly come here of her own accord? And what could she possibly want to confess that would need his immediate attention?

As they approach the reception area, Carter spots Molly sitting on one of the seats, looking a brew of nervous and resolute. Her long blonde hair falls around her shoulders, and her stunning blue eyes are fixed on the floor, but they snap up to meet his as he enters the foyer.

"Molly," Carter says gently as he approaches her. "You wanted to speak with me?"

Molly nods, standing up slowly.

"Yes," she says quietly, her voice steady but filled with emotion.

"I need to tell you something. About what happened... and about Gerry."

Carter exchanges a quick glance with Gilbert, who nods encouragingly. He turns back to Molly, his tone soft but firm.

"OK, let's go somewhere more private to talk. We'll get you a room, and you can tell me everything."

Molly takes a deep breath and nods again.

"Thank you," she whispers, and as Carter leads her away from the reception area, he can't shake the feeling that whatever Molly is about to reveal could change everything they thought they knew about this case.

* * *

Bonnie's gaze drifts out the classroom window, her mind wandering far from the droning monotony of her Maths lesson. She often daydreams about her Mum, especially when the subject matter fails to capture her interest.

Today is no different, and she finds herself lost in thoughts of her mother's comforting presence.

The whispers and sniggers of the girls seated behind her begin to seep into her awareness. Bonnie's attention is momentarily drawn back to her surroundings as she feels bits of crumpled graph paper hitting her hair. She turns, irritation flaring in her eyes as she sees the three girls behind her, their faces contorted into smirks of mischievous delight. The paper continues to land in her hair, and she pulls the pieces out with an annoyed flick.

Bonnie's usual seatmate, Amelia, is absent today due to a sickness bug, leaving Bonnie feeling more isolated than usual. She fumbles with her phone under the desk, trying to distract herself by sending a text to Amelia about how dull the lesson is without her friend.

Suddenly, a sharp, hard object strikes the back of Bonnie's head. Startled, she turns around, her eyes scanning the floor to see a pencil sharpener lying there, having been thrown at her.

The once manageable irritation in her chest boils over into

CHAPTER 25

anger.

Without a second thought, Bonnie stands up abruptly, her chair scraping loudly against the floor. She moves swiftly, leaning over the desk that separates her from the trio of girls behind her. With a fierce determination, she grabs the girl in the middle by the collar, her fingers tightening around the girl's throat. Bonnie's face is contorted into a fierce scowl as she shoves it close to the girl's face, her voice a harsh whisper filled with venom.

"You think it's funny to throw things at me?" Bonnie hisses, her voice low but seething with anger.

"Try it again, and you'll fucking regret it."

The girl's eyes widen in fear as she struggles to pull away, her face a mask of shock and distress. The classroom falls into a stunned silence, all eyes fixed on Bonnie and the girl.

"Don't you ever fucking touch me again, or I swear I'll make you regret it!" Bonnie snarls, her voice trembling with a mixture of rage and desperation. The girl's face pales, her eyes widening with fear and humiliation as she quickly raises her hands defensively, trying to signal a truce.

Bonnie's grip loosens, but she doesn't fully release the girl until she sees her nodding frantically and muttering an apology. The girl's shirt and tie are now askew, the collar twisted and crumpled from Bonnie's tight hold.

As Bonnie steps back, her breathing heavy and uneven, the classroom is engulfed in a stunned silence. Every student in the room stares wide-eyed, some with open mouths, others frozen in their seats.

Mrs Kastrova, who has been watching the scene unfold from her desk, stands up abruptly. Her face is a stir of shock and stern disapproval.

"Bonnie Chapman, gather your belongings and go sit outside the headteacher's office. NOW!" she commands, her voice booming across the room. Her authoritative tone leaves no room for argument.

Bonnie, her anger still simmering beneath the surface, collects her things in a hurried but controlled manner. Her cheeks are flushed, and she casts one last glare at the girl before storming out of the classroom. As she exits, the room remains eerily silent, the students whispering amongst themselves.

* * *

Ray pushes open the heavy doors of the school and makes his way to the headteacher's office. Mrs Kastrova, seated behind her desk, gestures toward Bonnie, who stands near the door, her eyes red and defiant. The meeting is brief but tense. Mrs Kastrova explains the situation: Bonnie is suspended pending further review, and Ray takes Bonnie into his care.

As they step out of the school, Ray's frustration boils over. The car park feels unusually quiet as he marches toward the car, Bonnie trailing behind him, her shoulders slumped. Once inside, Ray's temper erupts.

"What in the hell were you thinking, Bonnie?" he roars, his voice echoing off the car's interior.

"Attacking a girl like that, in front of the whole damned class!"

Bonnie's eyes flash with anger and frustration.

"For God's sake, Dad, she was throwing things in my hair and goading me the entire lesson. I lost it."

Ray's face turns a deep shade of red.

CHAPTER 25

"You watch your lip, young lady. You're not too old for a slap to straighten you out. Just shut up, will you?"

Bonnie's anger boils over.

"Well, they can't suspend me based on what I did," she mutters under her breath, barely concealing her bitterness.

Ray's face tightens.

"Are you joking? You grabbed a girl by the throat and threatened her in front of thirty-odd witnesses. Of course, you're going to get suspended!" He huffs.

Bonnie collapses into the passenger seat, slamming her seatbelt into place with a sense of resignation.

"I wish I'd actually fucking slapped her," she grumbles, her voice barely audible.

Ray's reaction is immediate and harsh. His hand snaps out, connecting sharply with Bonnie's cheek. The sting of the slap is instantaneous, like a wasp's bite, leaving a bright red mark and a lingering sting. The force of it causes Bonnie to recoil slightly, and a thin line of drool escapes from her mouth, smearing Ray's hand. He wipes it off on his jeans, his anger undiminished.

"I fucking told you to shut up," Ray growls.

Bonnie sits in stunned silence for the rest of the drive home. Her eyes remain fixed on the window, her mind a chaotic whirl of emotions. The sting on her cheek is a sharp, physical reminder of her father's rage, but it's the deeper ache of feeling misunderstood and isolated that cuts the deepest.

She's too upset to cry, her frustration simmering beneath the surface.

As they pull into the driveway, Bonnie feels a wave of resentment and sadness. She hates her father's unpredictability and harshness.

More than anything, she misses her mother's comforting presence, wishing she could be there to offer her some semblance of solace and understanding.

As each child processes their own experiences and the fragmented truths of their family, they slowly come to understand the reasons behind their mother's disappearance. The realisation that their mother's escape was not an act of abandonment but a desperate attempt to flee from an unrelenting nightmare reshapes their perspectives, allowing them to see their mother's actions through a lens of painful clarity.

As soon as Bonnie slams the front door behind her, the familiar thud reverberates through the empty house, marking the beginning of her desperate escape from the chaos. She kicks off her shoes in the porch and races up the stairs, her heart pounding with a combine of anger and sorrow.

Bursting into her bedroom, she collapses onto her bed and buries her face in the pillows, her sobs muffled by the fabric. The sting of her father's slap, and the unbearable tension of home life come crashing down on her all at once.

Eventually, her tears subside, leaving her exhausted and hollow. Bonnie shifts to sit up and, through her puffy eyes, catches a glimpse of her reflection in the mirror. The hand-shaped bruise on her cheek is a harsh reminder of her father's violence, and it fills her with a deep, seething hatred for the man who should have protected her instead of causing her pain.

Determined and numb, Bonnie scrambles under her bed and retrieves a large holdall, the same one she had used to pack their belongings during their previous stay at Uncle

CHAPTER 25

Reggie's. She moves methodically, collecting enough clothes to last her and her siblings until at least Sunday. She's relieved that she won't have to face school the next day.

Bonnie's task becomes more urgent as she heads to Oliver's room, gathering his weekend clothes and a fresh set for school, placing them carefully into the holdall. The reality of their situation weighs on her as she moves next to Lillie's room. Without pausing to inspect what she's packing, she stuffs some of Lillie's clothes into the bag, along with the comfort items that are vital to each child's sense of security. She retrieves Lillie's cherished blankie, Oliver's monkey, and places them gently into the bag, knowing they will provide comfort during this horrible time. With the holdall nearly full, Bonnie locates a rucksack in Lillie's room and adds it to her collection. The rucksack, along with the holdall, provides ample space for everything they might need.

Bonnie takes a deep breath, her mind racing with what to do next.

As Bonnie closes the rucksack and takes one last look around her room, the reality of their situation settles in. She feels a combination of fear and resolve, knowing that this is just the beginning of a journey toward finding a place where they can be safe and cared for. Bonnie takes a deep breath as she finishes packing the last of their belongings. She grabs her phone, her fingers trembling slightly as she types out a message to her Uncle Reggie, her hope pinned on his response.

»2:27p.m: Hi Uncle Reggie, I've been suspended from school today because I got into a fight. Dad picked me up and, well, he didn't take it well. He slapped me for speaking back. I've packed our bags and we're ready for

you to pick us up. PLEASE still come and get us. We really need you. xx

Her heart pounds as she hits send, and she watches the message bubble appear and disappear.

Bonnie sits on the edge of her bed, trying to steady her breathing, her mind racing through what might come next. She hopes her uncle will see her message and come through for them, as he has in the past. The thought of finally escaping their disjointed home and finding safety with Uncle Reggie and Auntie Yvonne offers her a sliver of hope.

Chapter 26

Thursday Afternoon

The interview room feels cold and sterile to Molly, its stark white walls and metal table far from anything she finds comforting. She sits down, her hands nervously gripping the edge of her chair. Gilbert, her support throughout this ordeal, takes the seat beside her.

"Are you sure you want me to stay?" Gilbert asks, her voice soft and reassuring, her concern evident in her eyes.

"Yes, of course," Molly replies, her voice firm but a bit shaky. "You've been with me since all of this started. I want you here."

Carter, seated across from them, leans forward slightly.

"Are you sure you don't want a solicitor, Molly? This is a really complex case, and I would highly recommend having legal representation. It's for your own protection."

"Am I under arrest officer?" she asks.

"No, of course not," he answers

Molly shakes her head.

"Then no, I'm fine, thank you, officer. I just want to get this over with."

Carter nods, respecting her decision.

"Alright, but I need to inform you that this interview is being recorded. Are you OK with that?"

Molly's eyes flicker to the camera mounted in the corner, its red light blinking steadily, a constant reminder of the eyes watching her from the offices upstairs. She swallows hard and asks, "Do you mean just audio recording or is there a video link to the rest of the team as well?"

"Both, if that's alright with you," Carter confirms, watching her closely for any sign of discomfort.

A shiver runs down Molly's spine, but she quickly regains her composure. She knows why she's here and what she needs to do.

"Do whatever you need to do," she says, her voice steadying as if steeling herself for what's to come.

Carter reaches over and presses the button on the recorder, which emits a small beep, signalling the start of the recording.

"This is a voluntary interview requested by Molly Chapman," Carter states clearly for the record. He glances at Molly, offering a slight nod of encouragement.

"Let's begin."

* * *

"Mrs Chapman, you have come to me because you want to confess something?" Carter asks, his voice calm yet firm, cutting through the sterile silence of the interview room.

I glance at him, momentarily distracted by his striking features. He's a handsome man, with a chiselled chin and dark, intense eyes that seem to pierce right through you. On the few occasions I've seen him, I've wondered if he

CHAPTER 26

might have been a model in a previous career, someone who effortlessly drew attention wherever he went.

"Mrs Chapman?" Carter repeats, his voice deeper this time, pulling me back to the present.

I blink, snapping out of my thoughts.

I need to focus.

The CCTV-style camera positioned directly above me is a stark reminder that this moment is being recorded, and scrutinized.

I can't help but wonder who's watching on the other end.

Is Chase there, his eyes fixed on the screen, waiting to see what I'll say next?

"Mrs Chapman, are you alright? Can I get you a glass of water?" Carter's voice softens, his concern showing through.

Despite the cold, impersonal setting of the room, his tone brings a surprising warmth.

"Thank you, no. I'm fine," I manage to say, trying to muster as much composure as I can.

I take a deep breath and look him straight in the eye, trying to steady my nerves.

"I would like to confess to withholding crucial information about this case," I say, each word measured, aware of the heaviness of my admission.

"Withholding crucial information? What information have you withheld from us, Mrs Chapman?" Carter leans forward slightly, settling into his seat, his curiosity clearly piqued.

I catch a whiff of his aftershave—sandalwood and soft musk. It's subtle but alluring, a scent that distracts me for a moment.

"Mrs Chapman?" he prompts again, his voice breaking through my thoughts.

"Please, call me Molly," I reply, a hint of a smile tugging at my lips.

"After all, that is my name, isn't it?" I glance up at the camera, my smile widening for a brief moment as if challenging whoever is on the other side.

"Molly," Carter says, pausing to gauge my expression.

"What have you withheld?" His tone is gentle but persistent.

I take a deep breath, carefully choosing my words.

"I have withheld all knowledge of who I am."

Carter furrows his brow, clearly confused.

"Please explain. I don't think I quite follow."

"On the 9th of November, two weeks after my accident, I woke up from a coma," I begin, my voice steady but laced with the weight of what I am about to reveal.

I can see the confusion etched on his face, the uncertainty in his eyes. He's trying to piece it all together, trying to understand where I'm going with this.

I glance over at Gilbert, who sits beside me. She offers a small, encouraging smile and nods, urging me to keep going. Her quiet reassurance is a comfort, a silent reminder that I'm not alone in this room, even if my story is one that no one else can fully understand.

Carter's expression shifts slightly, a flicker of anticipation crossing his face. He's expecting my version of events to mirror Gerry's, to be just another chapter in a twisted story he thinks he already knows.

But he's wrong.

Very wrong.

My version of events is not just a variation of the truth—it's a completely different story altogether.

CHAPTER 26

One that Gerry doesn't know, that no one could possibly expect.

It's a story of deceit, of survival, of a woman trapped in a nightmare and the choices she made to escape it.

"Go on," Carter instructs, his tone firm but not unkind, as he senses that what I have to say could change everything.

I take a deep breath, ready to dismantle the assumptions, ready to lay bare the reality that's been hidden for too long.

"When I woke up, I had forgotten everything, every detail about my life before the fall. But then later on I started to remember things. But I chose to pretend that I didn't. I pretended because… it was the only way I could keep myself safe from Ray."

Carter's eyes widen slightly, but he says nothing, waiting for me to continue. He knows better than to interrupt now.

"I didn't lose my memory as bad as they thought in the accident," I continue.

"I pretended to because I needed an escape. I needed a way out of the life I was living, away from Ray, away from the control, the manipulation, the fear. Gerry was my ticket to freedom.

He thought he was saving me, but really, I was using him to save myself."

Carter leans back in his chair, clearly taken aback by my admission.

"So, you haven't lost your memory?"

"No," I say, shaking my head.

"I played along with Gerry's delusion because it gave me a way out, a new identity, a chance to be someone else, even if just for a little while. And in that moment, being someone else felt like the only way to survive."

"So you knew who you were from when?" Carter quizzes

I lean back in my chair, feeling the weight of the truth pressing down on me.

"I've known for a long time who I am, Officer Carter. I never lost my memory completely. I remember everything— my name, my life, my family. I remember the arguments with Ray, and the nights I spent crying myself to sleep. I knew exactly who I was, even when I was with Gerry. I let him believe I had forgotten, let him think he could start over with me because, for a while, I wanted to forget. I wanted to be someone else, someone without the pain, without the memories."

Carter's eyes widen, absorbing my confession.

"So, you were aware nearly the entire time?" he asks, his voice now laced with disbelief and understanding.

"Yes," I admit. "I played along. And by doing so, I withheld the truth about my identity— from everyone. I knew exactly who I was, but I didn't want to be her anymore."

There, I have said it.

I've admitted it.

My heart pounds in my chest, each beat feeling like a hammer against my ribs. I'm terrified that I might have a heart attack from the sheer weight of my confession, but I can't let that stop me now. I've carried this burden for so long, and I need to lay it down.

I take a deep breath, forcing myself to stay composed, to push through the fear and anxiety that's threatening to overwhelm me.

"I remember everything, Carter. I remember waking up in that hospital room and seeing Gerry. I remember recognizing him eventually. I pretended not to know, but I

CHAPTER 26

knew. I knew everything."

Carter's eyes narrow, but he stays silent, giving me the space I need to continue.

"I played along because I didn't know what else to do," I admit, my voice wavering but determined.

"I was scared and confused, and the truth is, a part of me wanted to escape my old life. I saw an opportunity in Gerry, an opportunity to be free from Ray, from everything. But now, I realize that running away wasn't the answer. I've been hiding behind this lie for too long, and it's time to face the truth."

I take another breath, feeling a mix of relief and fear washing over me.

"That's why I'm here, Carter. I need to tell you everything. I need to tell you the truth about what happened and why I did what I did."

"Molly can you give me a moment I need to step out and speak to my superior about this case, this is extremely complex and I need to make sure it heads in the right direction."

"Of course," I reply.

"But please, can Gilbert stay with me," I ask.

"If that is what you want then of course she can stay with you," he answers.

"Can I get you a drink, tea, coffee, water?" he offers.

"I would love a strong coffee please, no sugar, just milk."

"I won't be long," he says.

As Carter leaves the room, I feel a wave of relief mixed with nervous anticipation. The silence that follows is thick, and I can hear the faint hum of the fluorescent lights overhead. My hands tremble slightly, and I clasp them together in my lap to steady them.

Gilbert shifts in her seat next to me, turning slightly so she can look directly at me. "You're doing great, Molly," she says softly, her voice full of encouragement.

"Just stay calm and focus on what you need to say."

I nod, trying to absorb her words and calm my racing heart.

"Thank you, Gilbert. I don't know what I would do without you right now."

We sit in silence for a few moments.

I glance up at the camera, its little red light blinking steadily, a reminder that everything I say and do is being watched, recorded, and scrutinized. It makes me uneasy, but I know this is necessary.

I have to see this through.

After what feels like an eternity but is probably only a few minutes, Carter returns, holding a steaming cup of coffee. He hands it to me with a small smile. "Here you go, just as you asked. Strong coffee, no sugar, just milk."

"Thank you," I replied, wrapping my hands around the warm cup. The heat seeps into my fingers, providing a small comfort amid the tension.

Carter sits down across from me, his expression serious.

"Alright, Molly," he begins, "I've spoken with my superior, and we both agree that this is indeed a very complicated situation. We're going to need to go over everything very carefully. Are you ready to continue?"

I take a sip of the coffee, letting its warmth spread through me, giving me the courage to nod.

"Yes, I'm ready," I say, my voice steady.

"I want to tell you everything."

CHAPTER 26

* * *

The team huddles around the monitor, their eyes glued to the screen. The room is filled with tension. No one dares to speak as Molly's revelation sinks in, each word echoing in their minds. It's a game-changer, and everyone knows it.

Lambert is the first to break the silence.

"You all heard that, right? This changes everything."

Poker, still staring at the screen, nods slowly.

"Yeah, and you know what this means now, don't you?" His voice is low, almost hesitant as if he's reluctant to say the words out loud.

Lambert sighs heavily, leaning back in her chair.

"Yes, Poker, I think we all have a pretty good idea of what you're about to say."

Poker takes a deep breath, preparing himself for what comes next.

"We're going to have to release Gerry," he finally announces.

Lambert rolls her eyes slightly, frustration and resignation on her face.

"Yep, I figured that's where you were going with this."

Sharpie, who has been quietly observing, chimes in.

"We have no grounds to hold him anymore. There's no crime here—at least not in the way we thought. Not unless Carter can get more out of Molly, especially about that night they left the hospital."

The team exchanges uneasy glances, understanding the force of the situation. They've been so sure, but now everything seems uncertain.

"Let's just see where this interview takes us," Sharpie adds, his voice filled with anticipation.

All eyes turn back to the monitor. The screen shows Carter sitting across from Molly, his posture calm but focused. The room is silent except for the faint hum of the recording equipment and the soft rustling of papers as Carter prepares for his next question.

The tension builds as Carter leans forward, his voice steady and probing.

"Molly, can you tell me who *you were* the night you left the hospital?"

The team's breath catches, each member waiting with bated breath for Molly's response, knowing that her answer could change the course of the entire investigation.

Molly takes a deep breath before she answers, steadying herself.

"I was myself. I left that hospital as Molly Chapman, but I was pretending to be Elizabeth Penwald. I left weeks fully knowing who I was."

The room upstairs falls into stunned silence. Poker is the first to react, slumping back in his chair with a groan.

"Damn, and there you have it," he mutters under his breath. "He's off the hook."

Lambert, still chewing on her BLT sandwich, nods slowly.

"He was innocent all along, really. Or was he? This case is more tangled than a bowl of spaghetti." She takes another bite, clearly frustrated with how things have unfolded.

Poker shakes his head in frustration.

"We should do her for wasting police time. Think of the hours we've poured into this case, running in circles," he grumbles.

Lambert, swallowing her bite, quickly retorts, "You can't

CHAPTER 26

charge her with that. Not with the state of her mental health over these past few months. She's clearly been through hell, and it's not like she did it on purpose."

Her tone is firm, despite the food still in her mouth, as she defends Molly.

Back in the interview room, Carter presses on, unfazed by the twists and turns.

"And the flashbacks, Molly—were they fabricated? Did you use them to make this all look more believable?" His voice is calm but probing, every word carefully chosen.

Molly shakes her head, her expression earnest.

"No, they're as real as you sitting there in front of me now. They're horrible, and I believe they're a symptom of the brain injury I sustained. I didn't make them up—they haunt me."

The team watches the monitor closely, some nodding in understanding while others remain sceptical.

"Molly, I need you to take us back to that night. Tell us everything that happened." Carter says.

Molly's gaze drops to the table as she takes a deep breath.

"I had a huge row with Ray. It was worse than usual—he hit me. I stumbled backwards and hit my back on the kitchen worktop."

She pauses, her hands trembling slightly as she recalls the events. "I went upstairs and changed, my mind spinning with dark thoughts. I wanted it all to end—the pain, the fear, the constant feeling of being worthless. I just wanted to be free of it all, even if it meant... ending my life."

Molly takes a sip of her coffee.

"I left the house that night, walked away from my children, from my life and my beloved dog Daisy. I climbed up onto the sea wall, I remember thinking how easy it would be to just let go, to let the sea take me."

Tears stream down Molly's face.

"I stood there, waiting for the waves to crash over. I wanted to drown. I wanted it all to end. But then… Gerry appeared. He was, like some kind of knight in shining armour, coming to save me."

She lets out a shaky breath.

"I tried to wave him away, to tell him to go back because the rocks were wet and slippery, and I didn't want him to get hurt. But his dog, Duke… Duke thought I was waving to him, and he came bounding toward me. It all happened so fast. One minute I was standing on the wall, and the next, I was falling into the sea."

The room is silent. Molly's voice drops to a whisper, choked with emotion.

"Duke found me. He swam out to me and stayed by my side. I clung to his fur and tried to hold on as he swam against the waves, but he was so heavy. I could feel him struggling, and then… I felt him slip away from my fingers. It was the worst feeling I've ever experienced. Watching him disappear, knowing I couldn't hold on any longer."

Molly covers her face with her hands, sobbing softly.

"I couldn't admit to any of this. I felt so weak, so… inhumane. I didn't want anyone to know how close I came to giving up. How much I wanted to end it all."

Carter sits back, letting her words sink in, the gravity of her confession clear on his face.

"We will conclude this interview once I've had a meeting with my team to see where we can go from here." Says Carter, is there anything we can do for you in the meantime Molly?

"Yes, when can I see my husband…" she asks.

CHAPTER 26

"Ray?" asks Carter shocked.
"No. Gerry."

Chapter 27

Thursday Late Afternoon

Reggie pulls up to his usual parking spot just outside the Chapman household. All the lights in the house are blazing, casting a warm glow that contrasts sharply with the cold, dark night outside. The brightness reminds Reggie of the "Blackpool Illuminations," a stark contrast to the tension he feels creeping up his spine.

He parks the car, takes a deep breath, and steps out onto the driveway. Making his way up to the front door, he hesitates for a moment, remembering the last time he was here. He had sworn he would never set foot in this house again after Ray had screamed at him to get out, but Yvonne had persuaded him otherwise.

"It's for the children," she had said, and that was reason enough for him.

Reggie reaches out and rings the 'Ring' doorbell, then instinctively turns his back to the camera. He knows Ray might be watching, and he doesn't want to give his brother-in-law any reason to be suspicious or more agitated than usual.

CHAPTER 27

To his surprise, it's Lillie who opens the door. Her face lights up when she sees him, and she quickly steps aside, waving him in.

"Uncle Reggie! Come on in," she says, her voice filled with an eagerness that tugs at his heart.

Reggie forces a smile but shakes his head.

"Thanks, sweetheart, but I'll wait out here."

"It's alright, Dad isn't here," Lillie assures him, her tone suddenly shifting to one of annoyance.

"He's meeting up with some woman named Tracy. I heard him flirting with her on the phone earlier."

Reggie can't help but mutter under his breath, "Sounds about right for your father."

"Huh?" Lillie asks, not quite catching his words.

Reggie quickly backpedals, realising his mistake.

"I'm sorry, Lillie. I shouldn't talk about your father like that. I'm sure it's just a friendly meeting, nothing more."

Lillie shrugs, unconvinced.

"Yeah, right. Dad's always 'meeting' someone," she says, using air quotes and rolling her eyes.

Reggie feels a pang of guilt. He knows how hard things have been for the children and how much they've already had to deal with. He's here to make things better, not worse. He places a gentle hand on Lillie's shoulder and says softly, "Let's not worry about your dad right now, OK? I'm here for you, Bonnie, and Oliver. Why don't you grab your things, and we'll get going?"

Lillie nods, a small smile returning to her face as she turns to head back inside. Reggie stays on the doorstep, glancing around nervously, still half-expecting Ray to come storming out of nowhere.

He knows they don't have much time.

As they step outside into the crisp evening air, Reggie takes a quick glance up and down the street, ensuring there's no sign of Ray. He doesn't trust him, especially after what he heard from Bonnie.

The children, though excited, seem subdued, their faces a mix of relief and something heavier. Reggie knows this isn't just a weekend escape—it's a necessary break from the tension and hostility that's been building up in their home.

Oliver and Bonnie climb into the back seat of Reggie's car, securing their bags and pillows around them. Lillie follows, clutching Daisy, who's already squirming with excitement at the prospect of a car ride. Reggie places the crate and blanket in the boot, making sure Daisy's things are secure before he turns to the children.

"Everyone buckled up?" Reggie asks, trying to sound upbeat. He knows these moments are critical—they need to feel safe and cared for, especially now.

"Yes, Uncle Reggie," the children respond in unison, combining exhaustion and anticipation.

As they drive off, Reggie tries to focus on the road, pushing down his anger towards Ray. He needs to be there for these children, now more than ever. They drive in silence for a while, the only sound being Daisy's excited panting as she sticks her head out the window, the wind whipping her ears back.

Finally, Reggie speaks up, trying to lighten the mood.

"How about pizza for dinner? We can even make our own if you're up for it."

Oliver's face lights up.

"Can we make pepperoni and pineapple?"

CHAPTER 27

Reggie chuckles.

"You got it, chef."

As they turn the corner and head towards Reggie's home, the weight in the car seems to lift just a little.

For now, at least, they're leaving their troubles behind.

* * *

Back in the office, the team gathers around a large table cluttered with papers, coffee cups, and the remnants of a long day's work. Lambert sits close to Poker and Chase, her face lined with tension, while Gilbert takes a seat beside Dixie and Sharpie, who look equally worn out.

Carter stands at the front of the room, leaning against a whiteboard filled with scribbles, case notes, and timelines. He rubs his temples for a moment, clearly trying to collect his thoughts. He then looks up at the team, his expression showing irritation and disbelief.

"Well, this is a right shit show, isn't it?" Carter finally says, his voice full of exasperation.

The team nods in unison, murmuring their agreement. The confusion surrounding Molly's case has thrown everyone.

"Where do we even start with this mess?" Lambert mutters, glancing around the room.

"We thought we had everything lined up perfectly, and now it's all unravelling."

Poker taps his pen on the table, his usual confidence replaced by uncertainty.

"We've been working on the assumption that Gerry was guilty, but Molly's confession flips the whole narrative. If she was fully aware of her identity the whole time, then what does that mean for our case?"

"Exactly," Carter replies, pushing off from the whiteboard and pacing the room.

"We can't hold Gerry if Molly's story checks out, but we also can't just take her word for it. There's still so much we don't know. Did she fabricate her flashbacks to fit the story she wanted us to believe? Or are there gaps in her memory we're not aware of?"

Dixie speaks up, his voice steady despite the fatigue.

"We need to consider her mental state after the accident. If she was confused or suffering from memory loss, she might genuinely believe what she's saying, even if it's not entirely accurate."

Sharpie nods.

"We need to dig deeper into her medical records and psychological evaluations. There might be something we missed."

Chase leans back in his chair, arms crossed.

"And what about Gerry? He's been through the wringer because of this. We need to get him in here and clear things up. If he's innocent, we owe him that much."

Gilbert, who has been quiet until now, finally speaks.

"We also have to think about the children. They're caught in the middle of this, and their statements will shed real light on what's really been happening at home."

Carter sighs, running a hand through his hair.

"Alright, let's regroup and come at this from a different angle. We need to release Gerry, and dig into Molly's psychological state maybe by contacting her doctor again, what was her name?"

CHAPTER 27

"Err, Gloria Tuffman," says Lambert looking at the case notes.

"Thank you," says Carter.

"And go through the children's statements. And we need to do it fast before this gets even more complicated," he says.

The team nods a renewed sense of determination in their eyes despite the overwhelming nature of the task ahead. The room falls silent for a moment as they all contemplate the work that lies ahead, the weight of the case pressing down on them.

"Let's get to it," Carter finally says, breaking the silence.

"We've got a lot to untangle here, and not much time to do it."

"In the meantime, Carter, I think we can allow a supervised visit between Gerry and Molly," Poker suggests, his tone cautious.

"Let's see how they interact with each other. They haven't had a chance to speak since all of this kicked off, and it might give us some insights."

Carter nods, considering the proposal.

"That's not a bad idea," he replies thoughtfully.

"If Molly's confession is genuine, watching them together could help us understand more about their relationship and what really happened."

Poker leans forward, his expression resolute.

"I'll happily handle the supervision with Chase," he offers, glancing over at his partner.

"We can keep a close eye on their body language, the way they speak to each other—anything that might give us more clues."

Chase nods in agreement, his arms crossed over his chest.

"Sounds good to me," he says.

Carter exhales deeply.

"Alright, let's set it up."

As the team starts to prepare for the next step, there's a sense of anticipation in the air.

This could be the moment that changes everything.

* * *

Gerry walks in silence down the long, corridor with PC Brighton by his side. The rhythmic echo of their footsteps on the tiled floor is the only sound breaking the silence. Gerry keeps his gaze fixed on the ground, feeling the weight of exhaustion. The earlier interview has drained him, leaving him feeling hollow and spent. He has no energy or desire for conversation, and PC Brighton seems to sense this, maintaining a respectful silence.

As they approach the door at the end of the corridor, Gerry's mind races with anxious thoughts. He half expects to find another pair of stern-faced officers waiting on the other side, ready to deliver bad news or perhaps even formally charge him.

His heart beats a little faster with each step, the anticipation almost unbearable.

Gerry glances around, searching for a familiar face—his solicitor, who has been his anchor throughout this ordeal. But she is nowhere to be seen.

A small knot of anxiety tightens in his stomach. Had she gone ahead into the interview room without him, like she had done before? Gerry's nerves prick at the thought, wondering if she had been called in early for some reason,

CHAPTER 27

or if something more ominous was at play.

PC Brighton pauses in front of the door, looking at Gerry as if to gauge whether he's ready. Gerry swallows hard, nods slightly, and steels himself for whatever comes next. He knows he has no choice but to face it, whatever "it" may be.

* * *

The door swings open, revealing Gerry standing in the doorway.

He looks utterly dishevelled, a shadow of the man I had once fallen so deeply in love with. His clothes are rumpled, his hair unkempt, and his face shows signs of weariness. For a moment, his eyes remain downcast, fixed on the floor as if he's afraid to look up and face what awaits him. Then, slowly, they begin to rise, travelling up my body from my feet to my face, taking in every detail with a gaze that feels both familiar and foreign.

When our eyes finally meet, the connection is instant and electrifying. A surge of emotion courses through me, making my heart skip several beats before it begins to pound furiously in my chest. His eyes widen with a marry of surprise and yearning, and before I know it, he is moving swiftly toward me, arms opening wide as he closes the distance between us. I barely have time to react before I am enveloped in his embrace. The intensity of his hold sends a shiver down my spine, and goosebumps erupt all over my skin, responding to the overwhelming energy radiating from him.

He pulls back slightly, still holding me close, his hands gently cupping my face. His touch is both tender and urgent as if he's trying to memorise every contour, every line, every feature. He tilts my chin up, and without a moment's hesitation, he pulls me closer and presses his lips to mine.

Poker and Chase exchange a glance, a silent understanding passing between them. They quietly step back, turning their backs to give us a moment of privacy. I'm grateful for the small kindness, and the chance to be with Gerry without the weight of their scrutiny, if only for a brief time.

"Elizabeth," he murmurs against my mouth, his voice thick with emotion. His kiss is fervent, filled with a desperate longing that matches my own. I sigh deeply into the kiss, my body melting into his touch, every fibre of my being screaming for this moment to last forever. But all too soon, he pulls away, breaking our embrace. The loss of his warmth feels like a sudden chill, and I am left standing there, breathless, my heart still racing from the intensity of his presence.

"Molly, it's Molly," I correct him softly, my voice trembling as I try to steady my emotions.

Gerry's expression shifts to one of confusion, his brow furrowing deeply as he processes my words.

"What do you mean?" he asks, concern and bewilderment flashing in his eyes.

I take a deep breath, trying to find the strength to continue.

"It's OK, my love. I know who I am." I say gently, though I can see my words sting him like a bee. The shock and hurt are evident on his face, but I need him to understand.

His head hangs low as he speaks quietly, almost in a whisper, "You know that I lied to you, Molly. You know about the story I made up to live this lie, to be with you?"

"No, my love," I say, my voice breaking.

CHAPTER 27

"Not you. I am the one who has lied. I created the story, I lied to you so that I could live this life, pretending to be Elizabeth, pretending to be your wife. I've known the truth all along."

Gerry steps back, his face a mask of confusion and disbelief. The way he looks at me now cuts deep, a brew of betrayal and incomprehension. I feel the weight of my confession crashing down around us, and it's almost unbearable.

"I've lived your lie as Elizabeth for my own reasons, for my own escape," I admit, my voice barely a whisper now.

"But I am Molly. I have always been Molly."

The tears I've been holding back finally break free, streaming down my face in hot, uncontrollable waves. I feel myself crumple, my legs giving way beneath me as the truth spills out, leaving me raw and exposed.

Gerry moves quickly to my side, his hands gentle but firm as he pulls me up from the floor. He wraps his arms around me, holding me tight against his chest, his own breath heavy with the weight of everything we've just shared.

Gerry leans closer, his lips brushing my ear as he whispers, "It is all going to be alright, my love. We will work this out." His voice is soothing, filled with a confidence I wish I could share. The reassurance in his tone is like a lifeline, and I want to believe him, to trust that everything will be OK but doubt claws at me from the inside.

"I love you, Molly," he murmurs, his voice cracking under the weight of his own emotions. "I love you."

His words pierce through the fog of despair, pulling me out from the depths of my anguish. I lift my head, my vision blurred with tears, and gaze up at him. His face is lined with worry, his eyes filled with love and pain, and it breaks my heart to see him like this. I can feel the sincerity in his words, the raw, unfiltered truth of them, and it gives me a sliver of hope.

With trembling hands, I reach up and cradle his face, my fingers brushing against the rough stubble on his cheeks.

"I love you too, Gerry," I whisper, my voice choked with emotion.

For a moment, the world outside this room fades away.

There's no past, no future, just this fragile, precious moment between us but in his eyes, I see a flicker of the life we once had, a glimpse of the love that somehow, against all odds, still binds us together.

I cling to him, feeling the familiar strength in his embrace, but everything feels different now—fragile, like a delicate thread that could snap at any moment.

Chapter 28

Thursday Late Afternoon

Chase and Poker turn back around. Giving us a moment to prepare for what comes next. Their expressions are a mixture of sympathy and professional detachment, a reminder that we're not here for a reunion but for answers.

"Molly," Chase says softly, trying to keep his tone neutral, "I need you to come with me. PC Lockman has a few more questions for Gerry before we can move forward with the investigation." His words are gentle, but there's an underlying firmness that tells me I don't have a choice in the matter.

I look at Gerry, my heart sinking. His face mirrors my dread, his brow furrowed in worry. We both know that this separation isn't just a procedural formality. It's the beginning of something that could be much more serious.

What are they going to do with us?

Gerry's hand finds mine, his grip firm and reassuring.

"It's OK," he whispers, squeezing my hand one last time. "We'll get through this. Just stay strong, alright?"

I nod, though my stomach churns with anxiety.

"You too," I manage to say, my voice barely more than a whisper.

As Chase gently guides me away from Gerry, I can feel the distance between us growing, each step a painful reminder of the uncertainty that lies ahead. I can't shake the feeling that this might be the last time we see each other for a while, and the thought terrifies me. But I have to stay composed, for both our sakes.

Gerry watches me go, his eyes never leaving mine until we're out of sight.

I can only hope that whatever happens next, we'll find a way back to each other.

The road ahead is unclear, but one thing is certain—we're in this together.

* * *

Back in the office, the team is working tirelessly. Everyone is trying to piece together the tangled mess of a case that has unfolded in front of them.

Dixie leans back in his chair, tapping a pen against his notepad.

"OK, so other than wasting police time, what have the pair actually done?" he asks, his tone sceptical.

Carter, looking tired but alert, sits down heavily with a coffee cup in hand. He takes a sip and then responds bluntly, "Nothing." His voice is flat, and a single word hangs in the air, capturing everyone's attention.

"From what we can tell, there's no crime that either of them has committed—at least not a crime we can charge

CHAPTER 28

them with."

He pauses, then continues, "It seems to me that the only person who has actually committed a crime is Ray Chapman."

Chase, who has just finished a call with Gloria Tuffman, the psychiatrist, nods in agreement. He hangs up the phone and turns to the rest of the team.

"I agree with Carter. I just spoke to Tuffman, and she says we wouldn't have a leg to stand on if we tried to charge Molly with anything. The CPS will throw it out due to diminished responsibility. Her mental state over the past few months has been all over the place. The best thing we can offer her right now is support."

Dixie sighs and rubs his temples.

"So, what now? We just let them go? After all this?"

"We let them go," Carter confirms. "And we focus on Ray Chapman. He's the one we should be looking at. Domestic abuse, assault… there's a list there that we can work with. But for Molly and Gerry, it's over. They've been through enough."

Chase nods again, and there's a murmur of agreement around the room. The team knows they've reached the end of this particular road. Now, they need to shift their focus to where it really matters.

"But what about Gerry?" Dixie asks, though he already suspects the answer.

His team looks at one another, each waiting to see who will speak up first.

Poker shifts in his seat, clearing his throat.

"I think we need to let Gerry and Molly go and play happy families," he begins, his tone pragmatic.

"At the end of the day, we're the ones who've kept Gerry

here. Now that we know the truth, there's nothing more to hold him on."

There's a pause as the team absorbs his words. It's clear that they've all been mulling over the same thoughts, but hearing it said aloud gives it weight.

"And Rachel?" Chase asks, leaning back in his chair.

"What about her?"

Poker shakes his head.

"Even Rachel hasn't had anything to do with it all. She was completely oblivious to the situation. From what we can gather, she had no idea what was really going on between Gerry and Molly. She's not involved in any of this mess, not directly anyway."

Carter nods in agreement.

"She was just another person caught up in the confusion."

Dixie leans forward, resting his elbows on the table.

"So, we're letting them both go? Just like that?"

"Just like that," Carter confirms.

"They're not criminals. They've been through enough, especially Molly. We focus on Ray Chapman now. He's the one who needs to answer for his actions."

The team sits in a brief, contemplative silence, coming to terms with the decision. It's not the outcome any of them had anticipated when they started this case, but it feels like the right one.

"Alright," Dixie finally says, breaking the silence.

"Let's wrap this up, then. Time to move on."

The team begins to gather their notes and close their files, shifting their focus to the next steps. There's still a lot of work to do, but at least they now have a clearer path forward.

CHAPTER 28

***

"Auntie Yvonne!" yells Oliver as he leaps out of Reggie's car. Daisy follows closely behind, her tail wagging furiously. Lillie and Bonnie climb out of the car more slowly, each grabbing bags from the back seat. Reggie lugs Daisy's crate and blankets, struggling to juggle everything in his arms.

"Damn," Reggie mutters under his breath as he glances back at the car.

"I forgot the bowls."

Lillie, catching on, starts to giggle.

"Just use a saucepan, that's what Mum used before she bought Daisy some new bowls," she suggests, her eyes twinkling with mischief.

"Yeah, right, Lillie. Can you imagine Yvonne's face if I pull out one of her fancy Tefal pans for the dog's dinner? I'd be dead meat!" Reggie chuckles, shaking his head at the thought.

"I won't tell if you don't," Lillie teases, a cheeky grin spreading across her face.

Reggie laughs along, enjoying the light-hearted banter.

The four of them make their way into the house, setting the bags down in the hallway. The familiar warmth of the home wraps around them like a comforting blanket.

Oliver dashes upstairs, eager to claim his favourite bed in the spare room. His footsteps thud up the stairs, and they can hear him whooping with joy as he reaches the top.

"See how much happier the children are the minute they walk through the door," Yvonne observes softly, her eyes following Oliver's noisy ascent. She turns to Reggie and leans in to give him a warm kiss on the cheek.

"Welcome back, love," she says, her voice filled with

affection.

Reggie smiles the tension from the day's events slowly melting away.

"I'm just going to set up the crate," Reggie says, hefting Daisy's crate under his arm. "That way, the dog has somewhere quiet to retreat to." He heads down the hallway, looking for a suitable spot, while Yvonne disappears into the kitchen to make everyone a hot chocolate. She knows how much the children love it, and she takes comfort in doing little things to brighten their day.

As Yvonne stirs the cocoa powder into the warm milk, her mind drifts to the children. She feels deep empathy for them, understanding just how hard things have been, especially with Ray's recent, completely unacceptable behaviour. It's clear to her that the best place for Bonnie, Oliver, and Lillie is right here, with her and Reggie, where they can feel safe and loved.

She hopes that if Molly decides to meet with them after the identification, having them all together under one roof will make things easier. Yvonne can't help but wonder what must be going through Molly's mind.

Does she even remember she has three children?

Or is she in complete denial of it all?

The police had been frustratingly vague about Molly's condition and what she might remember. Yvonne understands the importance of data protection and respecting a person's rights, but these are her son and daughters—her flesh and blood.

"So, we're having pizza for tea, yes?" Yvonne asks as the children pile into the kitchen, their faces lighting up at the thought of food.

CHAPTER 28

"Yes, please! Pepperoni and pineapple for me," Oliver chimes in, eagerly pulling out one of the bar stools tucked under the kitchen worktop. He climbs up and rests his elbows on the counter, already looking forward to his favourite toppings.

Bonnie and Lillie join him, each taking a seat. "I want cheese and tomato, please," says Bonnie, smiling at the thought of her comfort food.

"Can I have ham and mushrooms?" Lillie asks, her eyes bright with excitement. She looks around at everyone, grateful for this moment of normalcy.

Yvonne smiles warmly, taking in their requests.

"Pepperoni and pineapple, cheese and tomato, ham and mushrooms," she repeats, making sure to get everyone's order right.

"Alright then, pizza it is," she says as she goes to the fridge to get the ingredients to make the pizzas.

The children wash their hands and roll up their sleeves ready to dive in with the cooking.

* * *

Poker ushers Gerry back into the interview room.

Poker settles into his chair, the creak of the wood echoing through the room, as he prepares to officially discharge Gerry from police custody.

Gerry sits down across from him, visibly drained. His eyes are red-rimmed and weary, and his shoulders slump as though carrying an invisible weight. The events of the past few hours have clearly taken their toll.

Poker leans forward, trying to gauge Gerry's emotional

state.

"How are you feeling after everything that's come to light about Molly?" he asks, his voice calm but probing.

Gerry sighs deeply, his hands resting limply on the table.

"Honestly, I'm a bit numb," he admits.

"I feel like a complete fool. How could I not have seen it? All this time, she was just pretending to have lost her memory. But, you know what, officer? I love that woman with every ounce of my being. I can't bring myself to feel any anger toward her, despite everything."

Poker nods, understanding the complexity of Gerry's emotions.

"I guess both of you were deceitful in your own ways. Maybe it's a case of letting bygones be bygones," he suggests gently, trying to find some common ground in the confusion.

"Yeah, exactly," Gerry agrees, his voice tinged with regret.

"I just wish she'd told me the truth when she got her memory back. We could've avoided all this mess."

Poker leans back in his chair, pondering Gerry's words.

"That's the part that really gets to me, Gerry. Why the need for all this deception? She could have just reported Ray for what he did to her," he muses, with frustration in his tone.

"Maybe she was too scared," Gerry speculates, his eyes distant.

"Maybe she didn't want to go back to being that person. Maybe she wanted to start over, away from all the pain."

Poker nods slowly, considering Gerry's point.

"You might be right. Fear can make people do things they never thought they would. Maybe she was terrified of losing you and having to return to her old life with Ray and the children."

CHAPTER 28

He pauses, tapping his fingers thoughtfully on the table.

"But the children... that's the part I can't wrap my head around," he continues.

"Why let them believe their mother is missing?"

Gerry's face darkens with the thought.

"Maybe she was waiting for Ray to be taken out of the picture. Maybe she thought once he was arrested, she could come clean," he suggests, trying to make sense of it all.

"That's a possibility," Poker acknowledges, nodding.

"But we might never know the whole truth unless Molly decides to be completely honest. And given her track record, I'm not sure we can trust her word entirely."

Gerry feels a sting at Poker's blunt assessment.

He knows it's harsh, but there's truth in it.

Molly's actions have left everyone with more questions than answers. He sighs, resigning himself to the uncertainty.

'We may never know,' he thinks to himself.

There's a knock on the door, breaking the tension in the room. Chase steps in, holding a folder under his arm, his expression neutral but professional.

"Hey, Gerry," Chase says, nodding toward him.

"I just want to have a few words with you before Poker finalises your release, if that's alright."

Gerry looks surprised.

"Let me go?" he repeats, his voice full of disbelief.

"Yes, that's why you're in here with me," Poker replies with a light chuckle.

"This isn't another interrogation, Gerry. It's more of a formality at this point."

"Oh, right," Gerry says, his shoulders relaxing slightly as the reality of the situation sinks in. "I didn't realise I was going to be released." There's a flicker of excitement in his eyes now, a glimmer of hope that had been missing just moments before.

Chase gives a small smile, flipping open the folder to reveal a stack of paperwork.

"We just need to go through a few formalities, check some things, and then you'll be free to go," he explains, his tone reassuring.

"Fine with me," Gerry responds, sitting up straighter in his chair, with relief and anticipation coursing through him.

Chase takes a seat across from Gerry and gets straight to the point.

"How would you say your mental health is right now?" he asks matter-of-factly, his pen poised over the paper.

Gerry thinks for a moment, taking a deep breath before he answers.

"Right now, I'd say it's in pretty good shape," he admits.

"Earlier today, this morning… not so much. I felt like I was drowning like there was no way out of this mess. But knowing that I'm being released, that there's a light at the end of this tunnel—it's made a big difference."

Chase nods, jotting down notes on the paperwork in front of him.

"It's understandable, given everything that's happened. You've been through a lot."

"Yeah," Gerry agrees quietly, his gaze drifting to the table as the weight of the past few days settles in again.

Chase looks up from his notes, his expression serious but kind.

"Where will you be going after your release?" he asks, continuing with the formalities.

CHAPTER 28

"I'll be heading back to my home," Gerry replies without hesitation.

"The bungalow."

Chase writes down the information, his pen moving swiftly across the page. He glances up at Gerry, assessing him carefully, making sure there are no signs of lingering distress or uncertainty.

As Chase continues to fill out the forms, Gerry sits in a contemplative silence. He's ready to leave, but there's still a sense of unease—so much has changed in such a short time, and the path ahead is uncertain.

Chase finishes his notes and looks up, meeting Gerry's eyes with a steady gaze. "Alright, Gerry, just a few more things and you'll be on your way. We want to make sure you're leaving here in the best possible state, OK?"

Gerry nods, a small but genuine smile appearing on his face.

"Yeah, I understand. Thanks, Chase. I appreciate it."

Poker gives him an encouraging nod.

"Hang in there, Gerry. You're almost out of the woods."

Gerry takes a deep breath, bracing himself for the next steps.

"Almost," he murmurs, relief and resolve in his voice.

Chapter 29

Thursday Late Afternoon

After Gerry's health check clears him to go home, he is temporarily placed in a holding cell while the paperwork is finalised and his belongings are retrieved. Meanwhile, Chase walks down the corridor to conduct a well-being check on Molly. He approaches the interview room where she sits with Gilbert, who has been keeping her company.

Chase opens the door and steps inside, giving Molly a reassuring smile.

"Molly, how are you doing?" he asks gently.

Molly looks up at him, her expression a fusion of exhaustion and hope.

"Hi, Chase. I'm doing alright, thank you. A bit apprehensive, but I'm good considering the circumstances," she replies, her voice steady but with an underlying tremor of anxiety.

Chase pulls up a chair across from her and sits down, leaning forward slightly.

"How did you feel meeting with Gerry?" he enquires, watching her closely for any signs of distress.

CHAPTER 29

Molly takes a deep breath and smiles softly.

"It was like seeing my husband again after being apart for a long time. It was overwhelming but also really lovely. I didn't realise how much I missed him until we were face-to-face again. Thank you for giving us that time together," she says, her eyes glistening with joy.

Chase nods, understanding the complex emotions she's experiencing.

"That's alright, Molly. You'll be able to spend as much time together as you want once we finish up your well-being checks," he explains, keeping his tone calm and supportive.

Molly's eyes widen with surprise and relief.

"Oh my god! Really?" she exclaims, her face lighting up with a smile.

"I wasn't sure if I'd be allowed to go home, or if you still needed to keep me here."

Chase chuckles softly.

"Yes, really. There's no reason to keep you apart now that everything's been cleared up. You and Gerry are free to go home once we wrap things up here. We just want to make sure you're both in a good place mentally and emotionally before you leave."

Molly nods eagerly, the tension visibly draining from her shoulders.

"Thank you, Chase. That means so much to me. I just want to put all of this behind us and move forward."

Chase gives her a warm smile.

"I understand. We're almost there, Molly. Just hang in a little bit longer, and you'll be on your way." He turns to Gilbert, who gives him a nod of appreciation for his kindness and patience.

"Alright," Chase says as he stands up. "I'll go finalise the paperwork. We'll have you and Gerry on your way soon."

"Chase, just one more thing before you go." Molly's voice is tentative, stopping him in his tracks.

He turns back to her, his expression softening.

"Yes?"

"My husband, the real one, Ray…" Her voice trails off as if she's struggling to find the right words.

Chase nods encouragingly, sensing the weight of what she's about to say.

"Yes?"

Her voice is barely above a whisper.

"What he did to me, the abuse, the mental torture he put me through… Can I press charges for everything he did to me, or is it too late to do that now?"

Chase sees the tears pooling in her eyes, threatening to spill over. He quickly sits back down, leaning forward to close the distance between them.

"Molly, what he did to you was completely wrong and outside the bounds of the law. He has committed multiple crimes." He pauses, making sure she's absorbing his words. "Gilbert was planning to discuss the possibility of pressing charges with you after I left, but since you've brought it up, we can talk about it now."

Molly's eyes search his face for reassurance, her breath catching in her throat.

"Do you want your husband arrested and charged with physical and mental abuse?" Chase asks gently, his tone careful and measured.

Molly lowers her head, her shoulders trembling with the weight of the decision. Gilbert, who has been quietly sitting

CHAPTER 29

beside her, places a comforting hand over hers, squeezing it gently in silent support.

Chase continues, carefully choosing his next words.

"He's also interfered with the investigation and withheld evidence. We have everything we need to charge him with perverting the course of justice, among other offences." He stops, realizing he might be overwhelming her, but he knows she deserves to know the full extent of the case against Ray.

Molly lifts her head slightly, tears streaming down her cheeks. Her voice is shaky, but there's a newfound resolve in her tone.

"I… I want him to pay for what he did. I want to press charges."

Chase nods, feeling relief and respect for her courage.

"Alright, Molly. We will make sure Ray is held accountable for his actions. You don't have to worry about this anymore. We're here to support you through every step."

Gilbert gives her hand another squeeze.

Molly takes a deep, shaky breath, finally allowing herself to hope that justice will be served and that she can begin to heal from the trauma Ray inflicted on her.

"OK, leave it with me. I'll talk to the team," Chase reassures her as he rises from his seat.

"I imagine they'll be looking to make an arrest today."

Molly's eyes widen with sudden realisation.

"Oh shit, the children!" she exclaims, her voice filled with urgency.

"I need to speak to my brother."

Chase nods, understanding her concern.

"You're free to go now, Molly. If you come with me back to the front desk, we can make a formal accusation against your husband, and we'll take it from there."

Molly nods, her mind already racing ahead to the next steps. She knows she needs to call her brother, Reggie, and make arrangements for the children.

Chase gathers his papers, quickly organizing them into a neat stack. He senses Molly's anxiety and moves quickly.

Gilbert gives Molly a supportive nod as Chase heads toward the door.

As Chase opens the door, he looks back at Molly.

"I'll be just outside if you need anything. We'll sort this out together."

Molly takes a deep breath, steadying herself.

"Thank you, Chase."

He gives her a reassuring smile.

"We've got your back, Molly." With that, he steps out, closing the door gently behind him, leaving Molly and Gilbert to gather their thoughts before heading out to confront the next step of her journey.

For the first time in what feels like forever, she can see a glimmer of light at the end of the tunnel.

* * *

The team, startled by Dixie's raised voice, quickly turns their attention to him. A few of them put down their burgers, sensing the seriousness in his tone. The usual buzz of conversation in the office fades into an uneasy silence as all eyes focus on Dixie.

He clears his throat again, the discomfort evident in his face as he struggles to suppress another cough. His hand remains at his throat, gently massaging, trying to alleviate

CHAPTER 29

the tightness that seems to grow with every word.

"Listen up," Dixie says, his voice a little strained but determined to push through.

"I need to say something important."

Everyone waits, concern and curiosity crossing their faces. Carter leans back in his chair, arms folded across his chest, while Poker sets his food aside, wiping his hands on a napkin.

Chase, who had been quietly going over some notes, sets his papers down, giving Dixie his full attention.

Dixie takes a deep breath, wincing slightly as he does.

"I know we're all neck-deep in this case, and I appreciate how hard everyone's been working. But there's something personal I need to share."

Sharpie moves closer, his expression one of quiet support.

Dixie looks around the room, meeting the eyes of each member of his team.

"I've been battling some health issues for a while now," he begins, his voice low but steady.

"And I didn't want to say anything because… well, I didn't want to distract from the work we're doing. But I think it's time you all knew."

Sharpie stands beside Dixie, his presence offering silent support as he prepares to deliver his news.

The team senses the heaviness of the moment, a sombre anticipation settling over the room. They exchanged uneasy glances, noting the pallor of Dixie's face and the fatigue that has become more pronounced over the last few days.

Dixie coughs again, the rough, wet sound breaking the silence, and he takes a moment to steady himself. Lambert, who has always been perceptive to his needs, quickly moves to fetch a coffee, hoping the warmth will provide some comfort. As she hands it to him, Dixie gives her a grateful smile, acknowledging her kindness in this difficult moment.

Taking a deep breath, Dixie addresses the room.

"I've tried to keep this quiet for as long as I could, but it's time you all know what's been going on," he begins, his voice wavering slightly but growing stronger with each word.

Poker and Carter lean forward slightly, their expressions filled with concern. The rest of the team sits in stunned silence, bracing themselves for what's to come.

Dixie clears his throat again, the effort visible on his face.

"Recently, things have gotten worse." He looks around the room, meeting the eyes of his colleagues, who are now listening with bated breath.

"I've been diagnosed with prostate cancer. And it's aggressive. The doctors have told me that… I only have a few weeks or maybe days left."

The room falls into stunned silence, the impact of his words hitting everyone like a punch to the gut.

Lambert gasps softly, her hand flying to her mouth in shock. Carter closes his eyes briefly, processing the news, while Poker runs a hand through his hair, visibly shaken. Chase, who had been standing at the back, steps forward, his face showing signs of disbelief and sadness.

Dixie takes another deep breath, his eyes scanning the room filled with his team — his second family.

"I didn't want to keep this from you all, but I also didn't want it to distract from the important work we're doing. You're all like family to me, and I needed you to hear this from me, not from anyone else."

A heavy silence follows, filled only by the muffled sounds of the bustling station outside the office. The team members

CHAPTER 29

exchange looks of shock, sadness, and disbelief, struggling to come to terms with what they've just learned.

Because of my impending medical issues, I would like to take this opportunity to offer a promotion to Carter." he pauses.

Carter steps forward, his face flushed with surprise and a hint of embarrassment as he stands in front of the team. The sudden focus on him feels overwhelming, but he manages to maintain his composure. As the applause erupts around him, he takes a moment to absorb what's happening, the reality of a promotion slowly sinking in.

"PC Christopher Carter," Dixie continues, his voice steady but laced with emotion, "I would like to offer you the position of Detective Inspector. You'll be taking over from DI Sharpie, who will be stepping into my shoes when I am no longer here."

The room fills with renewed energy as everyone claps and cheers for Carter, their excitement mingled with the bittersweet undercurrent of Dixie's announcement.

Carter's eyes dart around the room, catching the proud smiles of his colleagues. It's a moment of mixed emotions—joy for the recognition and the opportunity, but also a deep sadness for the reason behind it.

"Wow, I don't know what to say, Boss," Carter stammers, his voice choked with emotion.

"Just tell me you'll accept it," Dixie says, a small smile playing on his lips as he watches the younger officer.

He takes a breath, trying to steady himself, his voice carrying the weight of his pride and affection for Carter.

"You can have a formal promotion when I've gone, but I wanted to be here to award you with it now. You've deserved it and worked so bloody hard running this case. It's not been easy, but you've kept going, and we are all so damned proud of you, lad."

Dixie coughs again, a light rasp that cuts through the applause. It's a stark reminder of his condition, and the room falls quiet for a moment, the team's attention shifting back to him with concern.

Carter nods, trying to hold back tears, understanding the magnitude of what Dixie is offering him—not just a promotion, but a legacy to carry forward.

"I'll do my best, Boss," Carter finally says, his voice thick with emotion.

"Thank you for believing in me. I won't let you down."

"I know you won't," Dixie replies, his eyes locking onto Carter's with a look of unwavering confidence.

"You've got the heart for this, Carter. And that's what this team needs. Heart, and determination. You've got both in abundance."

The room erupts into applause once more, the sound echoing with a mix of celebration and the poignant awareness of the changes to come.

Carter stands there, feeling the weight of his new role settling on his shoulders, but also the strength of the support around him.

He looks back at Dixie, nodding firmly, ready to step into his new responsibilities, not just for himself, but to honour the man who believes in him.

"So, we may have had the case blown wide open, but we've solved a missing person case, and that's rare nowadays," Dixie says, his voice steady but filled with a sense of finality.

"I want you all to give yourselves a huge pat on the back.

CHAPTER 29

You have been a tremendous team to work with, and I feel privileged to have worked with and to have known every single one of you."

As he speaks, Dixie's gaze shifts past his team to the doorway, where his sister Lucy stands, wiping away tears that she can no longer hold back. Her presence is a stark reminder of the reality that Dixie has been preparing himself to face. He knows it's time to go, to leave behind the team that has been his second family for so long. The weight of that realisation makes his shoulders slump slightly, the emotional toll of the day catching up with him.

Dixie staggers to his desk, each step a little slower than the last, his body betraying the strength of his spirit.

He picks up a small box containing his personal effects that he had carefully packed earlier. He makes his way to the centre of the room, where Lucy meets him with a wheelchair.

Relieved, Dixie gratefully sinks into the wheelchair, placing the box on his lap. His hands rest on top of it, fingers brushing over the items that have meant so much to him over the years—a framed photo of the team at a Christmas party, his first badge, and a few commendation letters. These small mementoes represent a lifetime of service and memories that are difficult to leave behind.

"Thank you, everyone, for everything," Dixie says, his voice soft but carrying through the room.

"I'm gonna miss you guys."

Lucy gently turns the wheelchair around and begins to push him out of the office. The room remains in complete silence, the gravity of the moment sinking in for everyone present.

No one dares to speak.

A tangible loss that each team member feels deep in their chest. The bond they shared with Dixie wasn't just professional; it was personal, built over years of trust, late-night shifts, and shared victories and defeats.

Tears stream down faces, and even the hardest among them find themselves blinking rapidly, trying to hold back the emotion that threatens to spill over. There isn't a dry eye in the room. They watch as Lucy wheels Dixie out, his figure becoming smaller until he disappears from view.

For a long moment, no one moves, the silence filled with the echoes of all the things left unsaid. They've lost more than a boss today; they've lost a mentor, a friend, a guiding light.

The team stands united in their grief, yet inspired by the legacy Dixie leaves behind—a reminder of the kind of dedication and heart that defines their work and the impact of one man's life on so many.

Chapter 30

Thursday Late Afternoon

The house is still brightly lit, glowing with the intensity of Blackpool illuminations, but as Ray slides his key into the lock, he notices something odd. The usual noise, the chaotic barking of Daisy, and the sounds of the kids bickering are all missing. Instead, he's met with an eerie silence that makes his skin prickle.

He pushes the door open and steps inside, calling out, "Oliver! Bonnie! Lillie!" His voice echoes through the house, bouncing off the walls without a reply. A cold dread creeps into his stomach as he waits, listening for any sign of life.

Nothing.

Growing more anxious by the second, Ray takes the stairs two at a time, his footsteps heavy and hurried. He swings open the door to each bedroom, scanning the rooms for any sign of the kids. One by one, he flings them open—Oliver's room, Bonnie's, then Lillie's—but they're all empty, each bed partially made, rooms in their usual mess.

His frustration mounts with each empty room, and he feels a wave of panic starting to set in.

Ray runs back down the stairs, his mind racing with possibilities. Maybe they're in the garden, he thinks. He throws open the back door and steps outside, the early evening air hitting him like a slap. But the garden is empty, too.

Desperation grips him.

Where could they have gone? There isn't even a note left for him, no explanation.

He runs his hands through his hair, pulling at it in frustration. Then, he remembers the Ring doorbell.

Fumbling for his phone, he quickly opens the app and rewinds through the footage, his finger swiping back through the recorded footage until he sees it.

There, on the small screen, is Reggie standing at the front door, ringing the bell. Ray watches as the footage shows the kids answering the door, bags packed and Daisy at their side. His heart pounds in his chest as he sees them leave with Reggie, disappearing out of view of the camera.

Ray's jaw tightens as he realizes what's happened.

His brother-in-law has taken them—and his dog, without a word.

Rage boils up inside him.

Why would they leave with Reggie?

Where have they gone?

Ray's mind races with questions, his body tense as he struggles to understand the situation. He knows one thing for certain: he needs answers, and he needs them now.

Ray's hands tremble with rage as he dials Reggie's number, his finger jabbing at the screen with barely controlled fury.

The phone hardly rings before Reggie picks up.

"Hello," Reggie answers, his tone calm and measured.

CHAPTER 30

"What the fuck are you playing at, Reggie? What the fuck are you doing with my kids, again!?" Ray explodes, his voice seething with anger, the words tumbling out in a vicious snarl.

Reggie doesn't back down.

"They wanted to come and stay with me and Yvonne. They're sick of how you treat them, Ray. You can't go around slapping your kids! You're a goddamn monster," Reggie shouts back, his own anger flaring.

"And in any case," Reggie continues, his voice dripping with disdain, "you'd buggered off with another one of your floozies. You think you can just come and go as you please, leaving your family in disarray? That's not how it works, Ray."

Yvonne, hearing the rising tension in Reggie's voice, quietly steps over and closes the kitchen door, making sure the children can't hear the heated exchange taking place. She knows this isn't something they should be exposed to—not now, not ever.

Ray is pacing now, his rage simmering just below the surface, threatening to boil over. "Look, they're all here until Sunday," Reggie continues, his voice steady but firm.

"So, you have a few days to get your shit together, Ray."

Ray's face contorts with frustration.

"And what about my dog? You can't just uproot my family and expect me to be alright with it!" His voice cracks, anger and desperation bleeding through.

Reggie sighs, his patience wearing thin.

"I am their next of KIN, Ray. Not you. And right now, it's in the children's best interest to be with us. They're scared of you, Ray, and you need to realise that. Unless you want me to call Social Services?" Reggie warns, his voice cold and serious.

There's a brief silence on the line as Ray processes Reggie's words, his breathing heavy and uneven. He knows Reggie is serious, and the threat of Social Services sends a chill down his spine. He clenches his jaw, feeling cornered, but he can't let Reggie see his fear. Not now.

"You wouldn't dare," Ray growls, trying to maintain a semblance of control.

"Try me," Reggie retorts sharply.

"You need to get help, Ray. For the kids' sake, and for yours. If you love them at all, you'll take this time to sort yourself out."

Ray grips the phone tightly, his knuckles turning white. He wants to scream, to lash out.

"This isn't over," Ray says through gritted teeth.

Reggie's tone softens, just a bit.

"No, it's not. But it can be if you make the right choices, Ray. Think about it."

Ray ends the call abruptly, slamming his phone down onto the kitchen counter. He stares at the silent, empty house around him, feeling the weight of his own actions pressing down on him, suffocating and inescapable.

∗ ∗ ∗

After making the formal accusation against Ray Chapman, Molly is finally released from voluntary police custody.

The weight of the day's revelations and the tension in her chest seem to lift slightly. However, her sense of relief is tempered by the knowledge that Gerry is still in holding, and

CHAPTER 30

it may take several more hours for his release to be processed.

Molly's heart races as she contemplates the next steps. She knows that the police are moving forward with her statement and the evidence they have gathered against Ray, but her immediate concern is ensuring that her children are safe and cared for during this dreadful time.

Chase, who has been instrumental in guiding Molly through the process, comes down to say goodbye. He finds her standing near the front desk, looking both relieved and anxious. He offers a sympathetic smile as he approaches her.

"Molly, I just wanted to say goodbye and wish you all the best as you move forward. If there's anything else you need, don't hesitate to reach out."

Molly takes a deep breath, mustering the strength to make one last request.

"Chase, I know it's asking a lot, but I need a favour. I want the children to be looked after by Reggie. He's been so supportive, and I trust him completely. Can you help me make sure they're settled with him?"

Chase nods, understanding the urgency in her voice.

"Can I please use your phone to call my brother? I don't have a mobile" Molly asks Chase, her voice urgent.

"Of course," Chase responds, taking his phone out of his pocket. He unlocks the screen and hands it to her.

"Here you go."

Molly takes the phone and dials her brother's number. She glances at Chase, who chuckles lightly.

"Oh, your memory is quite impressive," he comments.

Molly laughs softly.

"Oh shush."

The phone rings, and Molly waits anxiously. After a few rings, Reggie answers, his voice sounding strained and frustrated.

"Oh, for God's sake, Ray, just let up will you!"

Molly's face falls as she hears the unexpected response.

"Huh? Reggie, it's me."

There's a moment of confusion on Reggie's end.

"Sh—who's that?" he asks, realising the withheld number isn't Ray's this time.

"It's me, Reggie. It's Molly," she says, trying to keep her voice steady.

There's a stunned silence on the line, punctuated only by the sound of Reggie's heavy breathing and occasional sniffs. Molly can hear the emotional strain in her brother's voice as he processes her words.

"Jesus, Molly! Is that really you?" Reggie's voice cracks with shock and relief.

"Yes, it's me, Reggie," she says again, her voice trembling. The connection feels both comforting and overwhelming, as they share a moment of understanding through the phone.

The conversation falls into silence once more, with only the occasional sound of Reggie's muffled sobs filling the quiet. Molly holds the phone tightly, her heart aching as she listens to her brother's emotional response.

"Reggie, I need you to listen to me," Molly says firmly, trying to keep her voice steady despite the urgency in her tone.

"OK," Reggie replies, his voice full of concern.

"I need you to go and get the children for me and take them to your house," Molly instructs.

"They're already here, Molls," Reggie responds, a hint of

CHAPTER 30

confusion in his voice.

"How on earth are you? I thought you didn't remember us."

"I'll explain everything later, but I just need you to keep the children with you and don't tell Ray that you've spoken to me," she says urgently.

"OK!" Reggie agrees.

"Can you pick me up from the police station? Yvonne will be alright with the children, won't she?" Molly asks desperately.

"Of course I can. I'll leave shortly," Reggie assures her.

"We can talk in the car before I see the children," Molly suggests.

"Thank you, Reggie. I really appreciate it. I'll be waiting in the reception," Molly says, her voice filled with gratitude.

With a quick goodbye, Molly hangs up the call and hands Chase his phone back. "Thank you so much, Chase. You've been my rock through all of this—both you and Gilbert," she says sincerely, shaking Chase's hand.

Chase nods, understanding the weight of the moment.

"Just take care, Molly. We'll keep you updated on everything."

Molly heads towards the seating area of reception, her mind racing with thoughts of what comes next. She finds a spot to wait, trying to steady her nerves as she anticipates Reggie's arrival. The quiet hum of the police station surrounds her, offering a brief respite before the next chapter of her journey begins.

* * *

Emily walks down the corridor. She stops in front of the door to the holding cell and gives a light, respectful tap. The Custody Officer, a weary but attentive figure, opens the door.

"Hey Gerry, are you ready?" Emily asks, her voice warm yet professional as she peers into the cell.

Gerry looks up from where he's been sitting.

"Yeah, I'm ready," he replies.

Emily gives him a reassuring smile and gestures for him to follow her.

"Great, let's get you through the final steps of your release. We'll make sure everything is sorted before you head out."

He follows Emily down the corridor. The Custody Officer locks the door behind them, ensuring the cell is secured before they proceed.

Emily leads Gerry towards the administrative area, where the final paperwork for his release is being prepared. She makes small talk to help ease the tension, her tone light but focused on guiding him through the process.

As they approach the front desk, Emily gestures to a seat for Gerry to wait while the last details are finalised.

"Just a few more minutes, Gerry. We're almost done."

Emily busies herself with the final paperwork, ensuring all the necessary forms are completed accurately and efficiently.

***

Reggie strides into the police station, his eyes scanning the waiting area until they land on Molly. Relief washes over him as he spots her sitting on a chair. Without hesitation, he makes his way over to her, his steps quickening with each stride.

CHAPTER 30

"Molly!" he exclaims, almost breathless with emotion. As he reaches her, he throws his arms around her in a tight embrace.

Molly, her eyes glistening with tears, looks up at him. Her face reflects a mix of sadness and relief as she returns the hug, her arms wrapping around him.

Reggie pulls back slightly, cradling her face in his hands, his eyes searching hers.

"I never thought I would see you this soon," he says, his voice choked with emotion.

Molly gently wipes away the tears that have started to fall down his cheeks, her own eyes misty.

"Well, I'm here now, Reggie. I am here to stay."

With a soft, reassuring smile, Reggie places his arm around Molly's waist and leads her towards the exit.

"Come on, let's get you in the car," he says, his voice filled with affection.

They reach the car, and Molly takes a deep breath as she buckles herself into the passenger seat, letting out a huge sigh of relief.

As Reggie settles into the driver's seat, he glances over at her with a warm smile.

"I think you have some explaining to do, young lady." he laughs.

Molly chuckles softly through her tears, shaking her head.

"Oh, you have no idea."

Reggie starts the engine.

"So, where have you been?" he asks.

Molly looks out the window for a moment, gathering her thoughts. She turns back to Reggie, her expression serious but calm.

THE FOUND

"I have been with Gerry."

Reggie raises an eyebrow slightly, processing her words. "With Gerry? What's going on?"

Molly takes a deep breath, ready to unravel the complex and emotional journey she has been through. As they pull away from the police station, she begins to share her story, knowing that this is just the beginning of understanding and healing for everyone involved.

Reggie drives, his mind racing with the myriad of questions Molly's revelations have triggered. The silence in the car is heavy with unspoken thoughts until Reggie breaks it, his voice trembling slightly.

"Molly, we were informed about your situation, but it's still hard to understand. Why didn't you come home after you got your memory back? Why didn't you reach out to us? They told us you had lost your memory and didn't know any of us."

Molly looks out the window for a moment, struggling to find the right words. Finally, she turns to face her brother, her eyes filled with remorse and vulnerability.

"I lied, Reggie. Because I didn't want to come back to this life. When I had the opportunity to be someone else, I took it. The hospital told me that Gerry was my husband when I woke up, and they said I had lost my memory. Later on I just played along. Gerry made it seem like I was his wife, and he took me back to his home. I fell in love with him. It all got so out of hand. I was living the perfect life."

Reggie's grip on the steering wheel tightens.

"But Moll's, the children, me… your husband. How could you just leave us behind?"

Molly's voice wavers as she tries to explain, the guilt and

CHAPTER 30

sadness clear in her tone.

"I know how it sounds. It was never my intention to hurt any of you. But Gerry offered me something I hadn't felt in a long time—happiness, love.

It was like a fairytale.

I was scared and too deep into the lie to find a way out."

Reggie feels a pang of betrayal and hurt, but he also understands the depth of Molly's despair.

"But why not just get a divorce, leave him? There had to be another way."

Molly sighs, her eyes filling with tears.

"At one point, we thought you were dead." Reggie sniffs.

"I was too afraid to face everything, and the longer I stayed in the lie, the harder it became to break free."

Reggie's expression softens, and he reaches over to place a reassuring hand on Molly's arm.

"I'm so sorry, Reggie. I never meant to hurt any of you. I was just too scared and too deep into the lie to get out of it. I was happy, I felt loved."

Reggie takes a deep breath, trying to process everything.

"You know what, Molly? I can't dwell on this right now. The most important thing is that you're safe, you're well, and you're here with us."

Molly nods, grateful for her brother's understanding and support. As they continue driving, the silence is now filled with a sense of cautious optimism. The road ahead may be difficult, but Molly is relieved to be back with her family and ready to face the challenges together.

Chapter 31

Thursday Late Afternoon

"Would you like a lift home, Gerry?" Emily asks with a warm smile.

"That would be great, thank you. If you don't mind, of course," Gerry replies gratefully.

"I'm heading that way anyway, so it's no trouble at all," Emily assures him.

"Thanks, Emily," Gerry says as he gathers his things.

They drive in comfortable silence, the tension of the day gradually lifting as they near Gerry's home.

When they arrive at the bungalow, Gerry gets out of the car and turns to thank Emily for her kindness.

"Thank you for everything you've done," he says sincerely.

Emily nods, returning his gratitude with a warm smile.

"It's been my pleasure. Take care, Gerry."

As Emily drives off, Gerry heads up the path to his front door. The familiar sight of his bungalow brings a sense of relief. He opens the door and is immediately greeted by the excited meows of Era and the kittens.

"Hello, my little furballs," Gerry says as he bends down to

CHAPTER 31

their level. Era, with her distinctive fur, weaves around his legs, purring contentedly. The kittens, equally eager, bounce around his feet.

"Do you little kitties want some food? I bet you're starving," Gerry speaks as though he is talking to small children.

He takes off his shoes, and the black kitten promptly jumps into the warm spot left behind. Gerry chuckles, watching the adorable scene. The sight of Era and the kittens is a small comfort amid everything that has happened.

He heads to the kitchen, retrieves their food, and empties a couple of sachets into their bowl. He places it on the floor, and within minutes, the bowl is licked clean. The kittens meow contentedly, their tiny tails twitching in satisfaction.

Gerry watches them with a smile, feeling a sense of normalcy returning. The gentle purring and playful antics of the kittens provide a soothing backdrop as he reflects on the day's events.

For now, it's just him and his beloved pets, a quiet moment of peace.

Gerry walks through the bungalow and immediately notices that the drawers and cupboards are all open. A sense of confusion washes over him. He wonders if the police might have left it like that after they searched the place or if Molly had been looking for something.

He sinks into his familiar armchair, the cushions slightly worn from years of use. Furthermore, he stretches his leg over the armrest and lets out a sigh of relief as he settles into the seat. "Ahh," he says, trying to find comfort in the familiarity of the chair.

"What a bloody nightmare this has all been," he murmurs to himself, reflecting on the chaos that has unfolded over the past days.

Gerry's gaze drifts to the coffee table in the centre of the room. The flowers that had been bought by Rachel for Gerry's Mum are now wilting, their petals drooping under the harsh, dry air of the heating that's been left on. Despite the chill outside, it hasn't been cold enough to justify the radiators being on, leading him to wonder if Molly might have turned them on.

He misses Molly terribly. The emptiness of the bungalow without her presence feels lonely. Gerry's thoughts are consumed by memories of her laughter and warmth. He wonders where she could be, feeling a pang of anxiety. She has no transport, so she couldn't have gone far. He mentally retraces his steps, thinking back to the police station. Surely, if she had been there, he would have noticed her waiting.

Gerry closes his eyes, leaning back into the chair. He clings to a sliver of hope that Molly will find her way back to the bungalow eventually.

For now, he can only wait and hope that, somehow, she will come back to him.

* * *

Carter and Poker climb into their car, fully prepared for the arrest of Ray Chapman. The night is clear, and the promenade is bustling with the glow of illuminations, creating a surreal blur of lights as they speed away from the station. The decision to forego the blue lights is a strategic one, but Carter and Poker are ready to switch to them if traffic becomes an issue.

As they approach Ray's house, the surroundings are

CHAPTER 31

shrouded in darkness, except for a single light glowing downstairs.

Carter glances at Poker, a determined look in his eyes.

"He better be in. I want him in a cell within the next couple of hours," he says firmly.

The car comes to a halt outside the modest house, and they get out, walking up the path to the front door. Carter gives the door a firm knock, the sound echoing in the still night air.

Ray answers the door, his expression a mix of irritation and confusion. He looks directly at Carter, his eyes narrowing with suspicion.

"What are you here for this time?"

Poker, taking the lead in the interaction, maintains a professional demeanour.

"Can we come in, please?"

Ray raises an eyebrow.

"Why?"

Poker holds up a hand, trying to convey calm but firm authority.

"Well, we can do this out here if you prefer, but it's going to be pretty embarrassing for you," Carter says sternly, his tone leaving no room for argument.

Ray hesitates for a moment, then steps aside, begrudgingly allowing them entry. "Fine, come in. But make it quick."

As Carter and Poker step inside, they are greeted by the dimly lit interior of Ray's home. The atmosphere is tense.

Poker exchanges a glance with Carter, signalling that it's time to proceed.

Ray leads them into the living room, where Carter takes a quick look around, noting the disarray that hints at the recent upheaval in the house. Poker begins to speak, his tone both authoritative and composed.

"Ray Chapman, I am arresting you on charges of GBH, ABH, Emotional and Psychological Abuse, and Perverting the Course of Justice," Carter announces, as Poker stands by, ready to assist.

Ray's face goes pale, a mixture of shock and defiance evident in his eyes. He raises his hands above his head, trying to resist.

"You're not taking me in again," he growls.

Poker moves to secure one of Ray's wrists, but Ray evades the attempt, causing a brief struggle. Carter quickly steps in, grabbing Ray's other wrist. A slight scuffle ensues as Ray tries to wriggle free, but Carter's grip is firm.

With some effort, Carter successfully cuffs Ray, who is now subdued and visibly frustrated.

Carter and Poker exchange a look of relief and accomplishment before escorting Ray out of the house.

Ray is led to the police car, his mood sullen and defiant. Carter opens the back door of the vehicle and Ray is unceremoniously placed inside, the metal door closing behind him with a solid clunk.

Poker and Carter shake hands, acknowledging the successful completion of a difficult task. They exchange a brief nod of satisfaction before climbing into the front seats of the car.

The drive back to the station is filled with the hum of the engine and the occasional glance in the rearview mirror, where Ray sits brooding in the back seat. The street lights cast fleeting shadows over the car as they make their way back to the station.

As they pull into the station's car park, Carter and Poker

CHAPTER 31

prepare to process Ray and finalise the arrest, knowing that this case, fraught with complexity and emotion, is now moving toward a crucial resolution.

* * *

With Ray checked in and securely placed in a cell, Carter and Poker head upstairs to rejoin the team.

"We've got Ray," Carter announces as he walks in, his voice carrying a note of satisfaction.

Sharpie, who is meticulously tidying up paperwork and cleaning off the whiteboard, looks up with a tired but genuine smile.

"Oh, well done, lads. That is brilliant," he says, giving them a nod of approval.

The team gathers once more, their faces reflecting the fatigue and resolve of a long day. They dive into discussions about the charges, reviewing the evidence: Molly's diary, the blood-stained clothing, the children's statements and the details of Molly's fabricated new life. It's clear that the evidence against Ray is substantial, and they work with a renewed focus, preparing everything needed for the CPS.

As the team takes a moment to breathe and reflect, the phone rings, slicing through the quiet. Lambert answers it, her face immediately falling as she listens. The room tenses, with everyone exchanging worried glances, bracing for potentially bad news.

Lambert, after a few moments on the phone, nods solemnly and hangs up. She looks around at her colleagues, her eyes filled with sadness.

"It's Dixie," she begins, her voice barely above a whisper.

"He's been admitted to hospital."

A stunned silence falls over the room as the weight of the news settles in.

Chase, visibly shocked, is the first to speak.

"What, how? He was here only a few hours ago?"

Lambert takes a deep breath before responding.

"He's had heart failure. When Lucy got him home, he went to the bathroom and collapsed."

The room is filled with silence as the team processes the news.

His absence is deeply felt, not just for the work he did but for the personal impact he has on each member of the team.

As they grapple with the worry they know they need to continue with the work he was so dedicated to. The team gathers in a sombre circle, sharing a moment of reflection for their fallen leader, committed to seeing the case through to the end.

Chapter 32

Thursday Late Afternoon

During the drive, Molly gazes out the window, her mind racing with thoughts about how much her life has changed. The anticipation of showing Reggie her new home builds up inside her, nervousness and excitement showing.

"Reggie, before we go back to your's can we do something I think is a little more urgent first," Molly asks.

"What is that?" Reggie asks her.

"I want to take you to my home. My new home," she says.

"I don't know Molls."

"Reggie, please. It is important to me. I have kittens!" she says as if trying to persuade her brother.

"Like that is going to sway me." he laughs.

"But alright, if that is what you want to do first," he says.

As they drive through the winding roads leading to Lytham St Annes, Reggie glances over at her.

"You really live all the way out here now?" he asks, sounding a bit surprised.

Molly nods with a soft smile.

"Yes, Reggie. It's peaceful here, far away from all the chaos. I think you'll love it."

Reggie, still a bit sceptical but willing to trust his sister, continues to follow her directions. The car passes quaint cottages and the picturesque views of the seaside, the setting sun casting a warm glow over the landscape. The sight of the sea and the calmness of the area begin to put him at ease.

Eventually, Molly guides Reggie to a quaint, charming bungalow nestled in a quiet neighbourhood.

"This is it," she says, pointing to the modest yet cosy bungalow.

Reggie pulls into the driveway and turns off the engine. He looks around, taking in the peaceful surroundings.

"It's nice, Molls," he admits.

"I can see why you like it here."

They get out of the car, and Molly leads Reggie to the front door. As she unlocks it and pushes it open.

The house is quiet, except for the soft padding of kitten paws on the floor. Two little kittens and their mother, Era, trot out to greet them, their tiny meows filling the air. Molly bends down, scooping up one of the kittens, and looks back at Reggie with a smile.

"See? I told you I have kittens," she says, her face lighting up with a sense of joy and relief.

Reggie chuckles, the tension in his shoulders easing as he watches his sister cuddle the kitten.

"Alright, alright. You win. They are pretty cute."

Molly's smile widens as she motions for Reggie to follow her inside.

"Come on, I want to show you the rest of the bungalow."

Reggie follows her in, looking around at the cosy, well-kept

CHAPTER 32

interior. It's clear that Molly has made this place her own, with personal touches everywhere—a small vase of flowers on the table, a stack of books by the armchair, and a photo of her and Gerry together.

Molly watches him take it all in.

"This is my new life, Reggie," she says softly. "I know it's not what anyone expected, but I've found happiness here. Gerry has been good to me."

Reggie turns to her, his expression softening.

"I just want you to be safe and happy, Molls. That's all I've ever wanted for you."

Tears well up in Molly's eyes, and she quickly wipes them away.

"Thank you, Reggie. That means more than you know."

Reggie pulls her into a hug, holding her tightly.

"We'll figure this out, together. No more running, OK?"

Molly nods against his shoulder.

"No more running," she agrees, feeling a weight lift from her chest.

As they pull away, the kittens circle around their feet, their playful antics bringing a lightness to the moment. Molly reaches down to pet Era, who purrs loudly, rubbing against her hand.

"Now, let's sit down and talk," Reggie suggests, guiding her to the sofa.

"You can tell me everything, and we'll figure out the next steps together."

Molly nods, feeling a sense of relief wash over her. For the first time in a long time, she feels like things might actually be OK.

Reggie listens carefully, taking in everything Molly is

saying. He can see the determination in her eyes, a spark that wasn't there before. She seems different—stronger, more sure of herself. It's a side of her he hasn't seen in a long time, and it fills him with relief and concern.

"I'm glad you're feeling better, Molls," Reggie says gently.

He looks at her, searching her face for any doubt. All he sees is conviction.

"Alright," he says finally.

"I trust you. If you think this is the right move, then I'm behind you 100%. But promise me one thing—if it doesn't work out, you'll let me help. You won't go through it alone."

"What about the children, Molly? Where do they fit into all of this? How do they adjust to this new life you're planning?"

Molly takes a deep breath before answering, her tone steady and reassuring.

"There's plenty of space in the bungalow for all of us. Gerry has always wanted children, but he couldn't have any of his own. I believe he would welcome them into his life, and I think this could be a great environment for them to heal and start fresh. It will all work out perfectly, Reggie."

Reggie isn't convinced yet.

"And their schools? Their friends? What about their routines and their college plans? And then there's Ray. You can't just uproot them without considering all these things."

"I understand your worries," Molly responds.

"And I'll figure out those details soon enough. I know it's not going to be easy, but I truly believe this is the best decision for everyone. I feel it deep in my bones, Gerry is the right person for me, and he can provide the stability and love that the children need."

Reggie gives her a sceptical look.

CHAPTER 32

"And Ray? What's going to happen to him? He's their father, after all."

Molly's face hardens, her resolve clear.

"I'm going to divorce Ray. I've already pressed charges against him for everything he's done to me—both the abuse and the manipulation. The police have all the evidence they need, and it's time he faces the consequences of his actions. The children deserve a safe, nurturing environment, and he's never been able to provide that."

Reggie lets out a long breath, visibly impressed by her determination.

"Wow, Molly. You really have thought this through. It's a lot to take in, but it sounds like you've got a plan, and I'm here to support you every step of the way."

Molly nods, a small smile tugging at her lips.

"Thanks, Reggie. It means a lot to have you on my side. I know there's a long road ahead, but I'm ready to face it, for the sake of my children and myself."

Reggie gives her a reassuring smile.

"I'm with you, Molls. Whatever you need, we'll figure it out together. Just promise me you'll take it slow, OK? One step at a time."

Molly reaches over and squeezes his hand.

"I promise, Reggie. I'm not rushing into anything. I just... I feel like I've been given a second chance, and I don't want to waste it."

Reggie nods, returning the squeeze.

"Alright then. Let's get through tonight, and tomorrow we'll start figuring things out. No more looking back—only forward."

Molly takes a deep breath, feeling anxiety and hope.

"Forward," she echoes.
"I think I'm ready for that."
"Ahem, excuse me?"

A voice from behind startles both Molly and Reggie, making them jump. Molly quickly swings around on the sofa, her eyes widen with surprise as she sees Gerry standing in the doorway.

"GERRY!" she squeals with delight.

Without a second thought, she jumps up and rushes over to him, throwing her arms around him in a tight hug, holding on as if she never wants to let go. Her face lights up with joy and relief.

"Where on earth were you?" she asks.

"I was outside in the garden, having a moment at the spot where Mum fell," Gerry says.

Reggie, slightly taken aback by the sudden appearance of the man he's heard so much about, politely stands up. He feels a small tug on his jeans and looks down to see one of the kittens trying to climb up his leg. With a soft chuckle, he reaches out his hand towards Gerry.

"You must be Gerry," Reggie says in a gentle but cautious tone.

Gerry reaches out and firmly shakes Reggie's hand, his expression sincere.

"I'm Reggie, Molly's brother."

The two men stand there for a moment, both of them glancing at Molly, who is beaming with happiness.

"Shall I make some coffee?" Molly asks, breaking the silence, her excitement making her voice tremble slightly.

"Coffee would be good, please," Reggie replies, nodding with a smile.

CHAPTER 32

"Yes, please, my love," Gerry adds warmly.

Molly's heart flutters at his words, skipping a beat. She turns on her heel and practically skips into the kitchen, eager to prepare the drinks and give the two men a moment to themselves.

The realisation that her brother and her partner are in the same room together feels surreal but comforting.

Reggie watches Molly disappear into the kitchen before turning back to Gerry.

"So, you're the mysterious Gerry I've heard so much about in the last half hour," he begins, doing his best to sound polite.

It's clear he's trying to balance his protective instincts with an open mind, considering that the man before him had been at the centre of his sister's whirlwind experience over the past few days.

Gerry nods, understanding the apprehension in Reggie's voice.

"I am. And I can assure you, Reggie, I only have your sister's best interests at heart. It's been a complicated situation—messy, even—but it seems things are starting to fall into place now."

Reggie studies Gerry for a moment, then says, "I'm pleased to see my sister looking so well. She seems healthier, even—like she's put on a bit of weight. She was so skinny before, barely eating anything. Whatever you've been doing, it seems to be helping her."

Gerry's face softens, a genuine smile spreading across his lips.

"Trust me, I've done my best to take care of her. I know it's been a confusing time for all of us, but I'm committed to making sure she's happy and safe. She means the world to me."

Reggie nods slowly, taking in Gerry's words. Though still cautious, he feels a sense of reassurance in Gerry's sincerity. The man clearly cares for his sister, and that's all Reggie has ever wanted.

Molly returns from the kitchen, carefully balancing two steaming mugs of coffee in her hands. She places them gently on the table next to a vase of wilting flowers. Noticing how sad and droopy the flowers look, she quickly decides to clear some space.

"Let me move these out of the way," she says softly, picking up the vase and carrying it back into the kitchen. A moment later, she reappears with a third mug of coffee for herself.

Molly sits down on the sofa and gestures for Reggie to take his seat again. He nods and settles back into his chair, trying to relax. Gerry chooses the empty spot beside Molly and carefully sits down next to her. As he does, he places a comforting hand on her leg, a small but intimate gesture that reassures her.

Molly instinctively places her hand over his, their fingers naturally intertwining. They squeeze each other's hands tightly, then release, repeating the motion as if giving each other a silent, comforting embrace—a small exchange of reassurance in the presence of her brother.

After a few moments of this silent connection, Reggie clears his throat and speaks up, his voice calm but sincere.

"I was wondering if it might help if I kept the children with me for the next couple of weeks," he offers kindly.

"They were going to stay with us until Sunday anyway, and the week after next, they're on Christmas holiday. They'd be more than welcome to stay at our place during that time

CHAPTER 32

while you two get yourselves settled."

Reggie's tone is warm and understanding, showing he's genuinely trying to help make this transition easier for his sister.

"Oh, Reggie, that is so kind of you. That would be perfect," Molly replies, her voice filled with gratitude. She turns to Gerry, her eyes seeking his approval.

"Wouldn't it, Gerry? It would give the children a chance to get to know you without everything being too overwhelming for them or for you."

Gerry nods, appreciating the thoughtful suggestion.

"Absolutely. And it would also give us some time to get their rooms ready, make sure everything is comfortable for them," he adds.

Molly and Reggie share a warm smile, relieved that the conversation is moving in a positive direction.

"They could come here for dinner a few nights during the week," Gerry suggests, "ease them into it, you know, break them in gently."

Molly looks at Gerry, a hint of concern in her voice.

"Would you be OK with that? I know we haven't had much chance to talk about the children yet, and I don't want to rush things."

Gerry gives her hand another reassuring squeeze.

"Molly, I've always known this moment would come. I just didn't know when. I'm ready for it, for all of it."

Reggie stands up, sensing that his sister and Gerry need some time alone.

"I'm sure you two have a lot you want to talk about," he says, his tone light.

"So, how about I head home now? We were planning on

making pizza with the children. I could bring them over tomorrow after school. Or, if you'd prefer, we could wait until Saturday. They could spend the day with you then. Another few days won't make much of a difference to them, and it'll give everyone a little more time to adjust."

Molly nods, grateful for her brother's understanding and support.

"That sounds like a great idea, Reggie. Thank you so much for everything, but I'd love to see them tomorrow," Molly says, her voice soft with anticipation.

"And maybe again on Saturday." Her face lights up at the thought of reuniting with her children, a warmth spreading through her chest.

Reggie takes a slow sip of his coffee, his demeanour shifting to something more serious.

"There's something I need to tell you, Molly. The real reason I have the children with me right now," he begins carefully.

Molly's smile fades slightly, concern creeping into her expression.

"Oh, I thought they were just staying with you because they wanted to. What's happened?" she asks, worry now in her voice.

Reggie hesitates for a moment, choosing his words.

"Bonnie has been suspended from school," he finally says, watching Molly's reaction closely.

"She got into a fight with another pupil. Now, don't get me wrong—I don't condone fighting, but her actions were justified."

Molly's brow furrows in confusion.

"Justified? How?"

CHAPTER 32

Reggie exhales deeply, looking down at his coffee cup as if gathering the strength to continue.

"The girls had singled Bonnie out and were throwing things at her head, she just snapped." Reggie takes a moment before continuing.

"There is something else. It's Ray. He... struck her, Molly. Across the face. Left a mark."

The colour drains from Molly's face as she takes in what Reggie has said. Her hands begin to shake slightly, and her voice is filled with anger and disbelief.

"That pig!" she exclaims, her tone laced with fury.

"How could he? How dare he lay a hand on her?"

Gerry reaches over to gently squeeze her hand, offering silent support. Reggie watches his sister carefully, knowing this news has hit her hard but also recognises the strength she possesses.

"We've got them now, Molls," Reggie reassures her softly.

"They're safe. And with Ray being in trouble with what you have told the police, he won't be hurting anyone again."

Molly nods, her eyes burning with rage and determination.

"He will never have the chance to hurt them again," she vows.

"I know," Reggie says, his voice relieved.

"I kinda lost my shit with him tonight over it, but they're safe with me now. I've been looking out for them ever since you've been gone."

Molly feels a wave of gratitude washes over her. She jumps out of her seat and throws her arms around Reggie's shoulders, hugging him tightly.

"Thank you so much, Reggie. I don't know what I would have done without you," she says, her voice choked with

343

emotion.

Reggie downs the rest of his coffee in one gulp and stands up tall, stretching his arms over his head. He holds out his empty cup to Molly, who is already standing by, waiting to take it from him.

"Gerry, it was nice meeting you," Reggie says, turning to face him.

"Thank you for looking after my sister." He extends his hand to Gerry again, a gesture of respect and gratitude.

Gerry shakes Reggie's hand with a warm smile.

"It's been my pleasure. She's a special woman," he says.

"Right, I shall be off then," Reggie says as he makes his way to the front door. Before stepping out, he pauses and looks back at Molly.

"Shall I tell the children that you are home now?"

Molly nods, thinking it over for a moment.

"Yes, please do. I want it to sink in a bit before I see them tomorrow if that's OK?" she asks, her voice soft but hopeful.

"They're going to be over the moon," Reggie replies with a smile, knowing how much the children have missed her.

Molly walks Reggie to the front door and wraps her arms around him again, holding him close.

"I'll see you tomorrow, around 4:30 p.m.?" he suggests.

"That will be great," Molly agrees, pulling back to look at him.

"Thank you, Reggie, for everything." She gives him a quick kiss on the cheek, a gesture of deep affection and gratitude, before opening the door for him.

Reggie steps out into the cool evening air and waves goodbye as Molly closes the door gently behind him.

She takes a deep breath, trying to steady herself, then turns

CHAPTER 32

back toward the lounge.

She pauses, her heart skipping a beat.

There, standing in front of her, is Gerry.

The love of her life, the man who helped her find herself again. And now, she doesn't have to pretend to be Elizabeth anymore.

She's Molly—her true self—and she's exactly where she wants to be.

Gerry looks at her with a mixture of love and relief, his eyes softening as they meet hers.

"It's really happening, isn't it?" he says quietly, stepping closer to her.

Molly nods, a tear escaping down her cheek.

"Yes, it is. We're finally here," she whispers, stepping into his arms.

Chapter 33

Thursday Early Evening

Reggie's car pulls up to the curb, its headlights cutting through the dim evening light. As he steps out, he takes a moment to breathe in the cool air, steeling himself for what he knows is going to be an emotional conversation.

He makes his way up the path to the front door, where Oliver is already standing, waiting for him.

Oliver's face is mixed with anticipation and concern, having been told by Yvonne that Reggie had something important to discuss. As Reggie approaches, Oliver shifts nervously on his feet, his hands tucked into the pockets of his jacket.

"Hey, Uncle Reg," Oliver greets, trying to read Reggie's expression.

"What's going on? You sounded kind of serious on the phone."

Reggie gives him a reassuring smile, though it doesn't quite reach his eyes.

"Hey, Ollie," he says warmly, placing a hand on his nephew's

CHAPTER 33

shoulder.

"Let's go inside. We've got a lot to talk about."

Oliver nods and steps aside, opening the door wider for Reggie to enter.

"We made pizzas earlier, and Auntie Von saved you the same one as mine, pepperoni—your favourite," Oliver says, his voice bright with pride.

Reggie smiles warmly at his nephew.

"Sounds perfect. So, you've all filled your bellies up already, have you?" he asks, glancing around the cosy kitchen.

Yvonne wipes her hands on a tea towel as Reggie approaches. She tilts her head up, and they share a quick, tender kiss. Yvonne closes her eyes for a moment, savouring the closeness.

Oliver grimaces and rolls his eyes, making an exaggerated face of mock disgust.

"Ugh, you two are *so* in love," he teases, his tone dripping with playful sarcasm.

Reggie chuckles, reaching over to ruffle Oliver's hair.

"One day, you'll understand," he says with a wink.

"Now, why don't we all sit down? There's something I need to talk to you about."

Bonnie's eyes widen, her voice edged with concern.

"Is it about Mum?" she asks cautiously, searching Reggie's face for any hint of good news or bad.

Reggie nods, pulling up a chair to sit closer to them, his expression serious yet gentle. "Yes, it is. You all know that she's been found and has been living with someone because she lost her memory and couldn't remember who she was," he begins, speaking slowly to ensure they understand. He pauses for a moment, gathering his thoughts, then takes a deep breath.

The children lean in closer, their eyes fixed on him, nodding in silent agreement. They know this story well.

"Yes, we know," they murmur, their voices full of curiosity and anxiety.

Reggie looks at each of them, taking another deep breath to steady himself.

"Well, it turns out that your Mum has gotten her memory back," he says, his voice carrying relief and anticipation.

Lillie gasps, her hands flying to her mouth.

"Oh my god," she exclaims, her eyes wide with disbelief.

"She really is back, I heard you and Dad arguing about Mum this morning but I didn't know how true it all was."

Bonnie bounces in her seat, barely able to contain her excitement.

"For real? Are you serious?" she asks, her voice trembling with hope.

Oliver's face lights up, his voice filled with joy.

"Is Mum coming home?" he squeals, his small body nearly vibrating with excitement.

Reggie raises his hands, gently trying to calm them down.

"Hey, hey, hey, one at a time," he says, chuckling softly at their enthusiastic responses.

His mind is already racing ahead to what he needs to explain next.

He takes another breath and continues, "Your Mum wants to see all of you tomorrow after school." His words hang in the air, the room filling with excitement and anticipation.

"Oh my god," Lillie repeats.

She smirks a little and adds, "I bet she's still with that man, isn't she? The nice-looking one that she liked from the dog

CHAPTER 33

walks," she says, giggling to herself as if it's some juicy secret she's been dying to share.

Reggie's face tightens slightly, and he raises a hand to calm things down.

"Now, let's not get carried away, OK? Making assumptions like that could get your Mum into trouble with your dad," he says, his tone gentle but firm.

Lillie pouts a bit, feeling chastised.

"I didn't mean anything by it," she moans, rolling her eyes.

"I know, sweetheart," Reggie says with a small smile.

"But we have to be careful what we say. Things are a bit complicated right now."

Oliver tilts his head, clearly confused.

"Why? What do you mean?" he asks, his eyebrows pointing upwards as he tries to piece things together.

Reggie takes a deep breath, knowing he has to tread carefully with the next part.

"Well, that's the other thing I need to tell you all," he says, pausing to let his words settle in.

"With the good news comes some bad news," he continues, his voice softer now. The children fall silent, sensing the shift in his tone. Even Yvonne, who had been quietly observing, leans forward in her seat, her expression growing more concerned.

Reggie looks each of the children in the eye, making sure they're ready for what he's about to say.

"Your dad... he's going to be arrested by the police. For hurting your Mum all those times," he finally says, his words deliberate and careful.

Lillie's face hardens, and she mutters under her breath, "Good."

Bonnie nods in agreement, her face scrunched up in anger.

"He deserves to be arrested. And he should get done for slapping me too," she adds, her voice rising with frustration.

Oliver crosses his arms, looking equally upset.

"To be honest, he's been pretty horrible to Mum and to all of us. And don't forget he slapped me too, and he's always shouting at Daisy" he says, his voice firm.

Reggie listens carefully, noting how well the children are taking the news about their father.

There's a sense of relief among them, almost as if a weight has been lifted. Feeling it's time to shift back to more positive news, he decides to steer the conversation back to their Mum.

"Well," Reggie says gently, a small smile forming on his lips, "let's focus on the fact that your Mum is safe and wants to see you all. That's the most important thing right now. She's missed you a lot."

"So, your Mum is with another man," Reggie begins carefully, choosing his words. "And his name is—"

"Gerry," Lillie interrupts with a sly grin, rolling her eyes playfully.

Oliver and Bonnie giggle, clearly amused by their sister's cheeky confidence.

Reggie chuckles softly, shaking his head.

"Yes, Gerry," he confirms with a small smile.

"It seems like you already know more than I thought. After school tomorrow, you can all go and see your Mum and meet 'Gerry,' if that's what you'd like to do," he continues, glancing at each of the children to gauge their reactions.

The children nod eagerly, their faces lighting up at the idea of seeing their Mum.

"That settles it then," Reggie says, feeling a sense of relief

CHAPTER 33

wash over him. He turns to Yvonne, sharing a knowing smile with her.

"Do any of you have any questions?" he asks, making sure to give them space to voice any concerns.

"Nope," they all reply in unison, shaking their heads.

"Actually I do," says Oliver.

"Will we be living back with Mum or will be staying here with you and Auntie Von?" he asks.

"Your Mum would like you all to live with her and Gerry. They have a beautiful bungalow, but it is in Lytham St Annes, so you would most likely be changing schools," says Reggie.

"Bloody good!" exclaims Bonnie.

"Well, you might need another school if you keep beating up the bullies." laughs Yvonne.

"OK, any more questions, or are you all satisfied with what I have said tonight?" he asks.

"No more questions Uncle Reggie," says Oliver.

"Yeah, we're all good." Says Bonnie and Lillie.

"Well then, let's get ourselves washed up for bed and get a good night's sleep for school tomorrow," Reggie instructs, clapping his hands together lightly to signal it's time to move on.

"Except for me," says Bonnie playfully following her older sister's cheekiness.

The children scramble up from the sofa, immediately starting to bicker about who gets to use the bathroom first, their footsteps thundering up the stairs. Their voices echo down the hallway, playful teasing and mock arguments.

Yvonne watches them go, a smile spreading across her face.

"You did well there, Reggie," she says softly, her eyes filled with admiration.

"I'm really proud of you."

Reggie wraps his arm around Yvonne's shoulder and pulls her close, feeling the warmth of her body against his. He leans down and kisses her gently on the forehead, his lips lingering for a moment. As he pulls back, he lets out a big sigh of exhaustion and relief.

"It's been a long day," he admits, his voice low.

"But I think things are finally starting to look up."

* * *

Thursday Late Evening

The two of them snuggle together on the sofa, their bodies pressed close as the kittens curl up by their feet, purring contentedly.

Gerry's fingers caress the back of Molly's neck in a little tiptoe motion, sending shivers down her spine. He leans in and kisses the top of her head tenderly while stroking the side of her face.

"You really are very beautiful, Molly," he murmurs, his voice filled with admiration.

"You are not so bad yourself Gerry." Molly giggles.

Gerry presses soft kisses along the back of her neck and shoulders, his lips brushing against her skin. Molly responds with a delighted shiver, her body reacting to his touch, the goosebumps rising with the hairs on her body.

Molly turns her head to face him, her eyes meeting his with a mix of affection and desire.

Wanting each other.

CHAPTER 33

Needing each other.

Molly captures Gerry's lips in a kiss, her own lips moving in sync with his.

He cradles her face in his hands, his thumbs gently tracing the contours of her cheeks.

"I really do love you," he whispers, his words a soothing caress against her lips.

"I love you too," she replies, her body feeling like electricity is running through it.

He kisses her again, deeper this time, his tongue tracing a tender path across her lips.

Molly parts her lips slightly, welcoming the warmth of his tongue as it slips into her mouth. Their tongues dance together, entwining in a slow, passionate rhythm, each movement an expression of their loving connection.

Molly gently bites his bottom lip, pulling it away from his mouth, teasing it between her own lips as she sucks on his lip.

She giggles again.

The kiss deepens as they lose themselves in each other, the world outside fading away. For a moment, it's just the two of them, wrapped in the comfort of their love, while the kittens purr softly, a gentle reminder of the peaceful night they've created together.

Gerry's fingers trace a soft path along Molly's neck, their touch gentle yet electrifying. As his hand glides down her shoulder, he carefully slips her bra strap off, his movements tender and deliberate.

With a subtle but assured touch, he works the clasp of her bra free, letting it fall away and revealing the delicate curves beneath her top.

Gerry lets out a moan.

"Oh, Molly. I want you."

He moves with a sense of reverence, lifting her top slowly, exposing her skin inch by inch.

As the fabric clears her breasts, Molly instinctively shakes her hair loose from the small clip she has holding it back off of her face, allowing it to cascade down her back in a natural motion.

Standing before Gerry, Molly's bare skin is illuminated by the soft light of the room. Gerry's gaze holds a blend of admiration and affection as he gently cups her breasts in his hands. His touch is feather-light, exploring and savouring each sensation.

Molly's body is exposed and standing in front of Gerry, her breasts level with his eyes, he then cups her breasts in his hands and gently suckles on her nipples. They turn erect as he flicks them with his finger and thumb and then gently rubs them between his fingers.

Almost naked, Molly unzips her jeans and pushes them down past her waist, exposing her tummy and then her thin lacey black knickers.

Gerry takes his hand and strokes with a butterfly motion between her legs. She opens them partly while Gerry slides his fingers in between her legs and slightly inserts a finger inside her. He feels her dampness and it excites him. Feeling a wave of goosebumps covering his body, his hair stands on end with each touch of Molly's delicate fingertips.

Molly squirms against his hand as he plays with her. Gerry takes his shirt off and unbuttons his jeans sliding them down his legs and exposing his boxer shorts, inside them his hardness wants her.

CHAPTER 33

Gerry stands before Molly, he gently pushes her knickers down to her ankles, and she kicks them off delicately with her foot.

Now she is completely naked and standing in front of Gerry whilst he slides his boxer shorts down past his waist to his ankles. He steps out of them, and he, himself starts to giggle at their clumsiness of trying to get out of their underwear.

The two of them stand together and kiss passionately while they rub themselves against each other.

Molly forcefully pushes Gerry back down on the sofa and she kneels on top of him and gently lowers herself down onto his erection.

They passionately make love on the sofa. The world outside seems to fade away as they lose themselves in each other.

The evening passes quietly, filled with whispered words of love and shared moments of intimacy.

In each other's arms, they find not only physical closeness but also a deep, enduring emotional connection.

* * *

"Why don't you head home, Carter?" Poker suggests, concerned.

"It's getting late, man. You've been at it for days straight. You need to give yourself a break."

Carter shakes his head, a determined look in his eyes.

"I can't, lad. Not until we've got all the evidence sorted and ready to charge Ray Chapman tomorrow. I want everything squeaky clean, no loose ends, no bits of dirt hanging around anywhere. It's got to be perfect. It's what Dixie would have done."

Poker studies Carter for a moment, noting the exhaustion etched on his face.

"Alright, Carter. Just make sure you're looking after yourself too. You might not be alone in here much longer."

Carter glances over at the forensic lab where Lambert is still working diligently, her focus unwavering as she analyzes the forensic evidence. Poker nods towards her, a hint of reassurance in his gesture.

"Night, Poker. And thanks for everything today. You did a great job," Carter says, his voice carrying genuine gratitude.

Poker offers a supportive smile as Carter heads towards the lab, the weight of their shared responsibility still heavy on his shoulders.

Chapter 34

Friday Morning

Sharpie, Carter, Chase, Poker, Lambert, and Gilbert gather in the main office, each one clutching breakfast wraps and muffins.

The enticing aroma of fresh coffee mingles with the scent of warm pastries, filling the air with a comforting warmth that momentarily lifts the tension from the room.

In the centre of the table, a drinks tray is crowded with hot coffees, their lids gently steaming in the cool air of the office. The team huddles around, leaning in as they prepare for the day's work, the early morning light casting soft shadows across their faces. They all take a moment to settle in, the crinkling of wrap paper the only sound in the quiet room.

The whiteboard is now crammed with fresh leads and connections, each line and note tying Molly more closely to the evidence against Ray Chapman.

Diagrams, photos, and notes overlap in a chaotic but meaningful way, illustrating the full scope of their investigation.

Carter stands before it, pointing to various pieces of evidence with a marker.

"So, team, Lambert and I were up all night pulling together everything we have against Chapman. We've compiled enough evidence to go to the CPS, and we're confident we have grounds to charge him with domestic violence."

He pauses, his voice steady but intense.

"This covers the full spectrum of abuse: controlling, coercive, threatening behaviour, violence, and emotional abuse of someone aged over 16 in an intimate relationship."

Carter takes a breath, letting the weight of his words settle over the room. "Psychological, physical, emotional—this is gaslighting at its worst. Under the Domestic Abuse Act 2021 and the Serious Crime Act 2015, Section 76, Chapman could be facing a sentence of five to ten years."

As Carter speaks, Lambert steps forward from the back of the room.

She wipes a spot of ketchup from her chin and smiles at the team as she swallows the last bite of her breakfast.

"In short, we've got him. We're putting in the email to the CPS this morning and, with any luck, we'll have Chapman officially charged before lunchtime today."

A wave of satisfaction washes over the team. They exchange smiles and nods, acknowledging the hard work and dedication that Carter and Lambert have poured into this case, pushing through the night without a bit of sleep.

Carter winks at Lambert, a silent gesture of camaraderie and appreciation. The exchange doesn't go unnoticed. Gilbert glances at Poker, who raises an eyebrow and grins knowingly. She returns the smile, a shared acknowledgement of the sparks flying between their colleagues, adding a layer of warmth to the otherwise tense atmosphere.

CHAPTER 34

* * *

After dropping Lillie off at college and Oliver at school, Reggie heads into town with a purpose.

His mind is set on getting his sister a new mobile phone, something simple and easy to use. He walks into the mobile phone shop, his eyes scanning the rows of shiny devices displayed on sleek stands. Reggie knows his sister isn't one for flashy gadgets or high-tech features; she needs something straightforward that won't overwhelm her.

A sales assistant, a young man with a friendly smile and a name badge that reads "Tim," approaches Reggie, ready to assist.

"Can I help you find something today?" Tim asks.

Reggie nods, explaining, "Yeah, I'm looking for a phone for my sister. Nothing too complicated—she's not into gaming or streaming or anything like that. Mostly, she'll just use it for WhatsApp messaging. So, I need something with a simple user interface that she can start using right away without much fuss. Also, I need a SIM card, and she prefers the Pay As You Go type."

Tim listens attentively, nodding as he considers the options.

"Got it. We have a few models that would be perfect for her needs. Let me show you some that have a straightforward interface and are easy to navigate. Plus, they all come with Pay As You Go options. How does that sound?"

"Sounds good," Reggie replies, feeling a sense of relief that he's in capable hands. He follows Tim to a section of the store where the simpler, more basic models are displayed, hoping to find the perfect phone for his sister.

Tim stops in front of a small display.

"We have this Samsung A13," he says, pointing to a sleek, modest phone. "It's £155 for the model with the least storage, which is still plenty for photos and a decent amount of music files. It's got a simple interface, and it'll do just fine for WhatsApp and basic use."

As Tim rattles off the specs of the phone, emphasising its straightforward design and user-friendly features, Reggie listens carefully. By the time Tim finishes, Reggie is convinced this is the right choice for his sister.

"Alright, I'll take it," Reggie decides, nodding with satisfaction.

Tim smiles, pleased to have made a sale. He pulls a brand-new box from under the counter and slides it into a small bag, adding the Pay As You Go SIM card on top.

Reggie inserts his card into the card reader, the machine beeping softly as it processes the payment. He grabs his receipt.

"Thanks, Tim." He says and heads out of the shop, feeling accomplished.

Once back in his car, Reggie can't help but grin. He pulls the mobile out of its packaging and inserts the SIM card, watching the screen light up as he turns it on for the first time. As he waits for the phone to boot up, he chuckles to himself, the situation struck him as oddly amusing. Sitting in his car in a nearly empty car park, fiddling with a brand-new phone, he imagines how this might look to someone passing by.

"This must be what it feels like to be a drug dealer," he mutters under his breath, grinning at the absurdity of setting up what feels like a burner phone in the middle of the

CHAPTER 34

morning. His laughter fills the quiet car, with relief and humour at his own imagination running wild.

***

The doorbell rings, and Molly hesitates, a knot of anxiety forming in her stomach. She's worried it might be the police wanting to bring her in for more questioning. Taking a deep breath, she reluctantly makes her way to the door.

When she opens it, relief washes over her as she sees Reggie standing there with a warm smile, a bag in one hand and a bottle of milk in the other.

"To what do I owe this pleasure?" she asks, smiling back at him, feeling her tension at ease.

"I thought you could use a fresh bottle of milk since my coffee didn't taste too nice last night," he laughs, holding up the bottle playfully.

Molly chuckles, taking the milk from him.

"Come on in," she says, pleased to see her brother again so soon.

As he steps inside, she asks, "I was just about to make some cereal. You want some?"

"Good job I got the milk then," he jokes, his laughter filling the small entryway.

"I have a present for you," Reggie says, handing the paper bag over to her with a grin.

Curious, Molly peers inside and sees a brand-new mobile phone nestled in the bag. Her eyes widen in surprise.

"Oh, Reggie, this is too much! I can't take this from you!" she exclaims, her voice a mix of gratitude and shock.

"Call it a welcome home gift," Reggie insists gently, his eyes full of affection.

Molly's heart swells with emotion, and she throws her arms around him, pulling him into a tight hug. She plants a kiss on his forehead, overwhelmed by his thoughtfulness.

"Thank you, Reggie. This means a lot," she says softly.

They make their way into the kitchen together, side by side, the kittens trailing behind them, their little paws pattering softly on the floor. The room feels warmer, brighter, and filled with a sense of comfort and familial love.

The bathroom door unlocks, and Gerry steps out, making his way into the kitchen.

He looks well-rested, his hair still damp from the shower.

"Good morning Reggie. How are you doing?" he asks warmly, walking over with a welcoming smile.

Reggie nods and smiles back, reaching out to shake Gerry's hand.

"I'm good, thanks," he replies.

"Look what Reggie got me!" Molly beams, holding up her new phone proudly.

Gerry glances at the phone and smiles.

"Oh, what a lovely gesture. Thank you, Reggie," he says, putting his arm around Molly's shoulders. Together, they look at the phone, Gerry's arm a comforting presence around her.

Molly's eyes widen as she turns the screen on and starts tapping around, getting a feel for the device. Gerry reaches behind the kitchen door, grabbing a small business card off the noticeboard attached there.

Molly gives him a confused look as he hands her the card.

"The Wi-Fi code, dear," he laughs.

"Oh, yes, right," she giggles, embarrassed.

CHAPTER 34

"That would help."

"That's handy," Reggie chuckles, watching the two of them.

Gerry continues to prepare the drinks, setting them all on a tray. Once they're ready, he leads the way into the lounge, where they settle into the comfortable chairs. The morning light filters in through the curtains, casting a soft glow around the room.

"So, how did the children take the news?" Gerry asks as he sits down, handing out the mugs of steaming coffee.

Reggie takes a sip before answering, "Really well, actually." He glances over at Molly, who's engrossed in her new phone, scrolling and tapping with intense concentration.

"We probably won't get any sense out of her now," Gerry laughs, watching her.

"She hasn't had a mobile in quite some time."

Reggie chuckles, nodding.

"Yeah, so, the children took it pretty well. They're excited about meeting you later today." He pauses, his tone becoming a bit more serious.

"I told them about their father, too."

Molly looks up from her phone, concern clouding her features.

"And how did they take that?" she asks, her voice filled with worry. She's anxious about how her children might react to her decision to press charges against their father.

Reggie takes a deep breath.

"They were surprisingly OK with it. I think they understand why it has to be done. Lillie and Bonnie, especially, seemed relieved. Oliver took it a little harder, I could tell by the way he dismissed his father so quickly but I think he's definitely on your side and was also concerned about how

Ray treats Daisy."

Molly's shoulders relax slightly, and she nods, reassured by Reggie's words.

"I was so worried they'd be upset with me for pressing charges."

"They know you're doing the right thing, Molly," Gerry adds gently, reaching over to squeeze her hand.

"They just want you to be safe and happy."

Molly smiles softly at him, then at Reggie.

"Thank you, both of you. I'm just glad to have everyone's support."

They sip their coffees as Molly continues to set up her new phone, her fingers moving deftly over the screen.

The warm aroma of freshly brewed coffee fills the room, mingling with the soft hum of the aga in the background.

"So, what are your plans over the next few weeks?" Reggie asks, leaning back in his chair, watching his sister's face for any hint of her thoughts.

Molly looks up, her expression contemplative.

"Well, with Christmas fast approaching, I thought it would be nice to get the house ready for the children to come back on Christmas Eve," she says, a hint of excitement in her voice.

Reggie studies her, his eyebrow raising slightly.

"Are you sure? Didn't you want to get Christmas out of the way and then start fresh in the New Year?" He's trying to be careful, knowing how much she's been through, and wanting to make sure she's not taking on too much too soon.

Molly smiles softly, appreciating his concern.

"I know you're just trying to help, Reggie, but I've given it a lot of thought. I think it's important for the children to have some normalcy, especially after everything that's happened.

CHAPTER 34

I want them to feel like a proper family for Christmas."

Reggie nods, understanding where she's coming from but still wanting to be sure she's ready.

"No, I agree. I just want you to be certain, that's all. The children are welcome to stay with us for as long as they need. You don't have to rush into anything."

Molly turns to Gerry, her eyes wide and hopeful, a look that's hard for anyone to resist. "Will you be alright with that, Gerry?" she asks, her voice soft and earnest.

Gerry meets her gaze, his face breaking into a warm smile. He chuckles softly, unable to resist her pleading expression.

"Of course, Molly. I'd love to have the children here for Christmas. It sounds wonderful," he replies, squeezing her hand reassuringly.

Molly's face lights up with gratitude.

"Thank you, Gerry. It means a lot to me. I want this Christmas to be special for all of us."

Gerry nods, his eyes warm with affection.

"It will be. We'll make it a Christmas to remember."

Reggie looks between them and grins.

"Alright then, looks like we've got ourselves a plan. Let's make this Christmas one for the books."

* * *

Carter finalizes the case file for the CPS, carefully reviewing each piece of evidence and documentation one last time. After making sure everything is in order, he clicks "send" on his email, the sound of the mouse click echoing in the quiet office. He takes a deep breath, hoping that all their hard work will pay off and lead to a solid case against Ray Chapman.

Knowing it could be a few hours before they receive a response from the CPS, Carter decides to keep himself busy. He begins tidying up the office, organizing papers into neat stacks and clearing away empty coffee cups that have accumulated during their late-night work sessions.

Sharpie is sitting in Dixie's old office. The room remains untouched, with everything left just as Dixie had arranged it.

Feeling a blend of anticipation and concern, Carter decides to check in with Sharpie. He hopes to get any updates about Dixie's condition from Lucy, who has been by Dixie's side throughout his hospitalisation.

When he reaches the doorway, Carter knocks gently on the doorframe.

"Hey, Sharpie. Got a minute?" he asks quietly, not wanting to disturb Sharpie's thoughts.

Sharpie looks up from his seat, his face lined with worry.

"Yeah, sure, Carter. What's up?" he replies, setting down a piece of paper he'd been absently reading.

"I was wondering if there's been any news from Lucy about Dixie's health. Have you heard anything recently?" Carter asks.

Sharpie sighs and shakes his head.

"Nothing new since last night. Lucy said they're still running tests. Dixie's stable, but… you know how it is. It's a waiting game right now."

Carter nods, understanding the frustration and helplessness that comes with waiting for news.

"Yeah, I get it. I just hope he pulls through."

Carter gives a small smile.

He lingers for a moment, taking in the quiet determination in Sharpie's eyes, before turning back toward his desk. As

CHAPTER 34

he walks away, Carter can't help but feel a sense of purpose.

They have to make sure everything they're doing now honours Dixie's work and dedication.

Chapter 35

Friday Late Afternoon

The children are quietly chatting amongst themselves in the back of the car, their excitement surprisingly well-contained.

Lillie and Oliver whisper to one another while Bonnie gazes out the window, taking in the passing scenery.

In the front, Yvonne sits beside Reggie, looking as lovely as ever. She's made a real effort in preparation for seeing her sister-in-law and meeting Gerry for the first time. Her hair is elegantly styled, and she wears a warm but floral dress that complements her warm smile.

"You look gorgeous, Vonnie," Reggie says, glancing over at her as he drives toward Lytham. He places a reassuring hand on her lap, giving it a gentle squeeze. Yvonne smiles and places her hand on top of his.

"Thank you, love. I wanted to make a good impression," she replies softly, a hint of nervousness in her voice.

"It's a really lovely area they've moved to," she adds, looking out at the rows of quaint houses and the lush, tree-lined streets.

CHAPTER 35

"Yes, it is. Wait until you see their bungalow. It's huge inside—much bigger than the old place," Reggie says with a grin, eager to see his sister settling into her new home.

Yvonne laughs lightly.

"I wonder what Molly's going to cook for us. You know how much she hates cooking!" she jokes, her eyes twinkling with amusement.

Reggie chuckles, shaking his head.

"Honestly, I have no idea. Knowing Molly, she probably ordered takeaway. But whatever it is, it'll be fine. The important thing is we're all together," he says warmly.

Yvonne nods in agreement, feeling a bit more at ease.

She glances back at the children, who are still immersed in their conversation, and then turns to look ahead at the road.

As they drive, a sense of anticipation fills the car, mingled with a touch of nervous excitement.

Today is not just a reunion but a step toward healing and starting fresh as a family.

They pull up into the large driveway, and Reggie turns off the car's engine. As the doors open, the exterior lights of the bungalow automatically flicker on, casting a warm glow over the front of it. The soft light illuminates the carefully manicured garden and the charming stone pathway surrounded by a picket fence, giving the bungalow a cosy, romantic feel.

The children pile out of the car, their eyes wide as they take in the sight of their mother's new home.

Inside, Molly stands in front of a large mirror, adjusting her hair one last time. She takes a deep breath, feeling excitement and anxiety. Behind her, Gerry steps closer and places his hands gently on her shoulders, his touch both reassuring and steadying.

"You look stunning, Molly," Gerry says softly.

"The children are going to be beside themselves when they see you."

Molly turns around to face him, her eyes meeting his. There's a vulnerability in her gaze, of gratitude and lingering uncertainty.

"Thank you for this," she murmurs, her voice barely above a whisper.

Gerry tilts his head slightly, confused.

"For what?" he asks gently, searching her face for clarity.

"Well, a few days ago, we were living a lie," Molly begins, her voice trembling slightly. "Both of us were," she adds, her eyes flickering with the weight of everything they've gone through.

Sensing her nerves, Gerry quickly interjects, not wanting to dwell on the past or risk losing the hopeful momentum they've built.

"Let's not dwell on what we did or didn't do," he says softly, squeezing her shoulders in reassurance. He takes a deep breath, his voice steady and calm.

"Let's focus on what we are going to do," he continues, a small smile forming on his lips.

He leans in closer, his forehead almost touching hers.

"As a family," he adds, his words carrying a promise of new beginnings and a shared future.

Molly nods, her heart swelling with emotion. She wraps her arms around Gerry, holding him tight for a moment.

The sound of children approaching the front door pulls them back to the present. She pulls away, giving Gerry a grateful smile before heading toward the door.

CHAPTER 35

"They're here," she says, her voice filled with excitement and nervous anticipation.

Gerry follows her, his hand resting gently on her back, ready to welcome the children and begin this new chapter together.

The children stand on the doorstep, their nerves obvious as they look towards the front door. Behind them, Reggie and Yvonne offer encouraging smiles. As the door swings open, the warm light from inside spills into the driveway, casting their silhouettes against the soft glow.

Molly, standing just inside the entrance, gasps as she sees her children for the first time in what feels like forever. Her hand flies to her mouth, overwhelmed by emotion. Tears well up in her eyes as she takes in the sight of her children huddled together on the step.

Without waiting for an invitation, Lillie rushes forward, her voice breaking with excitement and relief.

"Mum!" she squeals, her arms flinging around her mother's shoulders in a tight embrace. Tears stream down her face as she clings to Molly.

Bonnie and Oliver are quick to join in, their tears mingling with Lillie's as they envelop their mother in a collective, heartfelt hug. Bonnie's voice quivers as she cries, "Mum, you are here."

Oliver's voice is choked with emotion as he adds, "Mum, you are back."

Molly wraps her arms around her children, her tears flowing freely as she holds them close.

The porch fills with fusion of sobs and laughter, the reunion marked by a powerful mix of relief and joy.

The warmth and love shared in that moment make all the

uncertainty and separation seem a distant memory.

Reggie and Yvonne stand back, letting the family have their moment.

As he watches Molly, Gerry's eyes are misty with emotion, touched by the depth of the reunion. Yvonne gives him a gentle, encouraging smile, understanding the significance of this first meeting and the new beginnings it represents.

As the embrace slowly loosens, Molly looks at each of her children with love and gratitude.

"I've missed you all so much, and how is Daisy, is she doing alright too?" she whispers, her voice trembling.

"We've really missed you too Mum," says Lillie.

"Daisy is doing great, we have her at Uncle Reggie and Auntie Yvonne's," she says.

"We're going to make up for lost time, I promise," says Molly.

The children, still holding onto their mother, nod in agreement, their faces shining with happiness. The scene is filled with the echoes of their joy and the comforting warmth of their family reunion.

Gerry steps back from the doorway, giving the family the space they need to enter their new home. He feels a surge of emotion, reflecting on how proud his mother would have been to see him welcoming his new family and imagining the joy she would have felt spoiling her grandchildren.

As the children, still wrapped in their reunion with Molly, begin to settle, Oliver looks up at Gerry and says, "Hello."

Gerry offers a warm, welcoming smile, extending his hand.

"Hi there," he says, his voice steady despite the emotions bubbling just beneath the surface.

Oliver, initially unsure, hesitates for a moment before

CHAPTER 35

reaching out to shake Gerry's hand. He grips it firmly, and Gerry returns the handshake with equal strength, a sign of his respect and earnestness in this new relationship.

As the children move further into the bungalow, followed closely by Reggie and Yvonne, Reggie takes the opportunity to introduce his wife.

"Gerry, this is my wife, Yvonne."

Gerry turns to Yvonne, a polite and genuine smile on his face. He extends his hand, cradling hers as he gently shakes it.

"Nice to meet you, Yvonne," he says warmly, making an effort to show his respect and appreciation.

Yvonne returns the smile, her eyes reflecting both gratitude and a sense of relief at this new chapter for her family.

"It's lovely to meet you, Gerry. Thank you for making Molly and the children feel so welcome."

Gerry nods, his emotions still close to the surface.

"It's a pleasure. I'm glad you're all here."

"Please, come on in and make yourselves comfortable," Gerry warmly invites, gesturing for everyone to step inside.

"Feel free to explore the place," he continues.

"We have two spacious bedrooms, a cosy lounge, and a large dining room that is separate from the kitchen. But the kitchen has enough room for a dining table in there, creating a great space for meals and gatherings."

Gerry stops talking allowing everyone to take his words in. Molly finds it funny as Gerry mimics an estate agent.

"There's also a quiet study filled with a huge collection of books, perfect for doing homework or just curling up with a good read."

Gerry pauses for a moment while he gets his breath.

"Upstairs, there's a converted loft space that we're considering turning into our bedroom. It used to be my Mum's sewing room, so it holds a lot of cherished memories for me. The loft is quite special, and we're excited about converting it.

Outside, we have a large garden with a lovely pond, surrounded by greenery. There's also a shed stocked with gardening equipment, though I'm thinking about building a bigger one—perhaps even a summerhouse. It would be a great addition to the garden, giving us more space to enjoy the outdoors."

Gerry moves around the lounge to light the fire.

"Please be careful in the first bedroom as we have a cat and her two kittens in there at the moment," he says.

"Kittens!" the children shriek together.

"Yes, kittens, just the two but they are mischievous at the moment, I will let them out later for you to have a play with them," he says.

"I see you have a motorbike as well, Gerry," Reggie remarks, noticing the bike with interest.

"Yes, it's my pride and joy," Gerry replies with a grin, then adds with a chuckle, "along with your sister, of course."

"Mum, what's going to happen with your car now that Dad's being arrested?" Lillie asks concerned.

"I'd like to get it back and start driving again," Molly responds thoughtfully.

"And Lillie, you're at the age now where I could start teaching you how to drive. How does that sound?"

"That would be so cool, Mum!" Lillie exclaims, her excitement bubbling over at the thought of learning to drive her mother's car.

CHAPTER 35

Molly smiles at Lillie's enthusiasm before turning to the rest of the family.

"Alright, everyone, go on and have a look around. Let us know if you have any ideas for the bedrooms. We can convert any of the rooms if needed."

With that, the children eagerly dash off, their laughter echoing through the bungalow as they explore. Gerry watches them with amusement, hearing snippets of their chatter, like "I want this room!" and "I bet we wouldn't be allowed to have this one," causing him to smile to himself.

"So, how are you going to divvy up the rooms?" Reggie asks, curious.

Gerry and Molly both start to answer at the same time, but Gerry stops himself, letting Molly speak first.

"I think the children should be allowed to choose their rooms," Molly says with a gentle smile.

"We'll be taking the loft space, so it doesn't really matter which rooms they pick."

"Anyway, come in from the chill. Let's get you both a drink," Gerry suggests warmly, ushering Reggie and Yvonne into the bungalow.

Yvonne, ever mindful of cleanliness, slips off her shoes at the door. Reggie glances down at her bunions, thinking to himself with a chuckle, *'I wouldn't have shown those off, love,'* as he removes his own shoes. He smiles at the pile of children's shoes already left at the entrance.

Barefoot except for their socks, everyone gathers in the cosy lounge. Molly soon appears, carrying a tray with speciality coffees for everyone. She's used the Tassimo coffee machine, hoping to impress her brother and sister-in-law with a perfect cup. The rich aroma of coffee fills the room as they all settle in, ready to enjoy the warmth and each other's company.

"So, what's on the menu tonight, Molly? Is it your famous à la carte takeaway?" Reggie teases with a laugh.

Molly meets Gerry's eyes and grins, "I told you he'd say that." Her laughter is infectious, and soon, everyone joins in.

"I was actually thinking of letting the children choose the meal," Molly continues. "Give them a bit of responsibility."

"You know they're going to choose pizza again," Yvonne chimes in with a knowing smile.

Gerry chuckles and adds, "Is that their favourite food, then?"

"How did you guess?" Molly replies, playfully rolling her eyes. She places a comforting hand on Gerry's lap, sensing how overwhelming this transition must be for him. They had talked earlier about how he was moving from a life of solitude to suddenly being thrust into the role of a father figure, along with gaining a new brother and sister-in-law.

The changes are significant, and she wants to be there for him.

Neither Gerry nor Molly have in-laws, a fact made even more poignant by the upcoming funeral of Gerry's mother. The loss is still fresh, and the absence of family is a stark reminder of the challenges ahead.

Unaware of his recent loss, Yvonne innocently asks, "Do you have any family, Gerry?"

Gerry hesitates for a moment, not wanting to bring down the mood. He offers a simple, "No, my family has all passed on. I was an only child."

There's a brief pause before Gerry adds, "I do have my Aunt Maud, though. She lives practically next door. She was

CHAPTER 35

my mother's midwife when I was born, and they stayed best friends right up until the end." His voice carries fondness and sadness, but he manages a small smile, grateful for the connection he still has to his past.

Yvonne immediately feels awful for bringing up such a sensitive topic. She shoots Reggie a quick, glance and squeezes his hand, a silent reprimand for not giving her a heads-up about Gerry's situation. Reggie winces slightly, realising he should have warned her, but he gives her a reassuring squeeze back, understanding her concern.

Oliver comes back into the room and quietly sits down next to his mother.

He looks up at her with big, sincere eyes and says, "I'm glad you're back, Mum. I've really missed you," his voice carrying the weight of a young child's emotions, unfiltered and pure.

Molly's heart swells with pride at her little boy's openness. At that moment, she feels deeply proud of him for expressing his feelings so honestly in front of everyone.

"I've missed you too, Oli, very, very much," she replies, her voice soft and filled with love.

Oliver wraps his arms around his mother in a tight hug, and she holds him close, cherishing the connection they share. After a moment, he pulls back and looks up at her, his expression shifting to something more immediate.

"I'm really hungry," he announces, his simple statement cutting through the emotional moment.

Molly smiles at the innocence of his words, realising how beautifully uncomplicated a child's world can be. In his eyes, there's no problem too big that can't be put aside for the more pressing matter of a rumbling stomach. She reflects on how, for children, the smallest things—like hunger—are often the most important.

Molly calls the children into the lounge, gathering them around with a smile.

"Alright, everyone, I need you to decide what we're having for dinner tonight," she says, giving them the responsibility she promised.

Without hesitation, the children shout in unison, "Pizza!"

Molly laughs at their enthusiasm.

"Pizza it is then," she agrees, reaching into her pocket to pull out her new phone.

"I'll use my new phone to go on Just Eat and order it."

As she starts to navigate the app, the children crowd around her, excitedly suggesting their favourite toppings and types of pizza.

The atmosphere in the room is filled with anticipation and the comforting promise of a familiar, well-loved meal being shared with family.

Chapter 36

Friday Early Evening

The day drags on, tension building with each passing hour as Carter and his team wait for the Crown Prosecution Service to deliver their decision.

Just before 6 PM, the email finally came through, granting permission to charge Ray Chapman. A wave of relief and excitement sweeps through the team as they realise their hard work has paid off.

"Finally!" Carter exclaims, and the team immediately begins sorting the evidence back into its designated places, carefully logging everything as they prepare for the next steps. The air buzzes with renewed energy.

Excited by the news, Carter turns to Poker.

"Come with me," he says.

"We're going to get ready to interview and charge Chapman."

Poker nods, fully aware of the significance of the moment. Carter picks up the phone and dials down to the Custody Suite. Biff, back on duty, answers promptly.

"Biff, can you please contact Ray Chapman's solicitor? We

want him in the interview room in an hour," Carter instructs, his voice steady but urgent.

"Will do," Biff responds, already making the necessary arrangements.

Carter hangs up the phone and motions for Poker to follow him into his office in the corner of the room.

The office feels stark and empty, a reflection of how chaotic the last few days have been. Sharpie moved his belongings out earlier, transferring them into Dixie's old office. However, he hasn't yet had the heart to unpack or make the space his own, the office still holding an aura of transition and uncertainty.

Carter's own office is equally bare, devoid of personal touches or belongings. He hasn't been at home much, too caught up in the whirlwind of the case to think about settling into the new space. The lack of familiarity in the room doesn't faze him, though; his focus is entirely on the task at hand.

As Poker steps into the office, Carter turns to him with a determined look.

"This is it," he says.

"Let's make sure we get it right."

After discussing the case in detail, Carter and Poker return to the main office, ready to outline their plan of action. They stand in front of the whiteboard, where Carter begins to write down the itineray.

"Here are the next steps for us after receiving permission to charge Ray Chapman," Carter says as he carefully lists each item:

CHAPTER 36

1. **Interview Preparation**
2. **Contacting the Solicitor**
3. **Setting Up the Interview Room**
4. **Briefing the Team**
5. **Conducting the Interview**
6. **Processing the Charge**
7. **Communicating with the CPS**
8. **Preparing for Court**
9. **Support and Follow-Up**

Lambert, who has been helping with the evidence, looks up and asks, "Is there anything that you want us to do up here now that the evidence is all back in its place, Carter?"

Carter glances at the whiteboard and shakes his head.

"No, we have everything in hand. We just need to go and charge him."

With a nod of determination, Carter and Poker prepare to move forward with their plan, ready to tackle the next phase of the investigation.

The phone rings, and Poker picks it up.

"Hello. PC Lockman here."

"Hey Poker, it's Biff. Just calling to let you know that Mr Roach is here to represent Mr Chapman," Biff informs him.

"Thanks, Biff. That's great news. Just out of curiosity, did Chapman request this solicitor, or did we assign him?" Poker asks.

"Let me check the paperwork... ah, here it is... We selected him," Biff replies after a brief pause.

Poker chuckles.

"Oh dear, that's the same solicitor Chapman got rid of the last time we arrested him."

Biff laughs.

"Well, shit happens and all that."

"Thanks for the update. We'll be down shortly. Can you get Chapman ready for the interview?" Poker requests.

"Will do," Biff confirms before hanging up.

Poker turns to Carter with a grin.

"Oh, dear, Carter, Chapman has Mr Roach again."

Carter chuckles.

"That'll certainly make things interesting. But to be fair, it doesn't really matter who he has. The solicitor is just there to ensure we follow procedure, which, of course, we always do."

"True enough," Poker agrees.

"Alright then," Carter says with a determined nod.

"Let's get the show on the road."

* * *

Everyone is waiting for the food to arrive, and Molly is busy collecting plates and condiments for their pizzas. Gerry is helping to find the paper napkins, which he is certain are in the cupboard next to the plates.

Suddenly, Gerry's phone rings. He glances at the caller display and feels a wave of unease.

"I'm sorry, love, I need to take this call," he says, his voice tight with concern.

Molly looks at him, puzzled, but nods as she opens the next cupboard and finds the napkins. Gerry gives her a quick kiss on the cheek before stepping outside with his phone.

CHAPTER 36

The garden path leading to the pond is illuminated by the automatic outside light. Gerry walks along the path, glancing over his shoulder to ensure that no one is within earshot.

"Rachel, what the hell are you doing calling me?" Gerry's voice is strained as he speaks into the phone.

"I think you have some explaining to do," Rachel replies, her tone bitter.

"Are you back home now?" Gerry asks, trying to gauge her mood.

"Yes, no thanks to you!" Rachel seethes.

"My Mum and Dad have been through the mill because of you," she adds.

"I'm sorry. I know it was all a big shock for you," Gerry tries to calm her down.

"A shock? That's an understatement," Rachel shouts, her voice rising with anger.

"Hey, calm down, will you? I have a houseful at the moment," Gerry says, his patience wearing thin.

"Oh, lucky you, playing happy families," Rachel retorts.

"Look, Rachel, it was a misunderstanding, that's all," Gerry explains, trying to defuse the situation.

"Just explain to me so I can make sense of it all. How did you end up with Molly Chapman? Tell me that, and you won't hear from me again," Rachel demands.

"I was there when she had her accident. We used to see each other while walking our dogs. She woke up with no memory, and I looked after her until she remembered who she was. She does now, so no harm done," Gerry offers.

"No harm done? Have you heard that she's pressed charges against Ray?" Rachel asks, her voice filled with frustration.

"How do you know that?" Gerry asks, surprised.

"Because I was the person he called from the police station this morning," Rachel explains.

"Listen, that man is a bully and a coward. Any man who slaps his children and wife around should be locked up. End of," Gerry argues his voice firm.

"Well, I hope you have a happy life together. Just be clear that I will never contact you again. I think you're a joke, Gerry, and I'm so glad I got rid of you when I did," Rachel says, her voice cold.

With that, she hangs up. Gerry stands alone in the garden, stunned and disheartened. Gerry kicks the ground in frustration, accidentally stubbing his toe on a rock by the pond. "Ouch, fuck it," he mutters, hopping on one foot and wincing in pain.

As he rubs his toe, he notices Molly approaching through the window. Realizing he needs to get back inside before she sees him limping, Gerry takes a deep breath and heads back toward the house. He composes himself, determined to put on a brave face and not let his phone call with Rachel spoil the evening.

Molly looks at Gerry with a curious expression.

"Who was that?" she asks, her gaze steady and searching.

Gerry knows he can't lie to her, so he decides to be honest.

"It was Rachel, love. She was calling to give me her two pence worth about me getting her arrested."

Molly's expression softens as she steps closer.

"Let bygones be bygones. Bite your lip and let's enjoy the evening, shall we?" She leans in and gives him a warm, reassuring kiss on the lips.

"Anyway," she continues with a smile, "dinner is here. Let's enjoy our food and talk about it tomorrow."

CHAPTER 36

Gerry and Molly head back inside, closing the back door behind them. They join the others in the kitchen, where the atmosphere is warm and welcoming. The table is set, and the delicious aroma of pizza fills the bungalow.

They sit down together for their first family meal. The children are already seated, eagerly sharing the dips and chatting excitedly about their pizzas. Molly smiles at the sight of them getting along so well and feels a sense of contentment.

As they all dig into their pizzas, Gerry and Molly exchange glances, appreciating the calm and joy of the moment. It's a chance to enjoy each other's company and celebrate the beginning of their new family dynamic.

* * *

"Mr Chapman," says Mr Roach as he offers a hand for him to shake. Ray takes it reluctantly and shakes the solicitor's hand.

Ray sits down next to him and folds his arms on the table in front of him.

Carter and Poker enter the room looking serious.

They sit down in front of Chapman and Mr Roach and start to read out the statement of charges against him.

"You are being formally charged with the following offences related to an incident of domestic violence:

Assault Occasioning Actual Bodily Harm (ABH)
Charge: Assault occasioning actual bodily harm under Section 47 of the Offences Against the

Person Act 1861.

Details: On 26th October, at 144 Wolverton Avenue, Bispham it is alleged that you assaulted Mrs Molly Chapman, causing them physical injury. This includes bruising, cuts and abrasions.

Coercive or Controlling Behaviour

Charge: Coercive or controlling behaviour under Section 76 of the Serious Crime Act 2015.

Details: Prior to 26th October, at 144 Wolverton Avenue, Bispham it is alleged that you engaged in a pattern of coercive and controlling behaviour against Mrs Molly Chapman, with the intent to make them question their perception of reality, erode their self-confidence, and isolate them from sources of support. This behaviour included repeatedly lying to the victim about their actions, manipulating situations to make the victim doubt their memory, or systematically undermining their sense of self-worth.

You do not have to say anything in response to these charges. However, if you do not mention something you later rely on in court, it may harm your defence.

- You have the right to consult with a solicitor before being questioned. You can contact any lawyer to represent you.
- You will be required to attend court on 13th January for a hearing where these charges will be formally presented and addressed.

CHAPTER 36

Do you understand the charges that have been read to you?"

Ray sits in complete silence, trying to process the charges brought against him.

"Mr Chapman, do you understand the charges that have been read to you?" Carter asks, his voice steady and formal.

Ray glances at Mr Roach, who gives him a slight nod, prompting Ray to respond.

"Yes, I understand," he says, his voice low and measured.

"My client would like to apply for bail," Mr Roach states firmly, maintaining his professional demeanour.

Carter exchanges a look with Poker before replying, "We are prepared to allow Mr Chapman to remain free until his court date, under specific conditions. These include reporting to a police station regularly, refraining from contacting Mrs Molly Chapman or the children—Lillie, Bonnie, and Oliver Chapman—and avoiding any places where Mrs Chapman or her children may reside."

Ray listens intently as Carter continues, "Mr Chapman may stay in the family home, but he must not visit any locations where Mrs Chapman or her children could be present."

Mr Roach reviews the paperwork carefully before turning to Ray.

"You need to sign these documents," he instructs, sliding the paperwork toward Ray.

Ray picks up the pen, his hand trembling slightly, and signs where indicated.

Poker leans forward, his tone authoritative.

"We'll sort out your discharge papers from custody. Please return to your cell until everything is finalised."

Carter and Poker rise from their seats, leaving the interview room together.

Once the door closes behind them, Ray turns to Mr Roach, a hint of frustration in his voice.

"Well, that was formal."

"It's always like that—by the book, no messing about," Mr Roach replies, packing up his briefcase.

Ray hesitates before asking, "So what now?"

"Now, you're a free man until the court hearing on the 13th of January," Mr Roach explains.

"That will be your plea hearing, where you'll declare yourself guilty or not guilty. But trust me, you'll get a lesser sentence if you plead guilty. It's something to seriously consider."

Ray nods, absorbing the advice as he prepares for what lies ahead.

Biff, standing just outside the door, enters the room as soon as Carter and Poker leave. He approaches Ray with a nod, indicating that it's time to return to his cell.

"Alright, Mr Chapman, let's head back," Biff says, his tone neutral but firm.

Ray rises from his seat, feeling a mix of emotions. He follows Biff out of the interview room, walking down the corridors of the police station. The reality of the situation begins to sink in, but Ray's mind is elsewhere.

As he sits alone in his cell, the door closing behind him with a heavy thud, Ray's thoughts drift to Molly. The charges, the bail conditions, the legal jargon—all fade into the background as his mind fixates on her.

He thinks about the years they spent together, the bitterness he feels toward her, and the resentment that has grown over time. In his mind, she failed as a wife, as a mother, and as a partner. He blames her for everything that's gone wrong

CHAPTER 36

in his life, ignoring his own culpability in the situation.

Ray sits in the silence of his cell, seething quietly, his thoughts dark and twisted.

He knows the legal battle ahead will be challenging, but what occupies his mind now is not the upcoming court case or the potential consequences—it's his lingering animosity towards Molly, a venomous disdain that fuels his brooding in the stillness of his confinement.

* * *

Carter and Poker step into the office met with an eruption of cheers and whoops from the team. Their faces light up with wide smiles, a reflection of the hard-fought victory they've just secured.

"Well done, lads. That was brilliant down there," Sharpie says, patting them on the back. He had been keeping a close eye on the proceedings as the charges were read out. "If anything more comes to light, we'll just contact the CPS and have the charges added. But for now, we've got enough to take this to court. He'll have no choice but to plead guilty, saving the taxpayers—and Molly—a lot of heartache."

Just then, Lambert enters the room, carrying a giant-sized Victoria sponge cake she had earlier picked up from the bakery. She places it proudly on the table, and moments later, Gilbert follows, balancing two large bottles of non-alcoholic champagne in her hands.

With a deft twist, Gilbert uncorks the champagne, the bubbles fizzing up as she pours the sparkling liquid into waiting coffee mugs. The team gathers around, holding their makeshift champagne flutes.

As the last drop is poured and the bubbly spills to the top of each cup, Carter raises his mug high.

"To Dixie," he says, his voice filled with both pride and a touch of reverence.

"To Dixie," the team echoes in unison, their voices strong and united.

They all take a sip, the celebration both a tribute to their colleague and a moment to savour the hard-earned success of the day.

The sweet taste of the cake and the fizz of the champagne add to the sense of camaraderie, a team bound together not just by duty, but by shared victories and memories.

Chapter 37

Friday Late Evening

It's late, and the room is quiet except for the soft crackling of the fireplace. The children have fallen asleep on the sofa and armchair, their faces peaceful and innocent in the warm glow of the fire.

Gerry gently places another log onto the flames, watching as they catch and flicker to life.

He glances over at the sleeping children, a wave of disbelief washing over him. In just a few short weeks, he will be stepping into the role of a father for them—a responsibility that both excites and unnerves him.

As he watches them sleep, Gerry is struck by how sweet and vulnerable they look, so different from the lively, energetic beings they are when awake.

He can't help but wonder about who they are as individuals, these small, growing humans with their own personalities, hopes, and dreams. They are miniature adults in the making, each one poised to explore the world in their own unique way.

Gerry has always wanted children, and while he regrets

missing out on their early years, he knows that being present during their teenage years is just as crucial. These are the years when they'll need guidance, support, and a steady hand to help them navigate the challenges of growing up. The thought of being there for them during this vulnerable time fills him with a sense of purpose, but also with the weight of the responsibility that comes with it.

He sits down in a chair by the fire, letting the warmth of the flames soothe his worries, determined to be the father they need as they journey into adulthood.

He falls asleep.

In the kitchen, the clatter of dishes fills the air as Molly, Reggie, and Yvonne wash up after dinner.

The evening has been warm and comforting, and Molly can't help but feel a deep sense of contentment.

"Maybe you could all stay the night since the children are already settled?" Molly suggests, wiping her hands on a tea towel.

"Oh, we better not," Yvonne replies with a hint of concern.

"We left Daisy at home alone, and someone forgot to put her in her crate."

"Don't blame me," Reggie jumps in defensively, "I was sorting the car out."

"Either way, she's probably wreaking havoc as we speak. I dread to think what the sofa will look like by the time we get home," Yvonne says with a sigh, glancing at the clock.

Reggie nods in agreement.

"Yeah, we should head back. But I'm happy to leave the children here if you are."

Molly smiles and excuses herself, heading into the lounge to check with Gerry. She returns moments later, beaming.

CHAPTER 37

"Come and look at this, but be quiet," she whispers.

The three of them tiptoe into the lounge. Bonnie and Lillie are curled up together at the end of the sofa, their faces serene in sleep. Oliver is draped over the armchair, snoring softly, and in the other armchair, Gerry is fast asleep as well. The fire is dying down, crackling quietly as it releases the last of its warmth.

"That is too cute," Yvonne whispers, her eyes softening at the sight.

"That's my little family right there," Molly says, her voice catching as she becomes emotional.

"He's a good guy, Molly," Reggie adds, his tone reassuring.

"I think you're going to be more than alright."

Molly nods, wiping away a tear.

"I'll just cover them with some blankets and let them sleep."

Reggie and Yvonne exchange glances and Reggie leans in to kiss his sister on the forehead.

"We'll love you and leave you for tonight, Molly. It's been a lovely evening, something we haven't done in years."

"You're welcome, and thank you both—for everything you've done for me and the children," Molly says, her voice filled with gratitude.

"You're worth it, Molly," Yvonne says softly, wrapping her arm around Molly's shoulder and kissing her cheek.

Molly quietly sees Reggie and Yvonne to the front door, trying to be careful not to disturb the kittens but they have woken them up and they are now playfully circling everyone's ankles.

They all exchange quiet goodbyes, and after a final wave, Molly closes the door behind them, the house falling into a gentle silence.

She returns to the lounge, where the soft snores of her children fill the room. Bonnie and Lillie are still nestled together on the sofa, while Oliver is sprawled across the armchair, his small chest rising and falling peacefully. Gerry is still asleep in the other armchair, his head tilted slightly to one side.

Molly approaches Gerry, and with a tender smile, she gently strokes his hair until he begins to stir.

"Oh shit, sorry, I fell asleep," Gerry mutters as he blinks awake.

"I was going to help with the washing up."

"It's OK," Molly reassures him, her voice soft.

"Reggie and Yvonne helped. They've gone home now, and I said the children could stay here tonight. I hope that was OK—I did come in to ask you, but you were sound asleep."

Gerry sits up, rubbing his face with a sheepish grin.

"Oh my god, I feel so embarrassed."

"Please don't be," Molly says, chuckling softly.

"They thought it was really sweet."

Gerry looks over at the sleeping children, his heart swelling with warmth.

"And of course it's OK. Your children are lovely Molly, and very well-mannered too."

"Thank you," she replies, her voice filled with gratitude.

"They've been brought up extremely strict, though, so it'll be nice to have someone as laid back as you helping to look after them."

Gerry smiles, feeling a deep sense of connection with Molly and her family.

"I'll do my best to be there for all of you, whenever you need me."

CHAPTER 37

Molly gently leans in and kisses Gerry on the forehead.

"I know you will, Gerry. And I'm really glad we're here with you."

With a warm smile, Molly heads to the airing cupboard and retrieves three soft blankets. She returns to the lounge, carefully draping the blankets over the children, making sure they're snug and comfortable.

Bonnie and Lillie stir slightly, shifting their positions to settle deeper into their cosy spots. Oliver stretches out his legs and adjusts himself under the blanket with a content sigh.

Molly and Gerry quietly sit together in the lounge, the only sounds being the soft crackle of the fire as it slowly dies down and the occasional sleepy murmur from the children. The room gradually grows colder as the warmth from the fire fades, but the peaceful sight of the sleeping family provides a comforting warmth of its own.

Once the fire has dwindled to embers, Molly and Gerry decide it's time to get ready for bed. They make their way to the bathroom, each taking a refreshing shower to unwind from the day.

After their showers, they head to their bedroom, feeling a deep sense of contentment and exhaustion. They retire to bed, the comforting quiet of the house wrapping around them as they drift off to sleep, ready to face whatever the new day might bring.

* * *

Arriving back at the Draycott household, Reggie and Yvonne exchange nervous glances, both apprehensive about what kind of chaos Daisy might have caused while they were out. Knowing her history with separation anxiety, they brace themselves for the worst, certain that she's chewed something up—or worse.

As Yvonne slides the key into the lock, they immediately hear frantic barking from the other side of the door. The scratching at the door grows more intense, as Daisy, desperate to reunite with her carers, tries to push it open from the inside.

Yvonne opens the door cautiously, only to be met by a horrid smell that instantly hits their senses. She grimaces, instinctively reaching for the hallway light. The moment it flickers on, she spots the culprit: a smelly present Daisy has left them, right in the middle of the hallway.

Yvonne sighs deeply as she takes off her shoes in the porch, noticing with dismay that the mess had been trodden through into the living room, streaks of it smeared across the carpets.

"Oh great!" she exclaims, her voice filled with frustration. "She's traced it all through the house!"

Reggie steps inside, holding his nose as he tries to avoid the worst of the mess.

"Oh man, that stinks to high heaven!" he complains, his face contorted in disgust.

Daisy, wagging her tail furiously, looks up at them with wide, innocent eyes, completely oblivious to the chaos she's caused. Yvonne and Reggie exchange exasperated looks, knowing they have a long night of cleaning ahead of them.

Yvonne, clearly less than pleased, grabs hold of Daisy by the collar. Despite Daisy's attempts to jump up and seek forgiveness, Yvonne holds her down and half-drags her to the backdoor.

CHAPTER 37

"I can't bear the smell," Yvonne mutters, wrinkling her nose in disgust.

"What have you been feeding her?"

The two of them march Daisy outside, shutting the door behind them, and then carefully navigate through the house, trying to dodge the mess that Daisy has spread across the carpets.

Yvonne, still fuming, heads straight for the kitchen. She pulls out rubber gloves, disinfectant, and a scrubbing brush and bowl from under the sink, preparing for the unpleasant task ahead. With a deep sigh, she gets down on her hands and knees, scrubbing furiously to remove the mess from the carpets.

Meanwhile, Reggie, feeling sorry for Daisy, decides to join her outside. He squats down beside her, gently stroking under her chin.

"You only did what dogs do, didn't you?" he says softly. Daisy looks up at him, her tail wagging with excitement, oblivious to the trouble she's caused.

A few moments later, Yvonne appears at the back door, holding a carrier bag full of the smelly remains. She opens the door just enough to hand the bag to Reggie, who takes it without a word and heads for the bin.

The house now smells strongly of disinfectant, and Yvonne has managed to clean the carpet to the point where it actually looks better than it did before they left. But the ordeal has clearly taken its toll.

"I'm sorry, Reggie," Yvonne says, her voice full of sadness as she watches him return. "But the dog has got to go."

Reggie looks at her, his expression softening.

"OK, OK," he concedes.

"But it was an accident. She was left alone, unattended, with the back door shut. She doesn't know how long she has to hold it in for. It could be a lot worse, Yvonne—she could have peed as well. Let's count ourselves lucky she didn't."

Yvonne sighs, knowing he's right but still feeling frustrated. She looks down at Daisy, who's now lying down quietly, her big eyes watching them both, and feels a pang of guilt.

"I know," she finally admits, "but I just can't keep going through this every time we leave her alone. She either chews stuff up or she pines in her crate"

Reggie puts an arm around Yvonne's shoulders, giving her a reassuring squeeze. "Let's not make any decisions tonight. We'll figure it out in the morning."

Yvonne nods, still feeling conflicted but grateful for Reggie's understanding. They both turn to head back inside, leaving Daisy to settle down in the garden, still wagging her tail.

After a few minutes, Yvonne feels a pang of guilt gnawing at her. She glances at Reggie, who is watching Daisy. With a sigh, she turns around and opens the back door.

"Come on, Daisy," she calls gently. Daisy immediately perks up, her tail wagging furiously as she trots over. Yvonne kneels down, holding the door half-open, and carefully checks Daisy's paws for any dirt or mess. Once she's satisfied that Daisy's feet are clean, she lets her back into the house.

"Alright, you can come in," Yvonne says, her tone softer now. Daisy bounds inside, her excitement bubbling, and heads straight for the lounge.

Reggie watches the scene unfold, a small smile tugging at the corners of his mouth. "See? She just wants to be with us," he says.

CHAPTER 37

Yvonne follows Daisy into the lounge, watching as she snuggles into her usual spot, curling up on the rug by the fireplace.

"Yeah, I know," Yvonne replies, her earlier frustration melting away as she sees how content Daisy looks.

"She's just a handful sometimes."

Reggie nods in agreement, but there's a warmth in his voice as he responds.

"She's family, though. We'll manage."

Yvonne smiles, giving Daisy a gentle pat on the head before settling down on the sofa next to Reggie.

Daisy, sensing the shift in mood, lets out a contented sigh and closes her eyes, finally at peace.

"You've had a long day," he says softly, his thumbs brushing along her collarbone.

"Come on, let's relax."

Yvonne lets out a small sigh and nods, leaning into his touch.

The room is dimly lit, the soft glow of a lamp casting a warm light over them. Reggie wraps his arm around Yvonne, pulling her close so that her head rests against his chest.

For a while, they simply sit there, the quiet of the house surrounding them. Reggie's fingers trace gentle patterns along Yvonne's arm, his touch soothing and reassuring. Yvonne lets her eyes close, feeling the steady rise and fall of Reggie's breathing beneath her. It is moments like these, when the world outside seems to fade away, that she cherishes the most.

Reggie shifts slightly, his hand moving to tilt Yvonne's chin up so that he can look into her eyes.

"You know how much I love you, right?" he says quietly,

his voice filled with sincerity.

Yvonne smiles, her heart swelling with affection.

"I do," she replies, her hand coming up to rest on his cheek. "And I love you too, Reggie."

Their faces are close now, so close that Yvonne can feel the warmth of his breath against her lips. Slowly, Reggie leans in, his lips brushing hers in a kiss that is as tender as it is full of love. Yvonne responds, her hand sliding to the back of his neck as she deepens the kiss, pouring all of her feelings into that simple yet profound connection.

They take their time, savouring the intimacy between them. The kiss is slow and gentle, a dance of familiar rhythms that speaks of years of shared memories, of hardships faced and overcome together. It is a kiss that reminds them both of the bond they have built, strong and enduring.

When they finally pull back, their foreheads rest together, and Yvonne lets out a contented sigh.

"I can't imagine my life without you," she whispers, her fingers lightly playing with the hair at the nape of his neck.

Reggie smiles, his eyes shining with love.

"You don't have to," he whispers back.

"I'm here, and I always will be."

With that, they settle back into the sofa, Yvonne resting her head on Reggie's chest once more. His arms wrap around her, holding her close as they both relax into the quiet comfort of each other's presence.

The world outside can wait; tonight is just for them, a night to remember how deeply they care for one another, and how truly they are in love.

As they drift off to sleep, the warmth of their embrace keeping them cosy, they know that no matter what challenges

CHAPTER 37

come their way, they will face them together—just as they always have.

Chapter 38

Saturday Morning

"Thanks, Gilbert," Poker says, nodding in appreciation. "Good to have everything squared away."

Lambert gives a small smile.

"It feels like we've tied up all the loose ends. Now it's just a matter of waiting for the court date."

Poker stretches, glancing around the office. "It's weird, though, isn't it? The way you get so wrapped up in a case, and then suddenly, it's over. Like you're supposed to just move on to the next thing."

Lambert nods in agreement.

"Yeah, but that's the job. We do our part and then let the courts take it from there. Still, it's hard not to get attached sometimes, especially with cases like this one."

Poker leans back against the desk, a thoughtful look crossing his face.

"I guess that's why we do it, though. You know, to make sure people like Molly and her children can finally get some peace."

Gilbert steps further into the room, dusting off her hands.

CHAPTER 38

"And you guys did a damn good job on this one. It's not just about solving the case—it's about making sure justice is served."

"True," Lambert agrees.

"But now we need to refocus. What's next on the agenda? Any leads on the new case yet?"

Poker shrugs.

"Nothing solid, but I've heard whispers of something brewing. Could be big. We'll know more once Carter briefs us."

"Well, I'm ready for whatever comes," Lambert says, determination in her voice.

"Same here," Poker adds.

"But for now, I guess it's just back to the grind, getting everything in place for the next round," he says.

The three of them continue tidying up, the sense of closure from the Chapman case mingling with the anticipation of what's to come.

The office feels quieter, almost like it's catching its breath before the next storm. But the team knows that in their line of work, calm moments are fleeting, and soon enough, they'll be diving headfirst into another whirlwind.

As Sharpie answers his phone, the rest of the team quiets down, their conversation tapering off as they watch him. Sharpie nods a few times as he listens to the caller, his expression shifting from casual to serious.

"Understood," Sharpie says into the phone before hanging up and turning back to the team.

"Well, it looks like the new case is about to kick off sooner than expected," he says, his tone indicating that whatever the call was about, it was urgent.

Carter steps forward, sensing the shift in the atmosphere.

"What's the situation, Sharpie?"

Sharpie takes a breath, clearly ready to dive into work mode.

"We've just received a call from the Chief. There's been a major development in the case we're about to take on. Apparently, there's been an incident tied to the new investigation—a potential lead that needs to be followed up immediately."

Poker glances at his watch, calculating the time before his dentist appointment.

"I guess we're not wasting any time, then."

"Nope," Sharpie agrees.

"We'll have to jump right into it. I'll need everyone on their A-game. This could be a big one."

Lambert, always eager for action, steps forward.

"What's the plan?"

Sharpie looks around at the team, gauging their readiness.

"First, we'll have a quick debrief to get everyone up to speed on what we know so far. Then we'll divide up tasks and hit the ground running. Carter, can you set up the briefing room?"

"On it," Carter says, already moving towards the briefing room to get things in order.

"Alright, everyone," Sharpie says, his voice steady and commanding.

"Grab your notebooks, get what you need. We're diving in as soon as Carter's ready."

The team disperses, their earlier chatter replaced by the focused energy that always comes before a new case.

As they gather their things, Sharpie heads toward his new office to quickly drop off his belongings, his mind already

CHAPTER 38

shifting gears to the task at hand.

A few minutes later, the team reconvenes in the briefing room, ready to tackle whatever this new case throws at them. The sense of anticipation is noticeable, each member knowing that whatever lies ahead, they'll face it together.

Sharpie's phone rings again, the sudden sound slicing through the hum of the office. He pulls it from his pocket, the screen casting a soft glow on his face as he glances at the caller ID.

"Hello," he answers, his voice calm and professional as always.

As the person on the other end of the line begins to speak, Sharpie's expression shifts. At first, he nods, his face a mask of concentration as he listens, but then, something changes. His eyes widen slightly, and the colour drains from his face. He glances up at the rest of the team, his gaze sweeping across them as if searching for the right words, though none seem to come. Slowly, he shakes his head, a silent gesture that sends a ripple of unease through the room.

Finally, he hangs up the call, the action feeling more deliberate, heavier than usual. He doesn't move for a moment, just stands there, his phone still clutched in his hand as if he's unwilling to let go of the connection, the last thread to the normalcy they had known just moments before.

When he finally does slip the phone back into his pocket, his movements are slow, almost reluctant, as though he's trying to delay the inevitable.

Sharpie looks at the team, his eyes filled with a mixture of shock and sorrow that he can't quite hide. He draws in a deep breath, trying to steady himself for what he has to say.

"It's Dixie," he begins, his voice low and thick with emotion.

He hesitates, the weight of the words he's about to speak almost too much to bear.

"He's passed away."

The room falls into a stunned silence, the reality of the situation hitting everyone like a physical blow. Disbelief flickers across their faces as they exchange glances, each of them grappling with the news.

How can Dixie be gone?

It doesn't seem possible, he was there only a few days ago, leading them, guiding them with his steady hand and warm smile. The idea that he's no longer with them feels surreal, like some kind of cruel joke that no one can quite believe.

Carter's usually steady composure cracks first, his expression sad as he tries to process the news. He shakes his head slightly, as if denying the truth will somehow change it.

"Dixie... gone? It just doesn't seem right."

Lambert feels her throat tighten, tears welling up in her eyes. She had always looked up to Dixie and admired his ability to balance strength with compassion. The thought of never hearing his voice again, never seeing his reassuring smile, is almost too much to bear.

"He was just here with us recently," she murmurs, her voice barely audible.

Poker, normally the one to lighten any mood with a joke or a sarcastic remark, is silent, his usual bravado nowhere to be found.

He stares at the floor.

"He was like family," he finally says, his voice low and strained.

"This isn't fair."

The room is heavy with grief, the air thick with the

CHAPTER 38

collective sorrow of the team. They all knew the risks of the job and knew that loss was an inevitable part of their line of work, but losing Dixie—someone who was more than just a boss, someone who was the heart of their team—felt like a cruel twist of fate being taken by Cancer.

Sharpie, struggling with his grief, knows he needs to pull them through this, to be the leader Dixie would have wanted him to be. He clears his throat, though the sound does little to break the oppressive silence that has settled over them.

"I know this is hard to take in," he says, his voice cracking slightly before he steadies it.

"Dixie… he was everything to this team. He was our leader, our friend, and he made us better at what we do—better people, even. Losing him like this… it's a huge blow, but we have to keep going. That's what he would want."

The words hang in the air, a call to action that feels impossible to heed in this moment of raw grief. But they know Sharpie is right. As much as it hurts, they have to continue. Dixie would never forgive them if they let his passing derail them. He would want them to push forward, to carry on his legacy with the same dedication and passion he had always shown.

Gilbert, who had been standing quietly in the corner, her face pale with shock, finally finds her voice.

"I bet Lucy is beside herself right now. What do we do now, it is such a shock."

Sharpie meets her gaze, his grief mirrored in her eyes.

"We keep going," he says firmly, though the grief in his voice is unmistakable.

"We do the work he taught us to do. We start this new case. We honour him by being the best team we can be."

THE FOUND

The team nods, though the sadness is still etched deeply into their faces. The loss feels overwhelming, but they know they have to keep moving forward, to carry on for Dixie. Slowly, they come together, each of them trying to find the strength.

Carter, his voice thick with unshed tears, lifts his coffee mug in a quiet, heartfelt tribute.

"To Dixie," he says, his voice trembling slightly.

One by one, the rest of the team follows suit, raising their mugs in a solemn toast.

"To Dixie," they echo, their voices filled with sorrow and determination.

As they sit together in the quiet that follows, the reality of what they've lost begins to settle in. They know the road ahead won't be easy, but with Dixie's memory guiding them, they'll face whatever challenges come their way.

Together, as a team, just as he would have wanted.

* * *

Oliver tumbles off the armchair with a soft thump, startling awake as he hits the floor. The kittens, nestled comfortably by Lillie's feet, jump up in surprise and begin to meow. Instinctively, Oliver rushes over to them, his small hands reaching out to stroke their fur. The kittens respond immediately, their meows turning into soft purrs as they nuzzle against him.

Lillie is the next to stir. She stretches out her arms and yawns, inadvertently pulling the blanket off of Bonnie, who wakes up moments later. The three of them, still in their clothes from the night before, sit up and blink in confusion,

CHAPTER 38

trying to make sense of their surroundings.

Lillie glances at the clock on the wall, her eyes widening in surprise.

"It's already 10 AM," she announces.

"Mum and Gerry aren't up yet."

"How did we all fall asleep here and not wake up?" Bonnie asks, her voice still groggy from sleep.

"God knows," Lillie replies, rubbing her eyes.

Oliver, still crouched by the kittens, looks up and asks, "Did Uncle Reggie and Auntie Yvonne stay here too?"

Bonnie rolls her eyes.

"How would we know? We were asleep, too, stupid!"

"I was only asking," Oliver mutters, a bit defensive.

The children become engrossed in watching the kittens chase each other.

"Good morning," a familiar voice says from the corner of the lounge. They turn to see Gerry. He smiles warmly at the children, his hair slightly tousled.

"Mum's still asleep," he adds, noticing their questioning looks.

"But it looks like we all had a good rest."

The children smile back, their earlier confusion giving way to a sense of comfort. Despite the unexpected start to the morning, they feel a warmth in knowing that they're all together, the kittens' soft purrs and Gerry's reassuring presence making everything feel right.

"Who would like some breakfast?" Gerry asks as he heads into the kitchen, his voice cheerful and welcoming. The kittens trail behind him, their tiny paws pattering on the floor as they eagerly anticipate their morning meal.

"Me!" Oliver shouts.

Bonnie and Lillie exchange sleepy smiles before getting up from the sofa and following Oliver into the kitchen. Oliver's eyes widen with wonder as he looks out the large kitchen window.

"Wow, look at your garden!" he exclaims, his excitement bubbling over.

Gerry chuckles softly and corrects him, "No, Oliver, look at *your* garden."

Oliver's face lights up even more.

"Oh wow, we can have so much fun out there! And the beach is just over the road too!" His voice is filled with pure excitement as he imagines the adventures he could have outdoors.

Bonnie and Lillie share his excitement as they take in the view of the garden and the promise of a day filled with play and exploration. Gerry smiles at them all, happy to see the joy in their faces.

"Right, you three—food!" Gerry declares, eager to get them fed and watered before Molly wakes up. He wants to impress her with his thoughtfulness, a small gesture to show he's on top of things.

"What would you all like?" he asks, glancing around.

The selection proves too overwhelming for Oliver, who hesitates before shrugging and looking up at Gerry.

"You choose for me," he says, unable to make a decision.

Gerry smiles and decides on Weetabix for all of them to avoid any potential arguments. The children nod in agreement, content with the choice, and soon they're all quietly eating their breakfast, watching the kittens and Era happily munching on their food as well.

Molly appears at the kitchen door, her hair slightly messy

CHAPTER 38

from sleep.

"Why did no one wake me?" she asks, her voice a mix of surprise.

Gerry looks up with a soft smile.

"You were like Sleeping Beauty. I didn't have the heart to disturb you. Besides, we've been just fine out here together."

Molly's expression softens as she takes in the scene—the children happily eating, the peaceful morning air, and Gerry's thoughtful planning.

"Well, it looks like you've done a wonderful job," she says, touched by his effort.

"So, what are we going to do today?" Lillie asks politely, her eyes full of curiosity.

Molly smiles at her, pleased with the children's excitement.

"I thought we could start moving some of the furniture in the rooms so that over the next few weeks, you can start having some space to yourselves. How does that sound?"

The children's faces light up at the idea. They're thrilled at the thought of making the bungalow their home, a place where they can settle in and feel comfortable.

"When are we going to come home, Mum?" Oliver asks, his voice tinged with a bit of sadness as he processes the transition.

Molly kneels down to his level, brushing a hand gently through his hair.

"I thought Christmas Eve would be a wonderful day to move in. That way, we can wake up on Christmas morning as a family, right here. We could even invite Uncle Reggie and Auntie Yvonne for Christmas dinner and make it a real big family celebration."

The children beam with excitement, the idea of spending

Christmas together in their new home filling them with joy. They eagerly run off to play, the thoughts of their own rooms and a special Christmas morning fueling their imaginations.

With the children occupied, Molly and Gerry find a quiet moment together. They sit down at the kitchen table, where the remnants of breakfast still linger, and begin to discuss the formalities—how they'll handle the move, the logistics of getting everything set up, and how they'll make sure the children feel settled during the transition. The conversation flows easily, filled with plans and hopes for the future, each step bringing them closer to becoming a family in every sense of the word.

Chapter 39

Saturday Afternoon

"As much as I love her, Reggie, she has got to go. Daisy needs to be with someone who can be with her all the time," Yvonne says, her voice laced with frustration.

"And knowing Molly, she'll probably let the dog sleep on her bed now that Ray isn't around, digging his claws into her back."

Reggie, feeling a bit cornered, tries to reason with her.

"Look, I'll clean up the mess this time. I don't know why Daisy's doing it in her crate—maybe she's sensing something's off?"

Yvonne lets out a sigh, still upset but softening slightly.

"We'll take her back today. I'm sure they'll be pleased to have her."

Reggie nods, trying to ease her anger.

"But what about the kittens?" Yvonne asks her tone more thoughtful now.

"Daisy will be fine," Reggie reassures her.

"She doesn't chase the cats outside, which is a good sign."

"OK," Yvonne concedes.

"When we go over later to pick up the children, we'll take Daisy too. Let me give Molly a quick call to make sure it's alright."

Reggie pulls his phone out of his pocket and dials Molly's new number.

"Hello?" Molly answers, her voice warm.

"Hey, sis, it's me," Reggie says.

"Sorry, I should've saved my number in your phone." Molly chuckles softly.

"Oh, it's OK. I know your number off by heart."

"I best learn yours then," Reggie chuckles, his voice lightening up.

Molly smiles on the other end of the line.

"What can I do for you?"

Reggie takes a breath, trying to keep his tone casual.

"Would it be alright if we brought Daisy home to you later when we come to pick up the children?"

He hopes Molly agrees, knowing Yvonne won't be thrilled if Daisy has to stay with them any longer.

"Of course," Molly responds without hesitation.

"I was going to mention her to you anyway. We'd be happy to take her back." As she speaks, she looks over at Gerry and playfully mimics a dog, making him laugh.

Relieved, Reggie smiles.

"What time were you thinking of coming to get the children?" Molly asks, wanting to make sure everything fits into her day.

"Around 5 p.m.," Reggie replies.

"Don't worry about cooking for them—Yvonne's boiling up some gammon later."

CHAPTER 39

"OK, I'll have them ready for 5," Molly says, nodding to herself.

"And don't forget to bring Daisy's crate, though we probably won't need it much," she adds, echoing Yvonne's earlier prediction.

"Alright, Molls. I'll see you later. Do you need anything?" Reggie offers, his voice full of brotherly concern.

"No, we're all good here. Thanks," Molly replies warmly.

"OK, see you then," Reggie says, ending the call with a sense of relief. He turns to Yvonne.

"All sorted—we can drop Daisy off later when we pick up the children."

Yvonne, finally easing up, gives a small smile.

"Oh, that's good. See? That wasn't so painful, was it?"

Reggie nods, glad that everything is falling into place.

* * *

As the children play in the garden, their laughter mingling with the sounds of nature, Molly and Gerry find a quiet moment together in the lounge. Gerry has just finished a phone call with the funeral directors, finalising the last details.

Molly, sensing the weight of the conversation, gently takes the notepad and pen from Gerry as he enters the room.

"Did you manage to get everything set in place for Mum?" she asks softly, her voice full of concern.

Gerry nods, his expression serious but calm.

"Yes, we're all set for next Friday," he replies, settling into a chair.

"It'll be a simple send-off. Just one car for you, me, and

Aunt Maud. There aren't any other relatives, just a small handful of friends. The cremation will be straightforward, with a twenty-minute service conducted by the registrar. They'll say a few simple words about Mum's life."

He pauses, his eyes reflecting the depth of his emotions.

"It's what she would have wanted—no fuss, no expense," he adds quietly, his voice both sad and relieved.

Molly nods, understanding the importance of honouring his mother's wishes.

"She always said she didn't want a big fuss," he murmurs, his thoughts drifting to memories of his mother.

"I'm glad we're doing it this way. It feels right."

Molly reaches out, taking his hand in hers.

"We'll get through this together, Gerry," she says, her voice steady but filled with warmth.

"And afterwards, we'll take some time to remember her properly. Just us maybe a walk on the beach or something she would have loved."

Gerry squeezes her hand, grateful for her support.

"That sounds perfect," he whispers, his eyes moistening as he looks at her.

She gives him a small, reassuring smile.

"You don't have to do it alone. We're in this together, every step of the way."

They sit in companionable silence for a few moments, sipping their coffee and finding comfort in each other's presence.

The weight of the upcoming funeral still lingers, but in this quiet moment, they find a sense of peace and strength to face the days ahead.

"I'm just going to make some sandwiches to take out to the

CHAPTER 39

children. Do you want anything?" Molly asks as she heads towards the kitchen.

"No, I'm good, thank you," Gerry replies with a warm smile.

"Just focus on the little ones. We can grab something to eat later."

"OK, will do," Molly responds, opening the fridge to see what's left.

"What time is Reggie coming over for the children?" Gerry asks, leaning against the kitchen worktop.

"He said about 5 p.m., and not to worry about feeding them dinner since Yvonne's making dinner," Molly says, pulling out a few ingredients.

"I bet you didn't need to be told twice," Gerry teases with a chuckle.

Molly grins, shaking her head.

"Well, I didn't put up a fight, if that's what you're asking, cheeky."

Gerry laughs, the sound filling the kitchen.

"Oh, I want to bottle these moments, beautiful," he says, moving to help her prepare the sandwiches.

"We really must go shopping soon, though. We're running on the dregs of the cupboards."

"We can go Monday if you like, in the morning," Molly suggests, passing him a loaf of bread.

"Sounds good. I need to call the agency, too, to see if they have any photography work lined up for me. Probably won't be until the new year now—a bit late to pick up any Christmas work—but you could come on some more of the photo shoots with me if you like. Be my right-hand girl," he says, winking at her.

Molly smiles, but it's a little wistful.

"I have a college course I need to complete. Maybe when the children go back to school after the Christmas holidays, I could restart it."

"That's a great idea," Gerry agrees, slicing up some cheese. "It'll give you a bit of self-worth too."

Molly looks up at him, her heart warming at his words.

"I'm really proud of you, Molly. You've been through so much and always put everyone before yourself. I want this time to be about you—you're important too."

Molly pauses, touched by his sincerity. She reaches out and gives his hand a gentle squeeze.

"Thank you, Gerry. That means a lot."

They continue making the sandwiches in comfortable silence, both feeling the deep connection between them. As they work side by side, they share a quiet understanding that, despite everything they've been through, they're building something solid and beautiful together.

Molly calls the children to the back door, her voice carrying across the garden. Oliver comes zooming over on his newfound scooter, which would have once been Gerry's, narrowly avoiding one of the kittens who leaps out of his way and into a nearby bush, its tail twitching in agitation. Molly watches with a smile as Era meows at her feet, clearly intrigued by the commotion.

As she puts the cheese back into the fridge, she adds, "There's some Battenberg cake if you all want some after you've finished your sandwiches."

"Ooo, yummy!" Lillie exclaims, her eyes lighting up.

"I love that cake."

Molly cuts the cake into four equal slices, savouring the familiar taste of marzipan that lingers on her fingers.

CHAPTER 39

"Mmm," she murmurs, a smile of contentment spreading across her face.

"Been a long time since I've had that."

"Well, I can't say no to a bit of cake," Gerry chimes in with a grin, quickly snagging a slice before anyone else has the chance.

Oliver giggles at Gerry's playful eagerness, and Molly can't help but feel a surge of warmth as she watches the two interact.

She senses that Gerry and Oliver are already starting to bond, and it makes her heart swell with joy. It's all she's ever wanted for her children—for them to feel safe and loved. Watching them together, she feels a sense of peace she hasn't known in a long time.

As she looks out the window, her gaze softens at the sight of her children playing in the beautiful garden, sitting by the pond that sparkles in the sunlight. This is everything she's ever dreamed of—a home filled with love, laughter, and the promise of new beginnings.

Molly takes a deep breath, feeling the weight of her past start to lift. She knows she has a difficult road ahead in terms of her own struggles, but for the first time, she feels truly happy. She has Gerry, who makes her feel cherished, and her children, who are thriving in this new chapter of their lives.

She silently vows to herself that she won't slip back into her old ways of self-harm. It's a hard habit to break, but with so much to live for now, she knows she can do it.

The happiness of her children and Gerry is at the forefront of her mind, but for once, she's also thinking of her own happiness.

And as she stands there, looking out at the life she's

building, she realises that maybe, just maybe, she deserves this happiness too.

The future looks brighter than ever, and she's ready to embrace it with open arms.

Molly glances down at the scars on her arms, a sombre reminder of the battles she's fought within herself. Gently, she pulls her sleeves down to cover them, a protective gesture that signifies both healing and caution.

Those scars, though faded, are etched with the lessons she's learned—painful but necessary. They're a testament to her resilience, a mark of her past that she now uses as a compass to guide her forward. As long as she remembers where they came from, she's confident she won't make the same mistakes again.

In moments like these, when life feels both heavy and hopeful, Molly misses her Mum the most. Her Mother never had the chance to meet Gerry, a man who makes Molly feel valued and loved in ways she never experienced with Ray. Her Mum only knew the side of Molly's life that was clouded by Ray's presence—a relationship fraught with tension, where even Ray's rare moments of kindness felt tainted by his controlling nature.

Molly can almost hear her Mum's voice, always with something to say about Ray, never fully satisfied with him.

Looking back, Molly understands why.

Ray wasn't always a monster, but his narcissism coloured every aspect of their relationship.

What he did right often felt wrong because it was always on his terms, never theirs. Molly now realises it wasn't her fault; it was Ray's inability to see beyond his own needs, to compromise and share a life that should have been built

CHAPTER 39

together.

She knows now that it shouldn't have been "Ray's way or the highway," but rather "our way or no way."

That's what she has with Gerry—a partnership where both of their voices matter, where decisions are made together, with mutual respect and love.

As she reflects on her journey, from the shadows of her past with Ray to the warmth of her present with Gerry, Molly feels a sense of peace. She's moving forward, not just surviving but truly living, with a newfound understanding of what she deserves. And in this moment, as she watches her children play in the garden, she knows her mum would be proud. Proud of the strength Molly has found, the happiness she's embraced, and the love that now surrounds her.

Molly smiles softly to herself, her heart full.

The scars on her arms may never fully disappear, but they no longer define her. They're part of her story, yes, but not the end of it. The chapters ahead are hers to write, and she's determined to fill them with love, laughter, and the kind of life she's always dreamed of—one where she's no longer just surviving, but truly thriving.

Molly finds herself contemplating her future and whether she still needs the guidance of Doctor Tuffman.

Over the past few months, she has managed without her medication, a fact that has surprised her. She's come to a realisation: what she truly needed wasn't a prescription, but a profound change in her life.

The medication helped dull the pain, but it never took it away completely. And while the numbness brought temporary relief, it also disconnected her from the world around her.

Now, she understands that she'd rather endure the pain and keep her mind clear than float through life in a medicated haze.

This isn't to say that she'll never return to her medication if the need arises, but for now, love, happiness, and hope are proving to be the best medicine she could ask for. They are her placebo, her lifeline, and she intends to hold onto them for as long as she can.

She knows that as long as there are warm embraces, children's laughter, and the small joys of everyday life to lift her spirits, she'll be alright.

Molly realizes that what was missing from her life wasn't just love and attention; it was the simple, joyful moments that come with being surrounded by her children. The sound of their giggles, the sight of their smiles—those were the things that kept her grounded, that reminded her what it means to truly live. They've become her anchor, her reason to push through the difficult days without resorting to medication that numbs more than it heals.

In those moments of quiet reflection, Molly feels a deep sense of gratitude. She's found a way to navigate her pain without losing herself, and it's given her a new perspective on what she really needs to be happy. It's not about avoiding the pain at all costs, but about finding the strength to face it with a clear mind and an open heart.

With Gerry by her side and her children filling her days with light, Molly knows she's on the right path.

She's no longer just surviving; she's living, truly living, in a way she never thought possible.

And as long as she has those little giggles and smiles to hold onto, she knows she'll be just fine.

Chapter 40

Saturday Afternoon

I find myself wondering what's going through Molly's mind. I hope she feels even a fraction of what I feel for her.

The children are incredible, and I can already sense a bond forming between us. Oliver, especially, tugs at my heart. Being the only boy, I can tell he feels a bit lonely at times, just like I did growing up as an only child. Seeing him with my old scooter brought back a flood of memories from my own childhood. I was almost always happy back then.

My parents did right by me—I had everything I could've wanted. I never knew what it was like to go without, and I realise now how lucky I was.

But I didn't have many friends, so my Mum became my world. She was everything to me. God, I miss her so much. There's this ache inside me that hasn't gone away, and I know it's because I haven't had any time to process everything that's happened. It's been nonstop—losing Mum, moving in here, being arrested, adjusting to this new life with Molly and the children. And now, with the children around, it feels like I haven't had a moment to myself.

I think I need that right now—just a little time alone to reflect, to sort out my thoughts and grieve properly.

I glance over at Molly, and she looks lost in her own thoughts, her expression soft and distant.

For a moment, I hesitate. I don't want to disturb her, but I really need this break, even if it's just for an hour.

So I gather the courage and walk over to her.

"Hey, Molly," I say quietly, not wanting to startle her.

"Do you mind if I go for a walk for a while? Just over to the dunes?"

She turns to look at me, and the moment our eyes meet, I'm struck again by just how beautiful she is. Her gaze is warm, and understanding, and it hits me hard how much I love this woman—every inch of my being is wrapped up in her.

I see that same understanding in her eyes, that she knows exactly what I need without me having to say too much.

"Of course," she replies, her voice gentle.

"Take all the time you need. We'll be here when you get back."

Her words are like a balm to my soul, reassuring me that it's OK to take this time, that it doesn't change anything between us.

I lean in and kiss her forehead softly, a silent thank you for being my everything.

As I head toward the door, the sound of the children's laughter drifts in from the garden, and it brings a smile to my face. I know the dunes will give me the quiet I need to think, to remember, and to just breathe for a moment.

When I'm ready, I'll come back to this life we're building

CHAPTER 40

together—to Molly, the woman who has captured my heart, and to the children who are quickly becoming the centre of my world.

I grab my coat from the hook by the door and slip it on, feeling its familiar weight settle around my shoulders.

As I step outside, the air greets me—warm but with a crisp edge, a reminder that Autumn is giving way to Winter. The quiet road stretches out in front of me, empty and peaceful, and within a few strides, I'm at the edge of the dunes. The sand spills over onto the tarmac, a soft transition from the man-made world to nature's domain.

I step onto the sand, feeling it give way beneath my shoes, its softness enveloping my feet. The long grasses rustle in the breeze, brushing against my legs as I push through, the blades now well above my ankles.

The sight and feel of it all pull me back to memories I hold close.

I remember walking Duke along the promenade in Blackpool—his massive body moving with the steady, confident stride of a dog who knew his place in the world. His muscular legs powered through the sand and concrete alike, always eager, always ready for the next adventure.

As I walk through the dunes now, I can almost hear the soft padding of his paws beside me, his presence so strong in my memory that it feels real, like he's still here with me.

Those were simpler times, carefree in a way that feels distant now. But the memory is comforting, a reminder that even during change, there are constants—like the love of a good dog or the peace of a solitary walk along the dunes.

The landscape here is different from Blackpool, but the feeling it evokes is the same—a sense of freedom, of connection to something larger than myself.

As I continue through the grass, the sound of the sea becomes more distinct, its rhythmic crashing against the shore a soothing backdrop to my thoughts.

I climb the dunes, each step a bit heavier as the sand shifts beneath my feet.

When I reach the familiar spot where Molly and I sat talking about Mum, it feels like a lifetime has passed since then.

The weight of everything hits me all at once. I can't help but think about how different things were when Mum was still here, the longing to see her just one more time gnawing at me, taking its toll in ways I didn't expect.

As soon as I sit down, the tears come, unstoppable and heavy. They stream down my face, the gentle breeze catching the drops and mixing them with the sand, creating a slight sting where they fall. I wipe my nose with the back of my hand and take a deep breath, trying to steady myself. The air fills my lungs with a sharp freshness, but it does little to calm the ache inside.

The sun hangs low in the sky, casting long shadows across the sand, and the tide is steadily creeping in, the waves rolling closer with each passing minute.

The beach is empty except for me, alone on the dunes, surrounded by nothing but the vastness of the sea and sky.

It's just me and my thoughts here, with no one to interrupt the quiet, and no distractions to pull me away from the memories.

I've found the exact spot I've come to think of as my contemplation place, the place where I can let my guard down.

CHAPTER 40

I let myself reminisce, allowing the memories of Mum to wash over me like the tide that's inching closer to the shore.

I think about all the little things—her voice, her laugh, the way she'd always know just what to say when I needed advice. The pain of losing her feels sharp, cutting through the calm of the moment, but there's a strange comfort in it too. It reminds me that she was real, that she was here, and that I was loved by her.

The tears continue to fall, but I don't try to stop them. I just let them flow, letting the sadness and the longing pour out of me, mixing with the sand and the sea air.

It's a release I didn't know I needed, a moment of pure vulnerability that I've been holding back for too long.

Here, in this quiet place, I feel connected to her again, if only in memory, and it brings a sense of peace that I hadn't expected to find today.

For now, I just sit with my thoughts, letting the sun dip lower in the sky and the waves come closer, and I allow myself this time to grieve, to remember, and to just be.

Time seems to slip away as I sit here, lost in thought, watching the sun descend lower in the sky.

This place, with its quiet solitude and natural beauty, is the perfect spot to witness the sunset.

The sky is ablaze with hues of orange and pink, the colours deepening as the sun inches closer to the horizon. The stillness of the sea reflects the sky's vibrant glow, creating a shimmering path of light that stretches all the way to the shore.

The water, calm and serene, slowly creeps back in, reclaiming the sand it had left exposed. Each gentle wave catches the light, turning the ocean's surface into a canvas of liquid gold.

It's as if the world is holding its breath, just for a moment, in awe of the beauty unfolding before me.

There's something almost magical about watching the sun set here, in this spot where so many emotions have surfaced over the past few days.

The beauty of it all feels bittersweet, like a reminder that life goes on, even in the face of loss. The world keeps turning, the sun keeps setting, and the sea continues its eternal dance with the shore.

As I sit here, taking it all in, I feel a sense of peace settles over me. The sadness is still here, lingering in the background, but it's softened by the sheer beauty of this moment.

Watching the sun slowly disappearing towards the horizon, I can't help but feel a little lighter, as if the weight of my grief is being gently lifted by the tide, carried away with each passing wave.

I feel the hours have passed whilst deep in thought.

I can hear barking in the distance but see no one around.

Positioned with my back to the world behind this serene beach, I remain blissfully unaware of Molly's approaching from behind.

Taking the lead, Daisy ascends the dunes and ambles over to where I perch on the sloped dunes.

The massive Bordeaux begins slobbering on my arm, catching me off guard.

Startled, I look up and meet the affectionate gaze of the lovable giant.

"Hello there!" I exclaim, a mix of surprise and amusement in my voice, as Daisy bestows a lick on my face this time.

CHAPTER 40

"Daisy, come here, girl," Molly calls out.

Still recovering from Daisy's unexpected attention, I turn to find Molly standing less than three feet away.

The ironic re-encounter strikes me, causing my heart to skip a beat and butterflies to flutter within.

"Mind if I sit down, or is this seat taken?" Molly chuckles, gesturing to the spot that Daisy has now claimed.

I join in the laughter, my laugh adding a charming note to the moment, which Molly finds endearing.

My timid demeanour triggers memories for Molly, recalling our meeting back in October.

"Of course," I reply, drawing myself back to the present.

"But it looks like this seat is taken," I add laughing and stroking Daisy under her droopy chin. Daisy, seemingly unimpressed, side-eyes me as if to say, 'About time.'

"Thank you!" Molly exclaims, carefully settling onto the dunes before me and Daisy.

Despite a pang of jealousy over the dog's attention, Molly manages a smile.

"You're welcome," I say, a hint of shyness in my voice.

"Although I don't have any right to stop you," I add, averting my eyes from the captivating 'Mrs Perfect' before me.

I can't believe the unfolding encounter.

Molly extends her hand courteously towards me. Smiling from ear to ear recalling our first ever meeting.

"My name is Molly," she says.

As I extend my hand, I greet her, "Well, it's lovely to meet you, Molly; I'm Gerry."

About the Author

Born in the year of the Silver Jubilee, 1977, Louise (Lou) Eade grew up in Tonbridge, Kent. She went to college and then worked for her local council. Lou had always loved writing and had written a lot of poetry. At 20 years old, Lou had her first child, a daughter, Tianny. In 2003, Lou married and had two boys, Kieran and Thomas.

In 2005, Lou and her family moved to Blackpool to run a small hotel on Wellington Road. In 2008, another daughter, Emily, was born, followed by another boy, Benjamin, in 2010 when Lou and her husband decided to live in residential. The family welcomed another daughter, Amelia, in 2013 while running a successful Café on Holmfield Road.

In 2021, Lou decided she was missing her family and friends down south, so she decided to separate and divorce from her husband amicably.

In 2022 and now Settled in Hastings, East Sussex, Lou rekindled the love of her childhood sweetheart Andi, whom she married in 2023. They now share a home in Hastings with Lou's youngest two daughters and the family pet dog, Snooch, a Dogue de Bordeaux, and their two cats Looby, a Bombay and Enzo, a Maine Coon.

Sadly, three days after moving back home, Lou's family was struck with tragedy when her Mum Pauline was diagnosed with terminal stage 4 lung cancer. Within two weeks of diagnosis, Pauline passed away.

Lou and her brother nursed their Mum in her final days as she didn't want to go to hospital.

Now settled and very content with life, Lou has used her spare time to write her first book in the Molly Chapman Series, **The Fall**.

You can connect with me on:
- https://www.loueadeauthor.co.uk
- https://www.twitter.com/loueadeauthor
- https://www.facebook.com/loueadeauthor
- https://www.youtube.com/@LouEadeAuthor
- https://www.instagram.com/loueadcauthor
- https://www.tiktok.com/@loueadeauthor
- https://www.amazon.com/author/loueade

Subscribe to my newsletter:
- https://www.loueadeauthor.co.uk/contact

Also by Lou Eade

Lou Eade is a talented author known for crafting gripping fictional psychological thriller stories. Within the pages of Eade's novels, readers are taken on a thrilling journey filled with intricate plot twists and turns that keep them guessing until the very end. Eade has a knack for creating captivating characters whose complexities and secrets add depth to the narrative, drawing readers deeper into the intricate web of suspense and intrigue. With each story, Eade masterfully builds tension, weaving together a tapestry of mystery and psychological drama that leaves readers eagerly turning pages late into the night.

The Fall - Book 1

Molly Chapman, a mother of three, finds her once-loving marriage falling apart.. Struggling with her mental health and neurodivergence, she seeks support from her psychiatrist.

To escape her troubled home life, Molly walks her puppy along the beach, where she encounters a handsome stranger.

One night, after another fight with her husband, Molly contemplates taking her own life but falls from the sea wall under mysterious circumstances.

Injured and in a coma, Molly wakes up with no memory of her life and a stranger by her bedside.

As Molly questions her new reality, will she uncover the truth and regain her memory, or will she learn to live a the lie?

The Forgotten - Book 2
After emerging from a coma, Molly is thrust into a world of deceit, betrayal, and hidden truths.

Haunted by amnesia, she struggles to piece together fragments of her past, clinging to the one person she trusts implicitly.

Her previous marriage holds dark secrets of abuse and undisclosed conditions that remain shrouded in her lost memories.

As a team of detectives races against time to unravel the mystery of her disappearance, Molly's husband becomes the prime suspect in her supposed murder.

PC Carter harbours a gut feeling that Molly is still alive, sparking a relentless pursuit to uncover the truth.
 Will Molly uncover the truth of her disappearance, or will she remain ensnared in the intricate web of lies spun around her?

The Van
Contains Trigger & Content Warning 18+

AMAZON BEST SELLERS
  #1 in Erotic Suspense
  #1 in Erotic Thrillers
  #1 in Erotic Horror
  #2 in Kidnapping

Set in Hastings in the UK.

In the serene setting of Lucy's neighbourhood, an eerie presence looms right next door.

George, the seemingly ordinary neighbour harbours secrets darker than anyone could fathom.

As Lucy peers into his world, she uncovers a bone-chilling truth: George's friendly facade may be a mask for something far more sinister.

"The Van" promises a riveting read; in this twisted psychological horror thriller, Lucy's journey unfolds as she navigates the treacherous waters of suspicion and fear.

Brace yourself for a heart-pounding tale of suspense and horror, where the line between friend and foe becomes blurred, and nothing is as it seems.

A gripping read, "The Van", will leave you on the edge of your seat with its chilling twists and turns.

But heed the warning: as this gripping narrative delves into dark themes that may unsettle even the most resolute readers and is not suitable for the faint-hearted.

Printed in Great Britain
by Amazon

023f6c97-b59d-4c7b-a60a-8b90d9027f9eR01